D0651328

Ada Dallas

Books by Wirt Williams

THE ENEMY

LOVE IN A WINDY SPACE

ADA DALLAS

Ada Dallas

WIRT WILLIAMS

McGraw-Hill Book Company, Inc.

NEW YORK
TORONTO
LONDON

ADA DALLAS

First Edition

For Ann and Meredith

A story is better if it has a real place to happen in. So—though all its characters, of course, are completely imaginary—I have put this story in Louisiana because I know it well. For dramatic purposes, some very minor changes have been made in the statutes of the state and in the geography of the city of Baton Rouge. In these small alterations, I hope I will be indulged.

ONE

Steve Jackson

The tower. Driving 61, up from New Orleans, you could see it ten miles out: straight and sharp and converging to spearpoint, flagpole spurting out of the point and into the sky, the sky maybe flame-blue with sun or maybe tomb-gray with rain clouds hung low and dark over the low dark country.

Inside the tower, and this you could not see at ten miles, were twenty-four tiers of offices stacked one above the other. In the offices, papers were signed that gave and took away millions, and also in the offices, words were whispered that gave and took away more millions than that, and in at least one of the offices, papers were signed and words spoken that gave and took away life and death.

The last had been dealt and received three times within the tower itself, and marble walls had bullet streaks to prove it.

The first of the three who found death there was a doctor named Carl Weiss. The second was a United States Senator named Huey Pierce Long, who had taken the bullets inside the tower a heartbeat before the doctor but who had taken his death many hours later in a bed between white sheets. The third was a woman who had been powerful, pitiless, and beautiful, and who had made one mistake.

Today, watching the tower spear deeper and deeper into the gray as rubber tires drummed it closer and closer in a soft unbroken dirge, I remembered all the times I had seen it lancing into space from miles away, all the times I had followed the highway to see Ada. To see Governor Ada Malone Dallas, whose citadel was the tower which was the capitol of Louisiana.

And these times whirled back and back to another time: before Ada was Governor Dallas, when she was simply Ada, whom I loved and who in her fashion loved me.

This was what I had to think about, driving 61, up from New Orleans, watching the tower climb into the low dark rain sky, taller and taller, wider and wider, on my way to Ada's funeral.

I had been driving, too, the first day I saw her—but in another direction. That had been eight years ago; it felt like, perhaps, eight weeks. Once it has passed, all time is the same. If you have good enough reason to remember it, what happened eight years before is as close as what happened eight hours.

That Saturday noon, of eight years before, without purpose or even conscious volition, I had walked out of my apartment, across the blinding white shadow-rimmed concrete patio, opened the iron-barred gate in the grilled fence, and gone out. I got into my just-bought three-year-old Buick Super convertible parked at the curb, and I started driving down the one-way street. The car rather than I chose the direction, it seemed, and it crept out of the jail closeness of the French Quarter, and then was eastbound and running fast on Highway 90 paralleling the coast. First I could not see the water, but only the green land cut by the twisting gray ribbon of road; then I was sweeping the brown shore and could look right to the Gulf of Mexico, an unending flat dazzle under a blue-flame sheet of sky burning outward from the smooth orange coal of noon sun. I stared into the dazzle and drove on. I had no destination. I simply kept driving. I suppose I was hypnotized by the unchanging shimmer on the endless water, or by the burning blue overhead. At least I figure it that way now. I drove across the big bridge at Bay St. Louis, through Pass Christian and Gulfport and finally Biloxi, and then I knew I was going too far, much too far, but I kept going anyway in the mesmerism of sun and sky and dazzling sea.

Many times since, I have thought how much history and now many lives would have changed forever if I had turned around at Biloxi, Mississippi, and got back to what passed for home. But I didn't turn. I kept going.

I drove almost two hundred miles to Mobile, Alabama, and so blindly ordained almost eight years of the history of a state, and wrenched with violence too many lives to count. But I did not know what was already starting to happen because I had not turned around at Biloxi. I simply drove through the outposts of Mobile until I saw a commanding white motel, fronting a tan strip of beach and crested by an unlighted neon that ordered: STOP HERE.

I obeyed. I decided I had already gone too far to get back the same day, that I would spend the night, sun and swim the next morning, and go back in the afternoon. I pulled in, went into the office, and signed the register under the ravaged face of a woman who was the manager and who gave me the key. I went into the cabin and floated in a tepid bath for a long time.

When I finally kicked myself out, I saw through the window that the sky was quite dark. I tied the big bath towel around my waist, and pushed the buzzer for the porter, whom I gave money and asked to bring me a razor, cheap swim trunks, and a pint of Early Times from the supermarket down the highway.

Someone knocked on the door, I opened it, and standing there was not the porter but the woman manager. I started to close the door, but she said, "That's all right," and pushed in. She had the things I had ordered, and placed them with the change on the table.

Her eyes were on me in a stare that was not so much speculative as seeing.

"I won't need anything else," I said.

She laughed, quickly and without good humor. "You sure?"

Did I look *that* hard-up, I wondered. She was at least fifty, her hair was dyed a horrible purplish brown, and her face was corroded and evil.

"I'm sure," I said.

But she did not go.

"I just thought," she said. The steady unspeculative points of her stare burned into me. "I just thought you might be interested in passing the time with a very beautiful young lady. I have several friends who are quite beautiful young ladies."

"I guess not."

"These ain't the ordinary type girl at all, they are very charming young ladies."

"I don't think, tonight."

"One of my friends is very intelligent, I think you would enjoy chatting with her."

She said she could call her for a hundred dollars. For a whole night, you understand, not just a few minutes. I understood but I thought not, not tonight.

With one hand on the door, she turned, said, "Seventy-five," and I was very much surprised to hear my own voice dropping into a second's silence, "All right."

She smiled, not in triumph but in vindication, as though she had known my "all right" was inevitable, as though she had known it was the only possible termination to our dialogue, and she went out.

When she had gone, I wondered why I had said yes. I had not wanted to. Partly from ennui, partly from solitude, partly because she had come down twenty-five bucks, more than anything else from passivity. I was just riding with it. Again. Often, in the years since, I wonder at the X of luck, or whatever name there is for it, that made me say the two words. But of course X was only the small part of what produced them. The big part was me, Steve Jackson, and I said, "All right," because I was curious, because I wanted to pass the time, and because, as I say, I was riding with the play.

I shaved, put on the clothes I had taken off, and walked to the edge of the court to look across the sandstrip to the Gulf, black now with the yellow moon path cutting across it to the horizon and vanishing at the edge of sky. The night wind came soft but cold off the water. I shivered, went back to my cabin, and read the Mobile paper on the bureau, wondering what the girl would be like.

Half an hour later, someone knocked on the door again, I opened it, the light rushed through, and I was staring at a very tall, handsome girl in a classically loose white dress.

She stood in the frame of the doorway, perfectly still, smiling. I faced her a moment, not moving, not surprised for I had no image prepared for her to shatter, but for a moment frozen. At certain moments, part of the mind shorts out while the little wheels in another part record, compute, and transmit their data by unfailing impulse. So, while I stood dumb and possibly gawking, the impulses came on steadily: her face was perfect but possibly too strong to be truly beautiful (I decided later it was not; she was beautiful, all right); her body was heroic, capable of inflammatory prodigies and delights; her gaze was profound and intelligent. She saw. In the quick collision of our eyes, I knew she saw.

And before her seeing, I felt naked, defenseless, and numb. She smiled—trying to put me at ease—and I felt more revealed than ever.

Then I swallowed, and said, I hoped nonchalantly, "Hi, come on in," and my first razored sense of standing at judgment passed. Quickly, I reduced her, almost, to just a big and very good-looking girl.

She stepped inside, smiling. She wore no make-up except lipstick, and her perfume was fresh rather than aphrodisiacal. Her features were smooth, classic, and unrevealing: she might have been anything, a Sunday-school teacher, or a whore, which of course she was. She moved into the room with a slow long-legged grace, and it was exciting to watch her move.

She was quite tall, I noted again, but not slender. Nor heavy: simply full to go with her height.

"How do you do?" Her voice had not simply politeness but a modulated and careful elegance. "I'm Mary Ellis."

This too was a deviation; she was supposed to give only her first name. Mary Ellis of course was not her name. But using the full name was appealing.

"Steve Jackson." I felt at once angry and embarrassed at having blurted out my real name, which is never done, and excited by her garden-party manners and pristine uncoarse sensuality, and I felt myself coloring with the ambivalence.

"Nice to see you."

She stood directly before me, almost as tall, close enough so her nearness and scent were real, not close enough to be vulgar.

She was still smiling, very politely, and I knew she was aware of my sense of awkwardness.

"May I sit?" She was actually trying to put me at ease.

"Please do." I did not want to be outdone. "Like a drink?"

"Please."

I felt her watching me as I mixed, I felt the blood steady in my face, and I had an idea she was amused. It had been a long time since I felt so gauche.

I brought her the drink.

"Thank you." She offered me a straight view of her clear, lightly tanned Grecian cast of a face.

We were silent for a moment, she sitting, me standing.

"You've never called a girl before, have you?"

I hesitated. "No."

"How refreshing." She said it with not unfriendly irony.

"I'm glad you're pleased."

"I am." She tasted, and still smiling said, "An awkward but necessary circumstance. My ground rules specify the business arrangements in advance."

"Sure." I took bills from the wallet and handed them to her, I trust delicately.

"Thank you." She looked at them boldly and counted, one side of her mouth still smiling, then opened her bag and dropped the bills in decisively.

She put the drink down and walked about in the room. She moved with a firm brooding containment, as though at any instant she would shift suddenly into some dramatic climactic motion and was taking her time about coming up to it. The expectation of that imminent animal explosion was the thing she gave you instantly, and which, I was to learn, she always gave you. This carried all kinds of excitement, not the least of which was glandular.

As long as I was to know her, this quality of contained violence awaiting some trigger never changed. In fact, her body and all its presences and emanations never changed. I do not believe she gained or lost five pounds in seven years.

It was only the clear golden Minerva face that was to change: a hardening of cast, a grooving between nose and mouth (born, I suppose, of unceasing trials and triumphs of resolution), and a setting of the eyes into a bright and blinkless half-stare, which tried to assess by intensity, as though if they looked long enough and hard enough they could see through flesh to the wheels and gears of desire and deception.

But at that moment, in the Mobile motel cabin, I foresaw none of the changes and hardening of the hovering years. I had no idea I would ever see her again. I simply watched her move.

As I hope I have made clear, she had great and instant sex appeal. As I was to learn, she also had a high voltage of sex potential. But not so high that the current ever blew the knobs and controls. She never belonged to sex. It belonged to her. And she always knew what to do with it, one way or another.

She turned not languorously, but deliberately, and said, "It seems to be a very good night. Would you mind if we walked on the beach a while?"

"Why not?"

I followed her through the door into the night, and we turned out of the court on a stone walk that led to the beach.

The sky was high, swift-clouded, and a depthless star-flung blue rather than black. We walked along, and she said over her shoulder, "Just lucky, I guess."

She had read me, all right. "Okay," I said. "Okay."

She turned and looked at me, and I could see her strong face in the moonlight.

"Do you know, I like you. I like you and I do not have to say that. I am not saying it for any reason except I want to. I like you very much."

I started to say, "I like you too," but avoided it somehow, and said, "I'm very glad."

"Thank you."

We walked in the foot-sinking sand and then stopped to face the sea wind and the white open hand of a quarter moon. Her hair danced in the keening wind, and shone darkly in the moonlight.

"Aren't you cold?"

"No, this is fine."

I took off my coat anyway and put it over her shoulders, my hand brushed her arm, and it was firm and cold.

"Why, thank you."

I tentatively touched her shoulder, now inside my coat, and she leaned against me.

Next morning, the first thing I saw when I opened my eyes was Ada, to me at that time known as Mary Ellis. She was sitting in the chair, unbelievably immaculate in the white cotton, her clear gold skin unmarked by either sleep or fatigue. She was reading the morning paper.

"Good morning," she said, and I answered, "Good morning." It seemed almost natural.

We had breakfast at the coffee shop, and went swimming on the narrow beach behind the motel (she always carried a swim suit in her car, she said). Later, the two of us lying in the warm sand under the steady fire of the sun, she said suddenly, "You don't care about much, do you?"

I was astonished, so I answered almost honestly: "Not much."

"You ought to. It's very bad when you care about nothing."

That was a precise statement, I thought. For it was exactly Nothing that I cared about. I mean that I cared for Nothing in a quite positive and concrete way. I loved Nothing with a capital N, I was immersed in it, and I had no intention of swimming out. It was what there was, and I was the boy that knew it. They were not going to mousetrap me again.

"It's not so bad," I said, now with absolute honesty.

She looked at me very directly. "I think it is. It's almost better to care about something quite bad than to care about nothing at all."

"I don't think so."

"You need something to wake you up." Her smooth, young but not youthful face did not change or make lines, but was authentically concerned.

And I felt gratitude. I considered telling her the truth, that I was not asleep but after a fashion had already died, and that she would too, and damned fast. But I didn't. She would find it out soon enough. I said, now falsely, "Maybe so, maybe you're right."

"I'd like to see you again," she said. "May I?"

"Sure. I'm in the book. In New Orleans."

She was sharply surprised. "I didn't know you were from New Orleans. Your license—" She stopped and smiled again. "That's really your name? What do you do? You don't have to tell me."

"I work for a television station." Later, I would always remember she had said she wanted to see me before she knew I was Opportunity; that if I had been that, at least I was something else first.

But when she heard "television station," her face without changing went somehow alert; if she had had movable ears, they would have pointed forward. Her watchful gods, or perhaps simply her genius, had at that instant gestured at me and she had seen.

But she only nodded.

"What do you do? In New Orleans?" I hurried over the blunder.

She looked full at me and smiled. "I go to Sophie Newcomb College."

"I mean really." Sophie Newcomb is the most social school in the Deep South.

"I go to Sophie Newcomb College."

"Good God."

She laughed a very clear laugh. "I shouldn't have told you but it's true. I'll tell you all about it, next time I see you."

And that was in New Orleans. I had not thought there would be a next time. I had by no means forgotten her, but I never expected to see her again. I had viewed our encounter as one of those Aladdinish adventures that sometimes fall from the sky, complete in themselves and having no couplings in the sequence of life. When I heard her voice on the telephone two weeks later, I did not recognize it for three sentences until she said, "I told you I'd call." Then I felt the run of excitement.

"Can you see me?" Her directness would have overpowered me if I had been resisting, and I was not.

"Sure," I said. "Come down and have a drink."

She hesitated for a second. "All right."

That night, it seemed she did have in mind only a drink. But I have never relished the role of eunuch-confidant, and I persuaded her to change her mind, or thought I did; anyway, she changed it. It was understood our relations were no longer professional.

She came by a second time the same week, and then again the next. I started to wonder if I was not interfering with commerce, but did not ask. She clarified it on her own. She only went to Mobile on weekends, she said, or for very special summons. The volume low, the price high, she said, and that was how she worked her way through college.

She said, "When this little venture is closed, and it will be closed very soon, I do not mean for anybody to dig it up and hit me over the head with it. I mean to be rid of it for good."

"How do you like Newcomb?" I said.

"You mean how does Newcomb like me? It doesn't. This has been one hell of a four years, but I have proved something and I will get out this June with a Phi Beta Kappa key which seldom happens at that noble institution.

"But how I hate them there. Since they despise me. Not because I am a whore—oh yes, let's face it, I am a whore—but because I have no background. That is what they say when you come out of the Irish Channel. You know everything there is to know about the Channel when you know they talk with a pure Brooklyn accent there. Erl for oil and goil for girl, you know. Now this is something I obliterated a long time ago, and it was not my accent that gave me away, nor my clothes, nor even my address, for all these I had studiously corrected. It was simply the fact that I was born and half raised in the Irish Channel that led them to spit upon me. That fact could not be destroyed or even buried.

"My weekend vocation, that could be concealed with perfect success. Hasn't it been, hundreds of times? I have been very careful to—what is a good euphemism for it?—to be commercial only in Mobile, where nobody knows my name. Usually I wear a black wig, even. And I never have dates, and that's the official euphemism of the profession, with anyone with a New Orleans license. Your Texas license was why we met. You see, you were a mistake." She laughed; I told her I just bought the car there.

"No," she said, "it isn't Mobile at all, it is just the Channel. I was not invited to join a sorority, not even one where out-of-town transients who are themselves not really accepted gather for solace. I should have expected it, but I was wounded. I cried. And they have a way of speaking that dismisses me, it simply goddamn dismisses me. That is why I would like to nail every one of those sweet Jesus bitches and their sororities and their Sophie Newcomb to the cross, because they dismiss me. And don't ask me how I'll do it, because of course I never will, but it is a lovely, lovely dream to feed on, and may I have a drink, please?"

All this she told me the second night she came. She also told me her real name, which was Ada Malone, and she told me much more in pieces.

"You're the second man in my life who gave me something for nothing," she said (and I felt awkwardly guilty, for I thought it was I whom the balance favored). "The other was an old Cajun grocer named Robichaux, if it hadn't been for him God knows where I'd be now.

"My father, you see, was a drunken bum. He put my mother out in her younger years to support him by, his expression was, peddling her hips. When she got too old for that activity, he got her a job in a dime store. My mother wouldn't let him put me to work, and I got to the eighth grade. Then she died. It seems she had a heart condition she never had a chance to pay attention to, and then one day she just died. Behind the sundries counter. It took them two hours to sober my father sufficiently to tell him, then he cried very hard for a day and a night, then on the way home from the funeral he stopped to ask if the store would give me her place. They said no, I was too young, so he found something else, he found something much better, he found me a job as a B-girl in a Bourbon Street bar. For though I was only thirteen, with make-up I could look much older, as old even as seventeen.

"You know what a B-girl does. She has drinks with customers, except of course there is no alcohol in hers, and she sees that the customer has a great many drinks and that he spends all his money. If he has more money than he can spend, she slips him a sedative known as a Mickey, and then certain other employees of the bar take him outside and relieve him of what is left. These were my duties at thirteen."

I did not know what to say. I finally achieved, "That must have been great."

"Oh yes." She smiled brightly. "Oh yes."

This, she said, was where Mr. Robichaux intervened. Mr. Robichaux's daughter was Ada's friend, and so, it turned out, was he. He created a job for her after school hours, which would have made it possible for her both to continue school and to buy whisky for her father. But when her father learned she had left the comparatively lucrative position of B-girl for one which offered only the negligible consideration of enabling her to stay in school, he became quite angry. He beat her, then took her by the hand and returned her to the bar. It was one of several operated by one of the town's top hoodlums, Ricco Medina. Then Mr. Robichaux, who was fragile, bald, and middle-aged, displayed what none of his acquaintances had ever suspected him of. He went straight to the bar and led Ada back to the grocery. He even suggested to Ada's father it might be better if she did not return; the possibility of charges was mentioned. Two subordinate hoods paid Mr. Robichaux a call, but he refused their advice. Surprisingly, nobody threw bricks in the window, or spoiled the stock, or made any of the standard reprisals.

Ada worked in the store, bought her father cheaper whisky than he would have liked, and was valedictorian of her high-school class.

After graduation, she found a job as a secretary for a shoe manufacturing company. She worked there for a year, then got the same kind of job with an advertising agency. This was, for her, a decisive move. In a very limited way, she entered a new world. Sometimes she was called on to help entertain the clients, which she did decorously enough. But she saw her chances and she conceived a plan. After a very long and cautious investigation, she made the Mobile arrangements. Shortly after that she entered Newcomb. ("It's not a hard place to get into," she said. "All you need are the grades and the money. What's hard is to stay.")

The arrangement seemed ideal, almost. She could go to college during the week, she could support herself by working on weekends only, nobody would find out because it was out of town.

"I suppose I should say there was a great struggle, and that I felt quite badly over my decision, I mean that I felt badly about becoming a call girl which is after all a whore. But I did not feel badly at all. It was a sensible and practical thing, it made possible my education. Oh I know all the arguments. You can do it other ways, you can wait on table all night and go to school all day, you can work all day and go to night school and finish in ten years. But I did not choose to. I chose this. It has been frequently dull, it has been more dull than anything else, but it has worked."

"It—does it ever bother you?" I asked.

"Never."

"Why did you tell me?" I said.

"There comes a time you want to tell somebody and I trust you."

"It's a hell of a responsibility being trusted," I said. "I don't think I want it."

"You've got it." She smiled.

So that was how I met her, and that was what she was: Minerva sprung full-bodied from the brow of Omnipotence, one hundred bucks a night, seventy-five if you were lucky. (And I was lucky for once, I thought then, for now I did not have to pay, though later there was a long time when I thought quite differently. In the end, in the very end, I thought again I might be lucky, but then I was much less sure what luck was.)

Then, she had not exactly defined to herself the tangible shape and size and heft of the thing she was after. But it was only the package in which it would come that she did not know. She knew what the thing was, what it really was, right from the beginning, even if she did not know the name to put to it. And what was its name? Call it significance, importance, reality. She said it, somewhat later: *I want to make the world admit I lived. I want to make it say, yes, you lived, nothing I have done to you has been able to change that.*

She was after what everybody is after until they die the first time, which is very different and a long time before they die the last. What she was after was greatness.

And she always pursued it. She never quit as I did. For her there was no double dying. She never died the first death, but only the last.

When I first knew her, in those early days of platonic carnality, she had already taken the first steps. She had fought her way out of the squalid obscurity of the Irish Channel of New Orleans. She had clawed for herself an education formal and brilliant. She had tasted exploitation and betrayal and contempt, and, once, friendship. Not only had all of it compounded failed to inflict the secret and interior first death (which begins with the abandonment of will and surrender to circumstance), but it had not damaged nor warped the prehensile shining metal of her self and her resolve. All that was done to her only knocked off the encumbering packing and dust, and bared the metal taut and naked and ready.

She was on her way and knew it, even if she was not exactly sure where it would end. Much later, I often wondered if she was born knowing every turn and every fork in the road, or whether she intuited them as she went along, or whether every turn simply turned out to be the right one because she took it. I was never sure.

And she had already intuited that she could use me, that instant on the beach I said "television station." How I don't know. I do not know what plan she devised, or even if she had a plan. I doubt if she did. I think she simply moved at opportunity reflexively, as a fighter punches at an opening.

But somehow I found myself suggesting that she apply for a job at the station, somehow I found myself introducing her, somehow I found myself working very hard to get her on.

And she was hired, as a girl of all work, starting the week after graduation.

I had wanted to come out and see her walk across the stage in cap and gown, but she had asked me not to. So the night she was graduated, I met her after the exercises in the Caribbean Room of the Pontchartrain Hotel.

At the table, she said decisively, "And that's over," and I knew what she meant. She had folded both Newcomb and Mobile neatly and locked them away, and she never wanted to open the trunk again.

"So life begins?" I said, I hoped humorously.

"So life begins." She smiled, with part of her face.

She started the next week at the station, with unspecified but staggering duties. She tore yellow paper from the clattering teletype, fetched scripts back and forth, and did all the odd jobs there were to do. After a few weeks, she began to rewrite the news copy to slant it for New Orleans, and when it became acceptable I used it sometimes on my morning newscast. The station had only one copy writer, and he was glad to let her do some of it. Then one day, he quarreled for obscure reasons with Harmon, the station manager, and quit. Ada became the writer.

Of course Ada had maneuvered the writer into quarreling and quitting, though I did not know it at the time. Let it be said in her favor that she did not put the knife between his shoulder blades. She simply presented it to him handle first. He should have quit a long time before, anyway, and he got a better job on the other side of Canal Street.

We were together frequently, in our pact of friendship and flesh. I wanted no more. I did not think I could fall in love with her, or with anyone, but I might be wrong, and if I did I would have it all to go through again: the pain, the tearing, the grief. The only way to avoid these is to keep a firm hold on Nothing, to let nothing come between you and Nothing, because once you believe there is more, you have the dying to go through again.

So I erected high boundaries, and I kept them high, and if she wanted it otherwise, she did not show it.

We spent time together: sometimes afternoons, sometimes nights, once in a great while weekends. New Orleans is a good place to spend time: you can eat at Galatoire's and Antoine's and Arnaud's and Brennan's; you can drink in good quiet bars like the Napoleon House or good noisy ones like the Old Absinthe House and the Old Absinthe House Bar, which are next to each other but not the same; you can walk down Bourbon Street after dark; you can drive to places down the coast. You can do a lot to spend time, and we did it.

It didn't mean anything, but—

Sometimes she would kiss me, and then draw her head back and look at me with soft grateful eyes and a face that had nothing to do with the daytime Ada. She would touch my face, almost shyly, with her hand. And once she said, "You're good to me, you're too good to me. Nobody is this good to anybody."

I felt my face burning and I said, almost roughly, "No I'm not. Don't be so damned grateful."

"You like me too, don't you?"

"God, yes, I like you."

She whispered something in my ear that I could not understand and brought her face against mine. I patted her shoulder awkwardly. Five years before, it would have been hard work not to fall in love with her. Five years ago, I could not have helped falling in love with her. I suppose in a way I loved her now. There are ways and ways. But it wasn't the same.

I knew of course why she felt, something. I had been, as she told me, the second man in her life who had been unpremeditatedly kind to her; that is, I had no angle as far as she was concerned. But more than that, I gave her an opportunity to be uncalculatedly generous herself, and this she had for the first time. It was a luxury she had never been able to afford before. The little aloof jerk of a cynic inside me whispered that the luxury had simply gone to her head.

But with me, when we were alone, her whole face would change like that. The perfect sharp brightness that never otherwise altered slipped off like a Mardi gras mask; the shape of the mouth and the look of her eyes became trusting, humble, grateful, and—I sometimes thought—asking.

It would have been hard, all right. Five years before.

And another time she said:

"You've never done anything you thought was wrong, have you?"

"Don't talk fool talk. Everybody has done things they thought were wrong and a hell of a lot of them."

"But you never planned them." It was not a question.

"I guess not."

"And if you ever knew about them you were sorry."

"You going to award me a gold star maybe?"

"No." She laughed softly. "I'm going to award you something else."

Then we came to a certain afternoon.

Ada, Harmon, and I had gone downstairs to the bar of the hotel whose twelfth floor we occupied. It was a quiet, expensively dark, smooth bar, with two clashing clienteles: the tourists staying in the hotel, and business people who had offices in it. Now, at three in the afternoon, we were the only customers who were not tourists. We sat at a table in the corner, and Harmon was saying to Ada:

"You were great, sweetie, only great. *Terrífico*, all the way." She had just finished an informal kind of test, reading a press-service movie column into the cameras. We had watched it on monitors.

"Thank you, sir." Ada smiled at him dazzlingly.

He cooed throatily: "Only great. You'll be queen of NOTV one of these days, you wait and see."

"Quee-een?" Her voice rose ecstatically; she was playing up to him, and hard, not so much with her words as her face.

"Why, I predict it." He lifted his Old-fashioned. "I absolutely do. Don't you think so, Steve?"

"Oh, absolutely," I said. "I predict it too."

Ada threw me a glance which I could not read exactly in the blue bar-darkness.

"It'll just take a little time," Harmon said, ponderously. "Just a little time to get it rolling."

I looked at him: at the heavy jowled face, at the eyes staring at her from behind thick heavy-rimmed lenses, and at the moonish insincerity that he so clearly considered to be debonair deviltry. He wanted her, and was willing to do business, and he wanted her to know it. I felt angry, and chilled, and was angry because I felt angry. What was it to me if she took his deal?

Then he looked away from her, beckoned the waiter, and ordered again. I could see him being pleased about having made his point and not punched it afterward. He had made it before, often enough, the bastard. But what was I sore about?

Then, to show the subject was changed, he said, "Say, did you hear the one about the black *capeau?*"

I wanted to say, "Not for years," but didn't and he told it. Ada laughed delightedly at the punch line: *Quel sentiment exquis!* He told three more, and she laughed the same way.

Then Harmon looked at his watch, frowned a little, and said, "Well, I got to go, got to get home to dinner and the little wife and all that. Have fun. You were really great, hon."

I said good-by, Ada said good-by very prettily, and we watched his fat body move authoritatively between tables and out the door.

Ada looked at the door a moment, then turned to me and said, "We ought to roll that sonofabitch and get you his job."

"Sure. And why stop there? While we're at it, let's just get the owners to sign over the stock, too."

"Don't laugh. It could be done. I mean Harmon."

"I think not."

"As you wish. My benevolent and righteous."

I drank.

"How would you do it?"

"Ah. Now. Now. That's better. Much better. Now you show the beginnings of at least rudimentary intelligence."

"I hate to disappoint you. But I'm just interested in the mechanics. Frankly I don't think you could."

"My dear ingenuous and upright boy. You really don't know, do you?"

"Nope."

"It's ridiculously simple. You would—" She paused. "No. I shall not corrupt your pastoral innocence. It will not be me who does that. I'll preserve you just as you are, in your nice, pristine, vacuumatic container. You've nothing to fear from me."

"You're so good to me."

"Am I not."

She picked up the glass. I glanced around the room at the tourists. Straight in front of me was a heavy-set blond man clearly trying to sell the idea to a small and pretty Latin woman.

"Why don't you tell me?" I said.

"Don't you know?"

"No."

"Perhaps I don't want you to know what I can do, in certain directions. Perhaps I'm afraid you'll think less of me."

I studied my glass.

"You see I care, that is the annoying and unforgivable thing."

I was glad it was dark so she could not see me blushing.

"That face," she said. "That damned unbelievable face. Is it seventy or seventeen? How the hell old are you anyway?"

"Thirty-nine. Forty in seven months." It was true.

"Forty. My God. How did they ever get you back in the Army?"

"I thought they'd forgotten about me. They hadn't."

"No, they hadn't, had they? How did you get it?"

"The leg? I got it playing poker. I got blown up playing poker in an area supposed not to be under fire, while I held four aces, nothing wild, and while there was a six-thousand-dollar pot on the blanket. That's how I got it."

That was how I got something else, too, I thought, that I had no reason to tell her about. That was how I got The Word. And The Word was Nothing. It had taken me years and years to learn it, and it took a 90-mm shellburst to teach me good, but I knew it now, you could bet your soul I knew it.

I had not known it fifteen years ago, or even ten.

Then, and that was a long time ago, I had wanted to be great, and thought I had greatness in me. I had thought that the world loved me, and that I was Destiny's bright-eyed son. I suppose everyone thinks it, and you come of age when you finally know that the world does not love you, that Destiny does not maintain a special file marked URGENT: JUST FOR MY BOY, at least not for you, and that you are simply a molecule in a universe of molecules. When you finally learn this, you are of age, and when you learn it, you die the first death.

Before the big war, Number II, I had been an instructor (not a professor but an instructor) of dramatic arts at Louisiana State University. I had thought this was the way to find it, that I would stay there a couple of years and somehow become somebody in The Theater—a playwright-director-actor-producer—and that I would be great. I had not figured out how. I would just become.

Destiny would take care of the becoming, for I was a man of Destiny, and I would just ride the big D home, to where I was going.

At this time, I was engaged to a girl named Laura, who had been in my modern dramatic techniques class and who stayed for a radio job in Baton Rouge after she graduated, because of me. (It occurred to me that she was the same physical type as Ada, later when I knew Ada.) We were engaged for more than a year, and then, without a quarrel, she broke it off. "You expect too much," she said. "Not just from me but from the whole world. I'm not up to it, you want too much." I was hit by this, and hard, for I had loved her, I thought. But I accepted it.

And then I went to war, and after the war there was television. It was very new and wide open, and I got an offer, a very small offer, and I was sure Destiny had whispered from the wings. I did not come back to Louisiana, but stayed in New York, where the offer had come, and waited for Destiny to take off on the big hop. But it was slow revving up, it was damned slow, and I did not direct plays, or write them, or act in them, but somehow found myself writing and doing a local newscast. I tried to put more into the newscast than was wanted. "Steve boy, tone it down," said the boss. "Remember the audience I.Q." I told him I would do it my way, I did, and a little later I was fired.

I caught on with a smaller station, where it was understood that I would only write news and do small newscasts and maybe sweep the floor, and at thirty-two I was beginning to believe that the world did not love me, and that Destiny was taking no pains on my account.

Then the Army recalled me for Korea, even though I was not in the active reserve, and I felt more than ever that nobody up there even knew about me. Then I was blown up by that wild shell, losing the sure-thing six-thousand-dollar pot I could not have helped taking with the four aces, nothing wild, and then I knew Destiny was not just indifferent but out to get me.

It was out to get me, I decided, because I would not accept my status as a flyspeck. I had not kept my head down, but had stuck it up in the line of fire and been hit. If I had just faced up to the fact that I was a germ in a world of nothing, I would not have been hit.

Not to get hit, you had to keep your head down, to admit you were nothing and the world was nothing. That was the only way to survive. That was what I would do.

And with this acceptance, I felt wonderful. I was intoxicated. Nothing mattered, nothing was my fault. I was just a victim because I had tried to be, and thought I was, more than a molecule, and because I thought the world had a beneficent design. Now I knew there was only nothing. So I reveled in my nothingness and the world's, and I was thirty-five years old.

I was thirty-five years old, and I came back to Louisiana, to a new station in New Orleans that needed experienced talent, cheap. I came back and I immersed in Nothing. Now I swam in it, now I was drunk on it, now I knew it was all there was, and I was glad.

"What happened then?" said Ada across the table.

"Oh. Then? Then I came back. Here. Here I am. Here we are."

"Yes. Here we are." She lifted her glass to drink and set it down. "Goddamn you," she said. "I'm in love with you."

And there it was, and what was I going to do with it? I had not asked for it. I had not wanted it. I was a little angry, for this upset the balance. But at the same time I liked it. Anybody likes it even when they do not want it, for it flatters and soothes, it is balm and ointment. If you don't ask for it, it involves no responsibility. It is something for nothing. I felt bad and guilty and I enjoyed it.

This of course changed things. The absolute—I thought—absence of emotion was gone, and we phased into a new and ambivalent situation: we were lovers who were not lovers. We were together as before but things were different between us because now there was something between us: Ada's declaration.

She did not make it again. There it is, her attitude said—do with it what you will.

I felt the pull, the temptation to surrender. But I knew the issues and the consequences, so I resisted. And because she never pushed at me what she had offered, but simply let it lie there, it began to achieve the inertia of an iceberg. I had to resist harder and harder. But we went on, overtly, as before, and one weekend we found ourselves on one of the islands off the Louisiana coast.

We got there by ferry. The ferry made two trips a day, and we rode it on the last one, in the afternoon, me twisting my neck to look up to the pilothouse and the competent unreadable face of the pilot. When the gangway clanked in place, I drove off the ferry to the hotel.

The hotel was well back from the water, and from one window of our corner room you could look across the island to the sea. The island itself was low in the water, and bare except for a line of heavy-trunked bearded palms that stood on the seaward edge and leaned steep toward the mainland with the sea wind. It was the off season, and few people were in the hotel; that night I saw only two other couples in the small section of the dining room still open. The lobby was vacant and cheerless; Ada and I went up to the room and played gin rummy, for a time.

Next morning, I awoke before Ada, and tiptoed to the sea window. It was open a couple of inches, and the sea wind blew through my pajama tops and chilled skin and flesh. Down below, the gray water rolled and broke white on the brown sand, and I listened to its surge, steady and dead-slow, like the wide-spaced heartbeat of some leviathan.

I suddenly felt a warmth against my shoulder, and Ada stood beside me, awake and clear-eyed.

"Look at it," she said. "Nothing matters to that, nothing at all. Not your robberies nor your murders nor your immortal fornications nor even your basest or noblest suicides in whatever guise they take. That swallows them all, and how grand it must be. To be everything, to take all the pollution, to be touched by none of it."

"Nobody you know will ever make it, kid."

"No. They won't, and I won't most of all." I looked at her and thought how easy it would be to let go. But I held on.

We dressed and went down to breakfast.

Except for us, the dining room was empty. There were no waiters; the proprietress herself served us: a heavy tall black-haired woman, with a wind-reddened deep-lined face, who might have been forty-five or sixty. Her body had once been handsome. Now she moved it defiantly and arrogantly, daring anyone to say it was no longer so. Something tapped lightly at memory; she reminded me of someone, but I could not pinpoint.

I heard the wind outside, blowing over the desolate beaches, bouncing along the wooden sides of the old hotel, rattling the glass panels of closed windows.

"Will we have a storm?" asked Ada.

"Maybe. Wind's much stronger than early morning. Listen." Across the room the panes shook, very loudly, and I heard it mourn along the empty sand.

After breakfast, she said, "Would you mind very much taking a walk?"

"Let me pay the check." I beckoned, the woman came over, and said, "No check, it goes on the bill. Pay for it all when you go." She smiled, and was gone.

We walked through the room and then it focused: the proprietress reminded me of the woman back at the Mobile motel, the procuress. The difference was that this one looked benign. Perhaps the quality the two aging women had in common, whatever it was, existed only for me.

I followed Ada out of the dining room, into the gray daylight and cold wind. The sunless sky was low and pale gray, and under it, the sea dark and white-frothed. Over the dull brown sand the palms dipped in the wind, the dark green of their foliage lining sharp and dancing against the brown and gray.

"Let's go down."

She took my hand. We passed through the rows of palms, then we were out of the trees and on a narrow jut of sand that slanted down into the gray-and-white turbulence of the Gulf.

"Stop a minute," said Ada.

"Aren't you cold?"

"I don't care."

We stood close. I watched the tan firm lines of her face, the dark wind-driven gold of her hair, and the hard clear gray of her eyes, as she watched the rushing, mounting, breaking line of the waves as they struck and exploded on the sand.

Not turning, she said, "This close to it, this much a part of it, I almost know who I am."

"And who is that?"

"Almost, I said. Not quite. I guess you're not supposed to know. You can only know it's there, both loose and riding the elements and locked deep inside where you can never touch it. I suppose you must not know, quite, what it is."

I said nothing, but felt the heavy cold wave of the wind, and the thrust of her love, which was also cold because I feared it.

Now she turned. "Who are you, Steve? What do you want?"

"What do I want? Nothing."

I feared the love she offered and I wanted it. It was so close. All I had to do was stop fighting.

"Didn't you ever?"

"Oh, yes. Once I wanted a hell of a lot, a long time ago. That passed."

"What? Tell me."

"Something very simple. To be great. Not to be a great warrior, or a great statesman, or a great anything. Nothing so complicated. All I wanted was to have greatness, to hold it in my hands like a diamond or a bottle. I didn't care what shape it came in, just so I got it." I guess that was the first time I had ever said it out loud.

"Didn't you know, didn't you have some idea how you would try to get it, what you would do?"

"I only thought I did." I laughed, and she pressed my forearm with her fingers. I thought then I might surrender. I spoke rapidly. "I thought I would make it somehow in the thea-tah. You know." I laughed again. "I worked very hard at it as a matter of fact, but I never really made my move. I never really made my move at all, and making the move is what you have to do before you do anything else. You have to be completely willing to fail before you can succeed."

"What are you going to do now?"

"I have done it. Nothing. With a capital N to denote abstraction. I have become Your TV News Reporter."

"Is that so bad?"

"It isn't bad at all. It is, right now, exactly what I want." And then I was sure I would not give in, I would not take what she offered. Perhaps I could not take it. My resistance had been successful. I felt triumphant, and bereaved.

"Poor Steve."

"I'm doing all right." I was half angry. She was so obviously feeling sorry for me.

"Is that enough?"

"Who am I to get enough?" I am not even really alive any more, I started to say but did not. "For that matter, who are you? Do you think you'll get enough? Do you?"

"I don't know." And now she was not looking at me. "But I will damned sure try. I will make everybody in sight know I try."

"You. Where do you think all your trying will get you?" I suppose I said it brutally. I did not mean to.

"I'm going to make the world know I'm alive. I'm going to make it say, 'Yes, you're alive, nothing I have ever done to you has made you not be alive. Whatever I have done to you, you have done something to me.' I'm going to make it impossible for the world ever to fail to admit I lived."

"Is that all?" I laughed.

"Not by a goddamn sight. I'm going to pay back every sonofabitch who ever hurt me and who ever threw dirt on me. They're going to know who I am and what I can do and I'm going to step on them like that jellyfish there."

And she ground it into the sand.

The wind shook the leaves of the trees, and now the first lash of rain whipped our faces. I smelled the rain and the sea on the wind.

"It's going to pour," I said. "Let's get back."

Her fingers went tight on my arm. "Stay, please."

I felt the rain cold on my skin, and heard it fall on Ada's face. From very far, thunder rolled. Against the dark sky and sea and the heavy tossing line of horizon, light exploded yellow and long and jagged, filled the world for one incandescent instant, and was gone. The rain drove at us now in heavy sheets.

"We'll be drenched." I shivered inside the shirt now plastered cold against me.

She slipped backward into my arms. "I'll warm you." Her back pressed flat and hard against my chest, her breasts round, full, and hard against my arms where I held her. In the wet blouse, she too was cold. Then in my arms she began to grow warm, and I felt her warmth where we touched.

Her hair was wet and stinging against my face, no longer golden but dark and storm-tossed.

"Steve," she said.

"Yes?" I whispered it into her ear.

"Love me, Steve. Please love me."

I said nothing.

"Will you, Steve?" Her wet smooth face moved against mine.

I still said nothing.

"You didn't answer," she whispered.

"How can I answer?"

"You mean you don't love me?"

"No, I don't mean that. Not like that."

"How else is it? You mean you love me as much as you can love a whore? As much and no more? Is that what you mean?"

I felt a sudden spreading blow—of guilt? "No!" I insisted—to myself? "I love you as much as I can love anybody. I'm too late for that. You know it."

"Do you really believe that? Or do you know it's a lie?"

"It's not a lie."

"No." I heard the wrench of her breath. "You really think you believe it. And there's nothing I can do against that." She slumped against me, and for an instant, her body was dead and cold. "Nothing," she repeated. Then she moved abruptly and quickly from me. I raised both arms, toward her, then dropped them.

"Come on," she said. "Let's go back to the hotel."

The wind blew hard through the night, and the rain came hard with it. In the old big bed, before the closed double windows, I listened to the wind and the rain and the breathing of Ada, who I did not think was asleep. Before dawn, the wind blew itself out, and the rain died with it. The morning was gray, but calm, and we checked out early, to catch the ferry on its only morning trip. Ada and I stood apart at the desk. The heavy-browed landlady presented the check silently, and silently I paid it. As I took my change, I looked at her strange lined face, and tried to tell if she were smiling.

And that was over.

There was nothing more—no quarrel, no words, no scenes. Such things come to the point where they go ahead or they end; this had come to that point, and by my decision it had ended. I did not want to accept the end, and I tried to see her a couple of times afterward, but she preserved a distance, and I finally had to accept. After that, we continued to cross at the station, to smile after a fashion, to speak in the flat reverberating manner of ex-lovers that is death with echoes.

Looking back at it, some time after, I sometimes thought that I had once again pushed her along her course, and I thought that if I had behaved differently then, things might have been very different later. But then I would instantly realize I was kidding myself. There had to be an Ada Dallas. If I had behaved differently, she would just have become by a different process.

She was rewriting the regional wire for the local slant, and doing it well. She was very friendly with Harmon, she was going out with newspaper columnists and some well-heeled advertisers, and her temporary, incredible surrender of calculation to emotion seemed well dead. She was Ada again, and you were worth only what you were worth to her. If that was nothing, then the hell with you.

She had been rewriting the wire and the local dailies for several months, when she made her move, again. Quite unexpectedly, the station's fashion commentator got an extra two weeks' vacation piled on the basic two—for outstanding merit, she was told—and she took it chortling. She was serenely pleased, but not at all surprised, at this earthly manifestation of divine justice, and she went to Bermuda for a month. When she came back, red-faced and freckled and smug, she was no longer fashion commentator. Ada was. The now ex-commentator was a dowdy frump who had no business on a screen anyway. Harmon found other duties for her and gave her a raise, and she adjusted nicely. In time.

But that first afternoon, she waddled into the office like the number-one angel checking back in with the Boss, with just the right air of tolerant disdain for us minor cherubim in the outer circles, and she came out heavy-legged with a handkerchief to her eyes and making unpleasant noises. A couple of hours later, Ada and Harmon left together, exchanging glances and a smile of a certain significance, and I knew like a blow that she was sleeping with him and had been for some time.

I hated them both, quite coolly. But of course this was foolish, for of course I did not care one way or another what she did, so of course I put away the hate and was only amused. Sure I was.

So now I was out of Ada's life as an active participant. I was only a spectator. Still, I had a ringside seat, and I watched with more interest than I would have liked.

Once, I abruptly went into her office without pretext, hoping—I don't know what I hoped.

"Hello," I said.

"Hello, Steve," she said with perfect detachment.

"Let me buy you a drink?"

"Thanks so much, but I'm afraid I'm awfully tied up."

At that moment Harmon put his head in the door; she smiled at him very brightly, and said, "Well. I'd given you up," and as she walked toward him I thought that maybe the swinging hips were to give me the needle. But I could not be sure, and the possibility that they might not be was the biggest needle of all.

She moved ahead very rapidly; her show became a very hot property very quickly. First it was a fashion show once a week, then twice a week, then a fifteen-minute general women's show five times a week. The old show had never made money; Ada's new one made plenty by the station's standards. It turned out that Harmon was right, even if he had not meant to be. She actually was queen of the city's television, which was something like being middleweight champion of one block. Still, it was something. She was getting known.

She started pulling local celebrities in for guest spots, and one day the guest was Tommy Dallas, the Singing Sheriff.

Afterward I often wondered exactly how far ahead she saw when she invited him, how far into the time machine she was projecting. I never knew.

But this day, I looked through the glass pane of my office-studio, and I saw walking through the door into the reception room, in order: a tall handsome white-haired man in a gray suit; a tall heavy-set man in a green fancy-trimmed cowboy shirt and a gray Stetson hat, his face at once open and ambiguous; and behind him four junior-grade cowboys in the same kind of shirt and hat and carrying musical instruments.

That was Sylvestre Marin, Tommy Dallas, and company, and I was supposed to meet them and take them to Ada.

Being in the news business, of course I knew what was important to know about them. Sylvestre Marin was a former state senator from St. Peter's parish, and the Machiavelli of Louisiana politics. Tommy Dallas was his present contender for highest office.

I went out to meet them.

"Good morning, Senator," I said. "Sheriff."

"Hello"—the Senator paused for just a heartbeat, and I could see wheels racing—"Steve. How are you?" He smiled broadly, but I was conscious of only a great and overwhelming coldness. I was also conscious of something running through my body, like alcohol after a straight shot, and it took me an instant to identify it. It was fear. I had heard that Sylvestre Marin made fear, and that he knew how to use it, and now he had made it with me. I was shamed that he had, and I made my voice curt and tough when I said things to him that day.

So I said, curtly, "Very well, Senator," and, shaking hands with Tommy Dallas, "How's the next governor?"

Tommy smiled, and made amiable and incomprehensible sounds. I had known many politicians who could say whole sentences without making sense. I had known several who could say words without making sentences. But Tommy Dallas was the first I had ever seen who could utter sounds without making words.

And this was the supreme gift. It was better than perfect. Not only was there no chance of misunderstanding. There was no chance of understanding. The residue was wonderful and complete: nothing.

Then Tommy completed his scale of incomprehensibility with four absolutely lucid words: "How you doing, Steve?"

This was the Singing Sheriff of St. Peter's parish, a certified public idol, a law enforcement officer who could not have detained, unaided, a stray dog, and a two-to-one bet to be the next governor of Louisiana.

"Miss Malone will be right with you," I said to the Senator, still seeking toughness without actual discourtesy. "If you gentlemen will just make yourselves comfortable."

Sylvestre's head dipped perhaps two millimeters in a nod. The professional friendliness was dropped, not because I had bothered him but simply because that phase of the encounter was over. His face was hard but smooth, its only lines cropping out from his bleak eyes. He was standing perfectly still when I spoke, then his head swung and the eyes, pouched and black in the hard webbed flesh, settled on me. I looked into their blackness, and felt again the swift pulse of fear. Something in him reminded me of Ada: I groped, and then found it. He also saw. I forced myself to stare back into his black gaze, and he smiled, with ironic politeness.

Ada walked into the room.

"Senator," she said. "Sheriff Dallas. How nice of you to come."

The Senator inclined his head, in the same elegant ironic courtesy. "Nice of you to ask us."

Tommy said, "Why it's our pleasure, honey." He could talk plain enough to women, I thought.

"I certainly do appreciate it," she said warmly to Tommy, and I felt the stab that I did not like to acknowledge. Her face glowed, her smile was awed. She had the current on full, all right. "I've heard you so many times."

"Why, thank you, ma'am." Tommy took the whole force and obviously loved it. "Thank you very much."

"It's not often we get a governor on this program. But there's a first time for everything, I guess."

"You don't want to believe everything you hear, honey. I ain't no governor, yet."

"A technicality." Ada smiled brilliantly, and shifted gears. "Now this is what we do on the show. We don't exactly rehearse, but we do sort of, talk, a little before. I'll introduce you and you do the song and then I ask you a few questions, all guaranteed harmless. Then you wind up with the theme song again. That's all. Okay?"

"That all right, Sylvestre?" said Tommy. His amiable, sensual, semicomprehending face worked hard for competence and understanding. It failed, and then froze in the blurred desperate glaze of a man in the water a long time but only half drowned, looking wildly but reflexively for the life preserver which isn't there and which he hopes somebody will throw out to him, but which they won't because they aren't there either. I felt the quick flood of a substance stronger than sympathy, warmer than pity. I wanted to say, "Come on, kid. There isn't one. There isn't anybody."

But I didn't. I just listened while Sylvestre Marin said to Ada, "What are the questions?"

She told him, Sylvestre nodded and said it was all right, and then Tommy nodded and said it was fine.

Later, in the studio, the red second hand swept toward 60 on the clock dial, the cameraman moved in for a close-up, and the Tommy Dallas Four started to play and Tommy Dallas started to sing. He sang his hillbilly theme, *You and Me,* straight to Ada in its wolf-howl entirety. She sat forward in her chair, her face rapt and her eyes entranced upon him, except for a quick glance through the glass to Sylvestre, in which her expression subtly changed.

Sylvestre sat beside me outside the glass partition, a cigar bristling from the corner of his mouth, his eyes raking Ada and Tommy. I tried to read something from his face, but could not.

Tommy finished, and Ada asked the questions (how did such a talented entertainer get into public service, sheriff, how do you like being sheriff, sheriff, how did you ever become a singer in the first place, sheriff). Then Tommy talked to The Folks, then he sang again, then they were displaced by a pear-bellied rabbit extolling the sponsor's product.

Sylvestre stood and walked into the studio, me behind him.

Ada was shaking Tommy's hand. "That was wonderful," she said. "Really wonderful."

"Thanks, honey," he said, and seemed about to say something else when he saw Sylvestre and was quickly silent.

Sylvestre was looking at her searchingly—or maybe appraisingly? "I think we'll be seeing you again, Miss Malone."

"I do hope so, Senator."

"I'm sure of it." His eyes were recording her assets, I thought, and not in lust. Then he turned, said, "Come along, Tommy," and the next governor of Louisiana came swiftly to heel on an invisible leash and obediently followed the well-tailored back and handsome white coiffure out of the studio and down the corridor, the four green shirts and gray Stetsons a ragged peroration behind him.

But Tommy must have said what he was about to say to Ada, very soon. For almost from that day, he was chasing her, very hard.

It started that easy, and who was to know that X had made another move on the board? In point of fact, it was Ada who had moved, for it was clearly not without purpose that she had invited Tommy Dallas to appear. I do not mean she had already planned her whole line of action. She never suffered from the handicap of an excessively detailed operational plan. She knew the direction, and she moved steadily along it, but she received the high-frequency waves as they came. And she fought the battles one at a time. But looking back, I see this invitation of Tommy Dallas, like every other move she made, plotted on a curve in space and time, like the trajectory of a projectile. I can see her whole life on the same line, the nice rhythmic parabola of the ballistic charts. Maybe everybody's life plots a curve. Maybe I just see Ada's because hers is the one I care about.

So now I watched—unwillingly, painfully, but closely—as Ada

closed in on Tommy Dallas. I watched her, dressed higher and with more sex than her wont (for Tommy was not subtle), dash into the women's room to put on a face, then dash swiftly to the elevator and go down, for what I was sure was a rendezvous with Tommy. Once, feeling like the jerk I was, I followed her, skulking at the doorway of the cocktail lounge of the hotel to look inside. And there they were: Dallas leaning across the table with desire thick on his heavy, amiable, possibly furtive face, Ada smiling delighted and expectant across the table. I walked quickly from the door, my belly cold and hollow.

Once I passed them walking together on Royal Street, Dallas laughing and elementally pleased with something he had said, and Ada laughing appreciatively at him. She glanced at me only an instant as I passed, said, "Hi, Steve," as though it were a duty, and looked back up at Dallas.

Soon I started to see pictures of them in the papers: at the race track, at civic events in St. Peter's parish, at personal appearances of Tommy and the Tommy Dallas Four. He came back to her program twice. Columnists noted and commented—one speculated on Early Wedding Bells for What TV Glamor Girl and What Gubernatorial Hopeful?

I read that one and realized seismographically that this was what she was after. (Everybody else had known long ago. I had just shut out what I didn't want to see.) She wanted to be the wife of the Governor of Louisiana. And Tommy was an odds-on bet to be governor. So if she nailed him, she had nailed it: being what is quaintly and fairly inaccurately known as First Lady of the State.

It really could happen. A year ago she had been a weekend call girl. Next year she might be the governor's wife. As a proposition, it was incredible. As a possible fact, it was frighteningly real.

Why frightening? I pushed the question away quickly without an answer.

She had a chance. But not a really good one, for two reasons:

First. Tommy lived for women. They were not just a hobby but a vocation. His office just gave him the cash and the scope to practice it. He ran through dozens of girls every year, and none of them had ever come close to bringing him in. Sometimes they were able to make him for a nice piece of change, for they outlived their term of usefulness quickly, and in politics, silence can be an exorbitantly expensive commodity. But if general report was true, and here I think it was, he had never been in serious danger of losing his bachelorhood.

Ada of course would make no mistakes. I had absolute confidence in that. She would not let him have what he wanted but she would sure as hell make him aware of it. She would make him so aware of it he might go to extraordinary lengths to get it. But marry her?

Second reason: Sylvestre Marin.

He would not let Tommy take any step of political significance that he did not personally and completely approve. Getting married is politically significant. And I did not know if Sylvestre would completely approve of Ada as Mrs. Tommy Dallas. She was too independent for his taste, I was sure. And a beautiful woman is a dangerous political quantity. Sometimes her beauty turns out to be a startling asset for her husband. Sometimes the other women get so jealous they turn against her.

And Sylvestre in time knew everything there was to know, and he would someday know about Ada and Mobile. If he did not know already.

Certainly he would take no chances with Tommy. Tommy was his masterpiece, and Tommy was also the ace or the joker with which he meant to capture, at last, the state of Louisiana.

Sylvestre had been working up to the state a long time, inching up year by year. He had completed his acquisition of St. Peter's parish ten years before, had run it like a medieval fief, and had carefully expanded his operations from that base. Now he controlled fairly thoroughly the machinations and men of the three parishes adjoining it. And he was the richest man in Louisiana. His money—nobody was sure how many millions—had come from those opportunities that public office presents to the diligent. He had been a thorough law student at Louisiana State University. He had been such a thorough student that immediately after his admission to the bar, he had started to pile up his political capital. With the divining and direct simplicity of all great men, he had moved straight at the key to power: at the almost anonymous, grubby boards of the parish. He had become a member of the levee board at twenty-five, and caused the board to award to dummy corporations, which were finally himself, long-term leases on land that fortuitously produced oil. He repeated the process, with variations, with the school board and police jury, and after ten years or so of very careful and successful operations in the parish, he got himself elected to the state mineral board. From that position, he was somehow able to check bids for oil leases, and somehow a corporation named the Big-Deal-Development Company was frequently the successful bidder on the richest oil lands, and somehow Sylvestre found himself a middle millionaire quite shortly.

Then he was ready to complete what he had so well begun: complete control of St. Peter's parish. Once he had the bankroll, this was a simple thing to one of Sylvestre's complicated simplicity and devious directness.

He spread enough money around to get his men in the sheriff's office, and the parish attorney's office, and on the Democratic Executive Committee, and on the elections committee. Then he got his own people in as precinct commissioners, where they managed the balloting and counted the votes. That was the last nail. St. Peter's was all his.

Next he opened the parish to gambling. He admitted the Syndicate—but with the extremely clear understanding that it would have no monopoly. Any man who could finance a game could run it—provided adjustments were first made with Sylvestre's organization. This devotion to free enterprise gave passionate delight to the citizenry, who thenceforth made games of chance their principal industry. The arrangement was so thoroughly approved that Sylvestre and his men could easily have won an absolutely honest election.

But Sylvestre would have laughed at leaving such a consideration to chance: even staggeringly favorable chance. Sylvestre would have laughed at leaving anything to chance. Sylvestre made sure.

Now in his fifties, Sylvestre was tall, wide-shouldered, silver-haired, and handsome, gifted with an organ voice which possessed infinite and sublime variations. The voice could produce any emotion demanded of the situation, or the cause of the instant. Or rather to the tactical phase of the instant, for the cause was always the same: Sylvestre. One newspaper editor had compared him to Milton's Satan: "a total rebel of matchless gifts, consecrated to total dominion."

Sylvestre never thought, he never surmised, he never guessed.

In his head were wheels which whirred, clicked, and halted, and produced sums, losses, products, and quotients. Sylvestre was always sure.

And Ada would have to make Sylvestre sure of her before she brought Tommy Dallas to terms with herself.

One day I encountered her in the corridor, and I could not resist it.

"How are you doing with the Governor?"

She looked at me coolly. "All right."

"Think you'll make Mrs. Governor, or just vice versa?"

Her eyes exploded in gray bursts. "You're so goddamn funny. Well, suppose I told you he wants to marry me."

"You mean if Sylvestre will let him."

Her face whitened with anger, she swung violently on her spike heel, and she moved away in swift accelerating strides.

The shot had landed. So Tommy did want to marry her, and it did depend on Sylvestre. I felt as sick as a dog. I did not want her to marry Tommy or anybody else. Except—I pushed that away.

Sylvestre was the hinge.

I remembered that appraisal he had given her in the studio. He knew what was going on with her and Tommy. Did he see her as ally or adversary?

Of course he saw her as both. He saw everybody as both. They were all adversaries until he had lashed them into total discipline, and made use of them, at which point they became allies. If that was the word.

With the perspective of distance I look back and guess that he saw Ada as a definite if putative asset, and of course he was right about that. I also guess that he felt she could be brought to heel with no more, or without much more, trouble than the rest. I suppose that was his only real mistake, and even now I find it incomprehensible that he could ever make any mistake at all. But this is now and that was then. Then he was deciding what to do about Ada. Then he decided.

A couple of weeks after my nastiness and her outburst, Ada came into my office. She was smiling, almost shyly, almost humbly, and more than ever I felt like a bastard about what I had said to her.

I felt very awkward in her presence, and I started to tell her I was sorry.

"Ada, I—"

She stopped me. "It's all right. Don't worry about it." The smile widened, just for a moment. "Would you do something for me, Steve?"

"You know it."

"Would you listen to a tape for me?"

I felt let down. "Sure."

She must have seen my disappointment. "It's quite a tape, Steve. I got it with that handbag with the Minitape setup, you know the one. I use it for the interview roundups."

"I remember it."

She was setting it up on the player.

"What is it?" I asked.

"Listen," she said, still adjusting it. Then she finished, and turned to face me. "Just listen."

The spools whirled and accelerated, I heard a humming, then unidentifiable noises, then a man's voice, deep and smooth:

"Miss Malone. Good of you to come."

"Not at all." Ada's voice was faintly mechanized on the tape.

"Do sit down." The other voice, the deep one, probed at memory.

"Thank you."

"Well. I suppose you have an idea why I want to see you." In a dark combustion of recognition, I knew Sylvestre Marin.

I felt a quick spurt of the uneasiness he touched off. But Ada's voice coming from the speaker showed none; it was cool, cheerful, and unyielding: "Why, I have several ideas, Senator."

I knew then it was going to be a duel.

"Yes." A faint chuckle. "I rather imagine you have. I should be quite surprised and disappointed if you did not."

"Thank you." Ada's bright aloofness came through the filter of the recording. She had not lost anything so far, I thought.

I watched the two spools whirling, and I tried to vision the two together in his office. But I could not. All I had was the voices coming out of the box.

Sylvestre's had his almost mocking politeness. "Now. How do we begin?"

"Isn't that your problem, Senator?" Ada's voice was charming and gay, keeping him back, giving him nothing.

"Yes. Yes, I suppose it is." The deepness was perfectly bland. If he felt checked, he did not give it away. "Well. You mean to marry Tommy Dallas." It was not a question.

"I do?"

"Please, Miss Malone, let's be no less than frank. You mean to marry Tommy Dallas."

Again Ada's stabbing brightness that conceded nothing. "Very well then. According to you, I mean to marry Tommy Dallas."

Good for her.

But the smooth deepness showed no anger, no annoyance, nothing at all. "You mean to marry Tommy. You want to be the wife of the governor. I should guess you want to play a quite substantial role in the affairs of this state. All laudable ambitions."

"I'm glad you approve. Of the laudable ambitions you say I entertain."

"I haven't said I approve." A stop. "I haven't said I don't approve, either."

"So?"

"So. I wanted to chat with you a little. I wanted to see if we might not have a meeting of minds."

"And suppose we do?" Ada's voice was perceptibly more friendly, by exactly as much as she wanted it to be, still completely in charge of itself, giving only what she clearly wanted it to give.

"If we do." Another stop, decisive. "Well, if we do, some extremely interesting possibilities open up. Possibilities, I think, that perhaps go even further than those you envisage."

This must have gotten to her. God knows it must have gotten to her. The hardest thing there is is to preserve poise when it looks as if you are going to win something. But her control never wavered.

"I'm always interested in interesting possibilities. If you'd be kind enough to develop them a bit."

"Certainly." The voice was very satisfied now. He was getting to where he had wanted to go. "Now I doubt if you have been thinking beyond the consort thing. Am I right? I mean I doubt if you've been thinking of anything beyond being the governor's wife, and an influence, and"—he chuckled, and his voice parodied the words—"the power behind the throne. Am I right?"

"You say so."

"I daresay I am right. Now in the first place there isn't any power behind the throne." Again his voice mocked those words. "I am, you might say I am the captain of my team, and everybody in this state knows it. Nobody on my team ever forgets it. That is the first, last, and abiding fact. Is that clear?"

"Your meaning is quite clear," said Ada in the box, and in my fashion I applauded.

Abruptly Sylvestre Marin said, "I have a lot more in mind for you than you have. How would you like someday to be in politics yourself? I mean directly. As a candidate and officeholder?"

"Why me?" Her voice was absolutely indifferent. How did she do it? "I'm a woman."

The deep chuckle simulated warmth. "Things have changed a great deal in politics, a very great deal. It's later than we think. And why you? Point one, a woman can be a good candidate now, under certain conditions the best candidate. Point two, appearance on television, I think you professionals call it impact, is right now the most effective asset a candidate can have, and you have it, that's been proved. Point three, I've invested a lot of time and money in Tommy, bringing him to the public's attention, building him up, and so on. I want as much return on that investment as I can get, particularly on my time, which is worth more than money. Now you know all about Eva Perón of course, and perhaps you know about Pa and Ma Ferguson in Texas. Are you following me?"

"I'm following you," said Ada remotely.

"To spell it out. If Tommy had a wife who was, or could be, a political quantity, a great deal of his development would automatically extend to her. His wife would instantly be a figure. She would have the springboard ready-made for her own development. Again I cite Ma Ferguson and the Peróns. As Tommy's wife, and with certain other ... steps, you would be a very formidable personality. Politically." I noted that he had shifted from "his wife" to "you."

"Again," said Ada. "Why me?"

The deep laugh. "For one thing, because you're intelligent enough to ask 'why me?' I.Q. 159, Stanford-Binet test, Newcomb College freshman examinations." The laugh again, and I at least was shaken. He was thorough. "And of course Tommy's crazy about you." The voice indicated this was an afterthought. "If you marry him, he'll think it's his own idea."

"That is nice, isn't it?" said Ada.

He let it pass. The voice rolled on. "You have many, many desirable attributes as a candidate. Humble origin: you were born in the Irish Channel but rose by your own efforts. Fine. That B-girl interlude looks critical at first glance but actually it can be converted into political capital. Exploited as a child, saved by the kindness of a good man, and so forth. Very good indeed. Social presence and acceptability: graduate of Sophie Newcomb. But the masses won't resent it, because you worked hard and saved money to put yourself through. Also a plus. No previous political record, so no embarrassing positions or enemies. Except of course mine." The laugh. "So far you fill my requirements superbly, Miss Malone, you fill them superbly."

I was chilled. I wondered if he had learned anything about Mobile.

Ada's voice said, "And after so far?" It was neither dazzled, nor intimidated, nor unresponsive.

"The really important thing is after so far. I want everything to be completely understood. I don't want to waste any time impressing on you the facts of life or wondering about you. You play on my team, you have only one captain. Only one. Myself." A break. "You have to understand this clearly from the start."

"I'd say you make it pretty clear."

"I do hope so." The heavy voice had heavy irony. "I don't suppose I have to tell you I can stop this thing between you and Tommy this second if I want to. Or I can make up Tommy's mind for him the other way."

"No. You don't have to tell me."

"Good. I see those Stanford-Binet things were all right. You know you and I might go far, very far. Tommy's fine at the state level, just fine, but—but beyond that I really have no hopes for him. You—" The voice trailed off.

There was a silence of several seconds. He was clearly waiting for Ada to speak. She did not.

"All right then." For the first time his tone was preemptory. "How about it?"

And Ada said, as though she were accepting, or perhaps with less concern than she would have accepted, a date, "All right."

I looked at the whirling spools, silent now except for the electric hum, and I thought: *By God, he didn't beat her, she held him even, she got what she was after as much as he did.*

Then Ada, the substantial Ada of flesh, not the phantom Ada of the voice in the box, got up from her chair behind me and turned the machine off. "That's the important part."

"Yeah," I said. "I guess it is."

I looked at her: the tall handsome blond girl with the clear fine face, the round fine hips, the long lovely legs, and I tried to match all of it with the unshakable voice on the tape. I thought again, with something close to stupefaction, *He didn't really beat her.* And I looked at her as though I were seeing her for the first time. But then I was always seeing her, or new lights and currents in her, for the first time.

"Well." I tried hard to pour enough brightness over my misery to smother it. "I guess that takes care of all your problems. I guess you've got it all wrapped up now, everything you want."

"I guess I have."

We stood facing each other curiously, me with the disaster syndrome of bitter dryness in the throat, and cold tightness in the belly. I tried to swallow and couldn't.

"Well," I said. "Congratulations."

I saw her white throat working. "Thank you."

We continued to stare at each other.

"Steve." She stopped. "Should I do it?"

"Isn't it everything you want?"

"You tell me, Steve." Her lips were not smiling, but were apart, her eyes were locked with mine, and her voice contracted to a whisper. "You tell me."

Afterward, I was always to wonder how I had said it, to search for the hidden stairs I had climbed blind to the moment of saying. For not only was it beyond action; it was beyond idea. It was the last thing on earth I would have done, or could have done. And in one second I had done it.

I said:

"No, I don't think you ought to. I don't think you ought to marry Tommy Dallas. I think you ought to marry me."

Her face was frozen into an ice mask of astonishment, or horror, or ecstasy.

"Marry me." I felt a wild kind of freedom, as though I had smashed through a wall and into daylight. "Marry me."

The mask shattered like ice in a spring flood.

"Steve." And she turned her face down to hide it. She gripped my hand tightly, and pressed her face into my chest. "Yes." Her muffled voice seemed to come from deep in my own body. "Yes yes yes."

The funny thing was that this did not strike me as even slightly incredible. Not even slightly. It seemed perfectly plausible, I mean that Ada should give up being Ada Dallas, for me. Later, I could see how fantastic that idea was. How impossible. But at that moment, I believed it completely.

And so, it seemed, did Ada.

That weekend, we went back to the island. It had been a place of ending, so it ought to be the place of beginning.

We could look through the open window and bright air to the sea burning blue under the flame of an orange and climbing sun. The sand stretched, sun-yellowed, to the gray palms nodding green heads at the blue.

Inside the dining room, the sun torched sharp and yellow shapes on the bare wooden floor, and across the table Ada shone bright and virginal: in crisp white, her face above it glowing and unpainted except at the lips.

I felt glances upon us, for now it was the season and many tables were occupied, and I was proud. The proprietress drifted tall and secret through the room, her red dress falling like a robe about her heavy body. She paused beside our table, and smiled without voice as I spoke. I looked into her face and wondered: did it show amusement, or compassion, or simply the catalogue of distant memory? Then she was gone in silent pace, only the creak of an ancient timber marking her passing, and I looked at Ada and thought of nothing else.

After breakfast, or lunch, or whatever it was, we walked the hot sands to the tree-rimmed edge where the island met the sea. We stopped, and I remembered how we had stood before and looked into the storm. Now we faced a blue-mirror sea and a warm wind.

"I never loved before," she said.

"Neither did I, not really."

She was silent, looking not at me but at the clear knife-edge of the horizon.

"Are you sure? About what you're doing?"

"You know I am."

"I mean are you sure about giving up—what you're giving up?"

"As sure as I could ever be."

"Is that completely sure?"

She smiled gently. "Of course not. Nothing is absolute. I only know that at this moment I would rather have you than anything else in the world."

"And tomorrow?"

"Tomorrow is a chance I take."

She came back in my arms as she had before in the driving icy flood of rain, but now the flood was sunlight, hot and soft. I looked past the white curve of her face to the world: blue sea and sky, big white clouds floating high and weightless, and the long unending line of mainland across the water. Standing out from shore, lining distant and slow toward our island, was a high-prowed boat that glittered in the sun. Above it a dark banner curled thin before the wind.

"When can we do it?" she said in my arms.

"Five days from today. We can have the ceremony Friday night and have a weekend honeymoon. We can go to Mobile." I recovered and said swiftly, "Or Galveston. Or Miami, we could fly to Miami."

She turned; she had not minded the Mobile. "Maybe Harmon will give us the whole week off. Do you think?"

"No."

I felt her body ripple in laughter. "I suppose not," she said. Oddly, I did not feel particularly jealous.

Looking out at the water, I watched the yacht come straight and close and closer. I could see some fittings now, shining dark silver in the sun.

"A weekend is a long-enough honeymoon," she said. "We'll have the big one later."

"Think Harmon will give us vacations at the same time?"

"He'll have to."

Harmon did not bother me now. Nothing bothered me. Ada had turned her head to see the yacht, so the wind streamed her hair laterally across my cheek.

"A beautiful boat," I said.

Ada looked away from it. "Let's go back."

She took my arm, turned me toward the hotel, and we hurried through the crumbling sand toward its big soiled whiteness.

It was later, and I was standing before the window.

"She put in here, all right," I said, looking out.

"What are you talking about?"

"That boat. It's tied up at the hotel dock now."

"Oh." She said it from the depths of a supreme and languorous detachment.

I looked purposelessly at the dock. Then I felt my hand tighten on the window sill. "I'll be damned."

She was there fast. "What?"

"There."

I pointed at the long cream-hued hull with dark paneling and the trim that had looked silver across the water, at the slender blue pennant that hung heavily from her jack staff, and at a tall heavy-shouldered figure in a navy blazer and a dark yachting cap, standing immobile and commanding on the dock.

"Yes," I said. "It's him."

"What does he—" She stopped.

Then, as we watched, Sylvestre Marin wrote on a piece of paper and handed it to a boy in dungarees, who started up the boardwalk to the hotel.

She turned to me, and her face was bloodless. I felt her fingers dig the flesh of my forearm.

"You know what he's here for," she said.

"Come on." I took her shoulders between my hands. "So he's come after you. So you tell him it's still no. No deal. That's all you have to do."

"That's all I have to do," she said tonelessly, and I looked in her face and wondered what I saw there. She had proved she was not afraid of Sylvestre Marin. So it could not be fear of him— could it?

"That's all," I said. "Now get dressed and go down and send him away."

"Yes. I'll get dressed."

She was making up at the table when I answered the knock we were waiting for, took Sylvestre's note, and read it to her aloud.

"It's nothing," I said, feeling the paper in my hand like a gun, watching her touch rouge to her pale cheeks. "You just tell him again. You've changed your mind."

I watched her a moment. Then I said, "You aren't afraid of him, are you?"

She looked at me. "You know I'm not."

"What are you afraid of, then?"

She gave me a long level glance, and did not answer, and I knew the shape of my own fear.

She stood up, fully dressed now, fully made up, all ready, and faced me. Forever after, I was to wonder what was in her mind, or her heart, at that moment. I wondered then. But then, as now, all I had was a question mark. Maybe that is what every real move finally sifts down to: the question mark at the bottom. So staring at the question mark, I said, awkwardly, "Okay, now you just go down and tell him again and come back up. It'll be over in ten minutes."

She smiled, and touched my hand. "Of course."

"Want me to go with you?"

She shook her head, still smiling. "No. I'll handle it." She touched her hair, gave the mirror a final check, and started out. At the door she said, "Bye, darling. I'll be right back."

She opened the door and started out. She almost closed it behind her, then opened it again, and leaned inside. "Steve," she said, "I love you." Then the door closed, and I heard her footsteps fade down the long hallway.

Did I know then? I am not sure. I wanted so badly not to know that perhaps I did not.

I lighted a cigarette, sat in a chair, drew three times on it, then threw it on the floor. Then I walked to the window and looked out.

Sylvestre was still standing on the dock, still unmoving, at once vigilant and relaxed, waiting as a tiger waits on the rock above the trail.

Then Ada's back came into my field of vision as she walked out of the hotel onto the boardwalk that led to the dock. I watched her stride tall and white and full-hipped toward Sylvestre, until I heard her footsteps beat slow, distant, and receding on the wood.

He was facing her now; and not moving, not altering visibly in attitude, he was suddenly coiled and poised on the edge of action. Ada's back narrowed as she went further from me and closer to Sylvestre. He moved two steps toward her, easily and watchfully, and I saw his dark face flash its ironic smile. He bowed, almost imperceptibly, and Ada's burnt-gold head dipped in acknowledgment.

Sylvestre was talking now, without haste, and with the appearance of negligence. I saw the gold head above the white shake "No." Then the movement of her head and lips showed she was speaking fast, almost violently.

Sylvestre smiled and began to speak again. The smile never altered on his face. Ada's head shook again. She turned from him and took a step toward the hotel. His hand touched her shoulder, and, for an instant, she stopped.

Then she raised her shoulder, the hand fell, and she walked along the narrow boardwalk back to the hotel. Sylvestre walked just behind her, not seeming to hurry, yet not losing ground. I heard Ada's footsteps come toward me on the boards. Sylvestre's crepe soles made no sound.

Then they had passed under the window, into the hotel, and out of my vision.

So it was over. Like that. I seized the corpse of my fear, dragged it to the light and named it. Oh, I could name it now, for it was dead. I had been afraid she would go with Sylvestre, and marry Tommy Dallas, and leave me alone. I laughed in silent wildness. I could laugh, for I held reprieve in my hand. I could sigh, for I had not lost.

I had won, and I knew then that I had not believed I could win. I was weak with the winning, and shocked with it. I was afraid of the shapes of dead fears.

I felt a rock of coldness in my belly, and knew the luxury of dissolving it grain by grain. Then I felt sweat on my forehead, touched it, and found it cold. Then I poured a straight shot, drank it fast, and felt the fire consume all the coldness.

I fell backward into a chair, breathed hard and slow, and eased every muscle and nerve, one at a time.

It was all right, it was all right, and Ada was on her way up.

We would be married next week, I would work harder and play it smarter, and everything would be fine, it would all work out.

I lay my head back, and closed my eyes, and after an unmeasurable interval that might have been a second or an hour, I sat straight up. Ada was not back.

I looked at my watch, and saw it circle off five minutes. She was still not back. I stared at the second hand as it swept the dial several times. I started to go down to get her, and remembered I had promised I would not interfere.

Then, from a certain distance, I heard the noise of motors starting, and knew before I reached the window that they were marine motors.

I saw the man in dungarees stoop slowly, like an image in an arrested dream, toss the last line from the dock cleat to the boat, and leap—it seemed in slow motion—from the dock to the forecastle.

The motor hum deepened, the bow swung like fate toward the open Gulf, and the cream-and-silver hull crept with infinite slowness from the dock. I watched the sudden surge of water it drove at the pilings, heard the water suck at them hard, and above that heard the unrelenting beat of propellers.

And still breasting ahead with that fevered slowness of a third-sleep dream, in which every line is a knife, every hair a universe, the sharp prow moved clear of the dock and was in open water.

The bow cut again the spearhead of foam, receding now, and her dark pennant blew backward in the wind. In the open cockpit, behind the cabin, I saw Sylvestre in the sharp-billed captain's cap, and under wet gold hair that whipped hard in the wind, I saw Ada.

She was standing, very straight, in the white dress, her face unsmiling and trained on the sea. Then she turned, and for one instant she looked at the hotel and at our window. If she saw me, she gave no sign. She turned away, to look at the deep water through which she was about to pass, and to the sharp point on the mainland the boat would finally reach.

Then from the window, I could no longer see her face, but only her hair trailing dark gold in the wind as the boat went faster ahead.

The proprietress was blank-faced when I checked out. Two weeks later, I saw on page one of the morning paper a picture of Ada and Tommy Dallas. They were facing the camera and each had one arm around the other. Tommy wore his gray Stetson, Ada was bareheaded. Both were smiling widely. The headline said: SINGING SHERIFF WEDS TV BEAUTY. I folded the paper carefully, pushed it to the back of the desk, and started to edit the 10 A.M. newscast.

Tommy Dallas

The Cad floated around the corner towards the parking lot, and I looked out the window and straight up at it; I looked at it for the first time in Christ knows how many years, and there it was just like the last second I had seen it: jabbing stiff and tall into the sky. The sky was like it had been ordered special, dark and drooping. The lawns were dead green. And down at the foot of the building, making dark little knots, the mourners were already gathering.

To look at it, nothing had changed, except the mourners and what they came for. Well. I knew better. A hell of a lot had changed including me.

Earl eased the Cad down the driving lane towards the end of the lot where signs said SPACE RESERVED, and I couldn't help remember how I used to have the number-one spot down there under the building. A state trooper in a sharp-looking blue-gray uniform, he looked familiar, he waved us to one marked SPACE RESERVED GOVERNOR T. DALLAS. Earl swung the Cad into it.

I could afford to be seen in a Cad now. After what I'd been through it couldn't hurt me. Nothing could hurt me, for they thought I was a sufferer and blessed in the sight of the Lord. That was a kick. That was funny. Because by God I had suffered, I had been through a hell of a lot, and they didn't know one thing about it. What they knew was a lie, and what they didn't know was true, so they were right all the time. Figure it out.

"Okay, govnor." Earl got out and started to come around and open the door but I got out first.

"Nemmine," I said. "Don't spoil me, boy."

"Hell, govnor. You a big man."

"Shit," I said.

I wasn't no governor, I was an ex-governor. Though maybe I was going to do a little something about that ex.

The cars were jampacked together. I squeezed my way between them to the curb. And frogs flopped in my belly as we climbed over and up the white walk that cut through grass and evergreens and then went on and past Huey P. Long. A light in the building throws a spot on Huey's statue twenty-four hours a day, it never goes off, and in the gray daylight you could just see the pale yellow shaft on Huey's bronze face. He was looking out at the world like he was seeing maybe all there was or maybe nothing, and I walked past him, and then, up there on the wide white steps, I saw the long rectangle inside an American flag, and I knew that inside that was Ada. I saw it, and I felt my guts drop out from under me.

And on the other side of the green from Huey were two men in white coveralls and a pile of loose brown dirt. I felt empty with knowing it was Ada they were waiting for.

I had hated her, and what she had done to me nobody should do to any kind of animal, but I had loved her too, and I was all at once sick and scared about her going into that ground, even if I told myself I didn't give a damn.

I shouldn't have thought like that, not now, but I couldn't help it. I couldn't help thinking about all that woman, gone to nothing and into the ground.

And I didn't hate her any more. For the first time since it happened I didn't hate her. I could remember the good times, before she had done it. Well. Maybe they weren't really good times. But there was some goodness in them, and now I could admit it.

I could even admit Ada made me finally learn what I needed to learn. It took her, and all of what she did, for me to learn it. Or maybe to get to where I could do something about it. Maybe you're born knowing. Maybe the fight is to make yourself admit what you know. And then to do what you have to do about what you always knew. But I guess that is learning, too.

It took me all my life, and I didn't learn it until a lot of people were dead, and now Ada was dead, and I had almost died myself, and somebody else was going to die. But in the end I'd learned. In the end it was maybe even worth what I had paid to learn.

We'd got married in the First Methodist Church of St. Peter's parish on Sunday, June 11. That was fifteen months before the Democratic primary. The church was one of three Protestant churches in the whole parish; I wasn't Catholic and neither was Ada. It was funny that I wasn't, because nobody is supposed to be elected to anything in the southern parishes unless they're Catholic. I couldn't of been sheriff of course except for Sylvestre, Sylvestre could elect anybody he wanted, and he wanted somebody that wasn't Catholic so he could run him for governor. You can't get elected governor if you're Catholic. That was what beat Chep Morrison. He should of run for senator, a Catholic can make senator.

I stood up at the altar in a double-breasted blue suit, no cowboy stuff for this one, and I felt my legs shiver, and I thought, *Is this you, Jesus Christ is this you,* and I looked around and thought for just a flash maybe I would cut and run. But I didn't. It was too late. How had it happened, how had I got there? I didn't mean for it to be this, not ever. It wasn't real. It wasn't me, not at the altar in a blue suit.

But it was real, and it was me, and it was Ada coming up the aisle, in that white dress with the white veil, on Sylvestre's arm, the organ booming out in the old pants-wetting *tum-tum-da-dum,* and her face smooth and white like frosted ice. I tried to grin at her, I guess not very good, and she smiled back, and I wondered what she was thinking. I wondered then, and I wondered a hell of a lot of times after that, and I didn't know, while she came down the aisle like a white statue that could somehow move, and I never did know.

How did I come to it? Was it just that I was a dumb sonofabitch? Was it that I wanted it so much I would do anything to get it?

Both those were true. But nobody ever does anything for just one reason. I kidded myself for a long time that it was just that I wanted her so bad I would even marry to get her. But that wasn't true, or not all the truth.

The big thing was that she made me feel like I was standing on my hind legs and throwing a shadow. When I was with her, I felt like I was alive. I felt real in myself for the first time since I went with Sylvestre.

I'd been a zero and I knew it. After Sylvestre took me over, I was so much empty space. He reached through me for whatever he wanted; I wasn't there. But I always had the feeling, somewhere, that this was only temporary, that all at once I would come back, I would be as solid as a side of meat. It would just happen. One day.

And Ada made me feel like it had happened—almost. That I was there again, big and solid—almost. That pulled me to her. That was the thing.

I don't know how she did it. Part of it, I guess, was some things she said: *you can do what you want, Tommy, you don't have to be anybody else's shadow, Tommy, you don't know how much you can do, Tommy.*

This was the old bull. I am almost sure now she didn't mean it, or all of it, but in the end it turned out to be true. In the very end, I mean. And she may have meant some of what she said. I think she came to mean it, for a little while.

But it wasn't just her saying things, that was only a little of it. It was like she was a current of electricity, and when I was with her I cut into the current and felt it running from her to me. And then I had it, myself.

All of that changed a hell of a lot, but that was the way it was then, and that was most of all why I married her, and now I know it.

But that wasn't all of it either. Part of the other was true. She set me on fire, she drove me crazy that way, and I would have done anything to get it. And I hadn't ever been close, not once, in all those months.

I would kiss her, and pull her close, and she would let herself go for one second, and I would think I would die happy if I could just have her. Then she would break away, breathing hard and her eyes closed.

"No, no," she might whisper, and her breath would come, all heavy and working. "Don't. Please don't."

"Hon, come on, hon. We got to. We just got to."

"No, we haven't got to. We don't have to. I'll never do that for anybody but my husband."

"Hon. Please, hon."

"No, darling, no. I love you but I won't even for you, not that."

And I would beg her, and she would say no, and then she would break down and let me kiss her once again, and maybe even let me just touch her, once, real fast, and then she would be gone again.

Hell, I knew what she was doing. I knew she was no virgin, either. It was what all of them are always trying to do. This time it just got to me, is all. I never thought any of them could get to me with it, but she did.

I would look at her hips when she walked away, and they swung like nothing else on this earth; not wide, not rolling like the easy chippies, but tight, controlled, all power. You would look at them moving away and they had all the power in the world, you would die unless you tasted that power.

But you couldn't, not ever, not unless ... and that I thought was worse than dying.

And she knew how to use it. She knew how to turn the knife.

Sometimes she would be sweet but standoffish, she would talk to you in that cool, high-toned Newcomb way, and then all at once on purpose she would drop it and throw the grin at you and say something that was pure Irish Channel: "Geez, guy, what yez tryna do?" And one side of her mouth would curl up in a grin, and she would stand back and look at you like she was saying, "I'm on to you, you bastard, I know what you want and it's worth more than you got and you damn well can't have it." And this turned the fire up a few more degrees.

This got worse and worse, wanting her, knowing I could never get her, and one day Sylvestre said, real easy, "You know, you could do a lot worse than marry that girl," and I thought: *By God I will, if that's what I have to do to have it, I will.*

And before I knew it I had backed into it. It was like dying maybe might be, you are afraid of it but you think it is big, very big, and then all at once there it is, and you say, *Is this all?*

So I told myself I married her so I could go to bed with her. I told myself that was the reason. And it was *a* reason. But the big reason, and this one I didn't admit for a long time, was that she made me be real for myself.

So there I was at the altar and there Ada was. She squeezed my arm, and smiled, and even winked at me once or twice while the preacher was reading. I guess she knew I was scared. When the ceremony was over, she kissed me like she meant it or maybe like she was trying hard to mean it. When we walked down the aisle toward the door, she slipped her arm through mine and held it close.

After the ceremony, we had a reception on Sylvestre's big lawn, and it looked like all St. Peter's was there. Even the Governor came down from Baton Rouge, and he looked a little sour because his four years were more than half gone, and he knew I would be taking over, soon. All through the reception, she stayed close to me, touching me with her hand sometimes, blowing kisses sometimes, and if I wasn't her dream man nobody could of told it. Then the reception was over, and I was driving somewhere.

"Well baby, I guess we gone and done it." That was almost the first thing I had said to her all afternoon. "Huh baby?"

"I guess we have." She smiled, and I thought her smile was more friendly or brotherly than anything else. What I thought must have showed in my face, because she whispered, "Don't worry, Tommy," and kissed me in a way that didn't have a damn thing brotherly about it.

I got to say this for her, once she made a deal, even if it wasn't spelled out, she kept it. She didn't hold nothing back. She gave me what I wanted. I used to say that none of it was as good as it looked walking down the street, but with her it wasn't so. With her it was better.

That first night, she came to me, and this time she didn't move away, this time she stayed.

Hell, I never thought she was no virgin, but where did she learn all she knew?

It turned out she could do anything she wanted with me. Once she got sore at me about something, I forget what, something I had done, and just to punish me, she cut me off for a week. One day I left the house in a mad, and came back a couple of hours later, and slammed the door, and went into her dressing room to tell her to go to hell.

She was sitting there in a red satin robe, reading *Vogue*.

"Hello, dear." She didn't look up.

"Hello." I was getting ready to tell her off, but she didn't look up, she kept reading the magazine, and then she did look up. And she moved. Real slow and no more than an inch or two, but I looked, and felt myself turning over, and knew I was a goner again. That was all it took, with her.

So for a few months we lived together like that. For a while, it was the best time of my life. And then I felt things changing, I felt them slipping away, sliding out from under, and I not only didn't know what to do but I didn't know what it was.

Then I did know. I couldn't cut into the current any more. I looked at myself and I couldn't see nothing. I wasn't really there.

For a while she had made me come alive for myself. Now she didn't. I was like I had been before we came together.

Was it her fault or mine?

I guess it was mine. I got to say this for Ada, she kept her deals. There was no place I could say: Here, it stopped right here. It just whined and whimpered and faded out. But there was a spot I could say: By this time it was all over.

This was about four months after we had been married. This night, I felt like hell. Sylvestre had told me to fire my chief deputy, André Morere, because he had set up a little private pay-off thing with a new gambling house. André was as good a friend as I had. I didn't want to fire him. I didn't want to fire him a damn bit.

"Get rid of him," Sylvestre had said. "Right away. All arrangements in this organization are made at the top. Down the line they just follow orders. The man that forgets that is lucky to get off with just being fired."

"Hell." I felt miserable. "André's a good boy. Couldn't we just maybe give him, you know, a warning?" I felt my voice get lost and swallowed the last words: "Or something?"

Sylvestre was studying some papers on the desk. He didn't look up and he didn't answer.

"He—he's got a sick wife, he needs money real bad, the job—" My voice trailed off again.

Then Sylvestre did look up. He looked me in the eye for a couple of seconds, and I felt myself breaking up inside.

"That's enough," he said. "You do what I tell you." His voice was low, just above a whisper, and I felt weak and sick with being afraid. "You get all the deputies and all the town marshals and every police officer in the parish in your office at eleven o'clock tomorrow and you fire him in front of all of them and you tell them why."

Now my throat was all dry, my legs were fluttering, but I tried one more time anyway. "I—"

"Did you hear me?" Now his voice was a whisper and those black eyes had hold of mine, and I said, "I—I, oh, sure, Sylvestre, I got you, that's the way it'll be all right."

And I went home to Ada in that fine red-brick eight-room three-bath house I had bought for her at builder's costs in St. Peter's, the town, and I got around to telling her, and I waited for her to say something, but she didn't. She didn't say nothing. She just nodded her head a little and went on with her book.

I finally said, "Hell, I don't want to do that, not like that. André's a good friend, I wish—" And I heard myself fade out, again.

Ada looked up. She was not very interested. "What are you worried about? He took his chances, didn't he? And he got caught, didn't he? What the hell else do you think he expects?"

Then me: "Nothing. I just—nothing. You think I ought to do it?"

And Ada: "*He* said so, didn't he?"

Me: "Yeah, he said so, I just thought maybe—"

Ada: "Maybe what?"

Me: "Maybe you thought I ought to do something else."

I guess what I really wanted her to say was: What do *you* think you ought to do, Tommy? You're a great man, Tommy, you make up your own mind. You're just the greatest, Tommy, yeah, you are The Man on a stick.

I wanted her to say that, and I wanted myself to think it, and then I guess I wanted to feel good about doing what Sylvestre told me to do, because of course that was what I was going to do.

But she didn't say what I wanted. She didn't say anything like it. She said:

"You better do what he says." And in a flat voice.

Then she just sat there, looking at me with no particular interest, and I knew the big thing was already over. I don't mean over that second. I mean that it had been over. That she had given up on me, or got tired of fooling with me, or something. She was never going to say again, "Look, damn you, there you *are*. You are you. You are Tommy Dallas, you are real." (Not that she had ever said it like that, that plain, but she had said it other ways.) And I knew she had stopped believing something was there, and stopped caring, if she ever had.

And I felt sick and sad inside, like someone I loved had died, and I felt empty and relieved because now I didn't have to try to live up to it. I didn't have to try to make myself be, not any more. I could lie back and let things happen.

So that's how we were, and how had we got there?

We had got there because I was a zero inside and out.

That was one reason Sylvestre picked me. He *wanted* somebody he could reach right through and turn the knobs. I guess he seen I was it.

He got me when I was singing at a little station in St. Peter's three times a day, and doing a 6 A.M. farm show for a New Orleans station. It had taken a lot for me to get that far even. If I hadn't had something, I would of still been pushing a plow up in Winfield parish, where I was a kid in the thirties. Those years I been trying to forget ever since.

Daddy went busted with six-cent cotton, then we were scrabbling on shares and lucky to be alive, and little bits of that time I can't forget no matter how I try. The cold wind from Dakota rattling the boards in the shack and eee-eee-eee-ing through the broken windows we couldn't nail up tight. Sowbelly and black-eyed peas and fried corn bread twice a day and nothing else. Walking barefoot two miles to the school bus stop, my feet cracked and hurting with bruises and dead with cold. Wearing a scratchy shirt made out of crokersacks and one pair of jeans that Ma had to wash out and dry at night because they were the only ones. And in the morning, not at sunup or even daylight but before that, at the first rooster crow almost, but it still dark while I threw the stinking swill to the stinking pigs, forked hay for the one mule and one old cow, and felt my teeth clicking and my shoulders shaking and most of all felt the cold cowturds and muleturds squishing up through my toes. All of it that I hated got hooked up with that one thing: cold cowturds through bare toes before daylight in December.

A lot of kids had this ambition or that one, but not me. All I wanted was to get away from that cold oozy squish between the toes. My folks kept me in school, God knows how, and I knew I wasn't going to make no lawyer or doctor, but I knew I would rather die before I would farm. So I thought I would maybe be a schoolteacher and I even started at Lousiana Normal that is Northeast Louisiana State now. But up there was a guy, Smiley Sagram, and he had a gittar. He taught it to me, and we went around singing and playing, and we won an amateur contest at Shreveport. Then we picked up a couple other guys, and first thing we knew we were making a living playing at juke joints and on hillbilly radio shows. We were doing all right that way for quite a few years when they drafted us.

I was a private the whole war, and not only never got out of the States but for two years didn't even get out of Louisiana. I even picked up pocket money playing at the jukes. Smiley was with me at Polk all that time; then one day they zipped him out as a replacement and four weeks after that he got killed going in at Omaha Beach.

There he was. One day slapping the gittar, the next day it seemed like, he was dead. And all the things we had done together seemed like they had just happened, him being dead seemed a hundred years ago. Once something has happened it is like everything else that has happened; it's all in the same pocket. Reach down and drag out what you want.

What happened next was that I got out, picked up the other two boys and two more, and we came to New Orleans and then St. Peter's. I mean the town, it is the parish seat of St. Peter's parish. We got that 6 A.M. spot at WLND in New Orleans, and we got the three hours a day at the little station in St. Peter's. We were making the best money we ever made, I had more girls than I ever had, and I felt pretty good.

What I had, I had made by myself. I had a lot of luck, but I had by God made some of the luck, and I was proud.

Then, one night, we played at an election rally for Joe LeMeune. He was Sylvestre's man for sheriff. Elections didn't mean nothing in St. Peter's parish, Sylvestre's men were automatically elected, but he liked to give the voters a show. I sang before the speeches and after. Everybody had fun. Even the opposition candidate was there having fun; he was Sylvestre's, too. Sylvestre liked to have a couple of them go, so it looked bona fidey. But everybody knew who was supposed to win.

After the rally, Sylvestre sent word he wanted to see me in his law office.

How come? I wondered, when I walked to his office in the little one-story yellow brick building across from the big three-story white-stone Confederate-statue-in-front courthouse that he ran from the little building.

I knocked on the door, and waited a long second before a voice inside said come in.

I saw the back of Sylvestre's white head over the top of a leather chair. He sat there, not turning.

"Yessir," I said. He still didn't turn.

"It's me. Dallas."

He swung around all at once and his face pointed at me like a hatchet blade or a 105-mm or maybe like nothing else in God's world but Sylvestre Marin's face.

He didn't say nothing. He looked me up and down, like I was a slaughtered carcass he might be going to buy. Which I was. Only I didn't know it.

I felt myself cold inside, and under his face, hit by those black bullets of eyes, I felt it all go away: the red silk silver-trimmed shirt, the white fifty-dollar Stetson, the skin-tight black pants. All I could feel was the cowturds under my toes.

"You wanted. They said you wanted to see me." One of the eighty-dollar boots was toeing the floor, and I noticed and stopped it. I guess I blushed.

"Yes." His voice was low and soft, and like cold music. "I did." He looked at me, his face not changing, letting it soak in, and I was sure he saw inside me, that he knew everything I was thinking.

Finally he said:

"I liked the way you handled yourself tonight, Dallas. The people liked you. I've been watching you quite a while and I like the way you handle yourself most of the time."

"Thank you, sir." I felt the color getting thicker.

"I understand you've got a war record."

"Yessir. That is, nosir. I was in the army but I never got out of the country." What did he have on his mind?

"That's all right, I think it's better. People don't really warm up to a legitimate hero. He makes them uneasy. He is superior. People hate superiority, Dallas. A candidate should never be superior."

"Yessir." What was he talking about?

"On the other hand, it is bad not to have been in at all because then they think you got away with something."

"Yessir." I was still wondering.

"You're a Baptist." He didn't ask it. He just said it like he was ticking things off.

"Yessir. I mean I was a Baptist. I ain't really been nothing for a long time. That is I ain't been going to church."

"Start going."

Who the hell was he to tell me to start going to church, I thought, but I didn't say it. I knew who he was. I had been feeling great half an hour before while a thousand people were applauding. I had never felt better, I felt big and solid as the Confederate statue. But now I didn't feel like nothing.

"Dallas." He stopped a minute, like a judge about to pronounce sentence. "I can use you. In fact, and I tell you frankly, I have been in a manner of speaking waiting for you."

"Me?"

"That's right. You can get uncommitted votes from the platform, you're a Protestant, you're a veteran. You have the perfect personality for a candidate." He smiled to himself at that. "It is my considered opinion that you'll be the best vote-getter this state has seen since Jimmy Davis."

"Me?" I was scared. But at the same time, I was all at once a foot off the floor.

"You." He smiled just a little bit. "What would you say to being sheriff two years from now and governor four years after that? What would you say to fifty thousand a year?"

"I. I never thought about nothing like that, Mr. Marin. It don't seem hardly possible."

He laughed a cold, hard laugh. "I only deal in the possible, Dallas. And you don't need to think. I think."

"Well." I was still that foot off the floor, but— "I appreciate it, sir. I appreciate it an awful lot, but I like what I'm doing now, and I think I'd just like to go on doing that if you don't mind. Sir."

He smiled with his whole mouth now. "What did you think I meant for you to do? That's what we're selling. Remember Davis." He stopped and looked at me. "Tomorrow you'll go on the payroll as a deputy. But keep right on with both shows."

I wanted to say no. No I won't. I like it the way it is and I'm not going with you because I am scared as hell of you. You can't make me. But I wanted the other, too. What he said: sheriff, fifty thousand dollars, governor. I wanted it. I had never thought of anything like that before and now all at once I had the feeling of Santa Claus coming. And I could feel myself giving in to him. I had to do what he wanted. So when I opened my mouth what came out was:

"Yessir. I'll do it."

And he took me over just like that, and after that nothing was the same.

And here I was with Ada, and she finally knew what I was, and it was nothing.

The next day I fired Morere like Sylvestre said.

So one thing was over with Ada and me, and another had started. We were still friendly, we were still man and wife, and nothing you could see had changed much. But it was different, and we both knew it. I started doing a little tomcatting, just a little, on the side, very quiet, and I think Ada knew it and I think she did not care.

Anyway, the election was less than a year away now, and Sylvestre started to get busy. All I had to do was what he told me.

For headquarters, he got a couple of rooms on the fourth floor of the New Orleans hotel where Ada's studio was. This was on the north side of Canal, in the Quarter. People could come to see us there without making it a real big production. Sylvestre and me could drive over from the St. Pete courthouse in an hour, and Ada could take an elevator. She was her own boss now, with just the one show, and it was over at twelve-thirty. So she would come down and meet important visitors when they came in and they were just impressed as hell at talking to a real live TV star, even a local one.

A lot of people came to see Sylvestre. Some of them were Sylvestre's own organization people, parish precinct leaders and so on, that wanted to get checked. Others wanted to make deals, or make sure the deals they already made were still okay.

In two months we got some big ones.

The Old Regular leaders, Johnny Darro, Whitey Lambert, and Jack Watson, they came in. They shook hands, laughed with me, and then went into the inside office with Sylvestre to do their talking.

Two guys from the AFL came by. Sylvestre told them, "Tommy's a good union man himself, member of Actor's Equity." Then he took them inside while I waited.

Three top men from the oil companies saw him. They didn't even make like they were paying any attention to me, and they looked sour. When they came out, they did not look exactly happy, but they didn't look quite as sour, either. One said, "Well, Senator, I'm glad we could reach some kind of understanding, anyway. You know how we feel about the whole thing, but—"

After they were gone, I told Sylvestre, "I thought you was going to soak them."

"There's soaking and soaking, Tommy. Which would you rather get hit with—a fly swatter or a blackjack?"

And then the sheriffs came in. Dolph Cazadessus from southwest Louisiana, Bill Burns from the middle, and Freddy Rogers from up north. Freddy was a grinning little half-pint who had shot and killed nine men after they had shot at him first. They called him the toughest man in Louisiana.

This time I was mad when Sylvestre didn't take me in. I was a sheriff, too. They came out, and Cazadessus was saying, "At least three-quarters," and they all nodded.

One afternoon Jack Moore came in. With old Jimmy Morrison not running this time, Jack was the only candidate besides me and whoever the reform crowd would run. Jack had been a congressman for ten years, and it looked like he was going to be one forever. He had run for governor three times, and he had a pretty good state organization—he was able to throw the key people some very nice favors in Washington, even if he never got into the state capitol, so they stayed with him.

He never figured on making governor. He would just lose in the first primary, and make a deal to support one of the two that got into the second, and pick up a nice piece of change. It was strictly business; if he'd of ever got in the second primary he'd been scared to death.

"Just a courtesy call, gemmun," Jack said, a big wide grin under the black horn-rims and the red fringes of his bald head. "Just wanted to wish m' worthy opposition all the luck in the whole world. Never let politics interfere with friendship, that's my motto. Friends before the election, friends after."

"That's nice, Jack," said Sylvestre. "That's very nice."

He went on like that, and we went on like that, and he finally started to go. He turned at the door. "Just remember, gemmun, that you can always count on Jack Moore." That meant we could always count on buying him in the second.

While Sylvestre was fixing up the big lines, I was getting around as much as I could, making as many appearances as I could. Ada had me on her TV show half a dozen times. Since I wasn't an announced candidate and the campaign hadn't started, the FCC equal-and-opposite-time thing couldn't be dragged in.

She was calling herself Ada Dallas now instead of Ada Malone. I told her once, just joking, "Hell, by election time they won't know which Dallas is running."

And she laughed and said, "Does it really matter?" Just joking, too.

While the politics went on, the way things were between us got more so. I knew she didn't believe I was anybody any more. And knowing she didn't believe it, I couldn't see myself for real. I looked for myself and couldn't see nobody there, nothing but a Stetson Hat and a gittar and a voice that could sing a little and say, "Sure, Sylvestre. I got you, Sylvestre." I was as I said in a way relieved. I didn't have to try hard any more. It is goddamn hard work to try to *be* for twenty-four hours a day.

One thing was funny. Now that the important thing was over, now that I didn't have to work to try to make her see me, I wanted her a lot more. In a different kind of way, and I am not sure exactly how it was different. It was maybe that I felt like this: Okay, if I can't do nothing else I can sure do this, if I can't have nothing else I can sure have this, and I want it.

And it looked like she felt the same way. She let me have what I wanted. Like she was saying: Okay, you can have *that*. It isn't much, I don't care, but you can have that all right.

One night I saw her at the house, after she had spent a whole day of campaigning, first with the program, then talking to a couple of women's clubs, going to a fashion-show cocktail party and I don't know what else.

I said, "Well, I guess it was a kind of full day, huh? I mean for you."

And she said: "I guess it was."

"Well. You sure done fine."

I don't know who I was trying to kid. Me giving her the pat on the back. But I went on.

"You sure look fine after a day like that."

"Why thank you, dear, you're very sweet."

I went over to where she was sitting, and feeling very awkward, I touched her shoulder. She didn't move away and she didn't do nothing to encourage me. I just left my hand on her shoulder and then she looked up and smiled, a smile that was a little tired but not much, and said, "Sure, of course. Why not?"

By this time, Sylvestre's chauffeur was driving him all over the state in that big black Imperial three-four days a week. He could afford to have a chauffeur and an Imperial; he wasn't no candidate. He just owned the candidate.

Now it was seven months before the first primary, and we announced. Sylvestre started a twice-a-week throwaway paper called the *Free Press*. All it had in it was our own propaganda. The big newspapers were all against us, and he wanted something to hit back with.

Jack Moore, that us gemmun knew we could count on, was already in. And right after we came out, the opposition announced their man: Armand Lenoir.

Lenoir was the candidate of what used to be the reform group— the old Sam Jones-Jimmy Davis-Bob Kennon thing that got itself organized every once in a while. And he was a lemon. How come they picked him I'll never know. He was rich, he was Catholic, he wasn't only from New Orleans but he was an honest-to-god New Orleans blueblood. He had a great-great-great-granddaddy that had been a French governor of Louisiana before Louisiana was part of the United States. All this and they still picked him.

There was only one reason they thought they could get away with it. Lenoir was a combat infantry veteran and had lost his left hand in the war, and he had been active a little in the veterans' outfits. They thought this would take the curse off. And it would, some. But not near enough. He was still a Catholic French New Orleans society boy trying to run for Governor of Louisiana.

I wondered why they had settled on him. For one thing, it was businessmen's money behind that outfit, and they wanted a businessman candidate. Which he was: he had never been in politics before. He was head of something called Mississippi Valley Incorporated— MVI—that did a big export business with South America. He had made a lot of dough out of that, and he had a lot of dough of his own to start with, and he was willing to spend a lot of it. The grapevine said he wrote out a check for $100,000 for the nomination.

With Jones and Davis and Kennon out of it now, the power behind him was New Orleans power. They just couldn't believe how bad it was for a candidate to be from New Orleans because they were from there themselves. Oh, they had been told often enough, and they had seen what happened with Chep Morrison, but they didn't really believe it. They wanted him because he was one of them. And they could tell themselves that the shot-off left hand made everything all right, and their organization could put him over anyway. So they ended up believing what they wanted to believe.

He wanted to be governor real bad, and his wife wanted it worse. She was another French blueblood, she hadn't had any dough when she married Lenoir, she had it now, and she wanted to be on top of everything, where I guess she figured she should have been all the time. The word was that it had been her that pried him loose from the 100 G's.

I had seen her a few times, and she reminded me somehow of Ada, even if she wasn't the same type at all. She had black hair and white skin, and a long-legged look like a race horse. You could tell she had dynamite. I guess it was this that reminded me of Ada.

The funny thing was that Ada did not know her but hated her. I asked her why.

"Because," Ada said. "Because."

"That ain't a reason."

"It is for me."

"No it ain't. You hate her guts and I just wonder why. It ain't natural."

"All right then. I hate her because I've had to look at her picture in the *Picayune* society section ever since she had pigtails. I hate her because it was her and not me in the pictures. Does that satisfy you?"

"Yeah," I said. "I guess it does."

So that was their candidate. They had sense enough to pick the rest of the slate from the country, that is the rest of Louisiana. And they got a hell of a break when they talked William Lee, an ex-speaker of the house, from Bossier parish, up north, into coming out for lieutenant governor. He was a real pro, and I was surprised they talked him into it, but I guess they made it worth his while. They would of been better off running him in the number-one spot, but it was too late for that.

One day Sylvestre brought in our number-two man. He was stocky,

big-bellied, and bald-headed, with gold-rimmed glasses. I heard him
laughing outside the door, and the first thing I saw when he came in
behind Sylvestre was his belly shaking.

Sylvestre waved me over. "Tommy, meet our lieutenant governor.
Ronald Hudson, Tommy Dallas."

"Glad to know you," I said. "Any lieutenant governor of Sylvestre's is a lieutenant governor of mine."

"Say, that's all right. That's really all right." He laughed some
more, the belly still bouncing, the lens of the gold-rimmed spectacles
misting all up.

He was a Lake Charles contractor who had got himself a lot of
U.S. money for apartment houses, and some fat city contracts, and
he had a bunch of tract developments going for him all over the
state. We weren't going to be a businessmen's administration, not
by a damn sight, but I guess Sylvestre figured one on the ticket would
be good. And Hudson must have come up with a nice piece of change
for the spot, forty or fifty great big ones if I knew Sylvestre. He
probably wanted to be governor himself some day. Why not, it
looked like everybody else did.

The rest of the ticket had been picked a long time ago: Ward
Johnson, who already had the job and could be reelected, for secretary of state. Eugene Loveless, a professional hick from central
Louisiana with a nice following, for secretary of agriculture. John
Boudreaux from Donaldsonville in the southeast for public lands
commissioner, a smart lawyer and a Catholic, which for a minor
office is good. It was a good ticket, a nice spread over the state, and
plenty of organization muscle.

"Any chance of getting Leander Perez to come out for us?" I
asked Sylvestre one day.

"Leander says he isn't going to be active this time. Too many
friends on both sides. That's all right. The big thing is he isn't
going to be against us."

It sure was. Leander had plenty big medicine. I was glad we
didn't have to buck him.

So things rolled along, and one day the New Orleans League of
Women Voters had this big luncheon for all the prospective candidates. We were supposed to let them look us over, and tell them
how we stood for good government and so forth. The only guy they
would think about voting for was Lenoir. But Sylvestre didn't want

to give them no easy out, so Ada and I went. Lenoir and Mrs. Lenoir were there, goddamn she was a good-looking woman, and old Jack Moore and his wife, and we made a polite pitch.

And all at once somebody was introducing me and Ada to Mrs. Lenoir.

"How do you do," I said, watching Ada because I knew how she felt about the other one and I was afraid she might get a little bitchy.

But she couldn't have been sweeter. She smiled like there was nobody she'd rather see, and held out her hand.

It was Mrs. Lenoir who did it. She left Ada's hand out there for what looked like half a minute, I guess it was really five or six seconds, before she finally took it, held it between two fingers like it was a dead fish, and then dropped it.

Ada's smile faded, but I got to admit she still tried.

"Haven't we met somewhere or other?" she said.

"Have we?" said Mrs. Lenoir.

Ada lost color but still tried to be polite. "I knew your sister at Newcomb."

"Oh?" Mrs. Lenoir's laugh was like glass breaking. "Did *you* go to Newcomb?"

Ada's mouth opened but all at once she was looking at Mrs. Lenoir's back and Mrs. Lenoir was calling across the room, "Syl-via! Wait up, darling!" And she was pushing her way through the room full of women.

For one part of a second, I saw murder in Ada's face, and then she had forced it away and was smiling again as sweet as you could ask, while she whispered to me, "That bitch that bitching bitch I'll get her!"

And almost in the same breath, she was holding out her hand to some other dame and cooing, "How are you? How nice to see you again!" Just like she loved everybody in the whole wide world.

A couple of days later, the president of the League of Women Voters came out for Lenoir.

Sylvestre laughed when he read it. "That'll get us votes in New Orleans. When some of those ladies campaigned for Chep Morrison, they went around the Irish Channel and the water-front precincts wearing fur coats and driving Cadillacs."

He laughed again, dropped the paper in the wastebasket, and picked up the phone on the desk.

He was spending hours on the telephone every day now, talking to our key people over the state. He had everything right at his finger tips. He could tell you who our chairman was in every one of the thirty-nine parishes, he knew who was on every parish Democratic Executive Committee, and whether they were for us or against us, and he knew how tight our precinct organization was in every one of them, and how close we were to the sheriffs. He carried it all around in his head, he could sit right at the telephone and run the works. I only saw him bobble just once.

He had picked up the telephone and said, not to anybody but to himself, to help himself put his finger in that telephone-book memory of his and come up with the name he wanted, he said, "Who's our man in Lincoln parish, now, what's—"

Then Ada said without looking up, without having to dig, "Belford, Cecil Belford," and Sylvestre looked at her for what seemed a long time but was I guess four or five seconds.

Then he said, "Of course. Cecil Belford." He placed the call, turned the phone away from his mouth while he waited for the call to go through, and said to Ada, "You certainly have a capacity for organization, my dear."

"Just a memory," said Ada, and looked him in the eye and smiled.

I did not know what was really between those two. She did everything he told her, and not just that. She was working hard at being another brain he could count on, somebody smart. And he took her on those terms. I wouldn't say he trusted her, because he wouldn't never trust anybody, but he had respect for her. Of course she had for him. For Sylvestre Marin, who didn't? But she wasn't scared of him, like I was and like everybody else I knew was.

But under all this—her working so hard to be his right hand, him so respectful to her—I felt something hard in each of them hit the same thing head on in the other. This was the feeling I got. But it didn't make sense because who was a woman to ever bother Sylvestre Marin?

Anyway, we had a hell of an organization by this time, and it is the organization that wins your elections. The only thing was, Lenoir's crowd had a pretty good one, too. They had worked a hard couple of years patching together the old Jones-Davis-Kennon bunch, and they had a pretty good setup in the parishes. Jack Moore just had his own little organization, which was not solid enough to put him in, but would make his support worth something in the second primary.

"We ain't got it sewed up, I wouldn't think," I said one day. "We going to have to work like hell campaigning."

Sylvestre smiled. "By the time the campaign starts, we will have the election thoroughly won."

"How?" said Ada.

He smiled again. "The Forces of Law and Order."

"How's that?" I said.

He kept smiling, and didn't answer.

Three weeks later, we found out. We all went up to Baton Rouge to the annual convention of the Louisiana Peace Officers Association. This takes in the sheriffs, deputies, marshals, and so on. I opened the meeting with a couple of songs, then we heard speeches by the outgoing president and a professor of criminology at L.S.U., and that afternoon and night we had parties in the rooms at the Capitol House and around town. Next day we had speeches from the chief of the FBI's New Orleans bureau, and a New York ballistics expert.

That afternoon, Sylvestre invited a lot of, but not all the sheriffs, to a special meeting behind closed doors in one of the hotel banquet rooms. He talked, and they listened, and when it was over, I knew the sheriffs were going to win us the election.

When we started to come down to the lobby after the meeting, a bunch of reporters were waiting there. One of them stopped Sylvestre.

"What's all this, Senator? What did you talk about?"

Sylvestre was in a better humor than I had ever seen him. "Home rule," he said, very pleased, very soft, almost purring. "You can say we discussed home rule."

"Home rule," he said. "Home rule."

I was on one side of him and Ada on the other, in the back seat of the black Imperial that was floating or maybe flying down the Air-line Highway, Old 61, to New Orleans.

"Home rule." His voice was dripping honey, like he was a preacher in the pulpit or somebody's dear old daddy sitting by the cracker barrel.

He lighted a cigar, and the smoke drifted through the car, slow, good-smelling, smelling like all the easy good life there was caught in that one smell. The glass windows were closed tight for the air conditioning, even if it was late October it was 92 in the shade that day. I looked through the glass to the short heavy trees growing thick on the edge of the swamp, and over them to the fireball in the sky that was scorching everybody and everything outside the Chrysler. Then I looked ahead, past the back of the chauffeur's head down the long white road that got narrow and faded and finally blew up where the sun and concrete hit head on.

"Home rule." Now Sylvestre didn't sound like nobody's daddy. "The sheriffs can run anything or let anybody else run anything they can pay for. And that means racing books, slot machines, dice tables, or whorehouses. They can run anything they want if we're elected. In their own parishes they're king. If we're elected."

Nobody said anything. Then Ada stirred, deep down in those Imperial cushions. "I think we just won an election," she said.

"I think so," said Sylvestre.

Then all at once the getting ready, the organizing was over. The campaign had started, and we hit the road. We barreled over the state, Sylvestre in the black Imperial with his chauffeur, Ada and me in a three-year-old Pontiac with a new Cad motor slipped under the hood, and the band boys in a new Olds. It would of hurt me to be seen in a new Olds myself, but it helped to have my boys drive one. That's politics. We burned up the big wide roads that Huey and the ones after him built, and we screeched around curves of the asphalt market roads the county boys built, and we raised big brown dust clouds on the few dirt and gravel back roads still left that nobody would admit they built.

And these two months blurred together in one long streak of speed, and in the blur I see places and faces popping out and coming at me like headlights out of the dark, coming fast and fast and then almost hitting and then losing themselves as they streak past.

Through red clay bluffs and red cattle and green cotton fields with white just starting, to Shreveport. Across the state to Monroe in the northeast corner, with oil and gas derricks jabbing up everywhere. A fast three hours down to Alexandria in the middle of the state, the pine trees tall in the sky. Black Angus cows straddle-legged on the red-brown hills looking down at us going past. Cattycornering to Lake Charles in the southwest, through Bougalee country where the real mean Cajuns lived, the country low and flat and the night dark as hell will be when you get there. Short trees coming out of the dark pastures, fences like jail-house bars, and something standing up against the full moon like a gallows. Back east again to Donaldsonville, pretty and white on the wide slow river, the people soft-talking and French.

And a goddamn endless river of faces. I got a fair memory but I could never begin to remember them. Somebody local was always at my elbow to whisper who they were; the precinct leaders and sheriffs and parish attorneys and executive committeemen and police jury and local big shots and people who just wanted to shake hands.

It was good to get back to New Orleans on a weekend once in a while to catch our breath, and a TV speech is nothing compared to the other kind. We used TV, we used it plenty, but it was still no substitute for getting around. In Louisiana you always going to have to get around and make the personal touch.

Ada had had her show shifted to a one-and-a-half-hour thing once a week; she was big enough to get almost anything she wanted now. She could just rehearse it once Friday morning and then put it on. And even if she couldn't mention politics, it kept the name Dallas right out on the screen once a week, for free.

One week, I made six speeches in two days, and was supposed to make another the next day in Dry Prong, which is the parish seat of Caldwell parish in central Louisiana. I woke up in the Hotel Bentley in Alex without a voice. This was the middle of the week, Ada was with me, and she called the hotel drugstore and they sent up a sprayer and some goop, but it didn't work, and when we pulled into Dry Prong I still couldn't do much more than whisper.

"What we going to do?" I said.

Ada said, very easy, like she had already thought it out and made up her mind, "Don't worry. I'll make the speech."

"You? Maybe we better call Sylvestre—"

"No, there's no need in the least to call Sylvestre. I'll just go ahead and make the speech. Don't worry."

"But maybe—"

"I said don't worry."

So we sat up on the top of the courthouse steps together, and the boys played "You and Me," and a couple of other tunes, and then

Ada got up. "Ladies and gentlemen, I want you to meet my husband and your next governor, Tommy Dallas."

I stood up and bowed and waved while they clapped and yelled, and I pointed at my mouth and shook my head.

Ada smiled and put her hand on my shoulder. "Tommy has been working his vocal cords so hard this last week that they're just played out. So if it's all right with you I'm just going to talk for him today. I'll try to tell you what he wanted to tell you."

She stopped a minute and looked at them, standing absolutely still, smiling just a little, as though she was almost scared but not quite. Then she smiled wide, dazzling them with it.

And she said, "Is that all right with you?"

She had them. You know what I mean. You see it sometimes with people making a speech but a lot more often with a night-club act, where the performer comes out and does something and says something and in one second the contact is made and the current jumps between them and he's got them (or she has). That was the way. Ada had them.

Somebody yelled, "Talk to us, Ada!" and somebody else yelled, "You talk, Ada," and a lot of them just yelled "Ada!"

And she smiled again, and she started. "Ladies and gentlemen, you know what my husband would say to you if he could. He would say it is time for the government of Louisiana to go back to the people of Louisiana. And so I say it to you. It is time for your government to go back to you. You had it once. Then you lost it when they took it away from you, and you know who I mean."

I was damned if I did. I guess she meant the opposition. But they yelled. And she said, "The time has come for you to take it back."

She talked for twenty minutes, and she kept repeating the catch-words over and over again, like a chant or a commercial. "It is time for the government to go back to the people. You had it once and they took it away. It is time to get it back."

It worked. When she was done, they stomped and clapped and whistled and yelled. They most yelled *Ada Ada Ada,* though some, not near as many, yelled *Tommy, Tommy Dallas.*

Later, back in the car, her driving now because I had three-fifths a degree of fever, I said, "Durned if I don't think we got the wrong Dallas running. I believe you'd get more votes."

"Don't be silly, I'm just your pinch hitter." She smiled and patted my knee. But I looked at her face and for the first time ever I thought I saw behind it. She did wish it was her running. Somewhere way off I felt something cold wriggle.

We had two speeches in Baton Rouge the next day, one downtown and one up in the refinery section of North Baton Rouge, so we had to get there this night. It was solid dark when we curved onto the Mississippi River Bridge. The bridge climbed into nowhere, and then we were on top of it. I looked down at the dark water a hundred feet below, and I could see all the lights jumbled together that were Baton Rouge. Between the bridge and the city were gas flares from oil wells, burning like torches a hundred feet high.

Then I looked back from the torches and the river and the lights to Ada behind the wheel. I could see her face, pale in the light from the dashboard and then hard naked white when headlights coming from the other side hit us. She was very pleased and very set on something. Maybe it was the driving, and maybe it wasn't.

And all at once the campaign was over, the first primary was over. I had 311,000 votes, Lenoir had 190,000, and old Jack Moore had 130,000. So it was a runoff; me and Lenoir in the second, and he would have to pull a miracle to beat me.

The campaign went on just like before only now it was the second primary. Anyplace up north it would be the general election that counted, but not here. Here the second primary was the general election. In fact, anyway.

The Sunday after the first primary, Sylvestre came by the house. "It's really too good." He laughed, a little. "As of this moment we could win an absolutely Simon-pure election two to one. That's what the survey says." He had had one of those New York outfits come down to see if we had lost any ground. You had to hand it to him: he never did nothing half-assed.

"I guess we got no problems then." I started to drink some more coffee.

He looked at me, quick and hard. "Don't fool yourself. They're running scared and they're dangerous."

Then he wasn't looking at me any more but was looking off, way off, at space or the election or the world. He was standing very straight and thick, in a gray suit, with a black silk tie that had little gold things chasing each other down it. Then he came back from wherever he was, and he said, "This is the time to be careful."

"Oh, sure," I said. "Sure. But we got the sheriffs delivering and we bought old Jack Moore and we only needed a few more votes anyway. It sure looks like its arranged."

"Nothing ever stays arranged," Sylvestre said. "Between the Idea and the Reality is an ocean of nothing. You can't lay out a perfect course and forget about it. Things happen. You have to see. And to correct. Things always happen."

"What might happen?" Ada said it slow, deep in her throat, and I watched her leg move against the red satin housecoat.

Sylvestre's body swung at her now, slow, like the second hand of a clock. He looked straight down at her, and I wondered if he wanted her. He had to if he was human, but human was not the word, not for him. I had never seen him go after a woman, or take more than one drink, or even finish that one. I had never seen him make a real mistake. He must of made one. But nobody would ever know what it was.

Then he said, repeating, "What might happen?" He took a deep breath and then he said, "Catastrophe." And then nobody said nothing, and I heard the clock ticking in the next room.

But nothing happened. We never let up, and I didn't see how they could pull anything, or how they had any kind of chance at all, even with the newspapers against us.

And they were all against us. One called me a "clown with a banjo" (they should of known anyway it was a gittar). Another said I was a "stooge for machine politicians," and the last one said our campaign was "a travesty on political responsibility and an insult to the state's voters." This was in the city, but all the even halfway big papers over the state were against us. Only ones supporting us were some weeklies Sylvestre had lined up, and of course our *Free Press*.

This didn't bother Sylvestre.

"All to the good," he said. "We've told them often enough newspapers stand for big money. We'll keep on telling them. And we'll keep hitting the tool-of-the-rich pawn-of-the-interests thing with Lenoir. Oddly enough it's true." He laughed. "Even if abstract truth is not exactly our major concern. I never saw a reform candidate yet whose reason for existence was anything but the one thing. He's in there to protect the bankrolls of those who have them."

"Hell, how about you? You got the biggest bankroll in the state of Louisiana."

Sylvestre smiled. That made him feel real good. "Why, Tommy, you might say I'm unique."

He looked at Ada and they both laughed.

With less than a month to go until the second primary, it still looked like Sylvestre was wrong about something happening. The campaign went on fast and smooth and absolutely perfect. I was sure that nothing could happen, that Sylvestre was dead wrong.

And then, three weeks before the election, he turned out to be right. He was right like an earthquake.

A nineteen-year-old St. Peter's honky-tonk girl filed a paternity suit in Civil Court. She petitioned that the father of her two-month-old child be required to assume its support.

As the father, she named me.

It was the big headline in every paper in the city, and I guess the state.

"I knew it." Sylvestre was black mad, I could see the blackness boiling in him like pitch on a bonfire. But he looked almost glad, too. Because he had been right. "I knew they had to pull something. Things were too good. I knew they had to."

"What we going to do?"

I felt awful. I had given them the chance. I was sure the kid wasn't mine but I had given them the chance.

"Do?" Sylvestre's black eyes hit me and I felt like I was in the chair and somebody had thrown the switch. "Deny it, of course. Deny everything. They've been smart for once, though. If they had made her out a sweet simple girl, we could have discredited her by proving what she was. By making a point of it right away, they've simply made you and the whole business look sordid. No, this wasn't one of their mistakes."

He stopped for a second, and he burned me with the look. "I suppose it is true? Not that it matters anyway with three weeks left."

I felt the blood run to my face, and then I looked at Ada and she was not angry but only annoyed, not because I had cheated on her but because I had loused things up. I did not answer Sylvestre, and she said, and now maybe she was laughing just a little, inside, "Oh, grow up. Tell him."

"I don't really even know," I said. "Oh, I messed with her a couple times but so did everybody else who came in the joint. I really don't think it was me."

Sylvestre nodded, maybe an inch. "So I figured." Now he was not wasting any more time being mad at me, I was just a stupid buck private who had done something the general would have to fix. He was studying how to fix it.

"Couldn't we maybe get affidavits from some of the others?" I felt better now that he wouldn't hit me with the shock again.

"Wouldn't help." It was plain he had already thought of that. "It would only be an admission and it wouldn't matter how many to the voters anyway. You'd still be stigmatized."

"How about the boys in the parish? Can't they take care of it anyway when they count the votes? No matter what?"

"This may have turned everything upside down. I'm going to check. But I doubt if we can count on the sheriffs a hundred per cent any more."

He picked up the phone and placed some calls. The first to come through was Bill Burns. Sylvestre said hello, kicked it around a minute, then asked the big one. He held the receiver out so we could hear the answer:

"I tell you, Sylvestre, out here it's like this. You know we got a lot of country people and you know how country people are and it's like this. They're just kind of down on Tommy now until he makes them think it ain't so, and I don't care if it is or it ain't. You know I can swing the count, I can swing it a hell of a lot, but I can't swing it to Tommy with everybody down on him. If I did, they'd be down on me, too. But I tell you, you fix it up and everything will be all right. Prove it ain't so or something like that and everything will be fine."

"Okay, Bill. If that's the way it is." Sylvestre knew when to sweet-talk, and when to blackjack, and when just to leave it alone. "We'll keep in touch." Sylvestre hung up, and turned to us. "You heard it. And that's the way it's going to be, all over."

He checked. It was the same, almost everywhere. There were five or six parishes where the boys said, "The hell with it, we'll handle it." But they weren't enough.

"You see?" he said, after the last call. He looked at his watch. "And to make it really good, Little Boy Blue comes on in a few minutes."

He switched on the TV. We waited a few minutes, then Lenoir's campaign music and stuff came on, then he and his wife. Did he come out and call me a seducer and a fornicator, the way they would of twenty years before? Not by a sight. He and his wife just sat there for a minute, holding hands and saying nice things to each other. The faithful couple. So loyal. So homey.

I heard Ada say, "The bitch, oh that bitch—"

They never did mention me directly, but they sent the message, all right, and I slid down in the seat and wanted to go through the floor.

Lenoir said a few things about the girl and the suit, but he never mentioned me at all. He wound up, "Now let us not judge our fellow man too harshly simply because we are moved to pity for this poor girl."

It was like some of the 1956 Democratic telecasts where they said Eisenhower's health would not be an issue, and like that one of Nixon's where he said Stevenson's divorce would not.

Then Lenoir and his wife talked some more, and he said, "I know I can count on you," and she said, "Dear, I know I can count on *you*," and he put his arm around her and the camera closed up on them, true-blue, all Mr. and Mrs. America, and then it faded.

"That woman," said Ada. "That—" She did not finish it. I guess there were not words to finish it. Because of fifteen, or was it twenty, years of pictures in the *Times-Picayune* society section, and one snubbing, there would never be enough words. I guess no man can really know how a woman hates another woman.

"Well." Sylvestre cut it off. "That's what we have to fight. We can't file a libel suit against the papers yet because what they've used so far is privileged matter. We can sue the girl, which we will, and we'll sue Lenoir, though we really have no grounds, and we'll sue the papers and everybody else as soon as they repeat the charges without privilege, which they will. And that still won't be enough. We have to fight back. We have to discredit them so badly that they're totally destroyed."

"How?" I said. "How we going to?"

"That will take some consideration. Of course I have an emergency plan. I've got some tax fraud stuff on Bull Lee as well as the libel suit. But it's not enough. It has to be Lenoir. And on him there's nothing. I've had him checked out all the way a long time ago." He scorched me with a quick look. "You. You gave them the one

opening. The one thing I can't turn against them. The one thing."
His voice was not loud but low, and that was the one that froze me.
My hands were cold as ice, and I held them tight together so they
wouldn't shake.

"He must have done something," said Ada.

"No. He's too gutless to have done anything, damn him. If he
had just been in politics before."

He walked in short springy steps through the room, his forehead
creased, his mouth all pulled together. I had never seen him working
like this before.

"What?" he said. "What can we do?" He was not talking to Ada
or me but to himself. He stopped at the window, looked out a
minute, and turned around. He shook his head. "If he had just been
in politics." He walked to the middle of the room and stopped. I
heard his breathing, I knew he was deciding what he had to decide.
He pressed his lips together, hard, the lines cleared from his head,
and I knew he had decided it.

"It'll just have to be the libel suit," he said. "It's the best we can
do. We'll sue everybody in sight for a million dollars and we'll sue
Lenoir for two million. We don't have a leg to stand on, but that
won't matter. We'll just let it die after the election. Ada, you and
Tommy go on the air and call the whole thing a political canard,
and Ada will insist how she knows it isn't so and how much she
believes in Tommy. And so on. We'll call them every liar in the
book. We'll raise so much dust people will forget what's going on,
at least I hope they will." I saw the sureness coming back into him
like wind into sails. "We may pull this thing out yet."

"Why don't we make sure?" said Ada.

Sylvestre's face swung on her. For a minute he did not say anything. Then he said, "Certainly. By all means. Just tell us how and
we'll go right ahead."

"Perhaps I can," she said.

Sylvestre whirled around to look straight at her. I suddenly felt
my mouth open and closed it. Ada's face was wide and innocent;
she wasn't looking at either one of us but at her cigarette case while
she pulled one out. Then she looked up, smiled, and with her eyes
asked for a light.

Sylvestre picked up a lighter from the coffee table and gave her
the flame.

"Thank you."

"Not at all." His voice was heavy and sarcastic. "Now. Would it be too much to ask what you have in mind?"

Ada quit playing. "Are there any New Orleans policemen you can count on? Some assigned to the Quarter?"

"I think we could rely on the, loyalty, of three or four in the Quarter."

"This might work then," Ada said.

She told us.

"My God," I said. Had it just come to her that second? Or had she been dreaming about it a long time, letting it get bigger and bigger down where you dream, until it was ready to be born? "We don't want to do that. We . . ." Nobody was listening. I let it trail off.

Sylvestre turned. His back was square against the light of the window. His hands were together behind him, where he stood, looking out.

Then he turned.

"Yes." His voice was purring, and his face was happy, like a preacher who has Seen the Glory. "Yes. That is perfection. That is it." Then he said straight to Ada: "A magnificent conception, my dear. Magnificent." And he smiled.

Of course he went ahead with the other stuff, too. The papers printed interviews with the girl, and this wasn't privileged, so he slapped a million-dollar suit on them. He filed a two-million-dollar suit against Lenoir for that silly telecast. The suit came to five million dollars, and the papers had to carry the story. Sylvestre raised hell for equal and opposite time on the state network to answer Lenoir, and he got it for the same price. Then I went on and called Lenoir a liar, the newspapers bloodsuckers, and the girl a poor unfortunate who had been taken advantage of by the interests. It was a good speech; Ada spent a whole day writing it.

We didn't have a chance of collecting nothing. We didn't want to collect. What we wanted to do was raise so much dust nobody could tell one side from the other.

And it almost worked, by itself. But not quite. The sheriffs were still scared to deliver the way they had in the first, with fast counts where we needed them, and Sylvestre's survey outfit did a blitz job and said we weren't a sure thing. So Ada's plan would have to be used. If it wasn't, we were gambling.

I didn't like it. I hated it, it made me feel crawly and ashamed, even if they had asked for it by framing me. If I could, I would have got out right then. But I couldn't. And Sylvestre and Ada set it up. It was then thirteen days before the second primary.

We could look through the window across the narrow street to where it was going to happen; a two-story gray stone apartment house with an iron-grille gate opening to the patio court.

Sylvestre and I sat on a sofa under the window. We were in an apartment on a short two-block street that ran into Decatur. The apartment had been rented for us three days before. We had been in it since three in the afternoon and now it was eight-forty at night. Sylvestre was looking out at the street like a big owl waiting for a field mouse.

I felt tight inside, my breathing sounded to me like I was in an oxygen tank and my heart like it was coming through a stethoscope. But what did I have to be scared about? It was somebody else that ought to be scared.

"How can anybody walk into a frame like this?" I heard the not-understanding in my own voice. "How can they be so dumb, how?"

"How?" Sylvestre laughed. The laugh had things in it that I did not know but scared me. "Because they think they are framing you. They think they are conspiring to betray and destroy you. That is why they can be betrayed and destroyed themselves. You know what the con men say. You can't cheat an honest man. And you can't. But where can you find one?" He laughed the same way, and I felt myself shiver in the dark. "They all con themselves. They all cheat themselves and betray themselves and destroy themselves. You never have to do it, they do it for you. What is inside them does it. Their dishonor brings them dishonor and their evil brings them evil. You never have to. You never have to do it. They do it to themselves. All you have to do is give them a chance."

"You mean you think everybody's like that?"

"All of them." He laughed, longer than I had ever heard him. "All of them. Every last one of them."

That minute I hated him, and I do not think I ever hated him before. I did not believe everybody was like that. I didn't want to destroy nobody. Most people didn't want to destroy. They did not have in them what he said they had. I would not believe they did.

But he was sure he could find it. I thought for one second that maybe this was what he lived for, to find it and drag it out. I was almost sick, and I was afraid.

Now Sylvestre was leaning toward the window. "And here comes our awaited guest."

Not in front of the apartment house, but a half-block down the street a green convertible had stopped. Already out of and walking away from it was a figure in green: who we were waiting for. As it came closer to the iron gate, I saw that there were dark glasses on the face, like a tourist wears for the sun, only now there was no sun or moon either, but only the globes on top of the posts that threw down white pools on the concrete. The figure moved very slow, almost but not quite hesitating, into the big pool from the lamp at the gate. Then it stopped at the gate, pushed the buzzer, and turned, and we got across the street a full clear profile shot of Mrs. Armand Lenoir.

The answer buzzer must have sounded, although we didn't hear it, and the gate swung open. She stepped inside, and we watched her green back draw away from the iron bars that made stripes on it. I heard her sharp-heeled footsteps across the street, and they filled the world, they were the whole world, and I shivered in it.

"Just a few more steps." Sylvestre was breathing slow and deep. "Easy, easy. Just a few more."

So that was what it was with him. Now I knew.

Then the steps were gone.

Sylvestre picked up a long flashlight, pointed it toward the intersection of Madison and Decatur, and flashed it a couple of times. Then a police squad car parked on the other side of Decatur flashed its red light twice, real fast, and drew easy around the corner to stop half a block from the gate.

"Three minutes more," whispered Sylvestre. "Five in all."

He watched the second hand on his watch circle them off. Then he flashed the light again at the squad car, that was now almost right across from us.

In half a minute, another squad car turned in from Decatur, and another still from the other corner, both almost at once, quiet at first, and then they started the sirens. All three worked the sirens, and the first car pulled up in front of the iron-barred gate.

Two cops got out, and started, not fast, for the black iron-barred gate. They stood there. Then one set of sharp heels hit the patio concrete, and *clack-clacked* louder and louder, faster and faster, and the gate flew open, and through the space, right into the arms of the waiting cops, ran Mrs. Lenoir.

For one instant the three froze together in a still picture: the green-dressed woman in the middle, one cop holding each arm, and under the light her face turned up and contorted. Then the picture broke, she started to twist and turn to get away. But of course she couldn't. Then she started to scream. They handcuffed her, still screaming, and put her in the back seat of the squad car, and her screams came out of the car where you could not see her, like the squeal from a busted radio.

The four other cops from the two other cars went in. Three more cars pulled up and some more cops got out and followed the first ones. A few minutes later they all came out, herding a couple of dozen men and women, who were making noises but not really fighting. I saw some wild-looking faces and reversed sexes come out into the light, and I guessed this had happened before, to most of them.

The cops crowded them into the squad cars and they drove off. The sirens whined as they went around the corner, toward the First Precinct Station.

This was what had happened:

They had got a woman to call Mrs. Lenoir and say she had enough dirt on Ada and me and our upcoming separation to put the election on ice for Lenoir. She said she was afraid to talk to the men because somebody might kill her afterwards. But if Mrs. Lenoir would come to this party, she could tell her in the powder room. That way nobody would know. But Mrs. Lenoir had to promise not to tell anybody, anybody at all, and come alone, and bring two hundred dollars.

Of course it was just what a woman would fall for, and of course Mrs. Lenoir did. She promised, and she came.

And the party was a marijuana party, among other things, one that floated from apartment to apartment by the week and was easy enough to set up for our special purposes. Sylvestre's cops were ready to move in as soon as he signaled, and they did, and they arrested Mrs. Lenoir. They would book Mrs. Lenoir at First Precinct before anybody could spring her. It would be on the record: possession of narcotics, moral turpitude.

Our campaign paper would print it, so the others would have to print it, their frame would be canceled out by ours, we would win. And I felt dirty and crawly and worse than I've ever felt.

It was two in the morning and we were sitting in the suite waiting for things to happen, and it did not take too long. The phone rang. Sylvestre picked it up. "This is he. Yes. Yes." A long stop. "How unfortunate, I'm so sorry. Please extend my sympathy to Mrs. Lenoir. And of course Mr. Lenoir." Another stop. "But I'm afraid you do me too much honor. I don't have enough influence to keep this out of the *Free Press*. That paper as you know is interested only in the full and absolute truth, unlike the other newspapers in this city." I saw him smile. "I suppose there's nothing to do but let events take their course. I repeat, my deepest sympathies to Mr. and Mrs. Lenoir. Yes." And he said the last words like a song: "Good-by."

He turned to us, the smile still there. "Yes, that was Lancaster. They want to deal, oh so badly. They say they'll get the girl to withdraw her suit and say she made a mistake, that she was put up to it by gamblers who were out to get Tommy." He stopped, and the smile changed. "As you heard, I told them no. What we're holding out for is Lenoir's complete withdrawal from the race. I think they'll think of that quite shortly."

Ada stood up, and walked to the other side of the room. Her mouth was open and twisted up at one side, the bigness of her winning shining out of her face like a floodlight. I had never seen her feeling so good, or looking so cruel. "I wonder now." She walked back, her face full of the happy cruelty. "I wonder what is the going price on Miss McGeehee's and Pi Phi and a debut at the Orleans Club and the Krewe of Venus and the Spring Fiesta and the Junior League and all the pictures." She drummed them out one after the other, like a prosecuting attorney reading the charges. "All the lovely, lovely pictures in the *Picayune* society section. Now tell me. Tell me this. Do you think they'll have pictures of her being booked for possession of narcotics and moral turpitude? That would make a lovely picture. Now wouldn't it? Or rather won't it?" She was walking back and forth, and now her face looked sweet and dreamy. "A lovely picture for the Sunday section. I can just see the cut line. Mrs. Marianne Lenoir, well-known and gracious garden-district hostess, was among those seen booked at the First Precinct Station last night. After the delightful ceremony, Marianne and friends adjourned to charming cells so thoughtfully provided by the authorities where a festive time was had by all."

She was walking back and forth, faster, tasting it, drinking it, filling herself with it. This looked like the high point in her life, and I wondered: *Is it inside all people? Is Sylvestre really right?*

Then the phone rang.

"Hel-lo," said Sylvestre. "Yes. Why yes, Mr. Lancaster. Well, now, I must confess that does interest me. Let me discuss this a moment with my associates. I'll call you back."

He hung up. Then he looked at Ada, and Ada stopped walking and looked at him. They were both smiling, Ada like it was Christmas and Happy New Year, Sylvestre like he knew something nobody else in the world knew.

"He'll withdraw," Sylvestre said. "They can kill the entry on the police blotter and keep it out of all the papers. Except of course the *Free Press*. And if we take care of that they'll withdraw. That's their proposition. The choice is ours. Ultimately, of course, it doesn't matter which choice we make. They withdraw and we win. They don't withdraw, the story runs, and we win. Heads we win, tails they lose." He stopped a minute, still looking at Ada, the hard black eyes tickled about something. "Now, my dear. I put it to you. It was your plan and your triumph. You are entitled to the decision. What shall it be? Thumbs up?" And he pointed his right thumb at the ceiling. "Or thumbs down?"

His eyes and Ada's never left each other's, and they kept smiling. Ada touched her lips with her tongue. She raised her thumb slowly, so it was pointing toward the ceiling. She looked at it a minute, like it was something not part of her, then she made a slow half circle with it and jabbed it towards the floor, and smiled wider than ever. Her voice was soft and dainty as she said:

"Down."

Sylvestre kept looking at her, the secret thing running between them, and he said, "That's your decision?"

"It is."

Not taking his eyes off her, he picked up the telephone.

At that minute I hated her. I had known she was after all she could get, all right. But I hadn't thought she was cruel. Now she was operating just like Sylvestre. No, worse than Sylvestre. I didn't never want to touch her again.

But an hour later, when she was getting ready for bed, the wining and cruelty had gone from her face. She looked drawn, tired, and sorry, and I felt glad, and relieved. She wasn't like him after all.

I said, "Why—" and stopped.

She looked at me. "What?"

"Why don't you take an aspirin?" I said.

"I don't need one," she said, and cut out the light.

What I had started to say was, *Why don't you change your mind? Get Sylvestre and tell him you changed your mind.*

But I didn't say it. And by not saying it, I guess I was as much to blame for what happened as Ada. No. I know I was. By not fighting it, I became a part of it.

Lying there, feeling sick about what she had done, I heard her moving in the dark for what seemed like twenty minutes. Then I heard the switch, the light went on, and she was up and walking to the front room.

Through the door I heard her telephone Sylvestre, in his room down the hall, and said, "Can you come down? It's urgent."

I got up, put on a robe, and went in there. She looked at me, tired, but obviously feeling better than she had half an hour before.

"I'm chicken," she said, and grinned, shaky, at me. "Just plain chicken. I can't make it stick, I'm going to let her off."

I put my arm around her.

Sylvestre came in, in a deep-purple dressing gown, his white hair combed, looking like he had never been asleep.

He looked from one of us to the other.

"Well?" he said, very soft.

Then the two of them looked at each other, very different from the way they had looked an hour and a half before.

"I've changed my mind," she said. "Let's let him withdraw."

He studied her face for several seconds. Then he shrugged, "A woman's privilege. And I gave the decision to you. I think there's still time."

He picked up the phone and dialed. "Mr. Lancaster. We've reconsidered. We'll go along with your proposition." He stopped a minute, and I saw his face change as I heard the voice in the receiver. It was loud, and fast, and angry, but I couldn't understand the words. Finally Sylvestre said, very smooth, "Will he withdraw now? Well then, we'll just have to go ahead as planned."

He set the phone down. It went on the receiver with a loud click. He looked at Ada, almost curious. Then he said, "It seems that our reconsideration was just a little late. Not by much. But enough. Lenoir won't withdraw. You see,"—he stopped, and now his black eyes looked hard and deep into Ada's face, like he was trying to find something—"fifteen minutes ago, Marianne Lenoir took a forty-five service revolver and blew the top of her head off."

Ada's face went dead white, and blank. Her eyes were wide open and staring, and then they closed. Her breath made one quick gasp. "My God," she said. Then she walked into the other room, and closed the door.

For a minute I heard nothing. Then, through the door, I heard her crying, for the first and last time in our life together.

The *Free Press* printed the story, and the big papers had to.

We won by 127,000 votes.

Steve Jackson

The crowds were already on the streets, jostled tight against the heavy bright-pennanted ropes, and you could hear them waiting. The waiting of a crowd is a strange sound, somewhat like a wind in high grass or maybe even in the treetops, but not much like anything except itself: the static before the program starts. This was a quiet crowd, a docile crowd, but it was waiting, and it made static as it waited, for Tommy and Ada Dallas.

I had the mike on the sidewalk in front of the main entrance to the Capitol House on Lafayette Street. A long wire ran back to our wagon, which had a couple of cameras on top grinding. I was doing the color broadcast, and I said into the mike:

"This is a big and colorful crowd, eager to see the new Governor and his beautiful lady. The procession is formed. All the dignitaries are in their cars. So we need only Governor, correction, he won't be governor for a few minutes yet, we need only Mr. and Mrs. Tommy

Dallas to climb aboard the gubernatorial car and we're on our way."

A long line of bright-colored convertibles, all full of what were called dignitaries, waited between the ropes as far ahead as I could see, which was not far. A slender man with a black mustache and a big white felt hat, who was officially in charge of the ceremony, walked out of the hotel, his face looking importantly worried. Four state troopers, two on each side of the one-way street, wearing polished knee boots and knife-creased riding pants, stood outside the ropes to restrain the crowd if the crowd became restless. But the troopers had nothing to do and stood idly. It was a docile crowd, as I have said, and it waited patiently.

"Where's Tommy?" a voice in the crowd called out, and someone else yelled, "Where's Ada?"

How long ago was it that I had waited, that other time, for Ada? Alone, in the empty room in the old hotel that stood in a high wind and faced a whitecapped sea? Time rockets from past to future, being perceived for only an eye flick at the spaceless intersection that is the present. The past of ten seconds is the same as the past of ten years, if you have felt them equally on that streaking trajectory. So that wait in the empty hotel room might have been yesterday, or it might have been two decades. It was in fact two years.

I guessed she had what she wanted, now.

I looked at the car in which she would ride (for it had been announced that, contrary to precedent, she would accompany her husband. When I had read that announcement, I remembered the taped conversation between Ada and Sylvestre Marin). It was a Cadillac convertible, a kind of off-gold. Draped on it were ribbons of purple and gold—state colors—and the upholstery was black.

"Already waiting for Mr. and Mrs. Dallas in the gubernatorial car is the outgoing governor," I said into the mike.

I looked at him, slumped on the black leather cushions and clearly angry that he was kept waiting. I looked at the heavy dull-gray hair, the second chin folding over the first, the mouth turning downward and sour at the corners when he didn't remember to smile and wave at people calling things in the crowd.

It was clear. Leaving gave him a sickness in the guts. Leaving left him naked in the rain. He was the biggest man in the state, the titular boss of four million people, and in a very few moments, with the touching of a Bible, the speaking of incantations, and finally the shaking of a hand, he would shrivel into a small-town lawyer with offices on Main Street. And the big emptiness in the belly.

They none of them liked it, not the taking leave of their bigness. Would you like it? Hell, no, I wouldn't like it. But I will never have a chance not to like it.

"At the wheel of the car is the director of state police himself, Col. Robert Yancey."

And I looked at Col. Robert Yancey.

Chief of state police, Louisiana's second-to-most-glittering war hero, military prodigy, colonel of infantry, AUS, at thirty, holder of the Distinguished Service Cross with bar, certified fearless, resolute, and leader of men.

Suddenly he turned his head, the polished black visor of his cap caught the sun and flashed, and he smiled. He was a handsome man, no doubt of it: a smooth tanned face, a hard but somehow sensual mouth, dark blond hair. He looked so friendly when he smiled. He reminded me, very much, of an SS captain the boys had brought in one day in 1944.

I said: "We're all ready to start, and while we wait, we'll see what's happening out at Tiger Stadium. That's where the actual swearing-in ceremonies will take place. So, take it away, Jim Keeney at the stadium."

I breathed in relief. I looked at the faces, close together and composite and yet separate as leaves on the bough: dark Cajun faces over plaid shirts; red-brown faces over khaki (overalls long since obsolete), shopgirl and secretary faces, shipping-clerk faces, and Chamber of Commerce faces. But I saw no diamond stick-pin, forty-dollar hat, hand-painted-tie faces. These I had seen, jowly in importance and quivering in subordination, clustered around Sylvestre Marin in his corner court at the hotel lobby two hours before. For these, the inauguration had begun with the fraternal handclasp and exchange of passwords in lobby and bar, had continued through the night in an opulent haze of ransomed cigars, and had been consummated with the genuflection before Sylvestre. They had appeared, were thus in good standing, and might pass another night in incense of cigar, or might float away, in a cloud of black limousine and overage blonde, back to wherever they had come from. These faces I did not see above the rope. Nor did I see Sylvestre Marin.

Ada still had not come out. I looked at the door, waiting for her, and I thought: So now she has it. The big white house, first lady, and the rest.

Then I looked away, to the white tower soaring into the hot blue sky, and from the crowd I heard a voice cry, "Here they come!"

Turning, I heard it run like fire through the crowd, and I saw, passing through the revolving doors and onto the sidewalk, Ada in a white dress and walking very straight and smiling. Behind her came Tommy Dallas in a blue Palm Beach suit and a gray Stetson.

The crowd detonated into noise. I got the mike back fast from the stadium and started the patter and Ada and Tommy stopped on the sidewalk. They smiled and waved, and Tommy put his arm around her, and waved the Stetson with his other hand. She looked at him happily, lovingly, and I felt as though I had been hit.

They started for the car, and came abreast of me two feet away. And she looked straight into my face.

"Hello, Steve," she said softly.

I never missed a word in the mike, or slowed even. Our eyes met for perhaps two seconds. She smiled with one part of her mouth, and then she passed on into the inaugural car, the soon-to-be-Governor of Louisiana trailing behind her.

The parade started.

TWO

Robert Yancey

Of course I did not go to the funeral.

I looked at my watch: three minutes after eleven. Now it would be starting. The preacher would be saying the words, the choir would sing, finally the dirt would thump and spill on the lid of the coffin. Later the grass would grow and the marble marker would show white against the green, I suppose not far from the statue of Huey.

Was it me? Was I to blame?

Not all. I swear not all.

If I had had the chance to act clear and straight, it would have been different. Everything would have been different.

But they didn't give me the chance.

In the war I had had the chance. I had found out what I could do.

I had found out I could crawl into an area enfiladed by machine gun fire, listening to the *ah-ah-ah* out ahead and then the *per-ew per-ew per-ew* flicking by your ear, watching the fast winking orange and then the quick tiny jets of dust, not seeing how they could keep missing—I found I could crawl into this and bring out a man too wounded to move. I found I could lead a patrol, also on my belly, crawling dark where I could not see a foot ahead. I found I could come almost under the spewing threads of a tank and throw a grenade. Later I found I could send one man out to die to save ten, and that was hardest of all.

I did all those things, I did other things, and once I disregarded orders and did not shoot three Germans who were technically saboteurs but actually harmless, and when any fool could see the end of the war was a matter of days. (I did not think much about this for a long time. Now I think more about it than any of the rest. I remember their faces, the old man's, the son's, the son's wife's, and how they looked when they found they would not die after all, and I enter this on a kind of balance sheet.)

I learned what I could do, and that doing is the most important thing there is. You are what you do. To be alive, you have to do. To act.

I had had the chance to act, and I had acted, and I had made myself come alive for myself.

And then it was gone. And I couldn't really do any more, I couldn't act. I was no different, I still needed to act to be alive, but the opportunity was gone. Then whatever it was that had come out clear and hard in action was bottled up. It went sour, and a little of it dribbled off in little meannesses, and it finally exploded and blew the top. It blew like a wildcat gusher, and what it shot into wasn't good any more. But it had to come out. If it hadn't been bottled up, it would have been different, I would have been different.

I do not say this to make excuses. There are no excuses. I say it to explain. To myself.

That day that I first saw Ada was like the day we hit Omaha Beach. It was like it because I knew another part of the waiting was over.

All my life I had had to wait. I didn't know what for. But I knew something was going to happen to me, something big. My whole life was building up to whatever it was. I just had to wait.

I had waited at Istrouma High School where I was a refinery worker's kid and the blocking back in the single wing. And at L.S.U., where I got the full ride (expenses and thirty a month, you could live on that in the late thirties) and where I was still the blocking back in the single wing, second string now. And through

1940 and 1941, when I was a second lieutenant at Benning with an R.O.T.C. infantry commission. I was still waiting on December 7, 1941, but whatever it was felt closer. A week after that I was a first, and a month after that I was a captain, and I stayed a captain until June, 1944.

That first day. I sat forward in an LCVP, heavy with field gear, looking back to the round dark eggs of helmets in twin rows; looking ahead to the long gray sliding hills of water, to the long almost straight white line of surf breaking swirling on the brown beach; to the shapeless dark unmoving things lumping half-in half-out of the water; above them, to the orange flashes and black cloud curls that were enemy gun positions. Feeling the up-down up-down of the bucking steel bottom, tasting sickness in my mouth and salt on my lips, hearing the air above flap with the sixteen-inch stuff from the navy wagons way off there. Finally crouching behind the ramp so all I could see was the gray steel inches ahead, then hearing the sand crunch, feeling the boat lift and grind, then watching the gray ramp swing down and out and show an open-topped square of tan beach and white water and gray sky. I ran out, heavy-footed, sloshing, the Thompson bucking as I swung it firing, and I knew it had come. What I had waited for. I never felt so good; nothing in my life had been real, before.

I got a field promotion to major two days later, I was put in for the D.S.C. and Silver Star both the first week, and when we were at the Rhine I was a lieutenant colonel and battalion commander and I was twenty-seven. After Remagen, I had another D.S.C. and I had a foot that a .88 sliver had smashed up good.

And then it was over. What I had waited for forever had come and gone like a bird flying. I had nothing left.

Because of the foot I could not stay in, not as a regular. But I stayed on military government duty three years, and was a full colonel when I finally went back to Louisiana, where I found out I was about the most decorated hero next to Ray Hufft. For a while I was director of security for Lyons Shipping Lines, but it was nothing, nothing but a desk and sitting. Then the commandant job came along and I grabbed it, hoping. I was able to move around a little more, but nothing really happened there either. I was waiting again, and this time with the feeling that it had already happened, that it could never happen again. Korea came but I had too much rank and the technically bad foot, though it didn't bother me, and I volunteered, but they said no.

And then I drove Ada Dallas to the capitol for her husband's inauguration and the second time of waiting was over.

That day:

"Thank you, Colonel." She slammed the door of the convertible and looked across it to me at the wheel, she smiling a bright friendly smile, the crowd still yelling her name around us. "It was a fine smooth ride. Thank you very much."

"Yeah, it was fine, Colonel," said Gov. Tommy Dallas.

"My pleasure, Governor. Mrs. Dallas," I said.

Then they walked toward the high white steps and the double bronze doors of the capitol, and I watched her going away and knew my life had changed.

I felt myself gather and concentrate and aim, as though I had been all at once cast into a gun barrel and put on target. For the first time in God knows how many years, all of me wanted one single thing, bad, and with the wanting I came alive again.

What I wanted was Ada Dallas.

It was not just that I wanted *her,* although I did, and bad. But she was the Governor's wife. She was at the top. So I was going to have to do something big and maybe desperate to make it. I didn't know what. But I knew, sitting behind the wheel, watching her body in white silk move away in whipping rhythm, that it was going to be a war, that I had found something to do. I had wanted action, and now I had it. It would not be easy, it would not be quick, and I was glad.

It may not have been as important as taking a Rhine River bridge. But it was the first real thing I had had to do in more than ten years. Now that I had found it, and knew I was going to do it, no matter what it took, I felt easy inside myself, awake and alive. It was as though I had been under sedation for ten years and suddenly came out of it.

It started inside me, that second, and from inside it came out, into the world, where it did what it did and I did what I did, and what happened happened. Hell itself couldn't have stopped it.

My office staff noticed the difference right away, and the troopers not long after.

Like the next morning, when I called my secretary. "Marge, would you bring the traffic casualty recap sheets, please?"

She went to look, and came back white and trembling without them. "Colonel, I—" I heard her throat working. "I ... don't seem to find them. I guess I misfiled them, I'm sorry, I'm very sorry." I heard her voice climb, and was afraid she was going to cry.

"Don't worry," I said as easy as I could. "No problem. There's a carbon over at the duty office. I'll pick it up myself this afternoon. No problem at all."

I patted her shoulder, and her eyes came to my face and opened wide, as though she couldn't believe it.

"Why thank you sir, thank you very much," she breathed, still looking that way, and then she turned and stumbled away.

I felt blood coming to my face. Had I really been that much of a sonofabitch, that it was hard to believe I could do a two-bit decent thing? I guess I had. I remembered things, and I decided I had been a real triple-barreled sonofabitch.

I had fired two secretaries over less important fluffs than Marge's, and chewed out the office staff until they dripped blood, and I had made life hell for the troopers with surprise inspections, suspensions and fines, extra duty, reading out, and general meanness.

But it was not that I was really mean. The thing had gone into meanness because it had had nowhere else to go. It was all going to be different now. I had something to do. I had Ada Dallas.

That first week I found I could almost set my clock by her. The day's session of the Legislature started at ten, and she came out at nine forty-five every morning, never more than ten minutes off either way. She came alone, in her own car, and parked it out front rather than under the building, and she made the long walk up through the sea-smooth green gardens. The first day, I saw her when I happened to be standing before the window, the next day I walked to the window on purpose, and the third I had my desk moved so I could turn my head and look straight out.

The next Monday, the first day of the second week of the Legislature, I watched her inch by inch moving up through the green, and when she started up the steps she raised her face to the tower and it seemed for a second that she was staring right at me.

I felt my blood run toward her like the tide, that you can't hold and can't change, and I was on my feet and walking through the door and along the corridor, heading towards the Governor's office, and in the corridor I met Ada Dallas.

I tried to pretend to be surprised. "Good morning, Mrs. Dallas."

"Why, good morning, Colonel. Where are you striding so purposefully, so early?"

Could she know?

"Down for a cup of coffee," I said. "Join me?"

"Thanks very much but not this morning. Some people are waiting for me in the Senate gallery. Another time, though."

"By all means." I walked on.

After I left her, I kept on seeing her face with its smile. Did she know? Of course not. How could she?

Steve Jackson

Not completely to my surprise, I found myself with a front row seat for Ada's performance in her new role.

The station had sold TV coverage of the legislative session to six sponsors. I would stay in Baton Rouge Monday through Thursday as long as the session looked interesting.

The big story of the session was the social benefit bills: Tommy had promised $100-a-month old age pensions, $40-a-week unemployment insurance, and a big broadening of state health services. He had also promised a lot of public work projects: new farm-to-market roads, state aid on parish hospitals, recreation centers, and so on. It would be interesting to see if the administration, which of course was Sylvestre Marin, really meant the promises.

A governor can get anything he wants out of a Legislature if he presses for it. I mean if he really wants it. If he doesn't want it, or if he doesn't want it bad, he can just ask and stop there. But if he really wants it he can blackjack it out of them. The immediate issue of this Legislature was did the administration really want to deliver on the benefits? And if so, how would it pay for them?

This was what I was supposed to be watching. Of course, I was also watching Ada.

Until the inauguration, I had not seen her at closer than fifty yards for a year. I had quit my job with WJDL and gone to another station so I would not have to see her. Actually it seemed impossible that I should see her, that I would ever meet her face to face again.

God knows I did not want to. After she left me, I had gone into a new phase. I no longer pulled Nothing over my head like a blanket on a cold night and scrunched up under it, the way I had done before I met her. I had rediscovered Nothing, all right, but I had also discovered it was better not to be idle in it. Activity was if not a justification at least a narcotic. To paraphrase the play, I now tried to find in motion what had been lost in knowledge. I shifted from semi-indolence to strenuous activity. I took on extra duties, came up with new ideas. I was the top newscaster in town; I had a weekly program called *Magazine of the Air* on which I fearlessly investigated, sensitively probed, dramatically presented. Nothing over the heads of my audience, understand. I was a real hot-shot, all right. And it passed the time, and I had a lovely lofty detachment.

I was so hot they had even put out expense money to have me cover the Legislature. And so, once again, I was watching Ada.

Two days after the inauguration, she called me at my room and said come have a drink. I said I wished I could but I was just tied up day and night and I was sure she knew how it was, and she said she knew how it was. I hung up and was even impressed myself. Oh, I was a cool lofty detached sonofabitch; she couldn't get to me again.

I watched her from a distance. She seemed to be taking no part whatever in the politicking; she seemed oddly cowed.

And I wondered.

I had heard by subterranean grapevine that she had been hit quite hard by the way Marianne Lenoir had solved her problems, and that she had figured mysteriously in that fifth act.

It may have been true. If there had been manipulation, she very probably figured in it. And if so, she would certainly have suffered afterward, from the impact of the bloody denouement on that contrapuntal conscience she could never quite shake.

Perhaps that was the picture. And perhaps not. I wondered what it was that had shaken her. I wondered, too, how long she could keep under ground that severed and lethal splinter of herself, the call girl Mary Ellis.

On her side was the fact that it was buried in another state. The spots had been picked—she had said: the volume low, the price high. That was working for her. But working for her more than that would be her luck. Her luck was very, very good.

The administration apparently meant business on the benefit bills, and on those for local appropriations. They were introduced in the House the first day, and were moving fast through committee the second week.

The session had by this time become for me a tracer stream of faces and things and moments, rather than an ordered sequence:

The low-voiced, knowing-faced, head-bending consultations. At tables and counters in the hotels. In taxi or convertible or nondescript old car, rolling down shaded streets to the capitol. In dark corners and lavatories. At desks in the high open chambers.

Daily, at ten o'clock, the tiny belligerent *thump-thump-thump* of the gavel, not cutting or conquering the swirling murmurous clamor, but breasting it, nagging it, finally restraining it not to silence but discretion. The droning voice monitoring, coaxing, driving affairs to decision. And the decision itself shining on the electric board where by each name a red light meant *No* and a green *Yes*.

On the floor, whenever an administration bill was up for vote, was Sylvestre Marin: sitting solid and quietly elegant in a chair next to somebody's desk, almost never speaking though nodding or shaking his head when spoken to, the smile flickering soft, discreet and yet somehow threatening about the mouth, the eyes sweeping the chamber the moments before the vote, then leaping quickly to the big board when the lights flashed their answers.

The answers were always what he wanted, and there were few dissidents: only a scattering of red eyes among the green. I suppose he wanted to see who they were, so he could get to them if he ever needed to. Or decide that he could not get to them, for there are always a few you cannot get to.

I never saw the Governor on the floor. Jimmy Davis and Earl Long and the rest used to come out on the floor sometimes when their own bills came up. But Gov. Tommy Dallas never did.

Tommy Dallas

In the state speech, that first day, I said it just the way Sylvestre wrote it, that the watchword of the administration would be harmony. They busted into the speech to clap at that, they stood up and clapped when I said it again at the end of the speech, and they clapped like all hell when I sang some songs afterwards.

The session sure started harmonious. There weren't any fights between the city boys and the country boys, or between the Old Regulars and what used to be the reform crowd in the city representation, or between the old governor's organization and ours. While the session was on, we didn't fire any state employees except five or six department heads.

We even kept Yancey. Sylvestre said it looked good, not changing police heads. He said this would look like we did not want that kind of power, and Yancey was on our side anyway. Sylvestre had made sure of that.

The second week Sylvestre had me announce his own appointment as "special executive assistant." I knew they were laughing about this in the Capitol House lobby and bar, and laughing to kill themselves in the rooms upstairs. Sylvestre my assistant. It was funny, I guess, even if I couldn't laugh as hard as the others. It gave him an office in the governor's suite, of course, and everybody said this was mighty convenient.

So there I was, Governor of Louisiana, top man in the state, and I was nothing. A couple of times I started to come out on the floor of the Senate, just not to be alone, just to be able to reach out and touch something.

But Sylvestre said: "I wouldn't come out unless there's something big we're interested in, something really big. I'll let you know."

So during the day I stayed in the red-carpeted office like it was jail.

But I broke out in the nights.

The first week I would maybe stand in the deep rows along the bar in the Capitol House, or maybe sit at one of the tables in the corner, or maybe sit on a bed upstairs and hear the ice clink and watch the room fill with smoke. Later in the night there would be parties at the roadhouses on the Air-line or across the river. And they would coax me up to sing. Then me singing from the floor, bowing, grinning and feeling good at last, then back at the table feeling good with slaps on the back, drinking with the boys, good boys, show 'em I'm not big head just because I'm top dog in the state, who am I kidding, they know who's the man running things and it ain't Tommy Dallas. So drink up with old Tommy, guys, old

Tommy is a good boy even if he don't have nothing to say about nothing.

Then Sylvestre said: "I wouldn't pal around too much."

But late at night I could still get around, a little. I would dance with the legislators' wives, some old and fat, some young and pretty, some stiff and a foot away, some hot and asking. And I would think how easy it would be to knock off a few of them, how I could really knock off one or two because their husbands had too much on their minds to pay them any attention.

Except Sylvestre had said: "Don't take on any new girls during the Legislature."

I was not with Ada much. I had not been with her as man and wife for a long time. I guess it was about the time of the second primary. After that she hadn't wanted me to touch her, and after a while I quit trying to.

As soon as the Legislature started, she dove head-first into the First Lady thing: the teas, the bridge parties, all that stuff, for the wives of the legislators and officials. She dived deep, like it was something to do, to make her get over Marianne Lenoir.

"Forget it, it was an accident," I had told her once.

"Sure," she said.

"They started it, it was all their fault."

"Sure."

"You would have taken her off the hook, she just wouldn't wait."

"Sure."

She had been like that. Now I was glad she had something to do. Maybe she could get it off her mind.

Anyway, she left politics alone; she had quit trying to be Sylvestre's right hand the minute Lenoir's wife pulled the trigger. She went into the other stuff, the social stuff, a mile a minute. She had a luncheon for the legislators' wives, and a tea for the presswomen and the wives of the pressmen, and she went to all the other parties all the other wives gave. Almost every day the Baton Rouge papers had her picture on the society page. It pleased her some, and I could tell it took her mind off that thing. Some.

"You look like you been having a pretty high time of it, hon," I told her. This was when she came in one afternoon from a tea or something.

"Not so high." She was pulling off white gloves and her voice was a distance off.

"Oh, pretty high. First Lady of Louisiana, queen of Baton Rouge society."

"Baton Rouge." Her voice halfway liked it, and halfway said it wasn't near enough.

"You know you like it, hon."

"I like it. It just isn't New Orleans."

So that was the way.

She had a big dance—ball, she called it—about a month after the session started. All the legislators, the officeholders, the newspapermen, even the lobbyists and their wives were there. The Baton Rouge papers had two whole pages on it with pictures.

That ought to satisfy her, I thought.

The next afternoon I found her in the little sitting room. She was looking, not happy, at the wall, and newspapers were spread around her feet.

"What's the matter, hon?"

She looked at me fast, then away. "Not a line. Not one goddamn line."

"What? What you talking about?"

She didn't say anything. But I looked down at the papers and saw they were from New Orleans.

Robert Yancey

I had to think, I had to plan. The first thing was plain enough. I had to establish contact. So far I had only talked to her twice. I had to treat it like any other woman deal. The thing to remember when you pick up a woman is that it doesn't matter what you say. It is the way you say it, so you don't jar her sensibilities or make it obvious. She will know what you mean, she will bring you ahead with a green light or bounce you off with a red. You are not trying to fool anybody, you are just keeping it smooth.

Now. I had to come up with something to talk to her about that would seem okay. Smooth. What would the chief of police talk to the Governor's wife about? He could ask her help for some benefit or other. He could ask her to dedicate something. Or he could ask her to help him out with the Governor.

Either the first or second would have been better. But we had no benefits coming up, and nothing to dedicate. So I would have to ask her to help me some way with Tommy. This would have been stupid as hell if I really did want something. But of course I didn't, all I wanted was an excuse to talk to Ada.

I would just ask her to help me get more dough for the force. I started to write her, then I decided that was not such a good idea. I called her at the mansion twice that afternoon and caught her in the second time. I told her I had something I wanted to talk to her about.

She hesitated for one second. Then: "Why, certainly, Colonel." Her voice was quite brisk, and she was keeping any surprise out of it. "It happens I've got an hour this afternoon if you care to drop by. Fine then. At four."

She met me in a kind of office-sitting room at the side of the house. She was wearing a white linen suit, not built to show her off, but she showed anyway, and in a way was more exciting. She extended her hand, I felt blood rising as I took it, and I thought: *She must know now, how can she help but know?* But what I wanted was for her to show she knew, and for something to come of it.

"I'm sorry I had to ask you to come by here, Colonel." She was smiling, but without the encouragement I wanted. Still, there was no discouragement. "I naturally don't have an office or anything in the building, so—"

"That's perfectly all right, Mrs. Dallas. I'm delighted you could spare the time at all and as I said, at your convenience."

She smiled in a way that said, What can I do for you, and I went right to the point, which of course wasn't the point at all. "The truth is, Mrs. Dallas, I want to ask a favor as I imagine you guessed." I smiled, I hoped winningly. "I have some rather acute problems that are going to demand my pressing attention quite shortly, and I wanted to discuss them with you since you so kindly could spare me the time."

"Not at all, Colonel, but why me? I should tell you right now that I don't mean to take an active part in public affairs, not at all."

"I appreciate that, Mrs. Dallas. I know the Governor is so busy just now and I thought I might explain the situation to you in case the Governor might discuss it with you at some future date."

I wondered if it sounded as thin to her as it did to me. I looked fast at her face; she had it set in an absolute blank. She nodded, just a little. "Why, certainly, just so you understand the situation."

"I surely do." I stopped a minute, and went into what I was supposed to go into. "The fact is I'm concerned with the highway traffic situation, Mrs. Dallas. Violations are going up, accidents and fatalities are going up, and I'm naturally concerned." I came up with some figures, and some more explanations, and talked for several minutes. I finished, "I wish we could do something to check the trend."

She nodded. "And you think more men and greater authority and funds for the department would help." She didn't say it as a question.

"Why, yes, and I must say your grasp of the problem is remarkable."

"I'm glad you think so." Something, maybe irony, fringed her voice now. She looked straight at me, and there may have been a flash of amusement on her face. But I could not be sure. "I do appreciate your talking this over with me, Colonel, but as I explained I am absolutely without power to help you. I would suggest you discuss this with the Governor, or perhaps his assistant, and if you have a meeting of minds perhaps something can be drafted in the way of legislation. You understand this is only a suggestion."

"I value your suggestion, Mrs. Dallas."

"I appreciate your confidence, Colonel."

She stood up and held out her hand again, the smile curving light on her lips, her face wrinkling faintly at the eyes, both meaning I didn't know what. *She must know,* I thought. "Now if you'll excuse me. I must dress for a dinner engagement."

"Why, certainly, Mrs. Dallas, and may I thank you again for your time and suggestion."

"Not at all, Colonel. I'm sorry I couldn't really do something for you."

I felt the heat strike my face, but I could not be sure she meant what she might have meant. Her face was innocent.

"Let me know if I can be of any service, Mrs. Dallas. Good evening."

"Good evening, Colonel."

Driving to my apartment, in the shade of the June afternoon, poplars making long thin pointed shadows across the streets, the air still and heavy and breezeless, I went over every word and every expression. No green light, no red light, no yellow. Nothing at all.

What next?

Steve Jackson

The days crept through the sun-poured wet heat of May and June. It was the time both of sun's fire and season's rain; the last came suddenly, with no warning but the sudden cloud over the sun and the first whisper of the fall. Sometimes the whisper flared suddenly into violent drumroll that didn't soften until brown rivers streamed swift in the gutters. And sometimes the whisper remained a whisper, never louder, hissing fitfully for life until it was lost in the gray air. After the rains, if the sun fought free of overcast, it struck vengefully and steam rose from the wet asphalt.

Through this I watched the Legislature march through its days, passing or not passing hundreds of bills, some so obscure their origins and purposes could never be known, some so devious that their language-wrapped layer-buried meaning would not be apprehended for years, until an ax fell, a knife slipped in.

And it turned out that the administration had only appeared to mean business on the benefit proposals. The reality was something else.

The benefit bills had flown through committee to be reported favorably to both Houses. But on the floor of both House and Senate, they were strangled with cords of silk. No one opposed them, everyone was for them. But almost everyone, it seemed, wanted to amend them. And I saw they were going to be amended to death. It was an old device. The bills would be amended and reamended and re-reamended after that in both Houses. Finally they would go to a joint conference committee of both Houses to resolve the differences. This committee would try, or seem to try, to work out a compromise bill on each piece of legislation. Each would go back to the floor in both Houses and be debated again. Finally, the session would be over, the bills would not have been rejected, but simply would not have been passed, and nobody would have been visibly against them. Everybody would smell like a rose.

But it could not have worked unless Sylvestre wanted it. Why did he want it? That was easy, I thought. He didn't want to hand out all the benefits at once. He wanted to save some for the next session, two years away, and some more for the next election, four years away, and for his next governor, whoever he decided it would be.

By the last week in June, the only benefit proposal that had gone into law was one providing a five-dollar-a-week raise in unemployment payments.

Meanwhile, I watched Ada Dallas violate the hot murmurous stillness with relentless motion.

She raced frenetically through teas and coffees and lunches and cocktail parties and dinners with the legislators' wives, who called themselves the "Third House." She was queen of all of this, and I knew it was at once sweet to her taste and not nearly enough.

I knew she lusted for, instead, luncheons at Corinne Dunbar's, charity committees of the Junior League, Carnival balls and her picture with the Krewe of Venus; herself the center for tableaux of the Spring Fiesta; chaperoning at debutante parties, and playing hostess at garden parties in the Garden District. I knew she lusted for the *haut monde* of New Orleans.

We passed three or four times in the corridors of the capitol building. She saw me only the last time, her eyes widened and tried to hold mine, I smiled quickly and turned my head toward whomever I was talking to. I saw her again with a party of legislators' wives in the dining room of the Capitol House hotel. She was laughing conscientiously at something. Looking over the white-clothed table she saw me and for an instant something like sadness crossed her face, but then her expression slid back into whatever it had been before so swiftly that I could not be sure it had happened.

All at once the session was half over, and we were in the second thirty days. This Tuesday, after my newscast, I left the capitol to go back to the hotel. In my car, I pressed the starter but the engine would not ignite though the car had just been overhauled and was supposedly "like new." I could call the auto club from the hotel, I decided, and I started the mile walk. I was out of the capitol grounds and on the short shaded street that went into Third when I heard a car stop just behind me, turned and saw it was a yellow convertible with a woman at the wheel. In perhaps one-fifth of a second I saw the woman was Ada, who called, "Hi, can I give you a lift?"

I got in, I was too surprised to do anything else. The car started.

"Fortunate coincidence," I said. "Mine wouldn't start."

"Wasn't it?"

I watched her face against the sliding backdrop of trees and houses. I glanced at the full shape of her body behind the wheel and at the way her legs spread tightly under the skirt on the car seat. Her physical presence enveloped me like a hot wind: I felt my throat go dry, and my palms sweated. I shut my eyes to force the remembrance of the long empty boardwalk and the boat pulling clear of the dock. I opened them and saw only Ada's face, calm and lovely as though that day had never happened, as though nothing since had happened. The thought flickered that maybe all I had to do was wipe all that from my memory and it wouldn't exist, only Ada here and now would be real. All I had to do was use the eraser.

But it had happened. It was real.

Suddenly she smiled at me, at once shyly and wantonly, and I felt not only her physical impact, but the sympathy that had always been so strong between us pulling hard. She said, "It wasn't a coincidence. I saw you afar from my chamber window."

We were on Florida Boulevard now, in heavy traffic.

"Buy me a Coke?" she asked.

"Even a drink."

"Whatever we can get at a drive-in, I guess. Caesar's wife et cetera."

"Of course," I said. "By all means."

She glanced quickly at me and I saw her mouth curve.

We pulled in on the shady side of a fancy drive-in. A boy in a white triangular cap came for the order, then back with two Cokes.

We did not talk for a minute. Then over her straw she said clearly, "Why do you have to be such a damned fool?"

"Just lucky, I guess." The echo of the words, in her voice, floated back from Mobile, those years before.

Her face showed she heard the same echo—or so I thought. She smiled faintly. "A long time, isn't it?"

"A long time," I said inanely, and we were quiet again.

"I wish—I wish you wouldn't cut me off so completely." She was looking not at me but straight ahead at the rising wall of the building.

"Who cut who off?"

She smiled again, not happily, and didn't answer. We sipped through the straws. Finally she said, "I wish you were more of a realist."

"I'm a hell of a realist."

"No you aren't. You may look at things as they are but you won't take them as they are. If they fall short of what you think they ought to be, you won't have them."

"You say."

"I know. All-or-nothing Steve."

I felt more defensive and more angry. "Just for the record. From you I expect nothing and want nothing."

"That's what I mean." She stopped, then spoke carefully. "There could be something."

"As I said. I'm not notably interested."

"You still hate me, don't you?"

"I don't hate anybody. I wouldn't waste the energy." I felt trapped and foolish.

"All right." Her voice was tired. "Forget it."

We finished the Cokes and she drove me to the hotel. I stopped with one hand on the car door. I knew shamelessly that I wanted to use the eraser, to make the present moment all that was real. I would have given anything to kiss her or touch her. But I couldn't let myself. I said finally, "Thanks for the ride."

"Don't mention it," she said crisply.

I watched the car go ahead in a swift smooth speed burst, then I turned and walked through the revolving door.

Tommy Dallas

I was governor of the state and a zero. I was a nothing, I knew it, everybody knew it.

I didn't expect nothing else. I had been Sylvestre's for a long time, and when you were his you were all his. I knew that, I hadn't ever worried about it before, I had no reason to start now. But I guess the Legislature and all, so many people doing so much, all except me who was doing nothing, made me see it and feel it like never before. It hurt, and what could I do?

What I finally did was to start shacking with a north Louisiana legislator's wife, a soft round redheaded thing who was sweet as a barrel of honey. Her husband was chairman of one of the House judiciary committees, he was just swamped with work, and she was awful neglected.

Less than a week after I had been helping her not be so neglected, Sylvestre called me into his office. It seemed funny, and wrong, that the Governor's administrative assistant could call the Governor in and chew him.

But I went in.

"What did I tell you?" he said.

"What did you tell me about what?"

"I told you to keep your, proclivities, under control until this Legislature was adjourned. Didn't I?"

I didn't say nothing.

"Answer me. Now didn't I tell you?"

"I guess you did."

"You know I did. Now you listen. You are going to break off this situation right now. You are going to be an absolute Jesuit until this session is over. Do you understand that?"

"I got you."

I walked out. The only thing I could do and he yanked it away. But back in my own office, the Governor's office, pulling a bottle of Early Times out of the big space under the desk, it came to me that I had not been as scared of Sylvestre this time as I had others.

I broke it off, though.

Then, one Thursday noon in July the Legislature was over in a great big firecracker shot of harmony. I sang, the legislators sailed paper airplanes through the House chamber, there was a big barbecue afterwards. Out there, after we had eaten and were hitting the bourbon-and-Seven-up in paper cups, I heard one of them say to another:

"Good old Tommy, what a life, not a care in the world."

"Yeah, man, all the gravy, none of the worries. What a life."

Christ, I thought, people didn't know a damn thing.

Right after the barbecue, the capitol and the hotel were a couple of crazy houses, and then by nine that night Baton Rouge was a town an army had just pulled out of. I felt like—like what? Like a guy all by himself in a big room and he cuts the radio off. Before the radio goes there is anyway noise and it goes and there's nothing. He's the only thing in an empty world.

Robert Yancey

So I had tried and got nowhere. It was necessary to try again. If you can't take a position with one attack, you just have to come at it again from a different angle. I had to figure the angle.

One thing: she couldn't spend a whole day in the capitol without going into the coffee shop. So I decided just to go back and forth in front of the glass door, once every twenty-five minutes, until she was in there. Sure enough, at one thirty-six, on my ninth trip, I saw her sitting at a table with Hudson's wife. Her back was to the door, but I knew her hair and the shape of her head and shoulders. I walked into the shop and past her table, pretending not to see her, then sat at a table facing her, and tried to look suddenly surprised and pleased when she looked over.

I went over and spoke to them.

"Hello, Colonel." Her voice was flat and her smile not wide. "How've you been?"

"Join us, Colonel," said Mrs. Hudson.

Mrs. Dallas did not say anything.

"Why, thank you," I said. "If you're sure I'm not intruding."

"Not in the least," said Mrs. Hudson.

She still did not say anything but smiled just a little, as though her mind was a million miles away.

I sat down. "Well," I said. "This Legislature is over anyway."

"Yes," *she* said.

"I suppose you ladies have been very busy."

"It's been fun," said Mrs. Hudson enthusiastically.

We talked some more. I did not leave, I would stick it out.

It was Mrs. Hudson who left first. "Oh, I'm late," she said. "I've got an appointment at the beauty parlor at two-fifteen and it's that now. I must run, you two excuse me."

She left. A break, I thought, but Ada said, "I must go too, I've an appointment."

"Must you?" I said.

"Oh, yes." She looked at me hard, but smiled just a little. "I must. Thank you for the coffee, Colonel." Her voice was flat again, and stiff. I had the red light.

But I'd known at the beginning it wouldn't be easy. I did not want it to be. But Jesus I didn't want to just stand still. I wanted to feel myself moving, even a little. And I was nowhere.

I would keep trying. I was sure now that if I ever made it it would come out of something lucky and unexpected.

But luck comes from what you do, yourself. I don't mean you have to arrange it. But you make certain moves and these set things in motion and those things set other things in motion and they maybe make something happen. Maybe. You shoot a cue ball hard enough and it bangs around the table enough times and knocks something in. A football team goes out and rushes hard and tackles hard and it jars the ball loose in a fumble and recovers. Or you lay down a blanket barrage even if you don't know the enemy positions and you always get a few. Luck is like that only not so simple. I believe almost all luck, good or bad, starts somehow with yourself.

But not all. Not all by a damn sight. There is a margin in there that nobody can figure and that starts nowhere. It is just there, and things happen.

So now I had to do something else. It didn't have to be perfect. It had to be something. But days and weeks dropped into the big sack and I wasn't even close.

Tommy Dallas

The week after the session, the capitol was in low gear, and in a few days it seemed like there hadn't been any Legislature. All that was real was the here and now, and that was going to the office at nine, shaking hands with whoever Sylvestre brought in for me to shake hands with, signing what he put there for me to sign, and going back to the mansion at four-thirty, where I saw Ada, sometimes.

This night I was sitting in the living room listening to Ada on the phone. She was laughing that high, climbing, disappearing laugh that a woman has for another woman.

"Yes," she was saying. "What could I do? What else could I do?"

She was in a silver dress, silver silk. Her arm was bare and white against the silver, her long yellow hair just touched her shoulders, and she did look like one million dollars.

And she probably spent damn near that much on the get-up. The clothes, Jesus the money she had spent on clothes. The charge accounts, the checks. That dough would buy me enough whisky to keep me the rest of my life or anyway the next couple of years.

She laughed again, said "Bye, darling." Then she walked across the room towards me, still smiling, pink in the cheeks.

"Going out, doll?" I asked her.

The smile changed: to automatic and tired but I guess still friendly. "A tea," she said. "At Rosalie's."

"You look great. They'll wish they were you."

She was still smiling but thinking about something else when I said, "You're the queen, baby, you're my queen."

She patted me on the shoulder. "I must run. Don't work too hard, dear."

Now what the hell did she mean by that? Did she know about me and the brunette in Public Works?

Well if she did it was just too damn bad. She and I hadn't been together in God knows how long, and I was entitled to something.

Watching her going away, round and shimmying under the silver, I thought: She's still the best, I would rather to hell and gone be with her than anybody else. It wasn't my fault I had to settle for the brunette.

She was building up an awful pressure about something, and I didn't understand it, not all the way. Part of it was she was still trying to forget what happened to Marianna Lenoir. Part of it was something else, and this I didn't know.

Another afternoon she wasn't there when I got there, and I remembered she had a bridge party. Then later, with the world outside the window dark and cool with rain, the rain dripping soft like it might all night, I heard the big front door slam and those footsteps of hers coming and coming on the carpet, even on those deep carpets her walk was like the Devil himself coming and after you, and then she was in the room. Her lavender dress was spattered with rain, and I saw drops shine on her face and hair. Her face was pulled tight together and not happy.

"Looks like you got caught, hon."

She nodded, looked at me, and then looked away before her head stopped moving. "Yes, between the car and the door."

What was eating her? I thought she would be satisfied, now. But she wasn't. The pressure was still building. It wasn't the brunette because she wouldn't really care about the brunette if she knew. It was something else.

I tried again. "Good party?"

"All right." Her voice had nothing in it.

"What's the matter, hon? Getting tired of the bit?"

"Tired?" The word came up like a wall. "No. Not tired."

I shut up, walked across the room, and came back with a couple of full glasses. She took one, nodded thank-you, and drank some. She drank some more, and I watched her face and could tell she was about to talk. Not to me because I was me, but because she had to talk to somebody and I was there. Looking over her glass, not at me but at some emptiness in the middle of the room, she said, "It doesn't count. None of it counts at all."

"What do you mean?"

"I mean this is Baton Rouge and it's fine but it's not New Orleans. It doesn't count."

"Hell, baby, this is the capital of Louisiana. What does it have to be to count?"

"You know what it has to be."

I looked at her, at the down-turning line of her mouth, at her eyes gray and deep and staring. And I said, "Hell, go to New Orleans then. Go down there and make it count."

She didn't answer.

"You can make it count anywhere you want. You're the Governor's wife."

"Yes." Her eyes changed, and her mouth turned up. "I am. I can." It was like she had just discovered it. "I think I can."

"Arranged. Of course it can be arranged," Sylvestre said. It was a couple of days later and we were all in his office. The smooth lines of his dark silk suit weren't even touched by the heat. It never touched him; he went around in his own glass case. "Anything can be arranged, up to a point. Certainly the Orleans Club can be arranged."

"I mean. Can we, you know, arrange, for it to work out? You know. For—everything—to be successful?" I had never heard her ask anything like that before: just one step from begging, her eyes wide and anxious on Sylvestre.

He looked down at her, with that smile of knowing all there was to know. "Who knows? You're aware of the issues, my dear."

She nodded, her eyes still anxious. Then she said, "I'll do it. I'll go ahead." She turned her head higher towards him. "What time would you suggest?"

"I should say the end of November."

The summer eased into fall, what there was of it, and that wasn't much. L.S.U. beat Rice and Alabama under the big lights, we had some good parties afterwards, and Ada didn't think about nothing except going to New Orleans. Then, a couple of days before Thanksgiving, we went down to the big white house out on St. Charles Avenue she had rented through Carnival and into Lent. On Thanksgiving we went out to the Fair Grounds and sat in our box through all eight races. A lot of flashlight bulbs popped, and they ran a whole picture page of us in one of the papers. Ada was mad, though, because they didn't have anything in the society section.

After Thanksgiving I went back to Baton Rouge and left her down there. Seemed like she had an awful lot to do.

Steve Jackson

With the Legislature over I was back in New Orleans, eighty-two miles from her and it was not nearly enough. I could no longer maintain the half deception that I was totally indifferent. Baton Rouge had melted some of the ice I had packed around my nerve ends. Now I had to admit, again, that she existed for me.

But I worked hard and began to achieve again my splendid anesthesia. The earth turned, and the seasons changed, only in New Orleans they didn't really change. October was only a few degrees cooler than July, and November almost the same.

I awoke with a warmness on my face, and opened my eyes into the low sun. I sat up and looked through the window to the patio court, where the sun cut unnamable designs in gold on the chinked gray stone. Then I got out of bed and was drinking the second cup of coffee, reading the Sunday comics, when the telephone rang and I picked it up. "Hello."

"Hello, Steve."

Whose voice? I wondered, and before I guessed, I knew. My stomach dropped a great distance, I felt my hands go cold, and I waited a moment to be sure I had control of my own voice before I said, "Hello, Ada."

For perhaps seven or eight seconds the receiver was silent. "Steve." Her voice was strained, and from this I drew a strange and considerable comfort. "How are you?" Her tension was heightened by the banality, and this, too, made me feel better.

She asked me to come out, I said yes, and in one second surrendered completely a position carefully prepared and defended hard for two years.

The house was far out on St. Charles, past Tulane University and Sophie Newcomb, but it was unmistakable when I reached it: white and massive, colonial with Doric columns, and fronted by a deep and landscaped lawn reminiscent of Versailles. It was precisely the house she would pick, I thought: an archetype of what she would regard, in hate and aspiration, as the traditions of aristocratic New Orleans.

I turned into the drive, parked beneath a double carport, and walked to the door. Ada answered the ring herself.

"Hello, Steve."

"Hello."

I looked at her, framed like a portrait by the doorway: her skirt bright blue and tight at the waist, her blouse silk and white with full sleeves that came to her wrists, and above it, her face a smooth

white stone with red and gray insets. Her hair was parted in the
middle, and came to a bun behind.

She smiled, perhaps sadly, perhaps in supplication, and I took
her hand as she offered it. "It was good of you to come."

"No trouble," I said.

She looked at me levelly a moment and turned away. I tried, in a
last flopping attempt at withdrawal, to summon bitterness, which
until now had been my constant companion since that day on the
island. I didn't succeed; I had relinquished it for good when I rang
her doorbell and we both knew it. I did not know what would sup-
plant it, but it was gone.

She gestured with her head at the car already in the drive. It
was the golden convertible of the inauguration.

We started for it. "Do you mind if I drive?" she said. "I feel the
need."

The motor moaned deeply as we swung into the divided expanse
of St. Charles Avenue. Then the car rushed softly on gray streets,
overtaking and consuming traffic as if by its own appetite. I watched
the old houses retreat in shade, I watched the long yellow hood
stream over the dark pavement, and most of all I watched Ada.

She clearly welcomed the concentration on the wheel, seeking
immersion in it. But she did not completely succeed. Shadows were
moving in the depths.

The Cadillac swung into Lee Circle, past the archaic bearded
man on the horse, myth incarnate of a myth, and entered the narrow corridors of downtown New Orleans. Ada worked it through
the thin spaces, took it past a mountain of gray concrete that was
Charity Hospital, and slowed to let a crying ambulance pass. Then
we were on Tulane Avenue, and finally on Highway 90, the coast
highway.

The city thinned and fell back before our advance, and in time
we were clear of it and floating in speed along the edge of the Gulf
of Mexico. The Gulf was a winter green under the yellow cut of
December sun. An easy wind shimmied it into thin dark creases
that, far apart, flowered into white and vanished. The road curved
thin and gray against the brown beach, and receded twisting and
unescaping before the always-coming golden hood.

I looked at her face, itself intent on the gray beam of road ahead.

The face had not visibly changed; yet I knew something beneath had calmed with the rush of the car, the blackest of her broodings had burned out in the fire of speed.

We had been hurtling in soft golden flight for an hour, and were beyond all city traces. I saw her eyes search the highway, and felt the easing as the car dropped out of speed. Then it swung right from the pavement into a thin gravel splinter that cut through sparse brown grass, crested a dune top, and ended in a wide brown flatness that overlooked the green Gulf.

We sat, not talking. Except for an isolated word and reply, we had not talked all the way from New Orleans. In silence, we looked at the half of the world now clear to the horizon: green sea, light blue sky, wool-white clouds, and the sun a soft orange ball in its western meridian. I heard the breath-spaced roll of sea on sand, and the high thin cries of gulls planing dark and stiff-winged above the water.

"You were good to come, Steve." Ada did not turn but looked through the windshield at the world beyond. "I'm very beholden."

"It was nothing." I felt my awkwardness.

Now she looked at me. "You know better." And it was I who looked away.

We were silent again. I thought of the last time we had talked, with the world we could see so much like this, and of what we had said, and of what had happened since to make time a gulf as unbridgeable as this. And yet the other seemed only a heartbeat away. It was as though I were walking down a long hallway and had opened a door, just a crack, and could hear myself on the other side. If I could just open it wider, go in. But I could not.

She said: "I have no one. I have no one, except you. That is why I asked it."

We both knew what she had asked, and we knew that I had agreed to it, or to the bigger part of it, when I came to her.

"You see," she went on carefully, "you are the only thing for which I feel real guilt. I have done things that people would say are bad and wrong, and I feel badly about some, but I don't feel wrong about anything but you."

I wanted to comfort her, but something that was dying hard gave an expiring twitch, and I wanted to pain her, too. So I said: "Don't worry. It's all forgotten."

"Don't tell me it's forgotten." She looked at me, and her voice was dry and tight.

"I just meant it was all right." The thing that had twitched was still, almost.

"Oh, no. It will never be all right. But I couldn't change it. I couldn't change it then and I can't now."

I looked away. Distant in the eastern sky were three aircraft coming toward us, the flight V-shaped, the broad wings and deep bellies silhouetted black against the blue.

"You did what you had to do."

"Do you forgive me? I could never ask that of anybody but you."

The black and silent shapes were drawing closer: I could hear the deep swelling hum of their approach. I turned back to her. "Yes." I was surprised at the ease of the words. "I forgive you." I was surprised, too, to know that I spoke truth, and abruptly I felt forlorn and bereaved: I could never warm myself on the hate again.

Her hand touched my arm. "Thank you. Now." She had closed her eyes. They opened, almost as in pain. "If I could only ..." She did not finish.

I said nothing. She started again.

"But I can't. I would do it again. I would do it next week or next month or this next minute. I know it and you know it."

The motor noise was louder. I saw that the planes would pass a short space out to sea.

"And this is the only thing I really blame myself for."

I started to tell her that no one ever feels that they have done evil, except saints. But I did not. Instead I said carefully, "I think that's very natural."

"I don't know. I'm not sure it is. But we are what we are." She turned toward me. "Steve. Don't make a stranger of me."

"What else shall I make of you?" I was fighting a crude delaying action, and we both knew it.

"Anything else you want it to be."

I did not answer. She looked at me, I looked away, and she said:

"All right, it won't be that way then. But please will you see me now and then, just see me and talk to me."

"Sure," I said. "Sure."

"If I can just know you're there."

"You can know that," I said.

So we were not going to be lovers. I did not have the guts for that again, I did not want that particular exquisite pain. We were going to be friends. In the way that always seems so fatuous in a play. What a jerk I always had thought the man who got sucked into that arrangement. And I was in it now, with the woman who had left me at the church, almost, and by my own choice and limitation when I could have set it up any way I wanted. That was the kicker, all right.

I had the vague feeling of time repeated, of having come full circle, back to where we were before I asked her to marry me. But it wasn't the same. Too much had happened; there were complexities now I didn't understand myself. I wasn't going to sleep with her now because I knew what it would do to me. It was quite different from before.

"PBM's all right," I said incongruously, watching the three planes come on: snarling, heavy-winged, pregnant-bellied, not black now but silver glinting in the sun. Then they were gone, the thunder dying fast, the silver shapes shrinking and altering with the swift alteration of distance.

"Those? The hell with them." She moved toward me on the seat, checked herself, and moved back. "No, I'm not going to kiss you. I know a deal when I make it and with you I'll keep it."

She turned the key, the car curved backward for an instant, then swept forward again and into the road. "Steve," she said, "I really am beholden."

I looked from the gray road to the green sea and up and ahead to the blue sky where the planes were only black points above the horizon, dwindling out of sight. I could think of nothing to say that wouldn't have sounded fatuous in my own ears.

At her request, I saw her many times in the next few weeks. We had both accepted the new status: that there was something between us, but nothing would come of it.

One afternoon, we sat in the open air in the Court of Two Sisters, while the sun cut across the west wall, pale and warm to my cheek. Across the table, it flooded one side of her face and left the other in shadow.

"Of course I'm sure it's all right," she said. "You're explainable, you're public relations." She smiled.

But I saw she was not thinking of explanations, nor of me, but wanted only reassurance on her great venture: the ball which would, she hoped, Launch Her in New Orleans. So I—suddenly become confidant, convenient shoulder, and what the hell else?—was expected to insist on the certitude of her approaching deification.

She had spoken of little else this afternoon, and her anxiety was a solid and visible mass under the lacquer-thinness of manner and make-up. I had never seen her so readable, I thought, so uncharacteristically transparent. And she, who had performed what was not simply impossible but what was fantastic, was as concerned over a party and her social fortunes as any grocer's wife.

It was, then, only a week away.

I felt strange in evening clothes; putting them on two hours earlier, I had reflected that, after wearing them at least once a week for five years, I had not worn them at all for more than ten. And they were loose rather than tight, for I had lost weight instead of gained.

Now, with the stem of the champagne glass between my fingers and the decorous blare of the orchestra in my ears, I stood near the door of the ballroom of the Orleans Club. I was discreetly close to Ada, receiving at the door with Gov. Tommy Dallas, and I could watch her sidelong without appearing to stare. ("Stay close," she had whispered, "I need all the support I can get.") Once, between arriving guests, her eyes caught mine and her face released a small quick smile that mixed a little humor and irony with the anxiety I knew to be in her, building up the pressure inside as great as that of the Mindanao Deep.

Under the carefully light dusting of rouge, her cheeks showed pale, but her smile was perfectly controlled. Her gown was ice-blue, loosely fitted, and carefully high at the bosom—without cleavage. (She told me the week before she had wanted it even higher, but the dressmaker had resisted: "After all, madam. A ball.")

I heard Tommy Dallas say, "You look great, hon, only great," and she answered with the suggestion of a smile.

She extended her hand to greet some arriving guests, with carefully regulated welcome.

"Good evening, Governor. Mrs. Dal-las! You look just beautiful! Don't you, though!"

That was Mrs. Alva P. Boudin. Her husband was State Representative Alva P. Boudin; they were political, from an unfashionable district on the other side of Canal Street, and not Social. The Representative was a short round-faced man with dark horn-rimmed spectacles under wispy straw hair, and was in black tie instead of white; his wife was large, blond, and ballooningly shapeless in pink satin, and clearly considered her presence a triumph. She glowed as Ada murmured her pleasure, and with the Representative trotting behind, she propelled her bosom toward the dance floor as though a Medal of Honor had just been pinned upon it.

I watched the pink balloon bounce and sway among the dancers. Then, between nine and ten, I watched with disbelief shading into quiet horror as arrived, with their wives, or whatever they were: Louis Lamore, who was powerful in the Old Regulars and who had made his money in the old Storyville brothels; James J. Concannon, who had moved from receivership of stolen auto goods to preferential building contracts with many city administrations; Charles Lemond, bootlegger turned president of Lemond Breweries; Arnie Morris, night club operator and self-proclaimed Duke of the French Quarter; Charles Brandt, the city's most steadily employed lawyer for small hoodlums; Jimmy Lorraine, manager of the Crescent Gymnasium and controller of many votes; Charles Cegiano, owner of a celebrated restaurant and whispered a power in the Mafia; and many others.

How? How how how how how? She had cut her throat by inviting them. But of course she hadn't. Sylvestre Marin had invited them. And why? Why would he? What was he trying to do to her?

I puzzled over that one and watched arrive, after ten, from New Orleans society: Dr. and Mrs. Sterling Smith, he the director of St. Anne's Hospital; the Blair DeNegres; the Webster Reillys; the Benjamin Lewins, he the corporation attorney; the Herman Von Pauluses; Mrs. Dorothea Grant; Col. Richard Bartlett and his house guests, Gen. Gottfried von Altenburg, whom he had captured in the 1945 offensive and steered safely through de-Nazification, and the Baroness von Altenburg; the William diFrassos, he the president of New Orleans Bank and Trust; and many others.

Ada looked very happy as they came, and I was miserable that it was already too late. Why had Sylvestre destroyed her chance? I felt physically ill, as though I had seen someone give poisoned candy to a child, who ate it with delight. And why?

Ada was no longer receiving now, but was conscientiously mingling, and she came over and mingled with me. I started to ask, "What in God's name happened?" But I didn't. It was no use now. I only said, "You have a great diversity of guests."

"I know." And her face showed a trace of worry. "Sylvestre said we had to invite all of those or make enemies. Do you think any real harm is done?"

"No," I lied.

"Does it look all right?" she whispered.

"It looks fine."

"I'm so glad."

I looked at her face, shining, trustful, and grateful, and wondered what had happened to her, that all of her toughness and ferocity were so completely gone. Though of course I knew. It was the old New Orleans syndrome. Anybody who lived in the town long enough and who was involved with it deep enough always succumbed. The minute they met New Orleans Society head on, they went into shock and were not responsible. I had seen a couple of millionaire businessmen transplanted from the North ruin their business while trying to be Accepted. I had seen others with absolutely gilt-edged credentials—for anywhere else—eat their hearts out and leave town, and I had seen still others do fantastic things in an effort to make it. Ada was not alone. I was disappointed in her, but her desire was natural enough, and goddamn Sylvestre Marin forever for doing what he had done to her.

It was after eleven when he arrived himself, in midnight-blue evening clothes that showed darker and better-cut than any of the others. I was with Ada when he came to her.

"How is it proceeding?" he said, after the coolest of greetings to me.

"All right." Ada smiled. "I think."

Hilda Von Paulus was quite suddenly upon us. "Sylvestre! How lovely to see you. I'd quite given up on you."

His smile, I thought, was ironic. "How are you, Hilda?"

"Come by and chat," she said, and floated away.

"I see you have some distinguished guests," Sylvestre said to Ada.

"They did come," she said happily. "I'm so grateful."

"It's nothing at all." He smiled the same way.

He was so right. I wished I knew why he had gone out of his way to do her in.

I left them abruptly, and went to the punch table. Moments later, I saw Sylvestre bowing as he was presented to General and Baroness von Altenburg. They would have a great deal in common, I thought.

The dancers were spread through the ballroom and Representative and Mrs. A. P. Boudin almost touched the Blair DeNegres in one corner. But near the punch table, where I was, a space like a line ran between two groups. On the left hand, Carlos Cegiano, Arnie Morris, Jimmy Lorraine, and J. J. Concannon whispered softly and laughed loudly; on the right, Dr. and Mrs. Sterling Smith, the Webster Reillys, Mrs. Dorothea Grant, and three other couples clustered. They were smiling, regarding each other with glances amused and conspiratorial, and they spoke softly, not quite whispering. Twice a woman's laugh flew swiftly upward and vanished in mid-flight to leave incompletion poised uneasily in the air.

From the table, I watched Dallas and Ada drift near, though not quite upon them, just as the group rippled in secret laughter that halted raggedly as Mrs. Sterling Smith saw Ada and flashed a broad smile that was clearly a warning to the others.

"My dear." She moved toward Ada. "Such a lovely party. We're having such fun."

"I'm so glad." Ada said it urbanely, but her cheeks pinked with pleasure.

"Governor, your wife is absolutely ravishing. I declare, there ought to be a law against such a beautiful first lady. She shames all the rest of us."

"Not for one minute," said His Excellency. "But you're mighty kind."

Others in the cluster exchanged smiles and murmured courtesies, Ada flushed with happiness, then moved with Tommy back onto the floor. When I danced with her, Ada whispered. "A baroness. Imagine, a real baroness at my party."

After intermission, and the replenishing of the champagne and rum punch with the rum much heavier, the visible gulf cutting the guests appeared to close: the worlds ran together and overlapped. Representative Boudin danced with Mrs. Smith. Mrs. Dorothea Grant conversed animatedly with Carlos Cegiano, and several minutes later I heard her shrill: "I always wanted to meet a real live hood."

Soon after, Tommy was persuaded to sing "You and Me" with the band, on which the guests wildly applauded, demanded, and received encores.

Tommy hired the band for another hour, and it played until after three. The guests were very merry as they departed. They all said it was a delightful party.

Tommy Dallas

It was over. I was tired as hell, but she had done it like she wanted. I hoped. I wondered why Sylvestre had had all that political crowd in. Some of them weren't much better than gangsters. Still, she was happy.

After the party, in that big white house on St. Charles that was as big as the mansion, she sat on the edge of her bed in a plum-colored silk thing and said, "It was a good party. It was just fine."

"Sure it was, baby."

"Do you know?" Her voice climbed all the way up with feeling so good. "I think it was really a success. I think I'm in."

"Hell, baby, you were already in. You the Governor's wife."

"Oh, that doesn't matter, not in New Orleans. But everything's fine now."

I went back to Baton Rouge that Sunday. We had worked it out that I would come down on weekends. Ada was loaded with everything: racks and racks of new clothes, four servants, and a social secretary. I just hoped Sylvestre would keep the dough coming.

The arrangement was fine with me. While she was down there waiting for things to happen, I was all clear for the blonde in the Department of Commerce and Industry (I had gotten rid of the brunette in Public Works a while back) and for anything else that might turn up. Hell, they all of them ought to be real glad to get a chance to accommodate the Governor.

The first Saturday afternoon I came down, Ada was reading a list of parties in the social calendar of the *Times-Picayune*. "Here's a cocktail party by the Sterling Smiths for December twentieth. That's one we'll have to go to. And a Christmas Eve dance by the Blair DeNegres. That one too." I had never seen her look so satisfied.

But the next week, her face was tight and strained and I could feel her about to explode. So I didn't ask no questions. Late that afternoon, I said, "Hon, you look kind of peaked."

"It's nothing." Her voice was flat.

"Sure it is."

"No." It was an order, so I shut up.

Still later, I said, "Do we have to go to that party tonight? The one you were talking about last week."

"No!" Her voice was smoke from a volcano, and I got the hell back from the rim.

But I busted out, "How come?" before I could stop it.

She came up fast, and her face blazed like a gun muzzle. For a second, I thought I was the target. "Because we aren't invited, and we aren't invited to the DeNegres' next week, nor the Lewins', nor the Von Pauluses' on New Year's Eve nor anywhere else."

She walked fast toward the stairs but she didn't leave; she just whirled around at the carpet's edge and shot herself back. "Correction." Her voice shook. "We are invited elsewhere. To Representative Boudin's on Christmas Eve and Charles Cegiano's restaurant on Christmas Day and Arnie Morris's for New Year's and various other brilliant occasions. We're so popular. So sought after." She stopped for breath, and pulled it in while her body shook with little inside explosions. She seemed to move wild and fast, but she never left one place. "The Governor's wife. And they won't invite me to their stinking parties. Not one of them."

"Come on, kid. This is just a couple. Stick it out. You got plenty time."

"No, I haven't." The storm had all at once gone by. She sagged and almost fell down. "No. No more time. It's over. They won't have me."

I thought she was going to cry. But she didn't, and all at once the storm came back, harder than before, and she shook in it. "All right. All right all right all right. They'll get it their way. I'll give it to them I will I will I will!" Her voice went up like a rocket, not hurting any more but hating. Then it dived down and the softness scared me more: "They'll get what they asked for. Very soon I think."

She started up the stairs, not slow and not fast, and her head was high.

I felt my hands go cold, then I went cold all over. Jesus, I thought. Jesus.

It happened fast. Ada gave up the house on St. Charles on Christmas Eve, with five months of the lease still to run and still to pay for. Ten days after that, Sylvestre brought a big white piece of parchment into the office and said, "Sign it."

"Where?"

He pointed. I heard the pen scratch as I signed, and I remembered the story they used to tell about O. K. Allen, Huey's governor. They said a leaf blew in the window one day and he signed that.

After I signed it, I said, "What is it?"

"A proclamation for a special session of the Legislature."

"How come?"

"To raise some money."

That was all he said.

Steve Jackson

I checked in at the Capitol House for the special session with a partial sense of repetition: the past not recaptured but brushed in passing. In the lobby, I went to the telephone booths by the side entrance and started to dial Ada's unlisted number. I stopped on the fourth digit, and then dialed the listed, public number of the mansion. I told the butler to tell Mrs. Dallas she could reach me at the hotel if she wanted to go ahead with the story we had discussed. That left it up to her.

She called later, and I went out to see her just before midnight. She looked quite tired and quite pleased, her hair wisping limply about her face, and her mouth set in satisfaction. She greeted me with unchanged warmth; things were still on the same basis as they had been when she was in New Orleans for the party.

"I'm sorry it's so late," she said. "Sylvestre and I were chatting with some of"—her voice flicked the words deridingly—"the boys."

"Oh?" I noted she had not mentioned Tommy Dallas's name.

She smiled with sudden boldness. "It's going to be a very interesting session."

"Good."

She waited a moment, I suppose for me to ask why, which I did not, and then she said, "You might call this the session for the liquidation of debt."

She was clearly pleased with herself, and clearly wanted to tell why, so I cued: "State debt?"

"No. No, not the state debt."

Then she explained.

It looked as if the session was going to be very interesting indeed. The legislators trickled into town and were careful not to use the word "harmony." This was a very different proposition from the hot and hand-holding summer. The high happy even hum was gone from the air; now it was ominously silent and still, as in a low-pressure area awaiting the storm.

The storm came swiftly. The first day, Tommy addressed both houses in joint session to charge them with their responsibility: to bring enough money into the treasury to pay for the unemployment increase and the local benefices. He spoke quickly and soberly, and the Tommy Dallas Four was not behind him. When he finished, he sang no songs, and walked swiftly from the podium as though glad to escape.

The next day, the administration's floor leaders in the House introduced four bills.

One proposed to eliminate a special tax exemption for private hospitals with more than a hundred beds. It was explained that this would affect only three hospitals in the state, and only one of these seriously. It was not explained that this one was the St. Anne's Hospital in New Orleans, of which Dr. Sterling Smith was director and major stockholder.

Another bill completely redefined the specifications for the state's printing. It would end the awarding of a single contract for all the printing, and would provide for individual bidding in many categories. This would save the state more than a million dollars a year. It would also take away more than a million dollars a year from the firm which presently held the contract. This was DeNegre Printing Co., of New Orleans, which was headed by Blair DeNegre.

The third bill proposed a heavy "separation tax" on all canneries exporting more than $100,000 worth of canned sea food from the state annually. More than anyone else, the Gulf Canning Company would be hit if this passed. The Gulf Canning Company's principal officers were Herman Von Paulus and Col. Richard Bartlett.

The fourth was a one-cent increase in the state sales tax.

The bills dazed the Legislature. Except for the sales tax increase, few knew what was involved. But they all were alarmed by that one, and they intuitively distrusted the others. The bills were referred to the House Ways and Means Committee and the boys scurried home for a long weekend.

When they came back Monday, the battle had formed. Everybody was against the sales tax, or pretended to be. The other bills had stirred up the "reform" delegation from New Orleans, which translated as the old-line-families delegation. They were violently attacking the bills, and even the Old Regulars were neutral about them, though their commitments were with the administration. This neutrality was the result of instinctive political caution; the bills were confusing. Few could understand what was behind them. I was one of the few, because Ada had told me.

The three bills were spite bills, Ada's spite bills, and Sylvestre was supporting them. On the last, I did not know why for sure, but thought I had the reason. It was the same as the reason for the other: why he had destroyed her in her New Orleans adventure.

It was simply that he wanted her back in the politics business. She had been shocked out of it by what happened to Marianne Lenoir. All of her high-compression combustion had been diverted into something else: the social thing. Sylvestre wanted it combusting where he could use it, and he had taken steps.

And they had worked, boy, had they worked. Now Ada was the article that hell hath no fury like, and everybody in range had better keep their eyes open and their heads down.

As Ada said, it was going to be a *very* interesting session.

Tommy Dallas

"What do you want to do it to them for?" I said. "What you going to prove just doing it to them? To four people?"

"They are only representative," Sylvestre said, but not really against it.

We were sitting in the inside governor's office that evening after Ada's bills were read.

"I know they're representative," Ada said, the hate in her voice.

"Can't you persuade her otherwise, Tommy?" Sylvestre was silky polite, the way he was when he had an angle. "Can't you get her to call off the vendetta?"

"I guess not." I felt the blood in my face.

What did he say that for? He knew I couldn't do nothing with her. He was the only one that could stop her. He could stop her in five seconds if he wanted to. She couldn't have started if he hadn't said yes. Why had he said it? The bills would never have been gotten ready if he hadn't passed on them. Everything started with him.

"Then I guess there isn't anything we can do," he said. "Is there?"

The bills didn't pass but weren't dead, and the boys were called into the office one at a time. First was the Hon. A. P. Boudin. His tar-black hair was plastered on the side, his eyes were all big and owlish with the heavy glasses, and he looked like he was scared to death but hell-set on being brave as he walked into the office.

The Hon. sat on the edge of the chair. He crossed and uncrossed his legs, he kept working his hands together, and his eyes jumped around behind the glass lenses. They stopped on me for a second, then on Ada, and finally on the floor.

I heard my throat clear. "Uh, Mr. Boudin."

The Hon. wouldn't take his eyes off their spot on the floor.

"Yes, Mr. Boudin." Ada said it soft, and he looked quick up to her, she smiled, and his eyes switched down again.

"We, uh, got a little problem," I said.

He didn't look up.

"We need your help on this . . . legislation," I said.

He didn't say nothing and Ada said, still soft:

"You know, Mr. Boudin, we're very surprised at you. And may I say, very disappointed. We thought you were our friend."

Mr. Boudin mumbled something.

"We thought you were our friend," Ada said again, sweet and sad. "But now you've disappointed us."

Mr. Boudin mumbled something else.

"Mr. Boudin," Ada said, very soft, "don't you think you might reconsider and vote with us next week?"

He whispered.

"What, Mr. Boudin?"

"I. Can't."

"Oh, Mr. Boudin." Her voice said he had hurt her feelings something awful, but she was worried about him. "I wish you weren't so, so adamant. Because the Governor wants you to have the recreation center in your district, the one the Legislature approved last summer. But there has to be money to pay for it. And the Governor can't sign the appropriation bill unless he has tax money."

The Hon. looked at the floor.

"You see the problem, Mr. Boudin."

"_____," mumbled Mr. Boudin.

"If there isn't any center, everybody will blame you, Mr. Boudin." The softness went out of her voice. "How about it?"

The Hon. made a hoarse croaking noise.

"What?" Her voice was gunmetal now.

"All right," croaked the Hon. Mr. Boudin. "All right."

The Hon. Mr. Boudin was the first. After him we got Rep. Leon Levalle, who wanted state money for a reclamation project in the bayou country of his district; Rep. W. O. Blake, who needed state money for a parish hospital; Rep. Alton Webster, he needed new farm-to-market roads for his central Louisiana parish; Rep. James Gravier, who had three gambling houses going for him in southwest Louisiana and who wanted them to keep going; and five others who wanted or needed or were scared of one thing or another. They all came in looking just a little scared, working hard to look brave, and they came out looking plain scared and not brave at all.

We needed, that is Sylvestre and Ada needed, only six votes changed to win on reconsideration. Sylvestre said ten would make it safe. On the second Thursday, all four bills passed, not by ten votes but by thirty-five.

"I guess the word got around." Sylvestre smiled.

"I guess it did," said Ada.

I said nothing.

They decided holding back the old persuasion in the Senate was a waste of time; Ada called in a bunch of the senators the day the bills hit the Senate Finance Committee. The committee reported them favorably the next day, and the day after that the Senate passed them 27-10, 2 not voting. Now all they needed was for me to sign them.

Ada looked over my shoulder while I looked down at the four white crinkly sheets on the desk. I could hear her breathing, and I felt her breath hot on my cheek.

"This is all it needs." She was real contented.

I made out I was reading the papers.

"Come on, darling," she said. "What are you waiting for?"

I pulled out the gold pen the St. Peter's Democratic Club gave me. But I read some more before I put the point on paper.

"Oh, hell." Her voice was climbing. "You know what's in them. Sign."

I listened to the scratch of the pen as it put my name on the paper and the bills into law.

"And that's done." She smiled and picked up the sheets, that were acts now instead of bills, and ran her finger over them like she was stroking a sweetie's cheek, only she never stroked mine that way.

"Is there anything else?" I meant it sarcastic; it didn't come out quite right, though.

"Well." She was still smiling, still loving up the parchment with her fingers. "There is something."

"What?" I sounded to myself like a confused steer.

"The small matter of a state office."

"State office? For who?"

"For me."

I looked at her, holding the white sheets and smiling. I looked at Sylvestre, his lips twisting up, but so little you didn't know if he was smiling or not. Why don't he cut her off, I thought, and I hadn't even finished thinking it when I knew he was with her.

"You got a state office. You're first lady. Can't nobody appoint you to any office high as what you got now."

"You can." She said it so sweet. Then she dropped the acts on the desk and pushed them back with her open hand and pulled her hand back high. *I'm through with you, acts, go do your business,* the hand said. Then she said in the same sweet voice, "You can appoint me lieutenant governor."

There wasn't anything in the room but quiet. I heard the clock on my desk ticking, and down below somewhere I heard a car door slam. I looked at Ada, who looked back sweet-faced at me. I looked at Sylvestre, and he was enjoying some joke all his own. I swallowed, and that sounded like an underground explosion.

"We got one," I said.

"Have we?" she said.

Steve Jackson

I saw Ada twice more before the session was over. The second time was just after adjournment. Her vengeance bills were passed and signed, she was triumphant and happy, and she was very much back in the politics business. If my theory was right, Sylvestre had exactly what he wanted: the end of her long remorse (if that was what it was), and her return to action.

The papers of course attacked all the new revenue acts. But the sales tax was the only one the public cared about, and they would get used to it, for it paid for the local monuments. So: in the next three months, the Gulf Canning Company, Herman Von Paulus, and Colonel Bartlett all moved to Gulfport, Mississippi. With no prospects of payment, the American Bank called a $300,000 note on DeNegre Printing and foreclosed. St. Anne's Hospital sold its physical assets to a Dallas hospital, and the building was converted into medical offices.

The swiftness of Ada's retaliation shocked the *haut monde* of New Orleans which she had hated and coveted so long, and which had rebuffed her with such casual contempt. When the intent of her vengeance bills first became clear, the clamor at New Orleans cocktail parties—half amusement, half indignation—had been shrill and uninhibited. When intent advanced into consequence, it suddenly hushed to a careful half-whisper. "For God's sake, don't get her down on us," husbands told their wives, and the wives at least pretended to circumspection.

As at the clicking of a switch, Ada had blazed from bauble to blowtorch. In Baton Rouge, those with boons to ask or blows to fear began to petition her as well as Sylvestre. The word ran through Louisiana the way a high wind blows through a field of rice: Ada Dallas was to be feared.

And this made me more apprehensive than ever about the Mobile spectre. Nobody had found out anything, so far. This seemed a small miracle. But the more moves she made, the more unfigurables she set in motion, and the more enemies she made. One of these might ultimately wreck her. And she sure as hell was making the moves and the enemies.

Not too many weeks after the special session, she suddenly turned up as sponsor of something called the Young Louisiana League. She went through the motions of addressing it at the request of its leaders; actually, she had conceived and organized it. Age limits were seventeen to twenty-five, and the principal article of faith was that voting should begin at eighteen. Ada must have been reading intensively in the comparative-government texts; if this one didn't have quite the scope of the Hitler Youth, it suggested strongly certain organizations in Italy and the Argentine.

I was present at the first full-scale meeting in Jackson Square one day in April—privately and not professionally. The faces in the crowd said the membership was predominantly hot-rod, duck-tail, wild daddy-o wild, and maybe spiv-gun, though on the platform were certain sober and intellect-ish types who must be the theorists, the Alfred Rosenbergs as it were, of the movement. I saw that this was the kind of crowd she would want and would think she needed: fierce, intemperate, desperately in need of the emotional moisture of belonging; wanting achingly the aphrodisiacal security of fervor, discipline, and violence.

A horn-rimmed eighteen-year-old introduced her, and she was on the platform before the mike, smiling. Then she began to talk. Perhaps it was my position in the crowd, perhaps it was some acoustical oddity of the square. But for an instant, the white gold-crested figure and the amplified voice were things apart, with neither link nor common identity. The voice was a sudden dimension: from no spring or source, it flowed over us like warm pumped air. And through the electrical barriers it was clear and sweet and true.

The words she said were commonplace, even banal:

"You are the ones who count more than anything else. For you are the future, and the future is yours. You must claim it for yourselves, because no one else is going to give it to you."

But the totality of what she said was something else. This was not only the words, but altogether: their clear hypnotic melody; the white figure who seemed to witness rather than speak the words; the upturned, entranced, and seeking young faces on which they fell; the effigied green horseman who had once on the same ground commanded an even motlier crew; the fresh blue fire of sky threatening, or blessing, what was beneath. At that instant, all of this brought to spearpoint was Ada, who said only:

"The question is: are you going to take what belongs to you?"

They made a noise like surf, but higher.

I was purposely well back in the crowd, and she never saw me. And I did not seek her out afterward. I was not sure why.

Robert Yancey

Through the crawling desk-and-paper days I waited. And I wondered: *When?* I hadn't yet earned my chance with Luck. The fault had to be mine because Luck never really gives you anything free, you always have to beat or wheedle it out of her. And I hadn't done it. Sometimes I would manage to meet Ada face to face and speak a word or two. But all I got for it was nothing.

Then, one day. She called and asked for a driver and escort to take her to New Orleans. She was going to address something called the Young Louisiana League.

"I'll drive you myself, Mrs. Dallas," I said.

"Oh, that won't be necessary, Colonel." She sounded cool.

"It'll be my pleasure, Mrs. Dallas."

"All right then. Pick me up at nine, if you'll be good enough."

I put the phone down, and felt the coldness of my hands. This was it. I had worked for it and sweated for it and got nothing. Now it had dropped into my hands. It was the breakthrough. At last I had my luck.

As I waited at the door, I kept commanding: Don't let it show. Don't be eager. But it was hard.

Then the door was opening, she came out, I saluted. "Good morning, Mrs. Dallas."

"Good morning, Colonel. Let me say again that I am honored." The words could have meant something if she had said them another way.

This was outside routine. For the head of state police to drive somebody was like a two-star general to drive them. But if I wanted to do something myself, I did it. I made my own protocol.

I opened the back door for her, and held out my hand. But she didn't touch it as she stepped in. And in the car she didn't talk. I tried, and she answered pleasantly enough but stopped it there, and if I had gone on, I would have been too eager.

But I had arranged a little something. I had focused the central rear-vision mirror on the back seat instead of the road (I still had the one outside to drive with), and by moving my head just a little I could see her legs and maybe if I had some more luck I could see more than that.

I glanced into the mirror every few seconds while the big black car bulleted ahead and threw miles behind. For a long time I saw just the brown nylon-covered legs below the skirt, which she held carefully over her knees. But I saw her head sink back in the cushions and her eyes close, maybe sleeping, maybe not. After a while, I saw she was sleeping, and she moved around to get comfortable, and I saw above the brown nylon a strip of white flesh.

I felt heat run to my face, and excitement through my body. I felt like a fool or a twelve-year-old, but I was damn glad to have even that, after so long. I kept shooting looks between the mirror and the gray ribbon of road ahead.

Then, a few miles further, she moved on the seat, sound sleep now and my eyes jumped back and forth from the mirror to the road and the road to the mirror, and then against all my will they hung like death on the mirror and I felt the quick short drop of the wheels leaving the asphalt and punching the shoulder and I brought them back with a quick scared twist of my shoulders.

I heard her voice from the back seat, "Trouble, Colonel?"

"Just missing a possum. Did it wake you?"

"That's all right."

That ended that.

In New Orleans, in Jackson Square, I stood in the crowd and kept my eyes open for anybody trying to try something. And I looked at them while they listened to her, and I wondered what kind of fools they were to take it in.

Anybody who knows anything knows one thing. There are those who run it and those who do what they are told. The ones that command and the ones that obey. But fools never learn.

So they believed her. Maybe for that second she believed herself, I don't know. She stood there, reaching for the sky with both hands, while the noise they raised flooded her and everything else.

It was nine o'clock that night before we started back; she hadn't stopped talking and meeting with them for all that time. Now we were in St. John the Baptist parish: for miles no house lights broke the dark. Beside the thin pale road running from the headlights into the dark stood only the low dark trees of the swamp: flashlighted in the rushing yellow and then drowned again in night.

I knew where we were. "Mrs. Dallas." I turned my head halfway. "Would you like some refreshment?"

"You mean a drink? Heavens yes, but where?"

"I know a place right up here."

I took a curve, slowed and stopped by a little white box-house staring at the swamp with square yellow eyes. I knew the inside: a plank floor, a grocery counter, a little plank bar, but with a lot of fine bottles behind it.

"I'll bring them out." I left the car and came back with two Cuba Libres, which are the best there is for doing that particular job.

She took the glass and said, "Why don't you sit back here?" She said it as though she had to, and didn't really care, but I took her up.

So there I was beside her in the shadows of the seat. Outside, the pale light from the house eyes thinned and died at the edge of darkness. Through the car window came the deep rank smell of the swamp, crowding all around as though it might spill out and run over us any minute.

She drank. "I did need that."

"Me, too."

"I hope nobody arrests you for driving while drinking, Colonel." She said it with just enough politeness. In the near dark I saw her crooked smile.

"Maybe I can get away with it this once."

She raised her glass, and I heard her swallowing heavily. I tasted mine, and looked at her those few inches away. I could put out my hand and touch hers, I could stretch out my arm and drop it around her shoulders, with one strong move I could bring the two of us completely together.

She saw me looking. She moved an inch further away and said, very pleasantly, "They make a good drink here."

"This is quite a little place. Unique."

I was wondering what she would do if my fingers touched her elbow.

"I hope this hasn't been too dull a day for you, Colonel."

"Not in the least."

"But I'm afraid it has." What was in her voice?

"Oh, no."

Was she encouraging me?

Try it.

I put my hand on her arm, and she moved away, and I knew I had been wrong, but somehow I could not stop, and then I had both her arms in my hands, and I pulled her to me. She was pulling hard the other way, then she went all at once limp, and I half fell forward and before I saw her hand move I heard the slap, felt the sting, and saw orange bursts. I felt the tears come, and I felt a fool, and for a second I went crazy. I tried to pull her over again, and she said very calmly:

"You sonofabitch you stop that *now*."

And I stopped.

For a second I looked at her white face in the dark and I felt my face burning. "I'm sorry." The thing to do was to be so sorry and contrite for a manly impulse I just let get out of hand. "I'm very sorry. I just lost my head, I shouldn't have."

"You certainly shouldn't have." I could not get over how cool she was. "But maybe it's just as well because now we can lay the cards on the table. Look, Colonel. You aren't going to get anywhere. I know what's been on your mind and it's not going to happen, not ever. So forget about me. You're an attractive man. You can have

all the girls you want, so get them and stop hanging around after
me. You're wasting your time."

"Why, Mrs. Dallas." I was going to say: I had no such idea. But
I saw her look in the moonlight and I stopped. I said only, "I am
sorry."

"It's all right, Colonel." She was still very calm, not angry and
not upset at all. "Just so we understand each other."

At the door of the mansion, she said, "Good night, Colonel," I said,
"Good night, Mrs. Dallas," and she closed the door behind her. I
heard the lock click, and was looking at the big knocker on the
white smooth surface of the wood.

Tommy Dallas

The leaves ripped off the calendar and
blew away in the wind. I waited for Ada and Sylvestre to move,
and I tried to forget I was waiting. I had my trips—to New Orleans,
Houston, Florida—always with something nice, and I did quite a bit
of forgetting.

But I knew it was coming. And that May, when we had all had
one year in office, it came.

"I guess we'd better break it to Ronald," Sylvestre said.

"Suppose he doesn't want to?" said Ada.

"He's a businessman. When he sees we've got him, he'll go along."

"And how will we as you say, get him? Buy his notes?"

His face took on the look of one of those little Buddha statues,
only not so nice. "My dear. I've had his notes for more than a year."

They called him to the mansion to give him the word. He came
into that little sitting room of Ada's, his three chins shaking, the
white-shirted paunch bouncing. We shook hands, and said it was
mighty hot. Ada said she thought Baton Rouge was the hottest
place in the country. No, Hudson said, Shreveport and Dallas were.
Then the quiet in the room got as thick as crude oil, the clock ticked
away on the mantel, and way in the house somebody closed a door.

"Well, now," Hudson said. "What was it you gentlemen wanted
to see me about?"

His face was smiling, babyish, and tough. He was a cool one, nobody was going to just scare him off.

And I was sure he knew what was coming. It was kind of like a dance. Everybody had to make the right steps, but everybody knew it was a dance.

Hudson had started it, and Sylvestre picked it up. "Ronald." His face said he was thinking very deep thoughts. "We have ourselves a little problem. And we thought you might help us out a little bit."

"Glad to." Hudson went right on in the dance. "If I can, of course."

"I think maybe you can." Sylvestre stopped; his face was a show window of heavy thinking going on. "You see, Ronnie, it's like this. We need your office kind of bad just now, some things have come up, Ronnie, and we do need it."

"Mmmmmm-hmmmmm." The bald head dipped, the three chins came together, the voice was so sympathetic. "Yes, sir, I see your problem. I certainly do."

"Now we thought you might be able to help us out," Sylvestre said, very pleasant.

The head nodded, the face was all sympathy. What he said was, "I sure wish I could help. Yes, sir, I really do. But right now I just don't see how I can."

"Now, Ronald, I'm sorry to hear that. I certainly am." Sylvestre's voice was all concerned. "You see, I thought you would be having so many business problems maybe you'd be kind of glad to get out right now."

That was the way. Never say it straight. Bank it on three cushions.

"That's mighty considerate of you, Sylvestre." Hudson said it just like he meant it. "And believe me I sure do appreciate it. Only right now I just don't see how I can."

"I know how you feel, Ronnie." Sylvestre was real solicitous. "But I thought with that big new contract on your hands and these new problems on your housing developments—" His voice stopped and pointed at things over some cliff you couldn't see.

"New problems?"

Sylvestre's face was polite and surprised. "Oh, you didn't know, Ronnie? I thought you did." He pulled a packet of papers out of his coat and handed them to Hudson. I knew what they were. They were Hudson's notes for $700,000, and they had been made over to Sylvestre Marin.

Hudson took them just as polite and began to run through them. "Mmmm-hmmmm," he said, very friendly, as he turned the pages. "Mmmmm-hmmmm. Mmmmm-h-mmmmm." He snapped his finger-nail against the packet, held it there a second, and handed the packet back. "Yes, sir." He was very friendly. "Yes, sir, I see what you mean."

Sylvestre bowed his head, oh so courteous, and didn't say nothing.

"I certainly do." Hudson's voice was soft. "Now this new contract." The voice trailed off.

Sylvestre did the big surprise bit again. "Why, they're going to let bids on that new mental hospital in a couple of months. And I thought that with your sources of information, Ronald,"—he laughed like it was a joke between the two of them—"you'd just naturally be low bidder. If, of course, you were eligible to bid, and being out of state office you would be."

Hudson stared off into space for a couple of seconds. "You know, you're right," he said, dreamy. "I am going to be mighty busy. I guess I just hadn't realized how busy I was going to be." The tummy quivered and rumbled with way-off laughter. "I guess I hadn't. Well, now."

He pulled a pen and paper from his coat pocket, and started to write. "My health is suddenly very bad, Sylvestre. I don't see how I can do much of anything except resign on account of my bad health."

"I certainly hate to hear that, Ronnie. They'll hold it against you next time you run for office." The words were a promise. "If it was your wife's health, now—"

Hudson shook his head, slow and solemn. "My poor wife. This female trouble just came up and hit her all at once." He shook his head, like she was about to die. "All at once. I hope you see how it is, Sylvestre, but a man's got to think about his family first."

He didn't crack a smile, and neither did Sylvestre. Sylvestre just bowed his head. "We understand."

Hudson shook his head. "Always been a big family man, Sylvestre."

Then his big belly started to shake, then it started to rumble with laughter, and Sylvestre joined in with his dry cough that was supposed to be a laugh. They both laughed very hard, each in his own way.

"You're a real businessman, Ronnie," said Sylvestre.

Now she had what she wanted, I guess. The hell she did. She was only starting to get what she wanted and I wasn't going to kid myself no more. I was just a rug for her and Sylvestre to walk on. They didn't even know I was there. If I could do something to make them see me. To make me see myself, again. But what?

After Sylvestre left, Ada left. She wasn't back for supper, dinner we called it now. But that wasn't nothing new. I saw her just at odd hours, now. She would come in late, and leave for appointments at night, and I would of been suspicious if it would of been anybody else, but you can always smell it when they're stepping out, and she wasn't. She just wanted to run as much of it as Sylvestre would let her, and that was all she gave a damn about.

She was late tonight. It was nearly nine o'clock when I heard the door open and her footsteps coming along the hall. Then she came into the sitting room, looking like a million bucks in some blue silk thing. She was still spending plenty dough on clothes, and it still goddamn was my dough.

"Hello," she said, friendly enough.

"Hi," I said. "How you doing? Late day at the office?"

"Yes. I had some of my children from the Young Louisiana League in the office and I had to entertain them for a while."

Children, hell. Gangsters. She had every zip-gunner in the state in that hairy outfit. How she had done it I don't know, but she had got them in all right, and when she gave them the word, boy, that was it. They went right down the line for her. I wished to Christ I had that kind of an organization.

"I know how it is." I looked at her. She was beautiful as hell, that blue silk fitted her like she had been shot into it with an air hose, her face was smooth and white, and her hair was as yellow and pretty as ever. I could remember how I used to think I would die if I could just have it. Well. You get over that.

She hadn't been up to anything. If there is one thing I can tell, it is when a woman has done that. She hadn't.

"Mix me a drink, huh?" she said, very pleasant.

"Sure." I was just as pleasant. That was the way we were now. Pleasant.

She tossed half of the drink I fixed straight down. I looked at her. I had made it pretty strong. "How is it," I said, "Governor?"

"Fine." Her cheeks started to flush at the word, but she let it pass. I had one with her, then another, then I had one quick big one by myself.

I looked at her, and she looked good, all at once she looked as good as she had two years before, and those two years were two minutes. Then they were two centuries and I hated her. Hating her and wanting her, I wanted even more to make her see me. I wanted to shock her, hurt her—anything to make her admit I was there.

I put down the drink and walked to her.

She looked at me, a little frown on her face, asking a question, and then her eyes opened wider, and she knew. She started to step back, but I had her. I pulled her close. She went stiff, her hands pushing against my chest, but this way I was stronger, and I pulled her tight and kissed her, feeling her warm and tight through the silk, even if she was fighting, and then she wasn't fighting any more.

I picked her up and carried her to the couch.

"Not now," she said. "Not here, you fool."

"Not here hell," I said.

It was a lot later. She was looking at me and seeing me.

"You know," she said. "You do have your points."

"You're damn right." I felt better than I had in six years. I had done something.

After that, I broke it off with my little blonde in the Secretary of State's office, and spent all my time with Ada. She was the best, no doubt about it. I had halfway forgotten, the way you forget when you got nothing to remind you, but now it all came back, and I remembered, and I made up for lost time.

Some days, I would stick my head in her office and wink, and she would wink back and touch her tongue to her lips, and I would know we could be together at home, and I didn't want to wait.

It was funny as hell, licking your chops like that over your wife. Your own wife. But I had made her admit I was something. Not a zero. I could look in the mirror and see somebody again. When the time came, I was even glad to appoint her lieutenant governor.

Steve Jackson

From high steps, I looked over the low dark arrowheads of evergreens and beyond Huey in bronze to the faces on the lawn, close together and pale in the jagged yellow rip of arc lights, not separate but all one. They were young faces: impatient, demanding, fierce, and they were the faces of a crowd, not simply of many people in the same place. They were a crowd because they were for Ada.

Into the mike, I said:

"The appointment of Mrs. Dallas has been under the heaviest kind of fire, from both political personages and the press. She was appointed to the second-highest office in Louisiana by her husband, Gov. Tommy Dallas. This has not happened in Louisiana before..."

Speaking, I looked at the white placards bouncing and twisting among the faces, sometimes leaping high, dancing on an airpeak, and diving downward. They said: ADA IS WAY OUT. ADA YOU'RE THE MOST. ADA ONLY THE GREATEST. And others said: YOUNG LOUISIANA LEAGUE.

I looked now at the light upcutting Huey's chiseled face, blank and noble and safe in metal, and I looked at the ribboned space at the top of the steps cleared for Ada Dallas. Six hours earlier, I— the certified friend, the not-quite lover, the useful news commentator —had looked at Ada herself across the desk in her new office.

"Let the bastards scream," she said. "I'm in. Let them scream all they want."

She was enormously pleased and not even vestigially contented. *I'm on the way at last, really on the way,* her manner said beyond mistake. *Everything up to now has been a nuisance, and now the nuisances are cleared. Get out of my way or take the consequences.*

That had been the afternoon, and now it was night. And the arc lamps threw dusty light on the dark lawns, a spot made a bright circle high on the steps, and the circle and the crowd and I waited for Ada.

They were shouting for her now: *"Ada! Ada!"* and I knew she would wait in the tower and give them herself at the magic instant, not one second before or after.

The shouts rang louder, they climbed higher, and I thought: *now.* Nothing happened and I thought it again and all at once she was there in the yellow circle. I had not seen her come to it. She was quite suddenly there, in a materialization, arms outward and upward in offering and triumph. They accepted her and gave themselves in a wordless shout.

You understand. This was not the Sportspalast and only a few hundred were here. But it was impressive.

Then Ada spoke. Her words were not important. I listened not to her words but to her voice, and I watched her face. I had seen the look upon it before, in other times, on other faces: on the mustached face before the Swastika in newsreels, on the smooth face under the cocked hat in the battle paintings, and on the long-nosed baldheaded statue of a face cast in white marble two thousand years before.

It was—how would you say it?—it was a look of certitude. As though the wearer knew by divination that his climb would be unstopping, that nothing would bar him from the absolute of absolute supremacy, of being the first in his world, and that the present passing moment was simply a footfall on a triumphal and unslowing march. Once I had had the feeling myself, but it was long ago and now I could not remember it.

Ada had it now. I looked, and knew that for her this was neither end nor beginning. I knew how it was with the Young Louisiana League, with the devout. We all had in common the absolute certitude in her absolute and unshakable destiny. And I could see now how ridiculous was the prospect of her ever preferring me to this, even those years before.

She spoke on, and they cried out and shook the placards aloft. Then I did not see the absurd inscriptions, but only the young falcon faces and the fire that she had lighted in them. They were hers.

At that moment, I thought, incongruously, that now she was surely safe, that now nobody would ever know about Mary Ellis and Mobile and a hundred bucks a night, seventy-five if you were lucky.

She had asked me to see her later. And, as the certified friend, not-quite lover, I said of course.

We drove in my Buick to a roadhouse across the river, parked, and I brought out a box of barbecue and two bourbons-and-water.

She ate, and drank, almost greedily. I could hear the quick swallows and in the half light I could make out the working of her throat.

"Nothing like animating the populace to work up an appetite, huh?" I sounded faintly malicious; I had not meant to.

Her mouth was full. She glanced at me, swallowed, and said clearly, "Nothing. Absolutely nothing. And that was pretty damned snotty."

"I guess it was."

"You know—" The sentence snapped and the two words filled the car. What I knew was that I had made my own terms. If I was not participating more fully in what was now a corporate institution, it was my own fault. I could change the terms any time I wanted. That is, I could slightly enlarge my small minority holdings. The hell with that.

But that was no reason to be a jerk.

I said, "I'm sorry."

She smiled, and put her hand very lightly on my arm. "It's nothing. Don't waste remorse."

I felt the warmth of her voice and smile like a physical substance, and thought that all I need do was gently extend one arm toward her and she would come to me. I felt the muscle tighten and lift, and my arm came perhaps an inch off the seat, and then dropped again.

"You were really very good," I said in the brisk, cheery, nonemotional voice of the friend who was not in.

She had seen the movement and the change, and her smile became wry and she said in the same brisk cheery nonemotional voice. "Thank you, it seemed to go well. It was a very responsive audience."

"They sure as hell respond to you."

She smiled differently, and her voice was proud. "Yes."

"Well. What's next?" Now I was safe on a safe impersonal plane.

"Don't you know?"

"Governor? Next election?"

She nodded. "Next election." Her inflection was curious.

"Do you think you can make it?"

"If I didn't, I wouldn't be wasting my time. Or more precisely. If Sylvestre didn't, he wouldn't be wasting his time."

"What's he after?"

Her voice was flat. "Don't you remember what he said? On the tape? He wants a double return on his investment. First Tommy, then me. And he thinks he can do something with a woman at the convention. One of these years." She stopped. Her voice was light and edged. "Oh he has it all figured out. All I have to do is learn my lines."

"It's like that?"

"Close enough to that. Not quite like Tommy though. He at least lets me"—the irony came back—"discuss things. How we do discuss things."

"This lieutenant governor business was Sylvestre's idea?"

She laughed, shortly. "He thinks it was. Or maybe he let me think it was mine. I suppose really it was his idea. Part of his master plan."

I did not answer, and she went on, the voice edging higher in its dry derisive lightness. "Did you know he had a little trouble with the plan? Just a little. With me. You see, I defected temporarily. I was somewhat, upset, after I caused Marianne Lenoir to blow her head off. Did you know that I caused it? It was my triumph." She was smiling and bright-eyed and one step from crying. "My great triumph. Only after that I wasn't interested in politics. After that I, you might say, I lost my taste for political action."

"Come on," I said.

"But he had the therapy for that. He has the therapy for everything. Dr. Sylvestre Marin."

"Come on," I said again, and I put my hands on her shoulders. I wanted to comfort, to solace her. But she moved away quickly.

"Oh no, Steve." Now she was mocking me. "Be careful. No intimacy. No awkward involvements. Don't forget yourself, Steve."

I leaned back in the seat. Neither of us spoke for a minute.

Then she said, conversationally, "I guess I had quite a little go there."

"No strain."

"Of course not. No strain, no pain. Why don't you get us another?"

On the bridge again, high over the slow dull-copper river, I looked at her. Her golden head was cushioned by the seat, her lovely face was pale and calm. I wondered again at what was beneath, at what combustible fuel it was that rocketed one woman against the universe.

Soon we were back in town, in the quiet half-lighted genteel streets.

"Home?" I added, awkwardly, "To the mansion?"

"No," she said. "I have to pick up my car. Take me to the capitol."

As we turned into the approach, I saw it standing alone in the dark and empty spaces of the deserted parking lanes: long and swift even in its stillness, shimmering and gold even by starlight.

I stopped. "Don't get out." She opened her door before I could move. But she lingered a moment. "Thanks for the drink." I saw her smile flash white in the darkness. "Good night, Steve. I'm sorry I was bitchy."

She came toward me, and put a kiss as light as breath on my cheek. Then she stepped out, called "Good night" again, and her heels struck sharply on the concrete as she walked to her car. To make sure she was safe, I waited until I heard the engine start its powerful whisper, and watched the yellow swiftness glide into the dark.

I drove to the end of the parking lane to turn. Coming back, I glanced out and up at the tower. It lanced straight and black and tall into the night sky, and came to a spearpoint somewhere in the stars.

I stopped at the edge of the street, looked both ways, and pulled into it. Ada's car had disappeared.

You look back through time to a sequence of connected events, and you are apt to see a unity that was not really there. You forget that things happened that were not part of the sequence, but actually consumed most of the time. The sequence is one thread in a big blanket. But looking at the blanket with a certain perspective, that thread is what you see.

The months after Ada became lieutenant governor, I did many things. I took up for a while with a red-haired widow from Venezuela, whom I met on the flight back from Caracas, where I had gone as a free-loader on the opening of a new Delta Airlines service. I nearly got thrown out of my apartment for an explosive scene in which she threw bottles, frying pans, and ash trays. I was "promoted" to be news director of the station, in lieu of a raise. I continued my *Magazine of the Air* series for which I wrote, and read over news films, a short feature story every week. I did dozens of these, and the only one I remember now was an interview with a cop killer two days before they burned him into nothing. I played a great deal of tennis at the New Orleans Lawn Tennis Club, I spent several weekends on the coast, and when I look back at those months, all I can see is Ada.

Ada was politicking full throttle. All at once, she was running as a Great Social Conscience, and this took some getting used to. She said nothing new: it had all been said by Huey Long or the New Deal or the Fair Deal. But she said it as if she meant it, and the voters listened.

I heard many of her speeches, and talked to her after, sometimes. She told me with what seemed complete candor—but maybe was not—what the strategy was. The congressional elections, Sylvestre thought, showed the time was ripe for a second coming of the New Deal, at the state as well as the national level. Of course it had to be a nice streamlined New Deal. Her job was to incarnate the approach, and get identified as its symbol, a long enough time before the election.

"Another part of Sylvestre's master plan?" I asked.

"What else?" Her mouth twisted.

I saw her regularly, if infrequently, and our status was unchanged. We both held fast to the same official attitude: that we were the kind of friends ex-lovers sometimes become. I was not sure how long I could keep it up; I felt my resolve weaken each time I saw her. And for a long time after that night across the river, she never indicated even by anger that she wanted it any other way. Maybe she didn't, now. This was not a thought that pleased me.

Then, a couple of weeks after my explosion with the Venezuelan widow, I met her in Arnaud's for a drink, one day when she came to town. She was at first quite distant, and then definitely cold. Just before we left, she said, "I hope this hasn't been too dull for you. I mean, having nothing to dodge or anything."

"What do you mean?"

"You know damned well what."

Clearly she had heard about my encounter with the widow. She was still quite cold when we said good-by, and I was very pleased that she could be jealous of me.

A week later, I produced some flimsy rationalization for the fact that I wanted to see her, and made an appointment to interview her about some humanitarian project of hers. The vacation Camp Fund for underprivileged delinquents, or bastards, or something. So I drove to Baton Rouge.

I walked through the lobby, glancing at the statuary of former governors, safe and rigid heroes sealed forever in bronze, and I passed through the entrance to the corridor that led to Ada's office. Coming out of the office was a woman. She was perhaps fifty, well if flamboyantly dressed, and with a small purple hat slicing hair unmistakably dyed to a dry red-brown. Her face was frozen in evil, or maybe only bitterness. She glanced at me idly and without interest, and walked past. Reflexively, I was sure I had seen her before, somewhere.

In the reception room of Ada's office, I tried to remember the face; I knew I had seen it. But identity danced just beyond reach. I picked up a copy of the *Morning Advocate* that someone had left. A headline read FOUR KILLED IN CRASH. I started the story and was well into it when I dropped the paper and stood up. Memory had shelled in.

I breathed deeply, and was sweating. I walked to the window for air.

"Come in, Steve."

Ada's voice was flat and dead, and I turned and saw her in the open doorway to her inner office.

I went in. The door closed with a distinct click.

I said, "Was that who I think it was?"

"Yes." Her voice was as full of nothing as death must be. "That was Mobile." A blade of sunlight cut a yellow scar on her cheek. "After four years. Not out of the past. *The* past. All of it come at once to kill me."

To be saying something, anything, I asked, "What did she want?"

"What would she want? Money. Lots of money."

From the other side of the wall, I heard the muffled beating of a typewriter, the hum of talk, the faint fall of footsteps. On that side of the door, the world was exactly as it had been before. On this side, one second had shattered it.

What was the measure? I wondered. A year could be lost and never missed. In a part of a second, the world could end. Which was the longer, the year of streetcar rides and clock punches? Or the fifth of a second of the drop to rope's end?

I said: "What are you going to do? What can I do?"

"What is there to do but pay? It seems she has pictures too. Candid pictures she called them."

I felt sick. "Call the police. Your police. They can keep her from talking."

"You know better."

I did. "I'll work out something."

She turned wearily toward me, and her face moved away from even the scar of sunlight into shadow. "No. No. This is nothing to do with you and there's nothing to do but pay."

"It is to do with me. You don't think I'll stand by—"

She went on as though I had not spoken. "It's a wonder she didn't turn up long ago. It seems she never saw the Louisiana papers. She didn't see any pictures until the wire services ran one last week. It wasn't until then that she knew Mary Ellis was Ada Dallas."

I said nothing.

"I had thought that now it was the same as never having been. You know. That was in another country and besides the wench is dead. But it doesn't die, and if you try to bury it, it comes at you one day with grave-earth in its eyes." She smiled, twistedly. "And what to do but to pay?"

"We'll come up with something." I felt a liar as I said it.

"No, Steve." Her smile altered, and became almost gentle. "I can make this payment, all right. But it isn't the end. Only the beginning."

For the second time she had shattered armor and touched nerve. I had to look at the hard shape of truth. I had not changed. I could not change. I loved her. From here in I would just have to take it as well as I could.

I saw her on TV the next week. She was dedicating a youth center in Elysian Fields, and she never looked better.

For almost three months after that, I tried to think of a way to stop the woman. I couldn't; nothing was good enough. I saw

Ada several times, but under semipublic conditions, and we couldn't talk. Most of the time, now, her face was dull with hard-masked worry. Once, after she had been interviewed on a TV press show in New Orleans, I was alone with her for a few minutes in the Monteleone garage.

"I'm still working," I said.

"Don't, Steve. It's a waste. She has me."

"There must be an answer."

"There is." Her smile was one-sided and tired. "Pay."

"Something else."

"Well, I'm considering every possibility." She said it as an unfunny joke. In the cavernous dimness of the garage, her face was suddenly white and frightening.

Then the attendant whooshed her car down the ramp and braked it hard. I closed the door after she got in, and our faces were a foot apart at the open window.

"Steve." The light was better, and her face human again. "I— please don't worry about this any more. Please."

I watched the big yellow car roll through the wide exit and into the street.

Robert Yancey

She hadn't let me get within a yard of her since that night I grabbed her in the swamp, months before. She didn't dodge me. She just acted like I was not there.

I would pass her in the hall (by my arrangement), and she would smile politely and not really see me. A couple of times I went to her office to talk to her about whatever I could come up with, and her voice would answer in a careful dead politeness that would let me know I was exactly the head of state police and nothing else. But I would sit there, looking at her across the desk, the shape of her bosom clearly outlined by the tight silk, and I would feel myself trembling. And I would watch her from behind as she walked away in the corridor, her high heels clicking hard on concrete, her hips curving and swinging above those beautiful silk-sheathed legs, and I knew I had to have her.

I wondered sometimes if she wasn't teasing me, just a little. Then

I stopped kidding myself. She simply wanted to show me I had nothing to look forward to.

Watching her, even from a distance, I could see she had something big on her mind. Then she was appointed lieutenant governor. And I was crazier to have her than ever. A big part of wanting her had always been that she was so high, and because she was so high, so hard to get. Now she was higher than ever.

I had to work it out, one way or another.

Sometimes I would wait—I would really hide—in the men's room down the hall from her office. I would watch for her, and then I would come out so I could pass her and look at her and maybe say six words to her.

It was no good. She might smile, but very politely and coldly, and she would say, "Hello," very stiffly, and she would walk away. Then I would have the hollow empty feeling in my belly for an hour afterward.

I couldn't stop. I wasn't fooling her. But I had to do it.

One day, I followed her from behind for two or three paces, and then called, very loud and very businesslike, "Oh, Mrs. Dallas."

She stopped, and turned around, and when she saw who it was, she frowned, not much, but mean.

"Yes?" she said. Her face was hard as a white rock; her eyebrows pulled together and her mouth turned down. I wanted to hit her and kiss her at the same time.

But I was still all business when I said, "May I see you a moment?"

"All right, Colonel." Her face smoothed out, a little, but she wasn't giving away anything. "What is it?"

I grabbed at the first thing I could think of. "About your trip to Shreveport." I was very formal. "Will you require escort?"

"No." She said it very shortly.

I inclined my head. "We'll have the usual staff on hand to take care of the crowd."

"Very well." She was not angry now or anything but cold rock, and before I knew it my hand was tight around her wrist, and I was whispering, "Damn you, you've got to see me."

She jerked her arm. Her face was white fire, and her voice was a water moccasin's hiss: "Stop it you fool!"

"You've got to see me!" I whispered, not letting her go.

"Get out of my way." Her voice was low thunder now.

"I said you've got to."

"Never never and never!" It was the hiss now. "And don't **you** ever bother me again. I mean ever."

I had been too rough. I tried it easier. "Ada—"

"Get out of my way!" She threw each word at me as though it was a dagger, and down the hall I heard a door open, and a voice talking, and I let her go. She walked away, her hips swinging hard with anger, and she went down the hall and into her office.

My face was hot, my ears were on fire. I had never hated anybody so much.

But I couldn't get her out of my mind. Whatever I tried. The burning white face and the packed tight body and the voice throwing hailstones: *Never never and never*. They were with me, every hour of every day. I would forget for ten or twenty and sometimes thirty minutes at a time, and would feel fine, not thinking of her at all, and then all at once it would come: "Great, you haven't thought about her for half an hour," and then there I was, thinking of her. She would be back and I could hear the ice-voice: *Never*, and I would be gone, all gone, with that big emptiness and a hard cold knot in my stomach.

I tried to drive it out with work. No good. Then whisky, then other women. No good, either.

When I was with them, she would come before me, and I would feel the sting of her cheek on my open hand, and see the red streaks on her whiteness, and I would bring the whip down on her flesh for what she had done to me.

If I could hurt her. Hurt her. And have her. But I would never. *Never never and never.*

And then one day I came back into the office from a trip down to the garage. Too damn many motor failures. I read them all off, and fired two mechanics who weren't under this new damn civil service, and I came back feeling better.

I sat down, and checked the phone pad. On the top sheet: "Call Mrs. Dallas." Nothing else. Not even the time.

What did that yellow-haired lousy bitch want? Was she telling me I was fired? That was it. She had pushed that jerk Tommy into firing me. She wanted to do it herself and rub it in. The hell with her. I wouldn't give her the chance.

I tried to write up some orders, but I couldn't. Goddamn her. Goddamn Tommy. Goddamn them all.

I heard my secretary's voice, stiff and detached, "Colonel. Mrs. Dallas on four."

"Tell her—" I was going to say to tell her I hadn't come back. But I stopped, switched to four, and said as tough as I could make it, "Colonel Yancey speaking."

If the bitch thought she could make me crawl, she better take another think.

"Hello, Colonel." Her voice came into my ear soft and pleasant. I wasn't going to fall for that.

"Yes?" I was still plenty tough. They might fire me. They weren't by God going to rub it in.

"I hope I'm not interrupting anything important, Colonel." She stopped, a second. "I was wondering if I could see you some time today."

I knew what she was up to. "If you want my resignation, I'll send it by messenger."

"Resignation? Colonel, what on earth are you talking about? Nobody wants your resignation. But I must see you."

What could I lose?

"All right," I said.

"Can you meet me in the coffee shop at two this afternoon?"

"All right," I said again.

Through the glass panel of the door, I saw her at a table, talking to her secretary. I suppose she had brought the secretary to make it look good. They had only coffee cups on the table, and she was not smoking. She never smoked in public, I guess she was afraid it would lose some country votes.

I pushed the door open, and came inside. For one second, she looked straight at me, then her eyes slipped away, and I knew the meeting was supposed to be an accident. I pretended just to see them as I was passing, said hello, and asked if I could join them.

"Please do, Colonel," said Ada.

I sat down. The waitress came up and I ordered coffee. I looked at Ada's face: fresh-powdered and smooth and telling nothing at all. What the hell did she want?

We talked a while, about nothing, and then Ada said, "Damn. I've got to go to town and my car is in the garage."

I saw what I was supposed to do.

"I've a car right outside, Mrs. Dallas. Let me take you."

"I couldn't think of troubling you, Colonel."

"No trouble at all."

So I paid and we walked out the side entrance to the black-and-white highway car I had parked out front.

She stopped when I started to open the door.

"That's a little bit obvious, isn't it?" Her voice was very low but not a whisper.

What the hell?

"We'll take mine," I said.

So I took her to my Chevy coupe. I never kept a fancy car because I had all of them in the department to pick from. But she looked pleased when she saw it. "Fine."

I waited for her to say where to while I backed out, and pulled into the street. She didn't, and I had to ask her. She did not look at me, but stared through the windshield. I thought she hadn't heard me, and I was about to ask again, when she said: "Across the river."

I didn't say anything. I didn't even want to think what I couldn't keep from thinking, that at last it was going to happen.

But why like this? It was a funny damn way to set it up. But maybe she was the kind that didn't mess around once she made up her mind. Don't crowd it, I ordered myself. Take it easy and pick up your winnings.

We were out on the highway now heading for the bridge.

I tried to make it businesslike. "What was it you wanted to see me about, Mrs. Dallas?"

She smiled a crooked little smile, and looked at me just a second. "Wait and see, Colonel. Then it'll be a surprise."

I felt my heart beat like a tom-tom. She couldn't mean anything else. It kept running through me like a brush fire: *now now now.*

I turned into the approaches, we made the curve, and then we were on the bridge. I felt it climbing, climbing like the *now now now* inside me, and straight ahead, over the dark iron frame of superstructure, the sun hung like a big red-orange ball on a string, all afire, and it hurt my eyes because I was driving into it.

I glanced away for a second, and saw through the crossed girders the dazzle on the flat shining brown water, below and far away, running wide and straight, and then curving into nothing in the green trees that made a dark jagged line against the blue sky.

I saw this from the top of the bridge in the part of a second I looked away. Then we were going down fast, like an elevator in a tall building, with the inside of you always a second behind the rest, the *now now now* strong with the drop, and then we were off the bridge and on the western bank.

"Where?" I said.

"Keep driving." Her face was the way it had been since we left town, cut out of marble, or of ice, and I wondered, what's inside her, and I thought, it's really going to happen. I drove for what seemed a long time, impatient, trying to hold back, and all the time feeling I'd won.

She said, not moving her head or anything but her lips: "Here. Turn here."

I saw a narrow road, twin tracks in soft dirt, going off the highway into the woods. I slowed and turned into them.

We bounced along the tracks, dark shadows falling from the west across the narrow road twisting into the dark woods, the rank woods smelling heavy in the cool air. In the heavy yellow grass and rolling ground, the road always vanished a few car-lengths ahead. You could see just so far on it. I could not tell where we were going. But the only way to go was straight ahead.

I drove for seven or eight minutes, probably a couple of miles off the main highway.

"How much longer?" I said.

"Not too much," she said smoothly, and I looked at her carved face and wondered again what was going on behind it.

We bounced on, deeper and deeper into the woods. We had gone maybe five miles further when she said, "There's a clearing right up ahead. We can stop there."

I saw it: a kind of glade, smooth green grass at the foot of a big black-trunked tree, with a thick limb coming straight out over the grass.

I braked, eased off the tracks, and I felt the soft ground sink a little under the weight of the car. I turned the keys and the engine made a whisper like someone dying.

Between treetops I could look off and see the sun, halfway to the horizon now, a big orange bowl pouring fire. But the clearing was shaded and cool and awfully quiet. In the trees, I could hear a jay *caw-caw*, and in the branches of the big tree the leaves whispered like scared women though there was no wind.

"Some road." I did not know what else to say.

"It's an old hunting road. Nobody uses it any more."

"I guess not." I laughed. The laugh sounded funny and hollow in the silence.

"We have things to ourselves," she said.

"Yeah." I felt good, I felt nine feet high, the way you feel only when you win.

We sure had it to ourselves. We were alone in the world. I glanced out the window, and half turned my head to look at the big black branch sticking straight out over us. Like a crossbeam, or a girder. I shivered. It was cold in the shade. I wished the sun would break through.

Well. I had her now. I had waited a long time. I thought I had ruined everything that day in the corridor. But this proved again something I had learned a long time ago. When you really move, you start things that you just don't know about. Anything can happen. It isn't brains that win. It is making a play, and if it turns out wrong, then making another. Make enough plays and you get what you want.

I lifted my arm to put around her but she moved away. She turned and looked at me and smiled. It made me uneasy.

"You've wanted me a long time, haven't you, Colonel?"

"One hell of a long time."

"Colonel, I think this may be your day."

She came closer, inch by inch, her eyes drilling into mine, the crooked half-smile still on her mouth. I listened to her breath, and my heart, and felt the *now now now* running through me like the Panama Limited, no, like an attack bomber.

Just before our lips touched, she stopped, for half a breath, then she came to me.

As she kissed me, now, inside the car in this dead-still place in the woods with the only sounds the jays cawing and the leaves whispering and my heart pounding, I knew I had never had this before in my life.

She stopped my hands when I tried to touch her, still kissing, and

I let her. Then we were apart. Looking straight at me, straight into me, she said:

"I said this may be the day. It depends on you."

"On me what?"

She did not answer, but came back again, and I was crazy with *Now*.

We were there, in the shadows, under the black limb, for what seemed a long time. I loved her as much as she would let me, which little by little was more and more, but never quite enough.

"You like me?"

"I've been in love with you for two years."

"No, you haven't. Nobody's been in love with anybody. You know what you want and it isn't love."

For answer, I kissed her.

Her breath touched my ear, and something inside drew so tight I could barely breathe. She whispered, "You know what you want. And maybe you get it. Today."

The hell with maybe. But I said nothing.

"Do you want me?" she whispered.

"You know I do."

"How bad? How much?" In that second, I hated her. With all that we had done, as far as she had gone, she still had herself under tight control. She was waving herself as bait to get something out of me. I wanted to hit her.

"What would you do?" she said. "For me?"

"Anything," I said, hating her.

"Anything's a big word."

"That's what I'd do."

"Would you?"

"Try me."

"All right." Her voice was very low and very soft, almost as though it were alive by itself and had nothing to do with her. "I'll try you."

I waited: three or four seconds, but they seemed like a month. Then she said in that same detached strange voice, "A very nasty woman is blackmailing me." She stopped. I waited. But she did not go on.

"Is that all?" I felt relieved, this was no problem. "I'll run her in so fast she'll think a truck hit her."

"I don't want her run in."

"Why not?" The relief broke up. I felt angry again. If she messed around much more I would just rape her.

"And have her spill her guts?"

"She wouldn't. I wouldn't let her."

"Yes, she would. What she has to say would get out one way or another, and this is what I don't want."

"What do you care, if it isn't true?"

"Don't talk like a goddamn fool." Her voice picked up an edge. "Of course it's true. That's why she's dangerous."

"What has she got on you?"

"You don't need to know that to help me."

"What do you want me to do?"

I said it in a kind of automatic question, uneasy but not thinking, and then I felt it hit. I know the punch, I have seen it land. You can see it land any time the prisoner stands before the judge and the judge finishes, "... until you are dead." This time I knew how the man in front of the judge with the black cap feels.

My face must have shown it. She smiled, just a little.

"What do you want me to do?" I heard it rising in my voice, and was ashamed. You do not let it show, in your voice or anywhere else.

Her eyes held mine, and she kept smiling.

"What?" I said again.

But I already knew.

She smiled.

"No," I said, making it tough. "I won't."

She did not take her eyes off mine. Her face was still ice-smooth and ice-hard, and I knew I had never really seen it before.

"I won't."

"You said 'anything.' "

"Anything else."

"She's an evil woman."

"No."

"The world will be better off without her."

"I'm not worried about the world."

"Are you afraid?"

"I'm not afraid. I don't want to sit in the chair, either."

Disgust came over her face. "The great hero. The brave officer. I owe you an apology, Colonel. I thought you were a man who would act to get what he wanted. I'm very sorry."

"I'll run her in for you."

"Oh, the brave man. He'll run her in for me. With a pistol and a badge. He's not afraid to arrest an old woman. He'll do that for me. How heroic."

Her words spattered like dumdum bullets.

I felt my temper climbing. "Look. I'm a soldier and I'm a cop. That doesn't make me a murderer."

She looked at me. "You better take me home."

I thought: The hell I will. Mrs. Governor Ada Dallas, you just bought yourself a first-class rape.

"No you won't." She talked calmly. I guess she had seen what I was thinking in my face. "You try it and I'll kill you."

I laughed.

"You think I couldn't?" she said in the same flat voice.

"That's right I think you couldn't. And don't dare me into it, Mrs. Dallas."

She changed it. "All right, then. Maybe you could rape me. You think it would be worth anything?"

"Maybe not."

She was right there. Mad as I was, I wasn't going to take her that way. Not unless she pushed me into it.

I thought for a second that I would tell her I would take her in for conspiracy to murder if she didn't. But before I had finished thinking it, I saw how ridiculous it was.

Goddamn her goddamn her goddamn her for promising and not letting me.

I started the car, backed it around, and started on the brown tracks in the yellow grass. It was going to be a different trip this way. Without the *now now now.* With only the *never never never.*

It had been mine, I was going to have it, now it was lost forever.

The car bounced on the tracks.

My breath was going fast. So was my heart.

No. I wouldn't. I wouldn't murder anybody. I had killed them in the war but that was different, like a football game only you killed them. You did not even know if you killed them. It wasn't murder. I would never murder.

"She's really a very bad woman," Ada said from the seat beside me. "Very bad."

I started. It was like she knew what I was thinking.

"*No,*" I said, as tough as I could. "Shut up."

She did not answer. I glanced at her. Her breasts were jiggling with the bumping of the car. She caught me looking, and I looked away fast.

A minute later she said, "Nobody would ever know."

"They always know."

"Only in the Sunday-school lessons."

I did not answer. The car hit a bad bump and I tasted the dust it knocked out of the seat.

"She's not even from Louisiana. Nobody will ever know she's been here. Nobody will ever find her."

"I won't."

"Even if they find her, they'll never know who she was, there's nothing to connect her with you and me."

"No."

I stopped the car at the edge of the highway. I saw my hands shaking on the wheel, and heard my heart kicking *bom-bom-bom,* and I felt the sick cold in my belly.

I had thought I was a tough boy. And I was. But nobody except professional killers are tough enough to murder, just like that. It is different in uniform. I did not even like to think of the word. And then all at once I knew that it was possible, that I might do it, and I was scared.

She was still talking. "They'd never find her. They'd never know. They'd never connect us."

"I don't want to sit in that chair," I said.

"You'll never have to."

I pulled into the highway, and saw it curving white through the green land to the bridge, the bridge high and sharp against the blue blanket of sky and crossing the river to the road back. I pushed on the gas. I wanted across that bridge.

I looked at the bridge, swelling steady as we got closer, and back to Ada. Then I glanced back to the road, and then to her, and then somehow the car had pulled off the road to the shoulder and stopped.

I had not done that. It was not me. The car had done it, itself.

I heard my breath going through my mouth like a bellows, and my hands were ice. My throat worked to say something. But nothing came out.

This isn't you, I thought. *No. Of course it isn't you.*

She was leaning toward me, smiling. I swallowed, and this time the words came out: "All right."

She kept smiling.

"All right all right all right," I said.

Of course it was not me. It was someone else. I was only listening. I heard the someone else say, "I'll do it."

She said, "You'll never be sorry."

"Where," said the someone else. "When."

Her voice was very soft. "Near where we were. In the woods."

"When," the strange voice said again.

Her smile changed. She touched my hand with hers, and said, "In an hour."

The punch hit again. My legs went to jelly.

She came close and kissed me, holding back nothing, nothing now, and I knew I would murder a dozen times for her.

"After," she whispered into my ear. "After."

She moved away and waited a minute. I guess she was waiting for me to get my breath. Then she said, very carefully, "Now, listen. I meet her in front of the Jax billboard, down the road three or four miles. She gets in the car and I pay her and I let her out a couple of miles down the road. She walks to her car and drives off and that's it till next time. Today I meet her at four o'clock. That's fifty minutes from now." She stopped. "How—" She stopped again. "What do you think?"

I ordered myself to think, but nothing happened.

"I—I don't know."

She breathed very deeply. "What do you think of this? You hide in the back seat. When she gets in and I drive off, you—you do something."

Wheels started turning. "I couldn't do anything there. Too dangerous." The sky above the bridge was pounding blue, the clouds were white and soft. I was sitting in a car planning a murder. "I'll arrest her. Then we'll take her somewhere—"

"Right back where we were."

"All right. We'll take her there."

Neither of us wanted to say the rest.

She did say, "That's wonderful, darling. I knew you'd know."

The car was all silent. Outside came the hum of an engine, the whine of tires. Some bird, not a jay, was twittering somewhere. Off in the green fields, a man was walking.

She said, "How? How are you . . . ? How will you do it?"

"Maybe I could shoot her while she's trying to hold you up."

"No, it has to be so nobody knows." She stopped a minute. "I don't guess you could just, just use the gun?"

"No. Ballistics marking. Noise. Everything."

"A knife?"

"A knife would do it. But I got a better idea."

"What?"

"I'll just twist her neck."

I heard her breath pull in, sharp. This was the first time she showed any of it had gotten to her. And the funny thing was I felt better. Getting ready for it was better than thinking whether to do it.

"If they find her, won't that connect it with somebody who knows judo or whatever it is?" she said.

"It would at that."

We were silent again.

I said, "I don't have a knife."

"I've got one." She opened her bag and took out a black-handled pocketknife. I looked at the chrome insignia on the handle; a boy scout knife.

"Where did you get that?"

"A troop visited the capitol a few months ago. I found this when they had gone. I just kept it, I don't know why."

I did not say anything. She said:

"I guess I did know why."

"We'll have to do something about her car," I said. I was feeling better. Now it was a police problem. Only I was looking at it from a slightly different angle. "Do you know where she parks it?"

"Right by the side of the road. We can get the keys and take it somewhere."

"Where's she from?"

She hesitated. "Alabama."

"I'll have to drive it back to Alabama then. And you'll have to follow and pick me up. After dark."

"All right." She stopped a minute. "Have you any civilian clothes?"

"I always keep a sport shirt and slacks in the back."

"Hadn't you better put them on, maybe?"

She was right. Why hadn't I thought of it? Then I knew I hadn't wanted to think of it. If you are in uniform everything is different. You are the soldier doing it, almost, or the cop doing it, almost. Out of uniform, you are just you.

I took the clothes from the back seat, went around behind the car, and changed.

We smoked a cigarette, and Ada said, "It's about that time."

"Okay," I said, and started the car.

From half a mile away, I saw her standing on the shoulder of the highway, a skinny woman in the brown dress and brown hat. I knew her the first second. I knew she was the one I was going to kill.

Ada was driving slow. The brown shape got bigger, and then I saw her face under the hat. It wasn't old and it wasn't not old. It wasn't anything. Except waiting. Like a chicken hawk. No. A spider. Only this time, baby, you don't know what you're waiting for. No you don't.

We were very close now and I could see it was a bad face. Like Ada said, she needed to be killed. I would be doing the world a favor. Killing the bitch. Old spider bitch.

It was no good, I couldn't work up a hate. I just looked at her, moving back and forth on those high heels, her ugly waiting face pointed straight down the highway, looking, not knowing it was us because she did not know my car, and looking myself, I could only think: *In half an hour you will be dead. Right now you are as alive as you will ever be and soon you will be dead. In one second you will go from alive to dead, and you can't go back. Not ever.*

I looked at her and for a second it was like I was looking at myself, standing by the road waiting to be killed.

I wished I was in uniform.

I was shaking, the way you do when you do not know if you are cold or afraid. But this was not a cold day. I touched the knife in my pocket, took the .38 out of the holster, and got down behind the seat. The .38 felt like a lump of ice in my hand. There on the floor,

I felt the car stop, I heard the door open, and through the crack by the seat I saw two skinny silk-covered legs and old white skin above them as they came inside, and then I came up with the gun in my hand and said, "All right. Just sit still." I showed my badge in the other hand.

She squawked like a hen buzzard, and the hard red ugly face turned the color of liver.

"You'll be sorry!" she yelled at Ada. "Goddamn you you'll be sorry. You wait and see. You'll be sorry."

The woman did not look at me after the first shock of the badge and gun. She just stared at Ada, her eyes wild and her face twisted crazy, and kept babbling, "You'll be sorry."

Ada drove, not fast, down the highway. The sunshine poured over the green cotton rows in the brown fields. We passed a low white house, one side shining with sun and the other in shadow. In the front yard a man and woman were standing close together, laughing. Buzzard-face kept whining.

"Shut up." I poked the gun into her skinny hard neck.

She was looking straight ahead now, saying only to herself the three words over and over again. I looked at the bony back of her neck, that was the spot, and then I looked at the rear-vision mirror above Ada and I saw the long straight black lines of the bridge pulling closer together as we went further away.

Then we were on that road, the twin tracks disappearing into the woods.

I watched the face so close to my gun, and the face changed. First it showed she was surprised, then it showed she was guessing, then that she was scared.

"This ain't the way. This ain't the way. Where you taking me?"

Then she yelled, and the face changed again. It changed to show that she knew.

I pushed the gun hard. "Shut up."

But she knew now she had nothing to lose. She kept yelling, and I hit her hard with the flat of my left hand right across the neck and she flopped in the seat.

She didn't come out of it until we were halfway there. Then she started moaning, not loud but deep, and she kept saying in a dead flat crying voice, "Please don't. Please don't." The voice didn't change, didn't go up or down, didn't stop. It just went on, "Please don't. Please don't."

Hell, I don't want to. I have to. I wanted to say it, to tell it to her so she would understand. But I didn't. And I felt naked in the floppy sports clothes.

It was like both of us were me. One me holding the gun. The other me feeling the muzzle in my neck and crying, *"Please don't."*

And neither one of them was me. Then we were back in the glade, and it was only the middle of the afternoon. Through the tops of the trees, the sky was still blue with white soft clouds, the leaves still whispered, in the woods the jays still cawed. The trees hid the hot sun, and under the tree it was shaded and cool. It was a good afternoon just to lie on the grass, or row on the river, I thought.

Then I looked up at the big black limb and knew what it had reminded me of all the time.

"All right," I said. I wanted to spit, but couldn't. "Let's go."

"No." She whimpered and blubbered. "Please. Please please please don't. I won't bother her. If you just let me go. Never. I won't never."

I pulled her out.

She crossed her hands over her shriveled old titties. "Honest I won't. I won't never."

I changed the gun to my left hand. My right found the knife in my pocket.

"Do you promise?" I pulled the knife out and held it behind me.

"Yes yes yes I promise. I'll do anything only don't kill me."

You wouldn't keep that promise any longer than it took you to make a phone call, I thought. I said, "You sure about that?"

I was her, an old bag begging not to be killed, not to have to go from alive to dead. I was me, who was going to send her on the trip. I was her waiting for the knife. I was me with it in my hand. And I wasn't either one. I was a big eye up in the treetop, watching.

None of these is you, something said, *not you at all.*

"Oh, you can trust me. Please believe me, you can trust me."

That was me begging, that was me who answered, "All right then. But if you ever double-cross us we'll know where to find you. Now turn around and get back in the car."

She turned her back, and I pressed the spring button, and she heard the blade snap open. She started to turn again, and I was her turning, seeing, knowing bursting like a shell in her face, but too late, too late to even move, while I was me stepping in fast, the hand moving fast and hard, and I was the eye in the tree looking down and not caring. The knife hit what felt like rock and went in with all my weight behind it, right at the spot, and she gave a quick little, "Aaahhh," just like she was making love, and then she was dead.

She was dead, and the eye in the tree closed, and I was only me, looking down at a pile in a brown dress, with a black-handled knife sticking up behind a brown hat, and a silver boy scout badge on the black handle.

I was a murderer.

I didn't feel any different. I was only out of breath. I leaned against the trunk of the big tree, and looked at the big limb coming out over me. I heard my breath wrenching. Then I heard the car door close, and jumped. It was Ada. She came up to me and stopped. She looked at what was lying face down on the grass, and turned her head away. Then she looked at me.

"Well," she said. "It's done."

"Yeah," I said, and took a step toward her.

"Now?" Her face showed fear. "Now? With that"—she pointed at it— "right there?"

"Now," I said. "Here."

I was furious with her, for making me do what I had done, and I wanted to shock her by taking her right beside it. I grabbed her hard, and I heard her whimper.

"Please. Please not here."

"Here by God."

But I couldn't. Not there.

So I lead her into the woods, where we could not see it. I kissed her and felt her body with mine. She shivered and moaned but did not try to move away. Then I took her clothes off, piece by piece, and spreading my coat on the rank grass, in the deep shade, I did what I had done only in my mind for the last two years.

The sun was slanting through the trees now, the shadows were very long, and I was cold and my legs weak. But she did not look tired. She was all business.

"Are we ready to start with that?" Her nose twitched as she looked down at what was under the coat.

"I have to fix it first."

I did something to it, so it would not swell with gas, and I put stones in it afterwards, and then I tied it up in an army surplus sleeping bag I had, and we put it in the trunk.

"Let's just hope nobody stops me," I said. "If anybody stops me, we're dead." The word fell out and it scared me. I hadn't meant dead like the thing in the sleeping bag. I had meant it just as a way of talking. But after I said it, I knew it was the same kind of dead.

We found her car keys in the handbag, and back on the highway we spotted her car, it was a '56 Olds, and Ada got out to take it, a scarf around her hair so nobody would recognize her easy.

We started. It was five then and past eleven when we got to the coast on the other side of Mobile. Ada knew a bridge over an inlet, and I dropped the sleeping bag over it, and then I took the license plates off the car and drove it down the bank and pushed it in. The water was deep and closed over the top.

Then I walked a half mile down in the road and got in my car, where she was waiting.

"And that's done," I said.

I put the uniform back on and felt like Colonel Yancey again, even if he was a murderer now.

I would have liked to take her again right there, but it was really too risky. I pushed the gas, and when we were back in Louisiana, almost to Baton Rouge, I pulled into the shadow of a country church standing white and tall in the dark. The night was turning gray when I pulled out.

I saw her in the corridor the next morning at ten, a stack of papers in her hand, looking cool as a daisy.

"Good morning, Colonel," she said.

"Good morning, Mrs. Dallas," I said.

THREE

Tommy Dallas

Since that evening, there'd been nobody for me but Ada. I had cut out all the playing around; things went on the way I had made them, and they were fine.

Then one day they changed again.

God knows they had changed between us lots of times. Before we got married, when she had been getting me so excited I would do anything to have her. Then we had the honeymoon, then she started running things, then I started running after other babes, and finally when we were just barely man and wife. Then after I raped her, we were together again and had a new kind of understanding. Now it was changed again.

Things can change two different ways. The first way is so slow you can't tell they're changing, until there it is; they are one hell of a lot different from the way they were, and you just don't know when it happened, or how, it has happened so slow and easy.

The other way is when it goes bam all at once and they have changed to hell and gone before you can draw a breath. Looking back, you can see one day or one hour, maybe even one second and one word, and know: This was it, this was when.

Those first changes with Ada and me had been the kind that slip up. The last one, when I took her in the mansion sitting room, had been the all-at-once kind. And the next one came in the same way.

It was the day after she had gone down to New Orleans for some meeting, she said—and came back the next day.

When I knew she was back, I popped my head in her office, and said, "Hello, Governor."

She looked up from some papers and smiled and said, "Hello, Tommy," and I heard something, like I had picked it up on an ear-set radio. But I pushed it away. She was probably just tired. Doing too much. I was going to have to make her take care of herself.

"How was the big city?" I said.

She smiled again, not very big, and said in a flat voice, "About the same, I guess."

"How are your juvenile delinquents?"

She smiled now like she was humoring me. "I wish you wouldn't call them that. The Young Louisiana League is fine."

"Hah," I said. She smiled again, and didn't answer.

"You going too hard," I said. "You better ease up a while."

"How?" She smiled the same way.

The old radio kept fizzing out something, but I wouldn't listen. I went back to my office and read some mail, then I started to read some reports from the Department of Highways but they were real stiff, and then I pulled *Variety* out of the top drawer.

I was on the third page, reading something about Sex Pix Stir Stix, when it got through.

Somebody had laid her down there.

My belly got all tight, and I could feel my breath coming fast. Goddamn her. Goddamn her to hell.

Then I thought: You don't really know she got it. You don't really know nothing. You just got some half-assed idea out of nowhere.

But that was one thing you could always tell.

Hell, that's one thing you can only guess. You don't know a thing. Not one damn thing.

So I told myself I didn't know, and pretty soon I believed it. Almost.

I took her to lunch in the coffee shop downstairs and she was the way she had been in the morning: tired and absent-minded, like she was thinking about something else, something a long way off.

And that night, when the time came, she said, "Not tonight, dear."

She had been so tired that I thought she would fall asleep the minute she pulled up the covers. But when I got in the other twin bed, two hours later, I could tell by her breathing she was still wide awake.

"Ada?" I said.

"Yes?"

"Want a sleeping pill?"

"No."

And that was all of that. But just before I dropped off myself I knew she was still wide awake.

Next morning at breakfast, her face was pale and drawn tight, but her mind had come back from that way off place. When I looked in her office toward noon, she was on the telephone, talking eighty miles an hour, and she was too busy to go to lunch. I did not see her again all day, and I did not sleep with her again for two weeks. When I did it was not like it had been, and I knew it wasn't going to be.

I tried hard not to believe the old radio, I kept telling myself I was just imagining. But I didn't quite make it. I wasn't sure she had and I wasn't sure she hadn't, and that was awful. I would rather have known she had than not be sure. Because this way I was jealous of everybody that even talked to her. I would see her smile at a newspaper man and I would think: *him?* Or I would see her walking to the door of her office with one of those wild-eyed Young Louisiana Leaguers and it would hit me: *maybe that one.* One day I was even suspicious of the Western Union boy. I even thought about whether it might be Sylvestre, but somehow he was the one guy I couldn't get worked up about.

I hated everybody, that is every man, I saw come out of her door; a young lawyer, the press agent for the Department of Commerce and Industry, an old lawyer, the superintendent of institutions. But I couldn't be sure. Not about any of them.

One day, I guess a couple of weeks after that first day I got the message, I saw Col. Robert Yancey close her door and start down the corridor. *Him?* I thought, the way I thought about everybody and I saw his face, not quite smiling, not even happy, but looking, I don't know, looking I guess satisfied.

It is him, I thought, *by God it is.*

He smiled. "Good morning, Governor." He was working hard at being cheerful. "How's it going?"

"Morning." I looked at him hard, hoping I could see something sure.

But I couldn't. After I walked past him, I had no real idea whether it was him or any one of a dozen, a hundred other guys. Maybe it wasn't anybody up here at all. Maybe it was her old boy friend, that TV fellow, Steve Jackson. Maybe it was somebody I never even saw.

That was a new knife.

I spied on her every chance I got. Once I would have felt like a jerk doing that, but now I didn't care. I saw her smile and be polite to God knows how many guys, and the second I saw it, I was crazy jealous, and ten minutes after, I knew I hadn't seen nothing.

Until I was sitting in the corner of the coffee shop one noon, halfway out of sight behind the boys in the band. I saw Colonel Yancey sitting at a table close to the door, and he looked up, quick, at the door a couple of times, like he was waiting for somebody.

A few minutes later, Ada walked in the door. She did not see me. She walked very close to Yancey's table, very slow, and his face turned up to look full at her. She gave her head the littlest "no" shake, so little you could just see it. But she had done it, I hadn't imagined it, and it was the kind of sign that goes between people who are cozy. A second after, she nodded at him, very pleasant, like he was somebody she just knew, and she moved along. Then she saw me, waved, came over and sat down.

I didn't have no doubts now. She had slipped me the horns, and the guy was Yancey.

That night, knowing both those things for sure, I slept better than I had in weeks. The next night I was out with a blonde from Commerce and Industry.

Right after that, I realized there was something else with Ada, too. She was running for office. I couldn't tell exactly when she had shifted gears, from just getting herself known to really running for governor, but one day I took a good look, and I saw she was running. I hadn't seen it before. I hadn't even known she wanted to be governor. At least I hadn't known it in the top part of my mind. Maybe I had known it, way down there in the dark. But now it was out on the table. She was running for office a mile a minute, a year and a half before the Democratic primary. The speeches she was making were the kind an unannounced candidate makes. Her charities, and that Young Louisiana League, and her buddy-buddying with the parish politicians didn't leave nothing to doubt.

I knew what she was doing, I'd been there.

And it was okay with me. Under the state constitution I couldn't succeed myself. More power to her. But she didn't have a chance. No woman had a chance in this state or any other Southern state, or maybe anywhere.

How about Ma Ferguson in Texas?

That was different. She wasn't a young good-looking tomato like Ada. It is fine if a politician's wife is good-looking. But if a woman is a politician herself, too much looks is a handicap. Ma Ferguson was past middle age and already governor when she ran. That was what had made the difference. She had stepped into the governor's office when Pa Ferguson got sick or died or whatever it was, it was so long ago I didn't remember or care which. But being governor when she ran was two-thirds of it. That was why she had been able to make it stick.

That was . . .

Then I saw it. I saw it coming, the way you might see that old Panama Limited coming way down the tracks. Way away, but coming faster and faster. While you are stalled across the tracks in the old pickup truck, and you can't get it started, and you hear the engine hum way down there, and you see that round silver head, swelling and shooting straight at you, and the hum gets louder and louder until it isn't a hum, it's a growl, and you push and push at the starter and the motor turns over and over but it won't catch, and the big silver bullet streaks at and at you. Then you either wake up in a sweat and take a deep breath, or you open the door and dive for the ditch, or you stay where you are and you hear the crash but you don't feel nothing because you are dead.

That was the way. I knew what she was planning. She and Sylvestre. I heard the roar, and I saw it coming down the tracks, and I knew I was running out of time.

Steve Jackson

I kept trying to come up with something to stop the Mobile woman, but I couldn't. Even if Ada brought hand-picked state police in, the story would get out. If she paid, she would have to keep paying. The only neat and conclusive solution seemed—execution. Which of course was impossible.

I finally arrived at a possibility. Ada and I could build up an overwhelming blackmail case against her. With marked money, pay-offs recorded on the Minitape in a handbag, me hidden to witness the pay-offs, photographs from a concealed camera, everything. When it was all there, Ada and I would confront her.

I would say, "This can send you to Angola for twenty-five years. The trial judge in this district is on our team. Now if any word of this ever gets out, I mean if it gets out from anybody, anywhere, we'll prosecute *you*. Understand that. No matter who talks or where, we'll hold you responsible, and you'll spend the rest of your life in a tough pen, and we have ways to make it tougher."

And then Ada would scare her, and I would scare her again.

I thought it would work, and the more I thought of it, the more certain I was. I went to Baton Rouge, and Ada and I talked in a corner of the Hunt Room in the Capitol House, me with my pad out and making notes as though it was an interview while I told her.

"Yes," she said. "I think it would probably work. I had thought of it myself. It would probably be five to one to work."

"Well then."

She looked at me directly. "I couldn't take the one chance in six."

"Would you rather keep paying?"

"I don't think I'll have to." Her tongue touched her lips, and her eyes moved from me. "You see, I gave her, one big payment. It'll keep her quiet for a while I think. I think it's all right now."

"I hope so."

She looked straight at me. "Steve, it's all right. Believe me."

"If you're that sure."

"I'm sure and you're not to worry about it any more." She pressed my hand very quickly, and drew hers quickly away.

We stayed there almost an hour. From the day the woman appeared, I had no more illusions about being over Ada. Driving back, I thought that every time I saw her, I moved another step toward— toward what?

The next time I saw her the circumstances were very different.

Robert Yancey

So I was a murderer. I had done murder. Not just killing that you do in uniform, but real murder. I wondered if I would be different. I had to know how it felt to have done that and to be that.

For one thing I was afraid. I was afraid of being caught and electrocuted. And I felt guilty. I found out that feeling guilty and feeling afraid aren't the same thing. When you are just afraid, you know what you are afraid of. But when you are guilty, you are afraid but you do not know what you are afraid of. You feel something is after you, you don't know what it is, but it is coming and coming and *after you.*

So that was part of the way I felt.

Did I feel sorry about the woman herself?

I really did not think so because she was a bitch, she had done very bad things, she deserved killing. But I could hear her voice, the one note, not changing, in my ear, "Please please don't," and I could see the knowing exploding in her face as I stepped in, and maybe I did feel sorry for her, too, even if I should not have.

So I was afraid and guilty and sorry a little bit for the woman herself.

What else?

I felt important. I had done something that just a few could do. I had proved I had the guts, I had proved to myself that I was somebody that counted again. If not for good then for bad, but I *counted.*

And I felt like I had won.

So that was the way it was being a murderer: afraid, guilty, sorry, important, and a winner. Because whatever else I was, I was somebody.

And Ada was mine, and I was hers. We both knew it. We both knew if either ever turned against the other, we were dead. This keeps a man and a woman together like nothing else. Passion and money get spent, and love is a word for fools, but necessity can go on forever.

Having done the thing we had done, together, we were part of each other. No matter how hard we tried, we could not have pulled out the part that each of us was of the other. Sometimes I wanted to kill her, even if I killed myself with her. I knew there were more times when she would have liked to kill me, just because I had become part of her. But neither of us did. We were bound. We were the same one.

When we were together it was more than just making love. It was being burned alive in a slow fire. It was the thing we had done going on and on.

Sometimes I could feel her hating me all the way through it. Once, afterwards, she said, "Damn you. Damn you to hell forever."

"You already did," I said. "And you'll be there with me."

She made a cry like something out of the swamp and slashed at my face with her nails, but I jumped back and they caught me under the jaw and raked my throat and chest. I felt the burning sting, and knew I was bleeding. I grabbed her arm, turned her over in one fast motion; my hand left red streaks on the whiteness, and I hit her again, and again. She cried out, but it could not really have hurt her. I did not hit her too hard. It made me feel good to hit her. "You son of a bitch!" All at once she was loose and on her feet. "Don't ever. Don't ever think you can. Not to me."

I could feel her hate streaming into me, like I could feel mine shooting at her. But it was the kind of hate you feel for yourself, or part of yourself, for we were the same one.

I served her. She also served me, but I served her more. I was a bodyguard, a chauffeur, a confidential counsel and messenger boy. I carried the word from Ada to various people over the state, I was always around for protection when she spoke, I gave her the dirt on plenty of people because I was the guy who had it. I would have liked to do more. I would have liked to work over everybody who got in the way, but she would not let me.

"I told you," she said, one day. "No violence."

"I could just scare them a little."

"No threats either. Implicit or otherwise. Except—"

"Except when?" I said.

"Except when we absolutely have to."

"Okay," I said. "If that's the way you want it."

"That's the way."

I never could figure where Sylvestre stood. She couldn't have been operating if he had not wanted her to. He was a deep one. With him, you only knew what he wanted you to know. I wondered if he really wanted her to be governor. Or if he had something else in his mind.

"Are you sure of Sylvestre?" I asked her.

"This is his idea as much as mine."

"I mean, do you trust him?"

"I trust nobody."

"Not even me?"

"Least of all you."

She smiled her crooked smile, and I kissed her. Her teeth clenched onto my lips, and then they opened.

First thing every morning, I went through the stack of newspapers on my desk, not really seeing what my eyes hit. But I was afraid to move straight to the one I wanted, the one from Mobile, Alabama.

I had gone to a lot of trouble to get that paper, every day. I knew how dangerous it would have been to subscribe to it. I did not even want to buy it from the newsstand. What I had done was subscribe to a whole batch of papers in Louisiana, Mississippi, and Alabama. For the department. To stay in touch with traffic and enforcement problems, I wrote on the requisition.

I would not let myself look for it, or pull it from the stack out of turn. I made myself wait. This time it was the sixth one down, and I looked through it inch by inch.

There was nothing in it.

I felt much better.

Tommy Dallas

I knew what was coming, and I waited. It would have to come soon, because she would have to have the job for at least a year for it to do any good. So I waited, and she operated, and Sylvestre smiled.

She had the word from him, all right. She couldn't have made the first move without it. And I was trying to figure where he sat in the deal, what he stood to make. Why her? He could run any one of a dozen guys next time and probably win.

Maybe he thought that he wasn't taking as big a chance, that by getting Ada in first and then running her he was putting it on ice.

But I thought it was a bigger chance. She was a woman. No woman had ever been governor of this state. There would be a lot of feeling that we thought the people were easy to jazz, and then they would be hell-bent to show us they weren't.

You can never let the voters think that you think they are easy. They are like a woman. They love it, but they got to insist that they are hard. You let it show how easy they really are and they hate you.

Why was Sylvestre so hell-set on it being her? I couldn't see. Unless he figured she was what he had always been looking for: the thing it took to wrap up the state for good and all. Like Huey had done.

But she wasn't that good. She was no Huey. Not by a damn sight. What did she have that . . . that I didn't have?

Then I thought of the faces turned up to her, standing there in the circle of light with the dark behind her, and something kicked in my belly.

Maybe she is the one. Maybe she can go on and on, and this is not the end but the beginning. Maybe she is the one, and Sylvestre has seen it, and he is going to take her to the end of the road.

And then I thought:

Maybe he figures she will go and go and never stop.

I thought it, and I felt goose-pimples on my skin, and I was afraid, and I waited.

I knew it was the time, when Sylvestre's voice came out of the telephone earpiece like Judgment Day, or maybe only like a diesel horn. "Tommy," it said, and I knew. "Do you have a moment?"

Knowing, I said, "Sure. Sure." And then the Governor of Louisiana went out of his own office into the one next to it, where he had been ordered by his administrative assistant.

They were sitting, waiting. Sylvestre was behind his desk, Ada in a chair by it, her legs crossed. I closed the door. I saw they didn't look at each other, and that Ada didn't look at me.

I sat and slouched down low in the chair. Sylvestre patted me with the old daddy-smile, and said, "Ah, Tommy."

Just like Hudson, I thought. Only I knew what was coming.

"Old Tommy," said Sylvestre, genially, and looked at me over the rims of his glasses. "Old Tommy."

By God, I thought, exactly like Hudson.

"Well, boy," said Sylvestre. "I suspect you can guess what this is about."

"I kind of got an idea."

Sylvestre laughed. Ada smiled, a little.

"I was sure you would, Tommy. I was sure you would. You're much too bright not to."

"Yeah," I said.

"That's what I told Ada. Why, Tommy's so smart he'll understand right away, I told her."

I smiled, and didn't say nothing.

"Yes, Tommy will grasp the issues. That's what I said. He'll grasp the issues."

"Is that right?" I said.

"Yes, boy, and what a time you're going to have." The voice was like a brush painting pretty pictures. "What a time. I have a couple of deals in mind for you that'll keep it rolling in. I mean rolling."

"Is that right?"

"No care of office. Nothing to worry about. Except living." That was some brush. "Except the finer things of life." He laughed, deep.

Ada was looking at some cloud or something, way off, her face dull and set.

"That sounds just fine," I said.

"Doesn't it though? And soon it'll be yours, all yours. Now. We can't waste time. Your term has just a little more than a year left, so we have to move fast."

I nodded, I was very polite.

"Of course, we have to have the right reason for you to step out." That was the first time it had ever come out into the daylight, and he said the words real careless, like a good actor throws a line away. "It ought to be health, it can't be anything but health, and yet it can't be anything that will impair your usefulness permanently. Like a heart attack. Do you agree?" He asked it real innocent.

"It certainly shouldn't be anything like that," I said, innocent the same way.

"Fine, now what do you think of this? We pile up your car. We plant you in it right after. Then we take you to a hospital, one where we've already made arrangements, and we announce that your condition is serious. Your condition is so serious you just have to resign. For the good of the state you have to turn the helm over to healthy hands. How about that?"

"Perfect," I said.

"You see, my dear?" He turned to Ada. "I told you we could count on Tommy. I know this boy like my own son, and I knew we could count on him. One hundred per cent."

Ada's eyebrows made an upward curve, that might have meant anything, or nothing. She had not looked at me since I'd come in.

"Sylvestre," I said. "My devoted wife."

I had expected big fear. Now it was here, and I wasn't afraid, even if I had been a few minutes before. Now the only thing I felt was good.

"Yes?" Sylvestre was all at once changed, and watchful.

"I got news for you." I stopped and watched their faces, something rising in me like a hot spring, and then I said it: "I won't play."

Afterwards, I always remembered that second as maybe the high point of my life. For the first time, I saw Sylvestre's face bust out of perfect control into anger and surprise. Ada looked like she was about to jump out of her chair.

But she didn't. She trained her eyes on me like a gun muzzle, the regret in them all gone now, and she said, "You fool. You utter fool."

"Nope." I was feeling better every second. "I won't."

Then I got up, walked out of the office, and down the corridor to the elevator marked *Governor Only.* I stepped inside, pushed the button marked *Down,* and felt the machinery start.

Of course that wasn't the end. Sylvestre gave me not one more chance but two, and I guess I was more surprised than he was when I wouldn't give in. After the second time, Sylvestre was real pleasant. He said, "All right, Tommy. If you feel that way."

Then I knew it was time to be really scared.

But day came after day, and week after week, with no trouble, no move, no nothing. And I could feel fear growing inside like a pregnant woman must feel a baby.

But I didn't do it.

Everything of course was all over with Ada and me. What had started the night I took her by force had ended that time she went to New Orleans. Any little bit left after that she wiped away when she tried to push me out of office. But I guess that last quick love affair between us, or whatever it was, was worth something after all. Without it, I wouldn't have been able to say no to Sylvestre. So it wasn't wasted.

Now I waited.

Five weeks and two days—I figured it out exactly, later—five weeks and two days after I said no, I had to go to New Orleans to address a meeting of big shots in the AFL.

I was afraid of what could happen in New Orleans. I called two of my old deputies in St. Peter's, and asked them to meet me in the Monteleone lobby. At first I felt better because I thought this made it safe. Then I remembered they were Sylvestre's deputies more than my deputies, and I felt worse.

The morning of the trip, my chauffeur called and reported sick, and I didn't like that, either. But I had to get there, and I figured I'd rather drive the limousine myself than get one of Yancey's thugs.

I had to go slow through town and fringe traffic, and I was fifteen miles out before it thinned enough to travel. The speech was set for ten-thirty; it was already nine. At last I got a good clear shot, and I pressed my foot to the floorboard. I felt the big steel shell take off, I heard the whispering climb of the engine, and I saw the white ribbon and green country come flying past me. I looked at the needle on the big dial, and saw it swing past 60 and 65, and touch 70, and I looked up and out toward the streaking road.

Then a tidal wave of sound was drowning me, blue sky and green grass tumbling end over end like a pin wheel, and the car top hit me, and the side, and the floor, and then I felt everything hit me, and then there was nothing.

Little pieces of myself were swimming together from some dark ocean that flooded the whole world. They would not quite come together, I ordered them to, but they still would not. Then I ordered them again, and they started, very slow, and I whipped them on, and all at once they came together and I was myself.

I was myself, opening my eyes to a great big spread of white. I closed them, then opened them again, and knew I was looking at a ceiling. I moved them: to white walls, to the foot of a white bed which I decided was mine, then to a woman in a white dress and white cap at the side of it.

The woman all in white smiled. I decided to say, "Hi, honey." That would get it started right.

I listened for the words, and it was funny when they did not come. It was even funnier when I knew my mouth was closed. It was funnier still when I found I could not open it. It was funny as hell when I found I could not move at all.

The nurse saw I was awake. She smiled. "Don't worry about a thing. Don't try to move."

It was two days after that Sylvestre and Ada came to see me. Sylvestre carried a big basket of white roses. Ada looked sad, and pretty, and dutiful. A crowd of reporters were clustered outside the open door.

They sort of, hovered, beside me.

Ada touched my forehead with her open hand. It was cool and soft, with just a scent of perfume. "My poor darling," she said.

I said: *You bitch. You buzzard bitch from hell.* But I said it only inside the white gauze that mummified my head; the words couldn't get to my lips.

"How could it have happened?" Her voice was sad. "But I suppose we'll never know."

"I suppose not," Sylvestre said, like it was a funeral, and maybe it was. "Old Tommy."

"The two of you," I said inside. "The two."

Even if I could of talked, I couldn't say no more. What I wanted to say was too big. There weren't the words.

"Don't worry about a thing, boy," said Sylvestre. "Not one thing. Everything's been taken care of."

"He's right, darling." Ada smiled a sad smile. "The only thing that matters is that you get well."

I couldn't even turn my back to them. I remembered the Indian torture, where they stake a man on his back, put a rat on his stomach, and a pot over the rat.

"If you only hadn't had to—make that damned trip," said Ada. And this she wasn't faking, I could tell. She looked older all at once.

If I had only got the hell out of the governor's office and let you in.

Sylvestre patted me on the shoulder. "Everything's in good hands. Your wife has taken over and everything's fine."

Ada said nothing. Her face was turned away from the door now, and she was not smiling.

"We thought you'd like to know," said Sylvestre. He patted me again. "Don't worry now." He looked at his wrist watch. "I'll wait out front, Ada."

Then he was gone.

My eyes went to Ada.

"Tommy. Tommy, I didn't—" she stopped.

I thought I saw her eyes cloud, but I knew I must be wrong. Not tears. Not from her. But there they were, on her cheek.

"Get well," she said, and suddenly left me.

Through the closed door, I heard her sharp heels hit the floor, and the buzz of voices, getting faint as they went away, and finally stopping.

The day after, the doctor told me I had a broken neck.

"But you'll recover," he said. "Completely. In time. Lots of time."

He tried to understand what I wanted to ask, and he answered:

"You lost control somehow. Maybe a blowout, your front tires were all busted up. You turned over three times." He laughed, like he didn't know what else to do. "It was really the damnedest thing. By rights you should be dead."

I blinked my eyes; the doctor understood. He said, "Six months. A year. All we can really do is guess."

The week after that, the state Supreme Court held that I was legally incapable of performing the duties of my office, and declared Ada governor.

The nurse brought in the papers and read them to me. Then she held up the front page so I could see. On one side was a picture of me in the cast. On the other was a profile shot of Ada going up the capitol steps, looking sad.

"You see?" said the nurse. "You don't have a thing to worry about. Everything's taken care of."

The newspaper boys wanted to see me the day Ada took over, but the doctor wouldn't let them. It wouldn't have done them any good anyway, I couldn't even make a sign for yes or no.

"You'll be talking in a few weeks," the doctor said. "That's mostly shock I think. Don't worry about it."

Don't worry, he said. That was great. Just don't worry. That was all.

He gave me a hypo at eight to make sure I rested, and it took me right out. I must have slept seven, eight hours solid because when I woke up it was that late late dark that is the darkest dark there is.

I was laying there wide awake when the door opened, the light from outside made a soft red rectangle in the doorway, and in it the night nurse was a big white box. She tiptoed into the room, to check that I was all right I guess, and I heard the stiff white dress rustle, and as she bent over I saw in the faint light her gray hair and top-kick face.

She saw my eyes were open.

"You should be resting, Governor."

I wanted to say: *I ain't no governor, didn't you hear?* But of course I couldn't.

"You need your rest." The top kick's voice. "Try to go back to sleep."

And she marched out, the uniform crackling, and then I was alone.

I was wide awake, in a hospital bed, and had a broken neck, and through the window I could see the night sky turning gray with the stars little pinheads spangled across it. Just like it had been a year ago when I was whole and governor, or five years before that when I was sheriff, or ten before that when I was a hillbilly singer and nothing else and happy about it. It was the same sky as when I was a kid in that sharecropper's cabin thirty years ago, and would wake up when the roosters crowed, and then look out and see the same dark gray sky getting light, and the same white pointed stars going off. It was the same. Only I was different.

Then by God I heard a rooster crow, and for a second I thought it was thirty years ago. It was like I had been walking down a long corridor and had found a door and stepped through it and inside it was any time I wanted it to be, any second of my life.

But then I came back from wherever it was, and the time was now, five o'clock in the morning, and I was in the hospital with a broken neck, and my whoring bitching murdering wife who had broken my neck had just taken my office.

After what seemed like a couple of weeks, the papers came in with my day nurse bringing breakfast. The day nurse wasn't Miss America by a sight, but after the sergeant she looked pretty good: plump and smooth-faced and dark-haired and still in her thirties.

She smiled and pinked a little when she said hello, and I thought in a distant kind of way someday I might make a play for her but that would be a hell of a long time off, and right now I just didn't care.

She spread out the front page so I could see a big picture of Ada standing at the foot of the big white steps, looking almost straight up to the double brass doors or maybe all the way to the top of the capitol. It was a good picture only it was fake. Nobody but tourists ever used the steps. Still it made a good picture. She looked sad, and alone, and brave.

Well she had it now. This was what she had been after always. Right from the start. What a chump I was not to of seen it or done something about it, before it was too late. She had just used me. She and Sylvestre. She had used me, and he had used me, and he had used her, only maybe she didn't know it yet. Sylvestre. I couldn't even call him a son of a bitch to myself, it wasn't enough. Nothing was enough. He had everything figured out. He always had everything figured out. Well someday goddamn it something was going to come along he couldn't figure out. I wanted to be there when it did.

I looked at the picture again, at Ada all by herself looking up at whatever she was looking at.

That was the way she wished it was. Only it wasn't that way a damned bit. The picture should have shown Sylvestre behind her, wiggling that little stick with the strings tied to her. The same way he did with me. And maybe the picture ought to show Col. Robert Yancey, that son of a bitch, and I could call him that, it was enough for him. Maybe it ought to show Col. Robert Yancey sniffing around.

You believe what you want to believe and you won't pay no attention to what you don't want to believe even when it smells like a mule dead in a ditch for a month. You put the clothespin over your nose, and one fine day you are going along and the bomb blows you up. I wondered which one had done it? Sylvestre? Yancey? Ada herself? All of them, probably. Every damn one.

The nurse was talking again. "Isn't it wonderful, Governor?" She was going on like it was her that had just taken over Louisiana and was getting tapped by Col. Robert Yancey. "You must be very proud," she said, and turned on a sweet misty smile.

I tried to say, "Honey, you just don't know." But nothing came out.

She smiled again and patted me on the shoulder.

Steve Jackson

Ada took the oath of office at her desk in the red-carpeted governor's office one morning at precisely nine-fifteen—a pile of papers stacked neat and white on the dark desk, her brown-haired secretary beside her in unobtrusive diligence. She was photographed in a string of tiny bursts of sound and light, and she put her hand on the Bible a second time on the request of photographers.

Then it was over, and the AP man said, "Thank you, Governor."

She said, "Thank you, gentlemen. And now I must get back to work. I fear this will be a working administration."

"Good-by, Governor. Good luck, Governor," they said in discordant chorus, and fled for telephone and typewriter. Except me.

And there we were.

"So now you're governor," I said.

"Governor." Her voice had a rind of sarcasm, a core of pride.

"How does it feel?"

She shrugged a shoulder and lifted her eyebrows. "Like nothing." Her face was strained, though faintly, and I wondered if it was from the responsibility, or from something else. Tommy's wreck fitted so perfectly into what she called Sylvestre's master plan. I was sure she couldn't have done it herself, or even had it done. Almost.

I probed. "How's Tommy?"

Her face showed nothing but concern. "Bad. You know, he's got a broken neck. It's a wonder he's not dead." There just might have been bitterness in the last words.

"He'll recover though?"

She nodded. "In time."

"Any plans? For your administration?"

"*He* hasn't told me yet." She didn't need to say who, and there was no doubt about the bitterness.

"Any news on the, other matter?"

She shook her head quickly, and touched a finger to her lips. "As I told you. I think it's closed, for a while."

"I hope it stays that way," I said, and shut up. Then, "I guess you're too august to let me buy you lunch."

Her face lightened. "August hell. It might not be a good idea though with Tommy and all. I'll give you lunch at the house. One o'clock." She meant the mansion.

"I'd be overawed."

But I went. She did not have much to say, she was clearly feeling the weight of something, but she was glad I was there. And so was I, even if her elevation had altered substantially the delicate balance between us.

Ada was accorded the usual honeymoon. Newspaper editorials expressed sympathy for Tommy's misfortune and her attendant sorrow, and for the ordeal of high office, so difficult for a woman— impossibly difficult without help, they hinted. They did not attack for several weeks. Not, in fact, until it became clear she was a candidate to succeed herself.

This revelation, or disclosure, or simply delayed perception of a fact already in full view, came when she called a special session of the Legislature in April. Uneasiness hung like a cloud over the capitol and its political avenues to New Orleans. As the legislators came to town, the question mark drifted through the blue fumed space of the nerve centers: the hotel lobbies and suites, the committee rooms and washrooms off the legislative chambers, behind the doors marked *Private* in the twenty-four-story hive of the capitol.

The newspapers were cautiously concerned and warily noncommittal. Nobody knew. Everybody wondered, and waited. The day before the session convened:

"What the hell is she up to?" the AP man asked me over the top of the Coke bottle while the state-wire teletype clattered in the corner of his office, in the capitol pressroom. "You used to be—you used to know her pretty well. Doesn't she cut you in on anything?"

"Not on anything," I said, and pulled on my own Coke.

For Ada's charge to the Legislature, the House of Representatives chamber was packed beyond capacity; at any moment, human bodies might have shot through the open double doors by pure compression. Members of both houses filled the business part of the floor; spectators jammed the galleries and the shafts of space behind the rails.

Finally Ada walked through a side door, the legislators on the first row stood, and the others followed like the inverted tumble of a deck of cards. She was in her public uniform of simple white, and she wore almost no make-up. At the rostrum, she turned and faced them.

You are kind and I am brave, her smile said, and they applauded.

Then they were still. And to the row of microphones just before her, to the faces in the chamber beyond, and to the world beyond the faces, she read her speech.

She read it in less than ten minutes. Then she was silent, smiling again, and she bowed her head. They applauded, neither more nor less than custom required, and they stood, still applauding, as she left the rostrum and walked down the long aisle to the double doors.

Then they sat, almost in silence, slowly apprehending that they had been hit by a shell with a proximity fuse.

Her speech had proposed:

Universal health insurance. Extension of unemployment payments from five months to a year. A state loan agency guaranteeing home loans for 90 per cent of value. A 50 per cent increase in old-age pensions.

And hooked with each benefit bill was a rider calling for a new tax to pay for it.

The bill for the hundred-dollars-a-month old-age pension also kicked the cigarette tax up two cents a pack, the proceeds being dedicated to the pensions. The new unemployment bill had incorporated with it a three-cents-a-gallon increase in the gasoline tax. A three-cents-a-bottle beer tax was dedicated to the new home loan agency, and a six-cents-a-fifth liquor tax was to pay for the health program.

In every case, the bill and the tax were packaged together, so that a vote against the tax was a vote against the benefit.

There was one exception. This was a bill providing for a 5 per cent state corporation tax, and it was not hooked to a special benefit. Its proceeds went "to the general fund."

Sylvestre's design was clear. Through Ada, he was going to give them an insurance state such as they had never seen. And he would simultaneously present the premiums. I was right; he had not pushed the benefits for Tommy because he had been saving them as a big blow for her.

The legislators were unable to comprehend at once what they had

been hit with. To reporters, they gave answers of reflexive caution:
"I'll have to have time to study it, I'll have to talk to my con-
stituents." They were all waiting for the signals; since it was Thursday, they recessed and went home.

The signals came down almost immediately. These were defined,
but by no means originated, in a front-page editorial in the most
conservative New Orleans newspaper. The editorial called Ada's
proposal "the most tyrannical taxation ever seriously suggested in
the United States." It would "bankrupt the state of Louisiana." "No
responsible adult [implied but not stated was 'adult male'] could
seriously expect the voters to allow it." The benefits were mentioned
briefly on the inside pages.

Other papers over the state said the same, businessmen bought
TV time to denounce it, and the opposition seemed, and sounded,
massive.

When the legislators came back Monday, the papers were all big
black headlines and all taxes. Monday's session was very quiet and
short. Immediately afterward, the House Appropriations Committee
met to consider all the bills. With Sylvestre Marin present, they
voted 10 to 4 to report them favorably.

The hotel post-mortems—or pre-mortems in this case—started
early. At three that afternoon, I was sitting at a table with an Old
Regular senator from the city who was a friend of mine, another who
was not a friend, and two from north Louisiana.

"I just don't know what to do," said one from the north. He was
a tall preacher-faced man with his brown hair almost gone in front.
"You can't vote for 'em and you can't vote against 'em. What you
going to do?"

"Nothing you can do," said the other north Louisiana one. "Except go along. You don't vote for those bills, you just better get out
of Louisiana. You better do that, because there sure as hell won't be
any point in sticking around."

"Why not?" I said.

"You don't support the administration, they sit on your local
appropriation bills and you're dead with the home folks. And if you
vote against the benefits, you're a sonofabitch."

"And if you vote for the taxes you're a sonofabitch," said the other.
"What are you going to do?"

"Gentlemen," said my friend from New Orleans, Senator Moriarity, "when it is inevitable you must relax and enjoy it. And, believe me, it is inevitable."

Before I left for New Orleans, I went to see Ada. We talked only about the bills and the legislators.

"They're scared, but they'll vote for them," I told her.

"I've no doubt. They're more scared of him."

"These are his?"

"His and mine. I contributed a certain amount." She was pleased about that.

Back in town, I did a little of what is poetically known as getting close to the grass roots. It is true that in a political capital you are, if not in a vacuum, at least on an island. Newspapermen interview themselves, politicians sample each other's opinion, and the whole affair is faintly incestuous. Getting out of it can be informative.

I rode some streetcars, ate a couple of lunches at Walgreen and Rexall counters, placed a bet in a horse-race parlor on Gravier Street, and had a couple of drinks in Exchange Alley. I heard enough to be quite sure of one thing:

In one week, Ada's romance with the voters had, in the public mind, ended with betrayal.

On the streetcars, I heard:

"Just who does she think she is, now? Her and all that big talking. Thirty-three cents for a pack of cigarettes. I don't want to pay no thirty-three cents for no pack of cigarettes. Who does she think she is, now?"

"Yeh. Somebody oughtta do something about that woman. That's what my husband said last night, he said somebody oughtta do something about that woman."

Pursed mouths and nods.

In Exchange Alley:

"That bitch. That filthy cheating fornicating bitch. A nickel more for beer!"

"You know what? Somebody gonna get that bitch, that's what."

At the Roosevelt Bar:

"Can you imagine?"

"Let's hope some of her staunch supporters will take it into their little pointed heads to eliminate her."

Of course it was just talk. But this was Louisiana, and the capitol corridor had been streaked and chipped by bullets.

Finally, painfully, both House and Senate passed Ada's bills.

That afternoon, Ada called and I went up to see her. She wanted to talk about the taxes. "What do you hear?" she asked.

I showed her the afternoon papers. I felt a flick of resentment that she seemed solely interested in her problems of state, if that's what they could be called. And I knew myself for a fool.

She nodded at the headlines. "I saw them."

"You know they'll keep the taxes red-hot and play down the other stuff."

She smiled. "Sticks and stones. Remember your Machiavelli. Do all the bad things all at once. Spread the good ones out as long as you can. Things will be fine once the benefits start."

"Your reasoning or Sylvestre's?"

Her smile was contained. "You might say both."

"I hope it works out the way you figure."

"What can they do?" she asked, now with a certain zest. The imminence of conflict always put a sharp edge on her. She said again, "What can they do?"

The first week in September, she found out. Until then, public resentment against the taxes had been a brush fire, which neither spread nor went out. The newspapers and the opposition kept it barely alive. Then on September 1, the taxes started, and the brush fire flared and exploded.

Café and bar windows bore signs: Beer, 30¢, Tax, 5¢, New Price, 35¢. Liquor stores flashed new prices and new taxes, and the thirty-three-cents-a-pack cigarette price was placarded on every tobacco counter and vending machine. Gas stations said in huge letters— Gas, 15¢, Tax 26¢, Total, 41¢.

Even the beneficiaries in her insurance state hated her, because she and Sylvestre made them pay their own premiums with the new consumer taxes.

Most important, of course, the corporations had been stung by the 5 per cent tax, and feared they might be stung much, much worse in the future. These were carefully organizing and harnessing the universal resentment.

Small crowds began knotting in streets near the windows with the largest signs. They did not, of course, happen to gather. They were planted. A goon whom I had seen try to break up an Ada political rally a year before was the center of one. "You know who's behind this," he kept bellowing. "You know who did it to you."

So the manipulation had started, I thought. And the opposition was throwing kerosene on the brush.

"Outbreaks" flared up all over the state: in Shreveport, Alexandria, Opelousas, Lake Charles, and other places. The "outbreaks" were of course phony in that they were arranged beforehand. They were not phony as manifestations of attitude. By September 8 the state of Louisiana hated Ada as it had hated nobody since Reconstruction.

The next move on the timetable was made by Armand Lenoir, who had picked up a great deal of second-reaction sympathy because of his wife's death.

Now perhaps Lenoir could see opportunity as well as the next man, or perhaps he simply had excellent instructions. Whatever, he came forward as the symbol of what regarded itself as the resistance. In a widely circulated speech, he said:

"It is now clear beyond all doubt that Mrs. Dallas has betrayed the people of Louisiana. So it becomes my duty to speak out. I call on the people of Louisiana to exercise their ultimate authority and depose this unelected incompetent woman by the process of recall."

Next day, the papers were splashed with his picture and his speech. They also carried Baby Ray-type articles explaining what recall was and how it worked: if two-thirds of the registered voters signed a petition that Ada be kicked out, she was out and a new election would be held.

The articles sent us pundits scurrying to the law books to see what was what. Nobody could remember recall of a governor ever having been tried in the state. The attempt to get Huey out had been by impeachment.

It turned out that the state constitution did not itself provide for recall. The constitution simply said it was okay for the Legislature to pass such an act. And the Legislature had passed such an act six years before, and buried it in the statute book.

I called my Old Regular friend, State Senator John Moriarity.

"Oh, yes," he said. "I remember the act very well. I helped pass it. I did indeed." He laughed.

"What was behind it?"

His laugh was in my ear again. "Hang onto your hat. That baby was pushed through by a gent who wanted a club over the head of the then incumbent administration. He was the gentleman from St. Peter's, Senator Sylvestre Marin."

I called Ada, who of course had been briefed by Sylvestre.

"Can they do it?" I asked.

"What do you think?"

"I don't know. There's a lot of pressure. What does *he* think?"

"Him?" Her voice held excitement, and she never answered the question. "It'll be interesting to see what happens. Won't it?"

The recall articles were the kickoff. All over the state, clubs were organized and called instantly, Out-With-Ada Clubs.

The papers, practically all of them, started to carry little daily boxes: So many signatures required locally, so many on paper. So many needed all over the state, so many on paper.

The whole affair had a very glossy finish, one that spelled big-time public relations. I suspected one of the top New York firms had been called in, but I couldn't tie this down.

Certainly, everybody was angry at her. And I felt it was only partly because of the taxes. I thought a bigger reason might be that so many voters had felt themselves in a kind of collective love affair with her. When she imposed the taxes, they had the outraged feelings of lovers betrayed. And this feeling of betrayal was skillfully utilized by those with more fundamental grievances (like losing money). Whatever the reason, the antagonism to her was sweeping, irrational, and great.

Even the sheriffs could not stop it in the parishes. Feeling was too high, and big money was behind it. Everybody hated Ada's guts because of the taxes. All the sheriffs could do was gently discourage it.

In the next month, I spent a great deal of time on the telephone, letting her knew all I could find out about the recall plans. But there was nothing else I could do. I felt ridiculously inadequate.

Out-With-Ada started on September 9. On October 2, Lenoir announced that the petitions had enough signatures and that they had been authenticated, they planned to take them to the Secretary of State in Baton Rouge in a big motorcade on October 4. Six New

Orleans policemen were assigned to guard the strongboxes containing the petitions.

I talked to Ada as soon as I got the news release, feeling I was pronouncing a court sentence. But she had the tough bright optimism she always showed in crisis.

"I still have some cards," she said, and I noticed she had said "I" instead of "we."

Robert Yancey

I felt good. Strapping on the gun belt at four o'clock that morning, I felt better than I had since Remagen, smelling the fresh-oiled leather smell of the holster, the greased copper smell of the shells sliding into the clip, and the steel and fine oil smell of the heavy-handled blue-barreled .45. In my mind I could smell the sharp, bitter, burning, fine old black powder smell, and I thought: Maybe I'll really smell it later today, maybe I'll get to expend a few rounds. I slid the gun into the holster, worked the round into the chamber, and slid on the safety catch. I felt alive.

It hadn't started to get light. It was still night outside, Louisiana night, very dark, the umbrella of the big willow outside my window making it as black as hell. I finished the second cup of coffee, and looked at my watch. Four-seventeen. I could have slept another two hours. But no use taking chances. I've seen too many operations loused up because something you hadn't figured on exploded, and then there wasn't enough time. Time is everything.

I drove my own car to the barracks, remembering what I had carried in the trunk, as I did every time I got in it, and as I did, every time, pushing the remembering away. They still hadn't found it. They would have to, soon.

I stopped thinking about that, and started to think about what I had to do today.

When I pulled into the barracks, they were still getting ready. I had ordered assembly for five o'clock, and when I got there it was only four thirty-nine. I would rather wait for them than have them wait for me.

I sat at the duty desk downstairs reading the New Orleans morning paper. It told me nothing I didn't know. The motorcade would start at eight from Jackson Square and get to the capitol before noon. Then they would deliver the Out-With-Ada petitions to the Secretary of State, and Ada would be out.

Only they weren't going to get to Baton Rouge.

At two minutes of five, I went outside. The men were already in ranks. They knew when I said assembly at five o'clock, it meant business started at five o'clock. At five sharp I was giving them their instructions, and at five after they were climbing into the patrol cars and pulling out one at a time for where they were going.

Where they were going was La Place, an hour's drive down the Air-line, thirty miles north of New Orleans, and where it was going to happen.

The last car was mine, alone. I got into it, drove off, stopped at a telephone booth by a gas station which had not opened yet, and made a call, to New Orleans.

"Hi," I said. "We're hitting the beach. Everything all right down there?"

"Everything's fine."

"Okay. Let's synchronize our watches." I laughed a little. "This time tonight it'll be all over."

"I hope so. Good luck."

"A breeze." I said good-by, hung up, and went back to the car. It was Ada I had talked to.

Another favor for her, I thought, and this would be the second time I had saved her. And the thing with Tommy, though that was a mistake, that was supposed to just scare him. The arming device had malfunctioned somehow. It was supposed to go off when he started the car and just scare him good. But the way it worked out, it put her right in, and she better not forget all she owed me. She gave me the feeling sometimes that now she was governor, she would like to be rid of me. But I would never let her; she could never break with me. And she still couldn't do without me; today proved that.

I drove out Florida Boulevard to the traffic circle, peeled onto the Air-line, and loafed south at fifty. No need to hurry.

The night was gone, and morning hadn't come. Through the window, the sky was fading from black to gray, but the stars were still yellow and sharp, and the fields off the highway still smelled fresh and wet with dew, the straight gray concrete was clear and with few cars. I like the hell out of this time, that isn't either night or day. You're all alone in the world; the world belongs to you. That was the way it was on the Air-line that morning. And I felt good because I was heading into something, the .45 felt heavy-good on my hip, and I sure as hell hoped I could expend some today.

We were going after those Out-With-Ada petitions. Once we got them, Out-With-Ada was dead. The signatures had been verified by the registrars for all the polling precincts. Now they had to be filed with the Secretary of State. Once we got those, petitions, everything would be fine.

It was after six when I hit La Place, which wasn't much more than four gas stations, one on each corner of the intersection. I drove through it and three or four miles down the highway towards New Orleans, then cut left on a dirt road. I pulled in behind a clump of oak. Fifteen troopers were there with their cars, standing around or sitting inside with the doors opened. They straightened up when I got out and walked over, not coming to attention, but straightening up. These were not the public relations men in uniform. These were my tough boys.

"All set?" I said. I could feel them relax. They could tell I was satisfied.

"All set, Colonel."

"Good deal. Now all we got to do is wait, so just take it easy for a while. You know what you got to do."

"Sure, Colonel."

I grinned. "How you feel?"

They grinned back. "Fine. Great. All right."

"That's good because you might get a little workout today. I just might give you a little workout."

"Hot damn!" That was a big redheaded boy named Paxton. He slapped his holster and said it again. "Hot damn."

"I said might. Don't count on it. Right now you just stand by."

"Yes, sir!"

I drove back to La Place. A lot of cars had pulled into the parking space by the service stations on the southeast intersections. They were old-model cars, but well painted, with white sidewalls and twin exhaust pipes, and some of them no hood. They were our Young Louisiana Leaguers; right on time. I pulled into the service station across the street. I could not be seen talking to them before the operation, but I had to check with them by radio.

"X ray from Charlie Yoke. How do you hear me? Over."

X ray was the contact in the cars across the street, the head of the Young Leaguers for this operation. He had his radio on my wave length, and he came in and acknowledged.

All set, he said. So my troops were ready. My troops. Once I had had as good a battalion as there was in Germany. Now I had punks in hot rods. Well, they were what I had, and I would do the best I could with them.

The plan was all right. Sylvestre had come up with the plan, Ada had worked out the details with the punks, and I would take care of the muscle work. It was really a very sound plan. I had to admit it.

Then I called the other two patrol cars.

"Able and Dog from Charlie Yoke, how do you hear me? Over."

"Charlie Yoke from Able, loud and clear, over."

"Charlie Yoke from Dog, loud and clear, over."

They were to the south.

I said, "Commence Operation Blockout," and they all acknowledged. There was nothing to do but wait. I was parked close to the edge of the highway, so I could pull right into it.

At ten-thirty, Car Able reported, "Suspect in sight." The convoy was coming down the road.

"Roger," I said. "All cars assume positions. X ray stand by. X ray stand by. Over."

"Roger." He was so excited he forgot procedure.

Across the road, an arm in a red sleeve came out the window of a hoodless black '46 Chevy and waved.

"Okay, X ray," I said into the radio.

Now. The hot rods full of Ada's young punks were ready, the patrol cars were ready. I was ready. Everybody but the fat dumb sonsofbitches in the convoy was ready.

I took my binocs out of the case and looked down the highway. A couple of cars were coming, quite fast, all by themselves. Not the convoy. I put the binocs on the seat. Across the road the hot rods were still quiet, but now full of heads and faces, many of them girls. The arm in the red sleeve waved again, and made the old middle-finger sign.

"Okay, X ray," I said. "Soon."

I looked without the binocs at the road, ending and burning in the dazzle way down there. Then I saw a car come black out of the dazzle, not fast, and it got bigger, coming on, and I thought others were behind it but I was not sure, and I put up the binocs again.

It was the convoy.

"Stand by, X ray," I said, and the red arm made a couple of circles in the air. All at once, I heard motors start, first one and then another, then all of them picking up until they sounded like a fighter squadron in a scramble.

Through the glasses, I could see the convoy lead-car plain now, flashing sometimes when the sun hit the chrome, coming on and on.

Across the road, the hot rods were making enough noise to shake the earth. I could feel it vibrate, the way you used to when a whole flight was revving up for take-off and you were down in the dirt ahead, and thinking, hot damn, wait till they hit those bastards.

The convoy kept coming. I picked a scrubbly little tree a half mile down the road.

The radio said, "Able and Charlie in position."

That meant the two patrol cars down the road were behind the convoy now, shutting them off.

The first car passed the tree, and I said, "Let's go, X ray," and the hot rods shot out across the road two and three at a time like somebody had pressed a firing key. They stopped on the slab to block it, and they filled up space on the shoulders so nobody could get by, and the motors were roaring and sputtering, and then they were dead. The punks poured out of the cars as the convoy braked to a stop with the first car a hundred yards away.

They were laughing and yelling. They had brass knucks and spiv guns that I could see and probably knives that I couldn't. They had been told absolutely not to shoot or cut, and they had damned well better not.

They started for cars in the convoy, yelling things to work themselves up. Men in business suits got out, surprised, stupid-faced, not knowing what to make of it, not even scared, yet. A couple of middle-aged women got out. If anybody tried to mess them up it would be too damn bad. I looked for Lenoir, but didn't see him. The kids milled up to the men in the suits and stopped. In front was the red flannel shirt, X ray. Now that they were up there, none of them knew what to do. They looked embarrassed. It was not that they were scared, they just did not know what was expected. I could feel my belly muscles hurt with laughing. X ray, with three or four others behind him started talking to a little knot of convoy men. You could tell from the faces that both sides were working up. The kid was pointing at the convoy, then clenching his fist. My eyes were watering from laughing.

Then the kid pulled back his right hand, very slow, as though he did not know what to do with it. It stayed there a second, like something that was not part of him. Then he socked the fat man in the belly. It did not look hard but the fat man doubled up. The other punks yelled a little now, as though it were something they ought to do but were still embarrassed about. They came in and started swinging the same way, as though they ought to but didn't quite know why or how. The men in suits backed up, scared now, and started swinging to protect themselves. From the third car back, three cops in blue uniforms jumped out.

They moved in, swishing the sticks, and a tall punk in a long blue jacket stopped one and went down to his knees. He crawled out of it, shaking his head, and came back.

That changed it. The hot-rodders were not embarrassed now but mad. They were fighting cops. They knew the cops were out of their territory. So they came in wild and mean. I saw brass knuckles on fists and I saw the spiv guns cutting the air like the cops' billies. One of these caught a cop at the back of the head, and he rubber-legged and staggered a few steps but did not go down.

It was fine, just fine, and I could not stop laughing. I would have liked to be out there myself, working them over, any of them, but I couldn't.

I let it go on a while. The cops knew they had no standing here and did not shoot. I watched them break each other's heads for almost ten minutes. I would have liked to let it run longer, but somebody might get killed.

Then I called the cars on radio and four of them came in, two from each side of the intersection, and I came in. The two behind the convoy came in, and shut it off from behind.

They stopped fighting as soon as they saw us, there were almost twenty-five of us. I walked to the middle of it.

"What's going on here?" I said.

The red-shirted kid had a mouse under his eye and blood on his face, and was breathing in gasps. The fat man was sitting on the ground with his back against the car wheel, his coat all ripped and his Bronzini tie torn off.

I still did not see Lenoir.

"I said what's going on here?" I made it real tough.

"They attacked us," said the fat man, panting, raising his finger to point at the kid. "Just stopped us and jumped us."

The hot rods were still there in the road block for any fool to see he was telling the truth.

"Oh no, sir," said the kid. "It wasn't nothing like that, sir. We just tried to talk with them a little, sir, and they attacked us, sir." His face was more innocent than you could believe while he pointed at the scratches on it.

"Now I don't know who's telling the truth, but somebody has been sure as hell disturbing the peace and I'm going to find out who." I turned to the troopers behind me. "Collect all the weapons and all the contraband."

"Yes, sir, Colonel!" said the big redhead.

They got all the knucks and spiv guns from the punks, and they, of course, got nothing from the Out-With-Adas, and then they started through the cars. Some of them hit the Young Democratic League cars, and I started on the ones in the convoy. The first was empty, and the second, and in the third, a big black Lincoln, was Lenoir, with a New Orleans cop on each side of him and a black box on the floor.

"Why, Mr. Lenoir," I said. "I'm certainly surprised to find you involved in this."

"Involved?" His face got red, and you could see him swell like a balloon. "Involved!"

"Yes, sir. I am certainly surprised. Now would you gentlemen mind stepping out. It's necessary that I search your car for weapons and contraband."

"Search! See here, Yancey, this has gone far enough. These young ruffians attacked us. I demand you arrest and book them."

"I'll decide who to arrest, Mr. Lenoir. And pending a complete investigation, I'm detaining everybody. Though I must admit you don't look very marked up."

That hit him. He got redder than ever, and said in a pompous kind of voice, "I have been protecting some very valuable documents which I am quite sure are what these hoodlums are after. Otherwise—"

I knew that voice so well. It was the voice of somebody covering fear.

I got your number now, Mr. Lenoir. War hero or not.

I smiled at him.

He got out of the car, his face all red. I suppose he felt at a disadvantage sitting while I was standing and looking down at him.

"Now, Yancey, I'm not going to fool with you. You and your men take these hoodlums in and get out of our way or Louisiana will be too hot to hold you. That's on the line." He moved his arm to show off his empty sleeve.

I smiled. I had his number. He knew it.

"Well, Mr. Lenoir, I'm sure it won't be necessary to detain you. I must examine your car, however. Please ask the New Orleans officers to step outside. They have no jurisdiction here."

"You men stay where you are," he bellowed. They looked uncomfortable. They did not know what to do.

"Please step aside, Mr. Lenoir." I hoped he wouldn't. My arm was aching for it.

"No!" His face had the look of a man who was scared and in a trap. These are much more dangerous than those who are not scared.

"Mr. Lenoir, I must ask you again to let me proceed with my examination." I knew now he wouldn't, and I could feel it bubbling up like warm water.

"No!" He was frozen now, leaning backward against the car, his arms spread-eagled.

He was mine, all mine.

"For the third time, Mr. Lenoir, I must ask you to let me proceed with my duty."

"Gentlemen." I turned to the troopers behind me. Paxton, the redhead, and a little Cajun named Beausang. "You have heard this gentleman refuse to cooperate?"

"Yes, sir, Colonel."

"Sure thing, Colonel."

"You see I have no choice except to take drastic measures?"

"Yes, sir, Colonel."

"That's right, Colonel."

"For the last time, Mr. Lenoir. Please step aside."

I would have been sick if he had. But he was too scared to move.

"You leave me no choice."

I pulled the .45 out of the leather. I could tell from his face he didn't think I would use it, but was scared anyway. I tried to look sad, and then whipped it fast so the barrel caught him behind the ear with a thump like a watermelon. His legs doubled, nice and even like they had been hinged at the knees, and he went over on his face like a trap door falling.

It was all hot and bubbling inside, and I could barely keep the lid on.

I took the safety off the gun. Then I opened the car door.

"You boys are a little out of your territory," I said, very friendly. "You better get out and let me have that box."

They hesitated a minute and looked at each other. One of them shrugged and started out on the other side. The other one did not move.

"Get out," I said.

He shook his head and grinned, mean.

"Give me the box," I said, I felt good.

He shook his head again. "Make me."

That was it, that was what I wanted. My finger flesh felt the cold ridged pressure of the trigger, tighter and harder, and then the .45 exploded.

His face went stupid with shock. The shot had hit him where I aimed, in the upper arm. And I smelled it then for real, the old sharp burning bitter black powder smell. The day was complete, almost.

"Boy," I said. "You shouldn't ought to have gone for the heater that way."

He looked at me, his face all twisting now with hurting, his hand holding the place on the right arm, the blood seeping through the blue cloth and making a spreading blot around his fingers.

"You sonofabitch," he said.

I smiled at him. "I'm sorry I had to shoot you."

Not taking my eyes off him, I said to the troopers. "You boys saw him make the move, didn't you?"

"Yes, sir, Colonel," said Paxton.

"We certainly did," said Beausang.

"Okay," said the cop, his breath going ah-ah-ah. "Okay, Yancey."

"Get him to a hospital right away," I said. "No hard feelings. And now let's have that box."

I met Ada in a motel north of Baton Rouge at nine o'clock that night.

She opened the door at my first knock, her face white and without make-up, her body straining like a quarterback just before the snap. Then she slammed the door and said fast, almost before it banged, not waiting for me, "It went all right then? You got them?" Her voice was small and tight and dry.

"It went fine." I moved, slow on purpose, to the big chair in the corner and flopped in it. "Just fine. Of course I had to slug Lenoir and shoot a cop." I meant to shock her and I did. Her face exploded, and then I said, "Not dead. Just in the arm."

"You fool. You simple stupid goddamn fool."

"I had to. Lenoir wouldn't give me the petitions and the cop went for his gun so I had to."

"I'll bet, I'll just bet." She was furious, but she couldn't really worry about anything but the papers. "You did get them?"

"I got 'em."

"That's what counts. We'll worry about the other later. There'll be an awful stink though. Now. What we'll do is, we'll keep a few of the sheets and finally return them through channels and call them liars when they say they had more. Microfilm by itself isn't legal for this and I doubt if they've got microfilm anyway. Then we'll burn the rest." She was walking up and down, her lips shut together and her face tight in concentration; she had already forgotten the slugging and the shooting.

"That's the way to do it," I said. "Then we'll have them by the old hairy."

She frowned. She did not like me to talk like that. I had not talked like that, before.

That was before.

"That's the way." She said it shortly. "Now I want to look at them before you burn them. In fact I think I'll burn them." She laughed a little. "It will give me great pleasure."

"Sure it will, hon. Sure it will."

She looked at me, hard. She knew now something was coming.

"Well." She was suddenly watchful, waiting for whatever it was going to be. "Let's have them."

I didn't move. I grinned.

She was looking at me very close, like a spring ready to jump if you touched it. Her voice was flat and low as she said, "Come on. Let's have them."

"Soon," I said.

"What do you mean soon? I said give them here."

"Maybe I will and maybe I won't."

That touched the spring. She jumped at me, all fury, and said not loud, the words spread apart and whinging at me like bullets, "What in the hell do you think you are doing?"

"Aw, come on, hon, don't talk like that to your old colleague."

"You sonofabitch you give me those papers and you give them to me *now*." Her voice was climbing.

"Now, hon."

"Don't you call me hon. You want me to get Sylvestre here?"

"Now you don't want Sylvestre to know all about something. Hon."

She looked at me, her face the slit of a not quite closed door to a furnace.

"You really want those things?"

She said nothing.

"You want 'em enough to ask real pretty?"

She did not say anything. The furnace door was wide open now and I had a good view of the fire.

I said, "If you ask real nice."

She was not talking.

I said, "If you really want them."

Something happened in her face. All at once she knew what she was going to have to do to get them. Before, she had not known and she had been absolutely sure I would not have the nerve to do whatever it was I wanted. In this second, she knew I did have the nerve, and she knew what I wanted, and she knew what she would have to do.

"You wouldn't want these things in the record, would you now, hon?"

Her shoulders shook, not from crying.

"You know what I could do to you." But her voice was dead, we both knew this was just a move she had to make before she surrendered, and she must have known what I would say before I said it.

Which was: "You'd be doing it to yourself, hon. You know that."

We sat waiting. I could hear my heart thumping *PAM-pam PAM-pam.* I had the whip hand at last.

Her face was frozen now.

I didn't say anything else. I knew I didn't need to.

I felt it warm and bubbling, like when I knew I was going to clip Lenoir, when I knew I was going to have to shoot the cop. I was on the top, the world was mine, I could act in it the way I wanted. I could do anything.

Finally she started it. "All right," she said in a very dead voice. "Will you please give me the recall petitions."

"That's not real nice," I said. "You ought to be more friendly."

She said nothing.

"Try again," I said. "A little more friendly."

She said it again.

"It still isn't real friendly. Say, please give me the papers, *darling.*"

I heard her breath rise and fall, twice, shaking hard. Then, not looking at me, she said, "Please give me the papers, darling."

"Say, I'll be a good girl and always do what you say."

"I'll. I'll be a good girl."

"Finish it."

"And. And always. Always do what you say."

She wanted to kill me very badly. I could feel her wanting to kill me. I liked feeling it.

"Now that's better. But I still don't think you want 'em real bad."

She jumped at me with her fingers out like claws, making noises that were not human. I grabbed her wrists, and heard her breath snarling and spitting, and felt the spit hit my face, and then she went limp.

"Now, hon. You won't get them that way."

And she knew she wouldn't. She knew I would make it stick. If she had not been absolutely sure I would make make it stick she would have laughed in my face. But she was sure.

"Coax a little," I said. "Just a little."

"Robert." Her voice was very soft, and I knew what it had taken to make it that way. "Isn't this enough? Don't make me do any more. Don't you have any feeling at all for me?"

"Course I do, sugar. I just want you to be a little nice to me."

"So it *is* that. I should have known."

I grinned. "Maybe if you begged a little."
She knew it was no use. She begged.
"Maybe if you got down on your knees."
She got down on them. I felt wild I felt so good.
"More," I said.
She begged some more. It was even harder for her than before because now she was about to cry. She was about to cry from hate and anger.
I knew when I got up that morning it was going to be a good day.

But I kept the petitions, myself. Sylvestre never asked for them, so I guess she told him she burned them.

Tommy Dallas

I read about it in the papers. Any fool could see what happened. The Louisiana Leaguers and Yancey had set it up so the Leaguers would stop the Out-With-Ada cars and Yancey would move right in, arrest everybody, and take the petitions. It was a hidden ball play you could see from the end zone, it wouldn't fool nobody. But it didn't have to. When you carry the referee and the head linesman and the time keeper around in your pocket, you don't have to fool nobody.

You can make them swallow anything if you smear enough sugar on it. And she and Sylestre would do it. She and Sylvestre would smear the pension money and the building money and the health money around so the suckers would gulp it down and squeal for more. They would forget the taxes.

The two of them had sugared their way and slugged their way out of it this time. This time, they were safe. Her slutting bitching whoring soul to hell. But there was no use lying. She had the dynamite and she was going to stay in office. My office. She was going to win next year. Getting me out of the way had done the job. She couldn't of made it if she hadn't of been governor already, but now nothing could stop her. Her and Sylvestre. Both of them to hell forever and ever.

"And ever." I realized all of a sudden that I had said it out loud, because the nurse looked up.

"Yes, Governor, what is it?"

Governor. Some kick.

"I wonder if I could have some coffee."

"Now, Governor. You've had your two cups already." She said it like a schoolteacher.

"Then how about a drink? Let's you and me have a drink and have a party."

She giggled and turned all red, but she liked it. "Why, Governor. You shouldn't even be thinking about such things."

"The hell with I shouldn't. Let's have a real party."

She giggled. "We'll have one later," I said, and she giggled again.

It would be a hell of a long time before I had any parties. I was all busted. Ada had used me, and gotten what she wanted out of me, and now I was out of it with a broken neck and lucky not to be dead.

The funny thing was I was not really sorry I had done it. For once in my life, I hadn't kissed Sylvestre's. They hadn't been able to make me. They had given me the business. I was busted up to hell and back, and I hadn't changed one thing. Everything was going like it would of gone if I had gotten out the first time they had told me. But they had done it to me. They hadn't been able to make me do it to myself.

And I was free. The *boom*, the car end-over-ending, slinging me off the sides like a roulette ball, shooting me out the slung-open door like dice, all this had torn me loose from Sylvestre and Ada. I was free.

I could of felt a hell of a lot worse.

And in six months or a year I would be back in business.

"Nurse," I said.

She was still blushing from what I had said about the party. "Yes, Governor?"

"When I get out of this thing, you know what we're going to do?" Then I told her.

She kept turning redder and redder. And she kept saying, "Why, Governor! You mustn't say such things."

But she stayed.

Steve Jackson

The Young Louisiana League and Col. Robert Yancey had pulled it out for her. Once the recall petitions were confiscated, that was the end of them. The attorney general, who was Sylvestre's, stalled and stalled on returning them, and then he said they weren't even legal. Lenoir and his crowd squawked like chickens, and yelled for Federal action, and for a minute or two things were very hot.

But they cooled off as if ice water had hit them when the first old-age pensions were paid.

Because then Ada, or Ada and Sylvestre, played an ace of trumps.

They made the first checks retroactive for four months, back to the date the bill was signed, rather than the date it specified. They did it by executive order, and it was of course unconstitutional. But after four appointments in four years, the Supreme Court was now Sylvestre's.

Those first checks were for $400 apiece, and after they dropped into the mailboxes, the Out-With-Ada movement was finished and the public's love affair with her was on again hotter than ever. She went on TV holding up one of the checks, explaining sweetly how they were the result of the taxes, and how the taxes were really not so bad, and that certain forces in the state just didn't want to see people taken care of.

She did not even have to pay for time for the speech, because she was not a candidate, but governor, and the speech was officially not a political speech, but a message of state.

In the next months, the old-age and unemployment checks poured out inexhaustibly, and the Department of Public Works exploded in all kinds of projects: highways, community centers, new health offices. Name it and they built it. And every one of them had a big sign: ERECTED BY THE ADMINISTRATION OF GOVERNOR ADA DALLAS.

All of these, and the retroactive pension payments, had turned the situation upside down. In two months, she had become a popular governor.

But the election was close now, and I suppose she and Sylvestre wanted to make sure.

So—

Four months after her new taxes had started, just when the voters seemed finally to have accepted them as the price of benefits, she abolished the entire general sales tax, which had been in existence for more than twenty years.

She did it by executive order. What she did technically was to direct the Department of Finance to cease collecting it. It was of course illegal. But who was going to complain?

It was the most popular single action by a Louisiana governor that I could remember. Sylvestre Marin must have planned it, knowing it would completely erase any popular disaffection over the other taxes. The timing was perfect. Now she would run for governor with two things uppermost in the minds of most voters. One was the benefits. The other was no more sales tax.

The day after the quick surgical stroke that terminated (I think that is the clinical word) the sales tax, Ada was at a pinnacle of— of what? I suppose adoration. I wondered what was next for her. No governor since Huey had ridden so high. The wheel had turned. Ada was now Joan of Arc and Santa Claus rolled in one.

Then I wondered how she was getting along with Sylvestre. Had she persuaded him to loosen the strings, just a little? Or was she simply very good at taking directions?

Robert Yancey

For a while, I was on top of the world. I had her the way I had wanted to have her for three years. I had her crawling.

She had used me. And used me and used me and used me. And when you use somebody, you belong to them more than they do to you. She belonged to me.

She wanted to kill me. I could feel her wanting to every time I made her crawl, wanting so she shook with it. I liked the feeling. You are more alive when somebody wants to kill you than any other time.

It didn't last, but I made the most of it while I had it. After she paid out the first big pension checks, I started to lose hold, and when she cut out the sales tax I knew those recall sheets weren't worth the price of the paper.

The day after, I brought the sheets into her office and handed them across the desk to her without a word. Her hand closed on them, and she looked at me steady for half a minute, her face a bare rock. Then, still looking at me, she opened her top drawer and put them inside and closed it, never taking her eyes off me, never opening her mouth. I turned around and walked out.

I did not even try to touch her again for weeks.

Then one morning she called with orders, and her voice was not mad, not friendly. I had to make a call for her on a guy in central Louisiana. I did, and came back with the report; unofficial, of course, because he'd gotten a little out of line, and that night we were together as a matter of course, even though she still hated me, and I could feel her still wanting me dead.

But the wanting was different now. It was not hot, but cold; not like ice to melt away, but like chunks of steel to last forever.

So we were still together, we were in everything together, and neither of us could get away. Not her and not me. For better or worse, we were welded. Of course I was no longer the boss. I had lost that. But neither was she.

One night I asked her if she was worried about any news from Mobile.

"Don't ever say that," she said. "Not out loud."

"They'll find something, sometime."

"It won't matter. There's nothing." She meant there was nothing to tie us to it. "Nothing. Don't talk about it."

So I guess she did worry. Maybe she lay awake in the night sometimes. Maybe she wondered what it felt like to have a couple hundred thousand volts hit you. Maybe she did, too.

In politics, though, she had nothing to worry about. With Sylvestre's organization, she couldn't miss getting elected. I was afraid for a while things would slow down.

But things were slow, and they weren't. Not an awful lot went on that you could see. Most the capitol was just marking time until the campaign, when all hell would break loose. Now, the office girls spent half their day in the basement coffee shop, and you could always see half a dozen people hanging around the Coke machines. From the pressroom, the newspapermen kept ducking out to the corridor to see if they could scare up something to fill a column.

But plenty of work was going on in private. The key people were getting their records ready for a turnover in case there was a turnover. Nobody was sure whether they would be back or not, if Ada was elected. Nobody but me.

I was always ready for inspection, anyway. First thing you learn in the army is to keep the paper work up. What you *do* doesn't matter to anybody but yourself; it's what the records say that counts.

A couple of times a week, I would go through the newspapers. I wouldn't let myself do it more often. Every time the Mobile paper came in, I wanted to dive at it, rip it open, and tear it apart. It was more than just wanting it with your mind. It was the kind of wanting you have for a woman, and it was hard to deny. But I waited.

I knew they had to find the thing sometime, and I would read about it in that paper. It was like going to the post office window every day to see if a package you ordered has come in. You ordered it, and sent a check, and you know it has *got* to come. Every day the clerk shakes his head and looks at you the way they look when they say no. And every day you go away without it. But you come back the next, and ask again, because you know it is only a matter of time, and in your mind it has already come, you have opened it, and you have taken out what was inside, the thing you have ordered and sent the check for, and you have examined it and held it. When it really comes, and you really open it, you feel like you are repeating something you did a long time ago, and you think: *This has already happened, how come I am doing it again?*

That was the way it was on March 19. On the front page of the Mobile paper was a picture of two thirteen-year-old boys with fishing poles. One had freckles and a cowlick, and they both looked embarrassed and excited at having their picture taken for the paper. Under the picture was a big headline:

BOYS CATCH SKELETON
ON FISHING LINES

And that was it. The package had come. *You're late,* I thought, *what kept you?* I was not afraid, or worried even. I was something else, I did not know what.

I read the story through. The boys had felt something on the line, had pulled it in, and there was the body, which was now a skeleton, give or take a few bones. The bag must have finally come loose, and the water carried it out. The body had not been identified.

I finished the story, and I was still not worried, or afraid. What was I, I wondered, how did I feel? And then I knew.

I felt relieved.

I was glad the package had come.

When I admitted this, I was afraid. I was afraid of where it might take me, of what the next step might be. If I was glad they had found it, maybe I would want them to identify it.

Something said, somewhere: *You already want them to identify it.*

Then I was really afraid.

The paper was already two days old. Today's would have fresh dope. I could go down to Third Street and buy one.

I went out the side entrance to my car, got in and drove downtown, parked in the hotel lot, and walked up one block to Third. I started to turn in at the cigar stand that carried all the papers, and then I walked past. I walked down the street half a block, and then I turned around and started back.

A suspicious action, I thought. Now I was a kind of referee, watching myself from just above, and giving myself a score: good—okay —not so good. The last was not so good.

I walked into the cigar store.

"Yes, sir," said the bald-headed clerk. In the commandant's uniform, you get all kinds of courtesy. Everybody is just as courteous as hell.

"Got a M—" I started to say Mobile paper, and then something hit me like a fist. I said instead, *"Morning Advocate,"* which is a Baton Rouge paper.

He gave it to me, and I gave him his nickel, and feeling weak in the guts I went outside into the street and the sunshine.

The thing that hit me scared the hell out of me. I had wanted him to notice I bought a Mobile paper and had wanted him to remember it.

Get off it, boy. Cut out the crap. You got to be careful.

I remembered some reports of murder cases where the criminal had left a whole path of clues, just like he had done it on purpose and was hoping they would find it. I had never understood this before. I had never understood how they could be so dumb.

Now I was beginning to understand.

You got to be careful.

Not knowing what I was doing, not really caring, I stopped on the sidewalk and looked at the front page of the *Advocate*. Then I almost jumped. I knew it would probably be in the Mobile paper, but this caught me off guard. Down there in the corner of the page was a little headline:

MOBILE'S SKELETON
FOUND TO BE WOMAN

It was an Associated Press story, just two paragraphs long, and it said the coroner had declared the skeleton found in the inlet to be that of a woman about fifty years old.

That would be all for a long time. Then finally they would find the car, and the license plates would be off, and the engine number rubbed off, and they wouldn't be able to identify the car. They would spend at least six months checking all the Olds sold in Alabama the year of the model.

Then they would maybe finally figure who bought it, and would put that together with the skeleton, and maybe they would know who it was. But there would be nothing to connect it with Louisiana, or to us. They would figure it was a gang killing.

There was nothing to worry about.

If I just didn't go around committing suicide.

All I had to do was be careful.

When I had not acted—I mean acted fast, hard, in a way I could feel all through myself—when I had not acted in a while I could feel it slipping close. I had to be in motion. Christ, it is so much easier in a war where you can act and still be good. Not any more, not for me.

But when I wasn't moving, I was nothing. All I could feel then was the whatever-it-was coming, and coming, and coming, after me.

That was my life now: waiting for things to be found in Alabama. No action, anywhere in the state. Nobody stuck their necks out. After what happened to Out-With-Ada, they were all scared. I had nothing to do.

And I couldn't handle Ada any more, like I had those short weeks. I couldn't command her. And she couldn't command me. We were stalemated.

Sometimes I would feel the warmness of her body and the thrust and drop of her blood pulsing, and I would hear myself whisper:

"You hate me don't you."

"Yes ah yes."

"You want to kill me don't you."

"Yes yes I'll kill you."

"You can't you can't."

"Bastard bastard ah I hate you."

That was all there was, that and the waiting. Sometimes I wished she really was trying to kill me. When you have to work not to be dead, you know you are alive. But she didn't try to kill me. She only wanted to. And I kept reading the papers from Mobile.

In the late spring, they found the car in the inlet.

I read the first of two paragraphs; not even on the front page, but stuck away inside, the headline so small I almost missed it, and I felt my blood run like hot water. I was afraid, but I knew in my heart I was more something else than I was afraid. In that funny, scary way, I felt *satisfied*. Another overdue package had come.

Then I read the last half-inch of gray type, and I felt cold.

The last sentence read: "Officers said the automobile was impossible to identify, and that no attempt would be made to do so."

I told Ada that night, and she breathed a deep sigh, and said, "That's good to hear."

"They still may find out about her. There's lots of ways."

"Don't sound so hopeful," she laughed, then stared hard at me, a funny look on her face.

Tommy Dallas

After all those months, finally, I was walking again, and I didn't really care about nothing else. I eased around the hospital terrace, my legs feeling not part of me at all. They were somebody I had just been introduced to. The only thing familiar was the cast on my back and neck. It was me.

I moved around, just a little at a time, and felt muscles I forgot

I had start to work. It was like being born again. You can't take too much of it, not at once.

I followed Ada in the papers: making the speeches and ending the sales tax and the big demonstration and all. It looked like she was on top of the world, but I knew better. I knew where the strings were, I knew who was pulling them, and I knew how it felt. They yelled for you like a hero, but you were a little stick with strings behind and somebody working the strings. You knew you were nothing and it ate your guts. It ate mine and it would be eating Ada's a damn sight worse. I had taken it. I kept on taking it right up to the end. But now I wondered if Ada would.

After I had got my voice back, the newspapermen started to come in to ask me what about this and what about that. I always saw them for as long as the doctor would let me, I was always friendly, and I always told them, "I don't have enough information on that to express an opinion. You see how it is, boys. I'm laid up this way and I ain't in touch. You see how it is."

It is always better to talk to them even if you don't say anything. Some fellows never learn that. Earl Long never liked to talk to them.

I saw them the day I left the hospital. I said I wished Ada luck in her responsibilities while I went away to recover my health. Ada came by and kissed me good-by for the photographers. "You're always in there, ain't you, kid?" I whispered to her in the clinch.

She pulled back and smiled so sweet while the bulbs went "pop" and made yellow flashes. "Remember the whole state is pulling for you, darling," she said out loud.

She left with the reporters and photographers.

I got a cottage way over on the north Florida coast, past Mobile, almost to Panama City, where anybody would have to go to hell and gone out of their way to bother me.

This cottage was in a little string of cottages, not close together, not close to anything else, on sand as white as snow and as hot as fire. Nobody would bother me there. I had a male trained nurse, or whatever it is they are, therapists or what, to take care of me. That was a hell of a note. But it wouldn't look good to have a woman nurse there. Wouldn't have helped either because I couldn't handle it yet.

Earl, the therapist, was a big black-haired bear who reminded you of a kid even if he was around thirty-five. He always wore a uniform of white slacks and knit white sport shirt that fitted him tight and showed his muscles. He walked around with his stomach pulled in and his chest pushed out; every night I could hear him grunting in his room, doing his push-ups and belly bends. He was good-natured and good company even if he was kind of simple (he probably thought the same thing about me). I liked him, only I wished he wasn't so hell-set on being cheerful and jolly. I guess he figured that was part of his job. Anyway, he had worked in good hospitals, he knew his job, and he took good care of me.

This was a nice little house: one room for me, one for the therapist, a kitchen, a living room, and a john. The house sat up on a little rise above the beach, and you could sit in the air-conditioned living room and look through the picture window at the Gulf rolling in to the white sand. You could sit nice and quiet, and see the world through the window without having to mess with it. It was a temptation just to sit in the cool room and look through the glass and never get out. But I made myself get outside and stay as long as I could, feeling that old sun hit me, feeling the bad things in my body sweat out, and the strength coming in like a drink. When you start from zero you can feel every inch you make.

A doctor came out once a week from Tallahassee.

"You doing fine," he said one day. "Can you swim?"

"Well," I said. "I'm not winning many medals."

"You ought to start swimming every day. It puts the old peppo back."

So I started to learn to swim again, it amounted to that. There was a nice lagoon where the surf didn't come, and I splashed around there for a month or so. The doc was right. I started to feel the old peppo.

From the window, I could see other swimmers sometimes come along the beach, and I would watch them swim out: their heads bobbing like balls, smaller and smaller as they went further out, then their arms stroking like hell and churning the water white when they came in fast on top of the swells.

I watched, and decided the trick was to figure the rhythm of the swells and figure your own rhythm and time them together and you were in business. I was going to try it, sometime.

One day Earl came back from town with a stack of newspapers.

He dropped them on the sofa, where I was sitting looking out the picture window.

"Thought you might want to see what's happening back there," he said, and I saw they were Baton Rouge papers.

"Sure," I said. "Sure."

I didn't give one flying jazz what was happening back there. I already knew, anyway. I just didn't know who it was happening to. What was happening was that Ada was giving somebody the business.

I looked at the first paper and saw why Earl had thought I would want to see it. On the front page was a big picture of Ada dedicating the new courthouse at Dry Prong. Col. Robert Yancey was standing at the very edge of the picture. Sylvestre was not in it at all.

"The little woman really looks great," Earl said.

"Yeah," I said.

"She's a great woman."

"Yeah," I said.

"You really got yourself something there, boss."

"Sure," I said. "Sure I have."

Steve Jackson

For almost a month after the end of the sales tax, Ada did nothing. Her quiet was the quiet that comes after the barometer drops and before the advance winds hit. The air is dead-still and weighs a ton and is poised like a hammer above your head. You see the little silver thread of mercury dropping and dropping, and you smell the storm, and you feel the electricity even though it has not erupted into lightning yet. You see and smell and feel, and you wait under the dark and dropping sky, and you know you do not have long to wait.

As are all calms, this one was brief. It lasted not quite a month. Then it exploded in a thousand pieces. The storm hit all at once, without warning, and it swept up and down Louisiana. Ada's campaign for governor was under way.

I trailed at a safe distance, observing phenomena and noting damage. Of course I talked to Ada a great many times. The feeling of the bond was there, with both of us. But for her it was more subordinated than ever to her commitment to action. *Nothing has changed,* her demeanor said, *but I have more important things to do, and remember you limited this thing yourself.*

What was between us had hit the kind of pitch that could go unchanged for years. And probably would. I had seen it happen. I once knew a bachelor and a married woman in Connecticut, who had maintained this kind of special cordiality for fourteen years and done nothing about it. Then one day, while her husband was in the city, her house caught fire, he rushed in to save her, and they consummated it in minutes while the firemen hosed another part of the house, where the fire was.

On those occasions we did meet, she was tired, in the temporary suspension of will and vitality that comes to an athlete after a contest. But the minute she stepped in front of a crowd or a camera, she was charged with a furious kind of energy. So many times I saw her in the white hard glare of a spot, or in sunshine, or in evening twilight. And I heard:

"You know what they tried to do to you!

"They tried to sell you out.

"They tried to keep you from what was yours.

"But I wouldn't let them!

"I'll never let them!"

And they answered every time with the noise the sea makes when storm rips it.

It was the same everywhere: the same speech (with variations), the same response (with accents).

In Winn parish, red-neck country and Huey's homeland: the sky a blue-hot sheet of metal crackling over the dark shapeless crowd animal. The faces red-brown and creased, maybe above blue denim overalls or khaki shirts or checked cotton dresses. But all listening, believing, as they had believed nobody since that day in 1935 when the doctor met the Senator in the corridor.

On the waterfront in Morgan City: the masts and yardarms of the shrimp boats bobbing in dark crosses against the blue white-pillowed sky. While the smell of fresh-caught shrimp, and of thrown-away time-polluted shrimp, and of uncaught wriggling shrimp waiting for the net down in the cool dark under the blue-green lid of the Gulf of Mexico, while the smell of all these floated like musk in the sun-shot afternoon air. The deep-tanned black-mustached black-sideburned faces, shouting, "A-*da Ma cher! Eh la bas!*"

In New Orleans: the knowing, smirking, razor faces of the quick and the young of a great city. Crowned with duck-tails, or Italian bobs, above gaudy jackets and blue jeans. Fanatically intent. Already dedicated.

In Bogalusa: the indescribable stink of the paper mills, filling the universe, almost blotting out the feebler dimensions of sound and sight and touch, blurring the faces of the mill workers turned upward upon her.

And in all the small cities and towns: pinched white faces above year-before-last's house dress, above the frayed white collar and stringy tie, the grease-streaked gas-station uniform and waitress blouse; faces, pinched and desperately thoughtful.

In the Railroad Avenue section of Baton Rouge: the sepia-chocolate-ebony faces, above anything at all: a Brooks Brothers shirt or one purple with yellow stripes, a custom-tailored raw-silk jacket or a dirty undershirt; flaming red satin or neat chaste blouse or cotton shift; all with the common denominator of darkness and dubious enfranchisement. These faces happy, these voices full of delighted acclamation.

And the women's clubs everywhere: all the girls (thirty to sixty) in their afternoon dresses and imitation pearls. You could see the dilemma on their well-powdered and innocent faces. Their husbands had told them that she was a dangerous subversive. But there she was, without horns, nodding and smiling over a coffee cup. *So charming. Why, just one of us.*

These were, of course, the women's clubs unrecognized by Social New Orleans. In the city, that is, in the thick-walled air-tight cell that was the Society of the city, she had the status of a low-caste Hindu, say, who had somehow become Mayor of Calcutta, if there is a mayor in Calcutta.

Since her defeat almost three years before as governor's wife, the warfare between herself and the New Orleans *haut monde* had been open and acknowledged. It was a good steady source for quips at the better cocktail parties and balls. But the quips were whispered. The memory of Dr. Smith and DeNegre and Colonel Bartlett was still vernal and twitching.

But there were other women's clubs in New Orleans besides the Orleans Club and its satellites. There were hundreds of completely humdrum little klatsches, with thousands of completely ordinary little women, who made the *Picayune* society pages only when they got married, and then in three paragraphs on a weekday. And oddly enough they seemed resentful of their enforced inferiority. They could not accept it as divine ordination. And I am sure they identified with Ada to a very great degree. When she won, they won. I had seen this on the unfashionable faces of countless unfashionable women.

For a long time, she had tried to play down the fact that she came out of the Irish Channel. But after her great defeat at the Orleans Club, she capitalized on it. The Channel hailed her as its St. George. She spoke there one night, and I wandered through the crowd, and heard its syllables, which were pure Brooklyn:

"Yeh, at's some goil. Lissen at 'er. Yeh, she's some goil awright. She'll show dem big shots. Ya know? She'll tell 'em off awright."

What I was seeing, of course, was the on-stage action. What I was not seeing was the director, Sylvestre Marin.

And so I followed her where I could. I was fascinated by the public Ada, and eager for whatever crumbs from the private Ada might fall my way.

One night in Buras, in the delta country south of New Orleans, she saw me and made a waving motion with her hand: an invitation. Twenty minutes later, I knocked on the door of her motel cabin, heard "Come in," and stepped inside.

Instantly I saw she was different tonight, somehow unarmored. Her face carried worry and something else, perhaps self-reproach, perhaps only fatigue. I wondered why. Maybe there was no reason. Maybe this was just a night when things well buried came out of the ground. She couldn't be the same woman who had stood under the lights thirty minutes before. I had the odd sense of unreality that came whenever this reversal of her selves hit me.

She was containing herself with a just-perceptible effort.

She gave me her hand. "Hello, Steve."

"Hi," I said.

We stared at each other a moment, and I said, "Nice speech."

"Why thanks."

"It really went very well."

"Why thanks," she said again, and silence became a solid element in the room. Neither of us was particularly well protected tonight, I thought.

"Drink?" she said.

"Sure."

She went to the dresser, where the bottle and the ice and glasses were.

"Only water I'm afraid."

"That's fine," I said.

We had the drink, spoke more inanities between heavy punctuations of silence. I felt the inescapable accelerating slide toward her, and I knew that it had already carried me a long long way. For a moment she turned her back, then came around again, quite suddenly, and the appeal I had not seen in a long time was naked in her face.

"Steve?"

"Yes?" Quite suddenly, I knew I was going to do whatever she asked me, and I hoped she was going to ask me again to come to her on the terms I had rejected.

"Nothing," she said, and I felt the bitter dullness of disappointment. Well, I had bought it, and if it was too late to change, it was my responsibility.

Her face swung away so I was watching it in profile, miserably. There was a line at the corner of her mouth I hadn't seen before. Then she was looking straight at me, everything I wanted to see was in her face, and she said, "Please come back. I need you so."

We both knew she meant on her terms, and I knew I was going to say yes, and I was glad. I took her shoulders, and pulled her to me, which was the answer. I did not kiss her but simply held her, feeling her tremble in my arms, while hers slipped around me, and we did not move. I am happy, I thought, and a quick double rap came on the door. Ada whispered, "Oh my God," and we parted just before Col. Robert Yancey stepped through the door.

There was no mistaking what he was there for. Nor, from the way their eyes clashed, that he had been sleeping with her for some time. His eyebrows pulled together, and he looked angrily at me. I looked at Ada, and she flushed. Her face was furious, guilty, and begging.

We all recovered at once.

"I just thought I'd look in and see if I could be of any, service," said the Colonel.

"Thank you very much." Ada looked at him murderously, and then back at me with the plea in her eye. "Now that you're here, do have a drink. Mr. Jackson and I were just having one."

I said, "I've got to go."

"Please don't." Ada's hand stopped me, and her face begged: *Please. Please accept this too, I can't help it.*

"I really have to," I said. I wasn't by God sharing her with Tommy Dallas and Sylvestre Marin and the voters *and* Col. Robert Yancey.

Her face went completely dead, and her voice was lifeless. "Good night then."

"Good night," I said.

Walking blindly to the car, I thought this was the third time I had lost her. That was enough. Except at a distance, I would never see her again. For a moment I tried to hate her, but it was no good. I could hate Yancey though. I could hate Col. Robert Yancey with no trouble at all.

Robert Yancey

I wanted to drive her to her appearances over the state, but being the commandant of police, of course I could not, not all the time. I did arrange her police escort, I did clear the routes, and sometimes I preceded her in my official car to wherever she was going. Sometimes, too, I could drive her. This was not officially a campaign, she was appearing in her capacity as governor, and she was entitled to all the formalities.

But we were very careful. I talked to her in public as little as possible, and just showed up at the right time and the right place. People are bound to talk about a good-looking tomato that looks like she's born to be laid, and if she's in the public eye, they're going to talk a lot more. And Ada was governor. Yes, by God, she was governor. Wasn't *that* a kick.

Officially she was still in a kind of mourning for Tommy, who was kind of half-dead. The poor slob. I wondered if he knew what hit

him? How could he help it? I wondered if he knew who. I was sorry
he got hurt so bad. I had only meant to scare him and shake him up.

Anyway, we were very circumspect. I didn't like it that that TV
bastard, Steve Jackson, had seen us in the motel in Buras.

"Don't worry," said Ada. "He's a friend. He can be trusted."

"One thing you learn in police work, it's nobody can be trusted."

"I said don't worry. Steve is okay."

"Well. He didn't really see anything."

Those very few times that I would break protocol and drive her
myself, she just had to keep telling me what to do. Like:

"Slow down, not so fast." Or, "Take that road, I want to go that
way." Even when it was the longest way.

She just had to prove she was calling them. And goddamn it, I did
what she said. That was what made me mad. Almost all the time I
did what she said. But not always.

Once she told me to take one road and I deliberately took the
other, that was rougher, but shorter.

Then her face went into that white blaze with the gray coals, just
like it had that time in the corridor, a long time ago.

"Goddamn you," she said. "Don't you ever do that again. When
I tell you to do something you do it. You hear?"

"You listen," I said. "Don't think you can boss me. Don't ever
try to boss me. Not ever. You just remember what we're in together."

"Don't *you* give me orders."

"Nobody gives anybody orders. We're in it together. Just remember it," I said.

Then I gave it gas, and I felt those 380 horses take off like a
guided missile. The road was shooting at us straight and white, and
the world was coming at us, green and wide, faster and faster, and
we were on top of it all and I was giving it gas and I had the wheel.

Steve Jackson

Although Ada had barnstormed like a
fury for almost a year, the campaign did not officially begin until a
couple of months before the Democratic primary. Against Sylvestre
and herself was the same line-up that had been against Sylvestre

and Tommy Dallas. This time, even in the face of Ada's gender, the opposition's chances were worse than four years before.

Lenoir was the quote reform unquote candidate again. At first he had picked up some popularity as the result of his wife's suicide. But after Out-With-Ada backfired on him, Ada and Sylvestre had successfully created the image of Lenoir as a big-money candidate. Which was exactly accurate. Jack Moore was running again, so he could sell his support to one of the candidates in the second primary. A couple of anonymities were in it for the publicity or whatever other reasons keep a hopeless candidate in a hopeless race.

Lenoir had the backing of some very large money, some very small reform groups, and of most of the newspapers. Against this, Sylvestre and Ada were throwing the coalition of sheriffs, the labor unions, the Old Regulars of New Orleans, the big syndicate gamblers, some small in-state corporations, and Sylvestre's own well-drilled organization. Ada was promising a brand-new New Deal and would finance it by raising taxes on oil, gas, sulphur, and timber. These would have to be paid by out-of-state corporations, and so would be popular with almost everybody else.

Naturally, those companies put up plenty for Lenoir, but Sylvestre's other sources came up with as much for Ada. With the bankrolls even, it was no contest.

The only thing that could win for Lenoir was a bombshell. Someday somebody would produce the Mobile episode—but nobody did. The election followed what Ada had called Sylvestre's master plan right down to the wire.

I could not separate myself from the campaign, I had to do a lot of shows on it one way or another. But I did not speak one word to Ada, or see her at a distance closer than twenty feet. Once at a rally in a K.C. hall in the Channel, I looked up from notes and she was looking at me. She smiled, and I was suddenly aware that I was smiling back. Quickly I ducked my head to the notes.

Election day in New Orleans. The bars are closed until six o'clock, which is alone enough to cut the cord to reality. Business almost but not quite congeals, and the town lies low. Except for voting precincts and campaign headquarters, where the purpose and motion that have been siphoned off the rest of the city spray wild and heavy and at all angles.

Then at six, the polls close, the bars open, and humanity swirls over streets and sidewalks and through cafés as though a dam lock has been opened. And the islands in it are the places, any places, where returns are compiled.

The foremost of these are the headquarters of the gubernatorial candidates. About eight o'clock, when the patterns of the vote were just beginning to cast shadows, I started with the crew and equipment on a round of these headquarters.

The first was Lenoir's: a converted banquet room on the mezzanine of the St. Charles Hotel. As I entered, the first thing I saw, at an angle of forty-five degrees, was a large blackboard, like the big board at Merrill Lynch. Beside it stood Lenoir and thinning out from it were perhaps fifty people. They were very quiet and did not look happy. Lenoir's white suit was badly rumpled and streaked. He was sweating heavily, and kept dabbing at his forehead with a wadded handkerchief.

On his face was the shocked and outraged look of a boy who has found the old swimming hole abruptly and completely filled with gravel, who has been told that the scout troop has been disbanded for all time.

I felt I was making some hideous joke as I asked, "How do you think the race is shaping up, Mr. Lenoir?"

He was not looking at me. He was looking at the board, where a bald-headed man sweating through his shirt had just written figures in the strip for St. Bernard parish. A couple of beads popped on Lenoir's forehead, and the outrage on his face changed to numb disbelief.

He did not answer, and I covered fast. "Some new returns have just claimed Mr. Lenoir's attention, and . . ." And so on.

Then I grabbed him and asked him again and mouthed silently, "TV." He looked at me, but for an instant did not see. Then he came back.

"It's phony and baloney." The parts of his face, which had for a moment been separate and without cohesion, regrouped. Now he was a man who had settled virtuously in his pew, and looked up to find a black mass being celebrated.

I glanced at the St. Bernard returns. They showed 2,018 for Ada, 123 for Moore, and 21 for Lenoir.

"Phony and baloney." Lenoir was not talking to me nor to the microphone and camera, but to himself. "Why I've got more than twenty-one close personal friends in that parish. It's phony. It's all phony."

This was crowding libel, so I changed quickly. "Do you expect the first primary to be close?"

He made a great effort then, and he managed: "Oh, yes. Very, very close. But I'm convinced the people of Louisiana will once again affirm their fundamental belief, their fundamental belief, in, in the fundamentals of good government."

"Thank you, Mr. Lenoir," I said.

He was dead, and knew it, and the knowing was in his face.

Arnold, the north Louisiana lawyer, had not even bothered to set up headquarters in the city. So I went next to those of Jack Moore, the old pro and percentage player.

I walked into a wake. Silence was as thick as fog, and one syllable, "Yeah," cut it as violently as a searchlight.

Less than a dozen people were in the office, all men except Moore's dumpy gray-blond wife. They had the apathetic uncomprehending look of disaster victims. Except Moore himself, who sat slumped in the far corner, and whose fat face was an unobstructed view of terror and ruin.

I suddenly saw what was the common denominator between Lenoir and Moore, besides defeat. Both had just been raped by their personal deities. The deities, of course, were different.

I felt like an undertaker as I talked to him.

"Mr. Moore," I said. "How does it look to you?"

He looked up. "What is it?" he whispered.

I said, "How does the race look to you?"

His eyes fell on me, and I could see his brain and body crawling toward articulation. He made a very great effort, and his voice cracked, "I. It's very early to tell anything. I ... Mrs. Dallas of course is making a fine race. But there are many parishes still to be heard from and nothing is certain and I, I refuse to concede until the last vote is counted."

Here sat a man (his face said) who had been violated by the universe. He had not placed his trust in such toys as justice, or morality, or luck. He had not expected to win. He had not expected, and absolutely did not want, to be in the second primary. He had only wanted there to be a second primary, so he could sell his support to one or the other candidate for a net profit reputed by the professionals to be in the neighborhood of twenty thousand dollars.

But now the twenty thousand profit was gone, and his investment of probably another twenty thousand was gone with it, and in his face you could see the forty-thousand dead loss. The show-bet sure thing had dropped dead on the track.

For at eight thirty-six by the clock, two and one-half hours after the polls had closed, the unbelievable fact was clear:

In the first primary, Ada Dallas had been elected governor of Louisiana.

Ada's headquarters were in the Monteleone Hotel, on Royal Street in the Quarter, but she was not there, nor was Sylvestre, nor Col. Robert Yancey. They were all in Baton Rouge in the governor's mansion.

Down here, State Representative Alva P. Boudin was the straw boss, and now he was swollen and strutting like a bantam rooster. I gave him the mike, and he rose to the occasion.

"The people have spoken. Now the state of Louisiana and its wonderful governor will go onward and upward together."

His turnip face was solemn, and he was enormously proud of having said something enormously profound.

It was a busy night, and it was after midnight when I got back to my apartment. I lay awake in the dark a long time. What was Ada doing now? I wondered. This very second. This was one of the nights when no anesthetic worked.

Tommy Dallas

I heard it election night on the black box radio. I knew she couldn't miss, I knew nothing could stop her and Sylvestre, only I didn't think she would take it in the first. That rocked me.

I cut off the radio, and stood up. I felt tight as a gittar string, I had to *do* something.

"Come on," I said to Earl. "We going to Mobile."

"Huh?" He looked surprised.

"I said we going to Mobile."

"Governor, you shouldn't—"

"Come on," I said.

So we went to Mobile, and got a motel cabin. The boy told me they had girls, and I had him get one. But I couldn't make it.

She saw I felt bum about it.

"Don't fret, hon." She patted my cheek. "Happens all the time, in the best of families."

"Sure," I said. I was scared, I almost wanted to die.

"I got to charge you just the same though. They make me, they figure you bought the night and whatever you do with it is your business."

"Let's have a drink then. Since I'm paying."

So I wasn't whole yet. Goddamn Ada. Goddamn her to hell forever. Suppose I never could again. Cut that out. Sure you will. Like she said, it happens, all the time.

But I felt gone, and I didn't think it would ever change.

The light was on now, we were sitting on a big white sofa, and I noticed for the first time it was a real fancy room.

She saw me looking around and grinned. "This is what we call the bridal suite. You really rated, hon."

She was a good kid, short, slim and redheaded, with a freckled face that looked homey and sexy at the same time. I saw she was trying to make me feel better.

"Yeah," I said. "Yeah, I see."

She looked at me hard. "I told you not to worry about that, hon. Happens to everybody one time or another."

"Oh sure."

"Sure is right. Here. Let me show you something. The old lady used to run this operation was a candid camera bug." She snickered. "She got some doozies, too. Somebody found her collection after she pulled out, long time ago."

She handed me a big scrapbook from the drawer of a table.

"Kind of moth-eaten," I said.

"It goes way back."

I opened it. "Jesus."

She snickered again. "Rugged, huh? The old lady had a real thing, you know, for pictures; she got her kicks that way. She had every room in the place fixed with little holes so she could take em every whichaway. New management had a hell of a time nailing those holes up."

"I just bet." I kept turning the pages, but they didn't do nothing for me, I didn't even like them. "She uses these little things to black-mail her customers, huh?"

"Oh no, no, hon, she didn't even know who her customers were. She had a real good thing going, she would mess it up by blackmailing customers. These was just for kicks, hon."

She laughed. I kept turning the big pages, old and crumpled on the edges, and then I stopped. I was looking at a picture of a man and a woman on a bed, and the woman's face was straight at the camera. Which of course she didn't know was there. Long black hair tumbled over her shoulders, her eyes were closed, and her mouth was open just a little. She was in heat all the way.

The little redhead laughed again. "You really dig that one, huh?"

"Not specially." I turned the page fast.

"That's good, because she ain't been around in an awful long time. I don't even know who she is."

I kept turning pages, but I wasn't seeing anything any more.

The redhead finally saw the pictures weren't doing it. "Scuse me a sec, hon." She got up and went into the bath.

I flipped the pages back quick to the girl with black hair, I started to tear the picture loose, then I pulled the whole page out, so no-body would know it was gone. I rolled it tight and slipped it in my coat pocket, and a few minutes later the redhead came out.

When I was leaving, she patted my shoulder and said again, "Don't you worry now, Daddy. You going to be just fine."

Earl was waiting in the car. He was grinning but stopped when he saw I had something big on my mind.

I couldn't wait to get back to the cottage to look at it again. Even if it was crazy. I had him stop at a service station a few miles down the highway. In the men's room, I pulled out the picture, covered the black hair with my finger, and imagined it yellow instead, and drawn back.

I looked close at the face a long time, and then the body. I knew them both like they were my own. There wasn't no doubt. For any-body else, maybe, but not me. It was Ada, who I had had to marry to lay.

Next day, I got up early, while Earl was still asleep, and went down to the beach. The big beach, not my lagoon. Nobody was there this morning, maybe because it was a dark day and full of wind.

The sky stretched out gray, the sea not blue but darker gray and full of whitecaps.

I had picked a day, all right.

I tried not to think of the picture, and this was hard because I hadn't been able to think about anything else since I saw it. It was the works. It was my chance to get back at her and Sylvestre for every stinking thing they had done to me. Now that I knew, there was sure to be some way I could get the proof I needed to back it up. I would have to wait for that, and for the right time. But it would come.

The thing now was for me to get ready myself.

I started to wade out. The water rose along my ankles and calves and knees and thighs like cool blood, and when it was at my waist, I flattened into it and started swimming. I could see the gray white-topped wall of the next swell coming at me, not fast when I first saw it but looking faster and faster as it bore down and down, not mean or mad but just not caring, not for me or for anything, and then it was straight above me and I ducked under at just the right time. It didn't throw me, I just felt a good strong surge at my body and then it was gone and I was watching the next one start, way off.

I took another, and another. I felt good taking them, I wanted to keep on, and on, and then I looked back to the beach and saw that it was quite a piece away and that Earl was standing there in a white T-shirt waving his arms for me to come back.

I turned around and started in, turning my head with the stroke to watch the swell coming now from behind, closer and closer, and I worked my arms fast so I could ride it in, but I couldn't go fast enough, and something picked up my feet and slung me sideways and end over end, like the car when it blew up, and I was swallowing salt water, and fighting to come up. Then the swell passed, and I was in the trough and my head out of the water, but the next one was coming fast, like an express train sideways. I saw it, and I rode it. When it passed on, I turned and swam as fast as I could for the beach, then turned around to face the next one coming in. It was the only way I could beat it.

I kept doing it that way, but I kept swallowing that bitter salty water every time I went under, and my arms were so gone I could barely lift them, and I was goddamn glad to see Earl's head all at

once bobbing out there next to me and his hand reaching out.
On the beach he said:

"Jeez, Governor, you shouldn't ought to of gone out that far. You shouldn't ought to of done it."

"Naw." I was trying to cough up the bitter stuff and fighting for breath, all at once. "Naw hah-ah, I hah-ah guess not."

He was half holding me, one arm around my waist, and I was leaning on him.

"You shouldn't ought to."

"I was doing all right out there till—" My breath was coming easier. "Till I started back. Couldn't go fast enough. Next time. Next time I'll—"

Then it came up, the bitter water and everything else, and after it was out and I had my breath, I felt better. I walked by myself up the slope and rested in front of the fire that Earl built. I listened to the logs crack, and smelled the wood burning, and felt pretty good. I hadn't done too bad. I would do better.

I would make it with the swells and with that same girl, too. The swells were nothing, the girl was nothing, but now they had come to stand for something. They were like highway markers along the way I had to go before—before what? I guess before I could see my shadow the way I wanted. Then I would move. And when I did —I'd have the ammunition.

Steve Jackson

Ada's inauguration came on a bright blue day in May—so bright, so blue, that human sin seemed wildly implausible, a campaign lie spun by the Opposition to win votes.

Ada herself looked cool and lovely—no, those were not the words —Ada was serene and pure in her white dress, sitting quite alone on the throne of a white leather seat of a white Cadillac convertible, courtesy Wild Bill Hickson Motors. She was in the tunic-like white, wore no hat, and her hair was long and gold and worn in a classic knot. In gilded shell the king's daughter... Sweet Thames flow softly. Only no king's daughter she, but an Irish Channel girl who had risen by what complots, what craft, what deeds. And her face showed none of them, none at all.

The inaguration was a re-released movie run from an old and faulty print. I had seen it all before, four years ago. But the images kept distorting. I kept wanting to say, *No, that isn't right, that isn't right at all.* Where is Tommy, and where is the old Governor? They cut them out somewhere. But there is Col. Robert Yancey, driving like before; there is that sonofabitch, all right.

It was the same except it kept getting different. The past recaptured, but not quite: the wrong cookie, perhaps. But the procession of Cad convertibles, glittering in the sun, again courtesy Wild Bill Hickson (the cars, not the sun), was the same, the route was the same, the amused profane faces in the press car were the same, and the destination was the same: the university stadium with the temporary bleachers and scaffolding.

The facilities, temporary, must have strongly resembled those provided in the tower court that morning for the farewell appearance of Anne Boleyn. But Ada, of course, was here for a different purpose.

She stood as before, speaking into a row of microphones. A gun fired in the distance, and I thought again of Anne Boleyn. Ada took the oath from a judge in black robes (and how he must have been sweating today), and she was the anointed Governor of Louisiana.

It was strangely anticlimactic. Instead of an old print of a feature film, the inauguration had become a newsreel of an event consigned to history long ago. *We have done this before,* I thought, *why are we doing it again?*

I had checked the mike for her speech, but had not met her eye. And she had not spoken, not to me.

Then it was over, she took her place in the white chariot, and the procession started behind her for the capitol.

Sylvestre Marin was not in the procession. I had seen him in the audience, and had seen him depart before she took the oath, doubtless to return in his own chauffeur-driven black Chrysler, which was not courtesy Wild Bill Hickson Motors.

I rode back in the press car, my broadcast done, with the feeling of empty release that comes after a wedding, or a funeral.

An hour later, both houses of the Legislature convened separately, then came together in joint session to receive Ada's message. The legislators gave her the customary standing ovation, and adjourned for the day.

So now she was, by the forms, alone, on the top of the tower—and she must be realizing that she neither had anything nor was anything. Between her and the reality of her appearances was Sylvestre Marin.

I stayed in Baton Rouge the first week of the session; nothing exciting came up, and it seemed that nothing was going on. Sylvestre's—and Ada's—program had been pushed through before the election. So the station brought me back to New Orleans.

For three weeks more the Legislature continued to be the quietest in years. Then one Saturday, Senator Moriarity, home for the weekend, invited me to lunch. We met at the New Orleans Athletic Club, and just before coffee he finally told me what he had called me there for.

"Did you know Sylvestre and your girl friend have been making some deals in town?"

"Who with?"

"Us. The Old Regulars."

"About what?"

He grinned, and his eyebrows lifted in a way that made his face puckishly satanic. "That's classified information, Stevie. I'll tip you before the fireworks start, though."

They were slow in starting. It was almost two weeks before Moriarity called and said, "Better come up next Monday." Then, that same night, something happened that neither the Old Regulars nor I nor anyone else had on the timetable.

There are people, places, and things that seem as indestructible as God and the devil. You cannot imagine any blow befalling them, any tumble from godhead, good or bad, that is signature to their mortality. Such a fall comes as a great personal shock, as a violent wrenching of whatever moral order exists. It even suggests that the world is a place not of design but of chaos. Its consequences are profound.

I picked up the *Times-Picayune* the next morning and felt the hieratical walls shake. There was a three-paragraph bulletin on the outside column of page one. Sylvestre Marin had had a heart attack.

The story said his condition was serious but not, presently, critical.

As soon as his personal physicians thought it wise, he would be flown to Boston to be under the care of the nation's top specialists.

I pushed the paper back. I had a definite feeling of deprivation. I hated Sylvestre Marin, but I had thought—no, I had absolutely believed—that he was impervious to the twitches of the human condition, that he was fixed in the sky. His toppling gave the feeling that nothing was fixed, that all was confusion. For a moment, I turned slow metaphorical somersaults in space, as though the law of gravity had been repealed.

I realized also that I felt a certain thrill of pleasure, even of unearned triumph, followed by a sudden shot of guilt. I sat still a few moments, adjusting, and then I called Ada.

It was the first time I had talked to her since that night Yancey had barged in. I heard the strain in my own voice, but hers was completely natural.

"I guess you know what," I said. "I need something from you on Sylvestre."

"It's already written. Quote I join the people of Louisiana in wishing a successful recovery to Sylvestre Marin, whose services have been of inestimable value to both this administration and the state. It is my understanding that Mr. Marin's condition is grave, but medical authorities are sure he will recover. Let us all pray for his speedy restoration period unquote end of statement. Okay?"

"Okay for the statement. Now, what's going to happen in the Legislature?"

Her voice might have been evasive. "We'll just have to go ahead with what's planned."

"What's that?"

"I'll tell you when I see you." Her voice was not evasive—I decided—only cautious.

But I heard it first from Moriarity. There was a note waiting in my box when I checked in at the Capitol House Sunday night: Urgent he said, when I called, and would I be waiting for him in front of the building in fifteen minutes.

He picked me up, drove a dozen blocks north, pulled in another side street, and stopped.

"Do forgive the precautions," he said. "I'm not supposed to be tipping you. But this is going to be a lot bigger than I thought."

"How come?"

With the street light behind him, his small mobile Irish face was dark as it turned toward me. "Bomb, kid, big bomb. You know what I told you about the Old Regulars and Sylvestre?"

"Yes."

"Well, he was going to push our baby through. You know the bill, the Commission Council one that fixes it to elect the commissioners by district instead of city-wide. Then the council elects the mayor. You know. It's been up before, it would hand us this town for good."

"I remember."

"Well, Sylvestre was going to go down the line for us on that, in return for certain, considerations. It was all set, then he had the heart attack. So we didn't know what was going to happen."

"I see."

"So some of us went up to see Madam Governor; Whitey Lambert and Johnny Daro and me. She was as cool as you please, she shook our hands like she didn't have a worry in the world. She might as well have said everything's under control boys and what can I do for you. We told her how we knew Sylvestre's loss was a great one and perhaps she would want to postpone the action we had agreed on. Why no, she said, I don't think that will be necessary. We're very pleased, Governor, Johnny said. Not at all, she said. Then she leaned back in the chair, and she said, I have some other legislation, gentlemen, that will help greatly in your problem. And we looked at each other, and I said, what is that, Mrs. Dallas? And she told us."

He stopped; his head was a dark circle with light behind it.

"Boy did she ever tell us. She has bills set up that would hand New Orleans to the governor on a platter. With some of it going to us, but she would damned well have the biggest half. It was good but just a little too good, you know. Finally Johnny said, I'm just not sure about all those bills, Mrs. Dallas. And she said, so sweet honey wouldn't melt in her mouth, Why, Sylvestre told me they were all part of the same project. I see, Johnny said. We all saw. It was everything or nothing and that was it boy. We were quiet for a second and Johnny finally said, Certainly, Governor."

I whistled.

"So you be all set tomorrow," Moriarity said.

"I will. And much obliged."

"Nothing, kid, nothing. Just keep that camera on me if I get up to talk. That's all I ask."

The Legislature convened next day like a well-worn record starting another turn. And then the fun began.

"Mr. Speaker," said a voice.

"The chair recognizes the gentleman from New Orleans," said the Speaker, and Representative Johnny Daro was walking up the aisle to the microphone facing the chamber.

Johnny smiled sweetly, with the utmost reasonableness, his teeth making an even white line under his short brown mustache.

"I have a little amendment to the bill appropriating state funds for the port of New Orleans," he said into the mike, still smiling, dimples showing at the corners of his mouth. "This amendment isn't a major item at all. It just brings the method of appointment of members of the dock board more in line with the main bill, the bill providing these state funds."

The page boys were swiftly distributing copies of the amendment, and one dropped on the press table. We all crowded to look.

"This amendment just gives the state some voice in the appointment of these port commissioners." The white line of teeth still showed even under the brown mustache.

I read the gray type on the thin white bond. When the three-corner shots of legal language were spent, the amendment had one intent: to give Ada and the Old Regulars complete control of the dock board.

The legislators had fallen into puzzled silence. Now they began to talk to each other, and the hum was loud. Johnny stopped talking, and continued to smile his serenely reasonable smile out at nothing.

Then a New Orleans "reform" legislator was on his feet. He clearly did not know, entirely, what was up, but he knew the Old Regulars had thrown a sneak punch.

"I move the amendment be referred to committee for further study," he called.

That was the best he could do, and it was not much. Johnny Daro spread his hands and inclined his head in generous agreement, his dimples deeper than ever. The Speaker sent the amendment to the committee.

That was just the beginning. Johnny presented the other bills. One would give Ada and the Old Regulars control of the levee board. Another was the Old Regulars' bill to have the Commission Council in cities above 250,000—New Orleans was the only one—elected by districts instead of city-wide. The next would have the mayor elected in such cities by the Commission Council instead of by the voters. And the last would set up a "police board" for the same cities, appointed by the governor and approved by the Commission Council. This would take the New Orleans police department away from the mayor and hand it to the council—and the governor.

The House was stunned as the Reichstag must have been stunned when it received certain proposals in 1933.

"Not even Huey—" somebody said at the press table.

Not even Huey had been able to take over New Orleans. This would give Ada more power than any governor in history. If she could make it stick.

The New Orleans papers screamed in black ink, New Orleans conservatives held "mass meetings" to protest, prayers were even said against the bills in certain pulpits, uptown. Telephone wires to Washington ran hot. But there was nothing Washington could do until things wound up in the Supreme Court. Meantime, Ada, and Sylvestre, owned 95 per cent of the country legislators, and the Old Regulars outnumbered their opponents from New Orleans almost two to one.

On the vote, all you could see were the green "yes" lights flashing on the big vote board. Ada signed the bills into law the next day.

"We will fight this illegal rape of the city of New Orleans with every legal means at our disposal," the mayor said. And he tried.

Injunction and setting aside followed injunction and setting aside. The city's suit testing the legality of the acts moved tortuously through the courts.

If Sylvestre had been around, he would have waited for all the courts to finish with it before he did anything. He would have known he couldn't lose anyway.

But he wasn't around, and I knew as I knew the earth turned and the tides ran that Ada would not wait.

Robert Yancey

About a month after the session, almost two after Sylvestre's attack, Ada called me in about the New Orleans thing. I had seen her the night before but we hadn't talked business.

She picked up a paper cutter and tapped the blade on her desk, looking past me to the wall behind. Then she dropped the cutter and her eyes swung down to me.

She said, "I don't see any point in waiting for the courts."

I said, "You know what he'd do."

"He isn't here."

"No."

She looked over and past me again, seeing something way off somewhere. "You remember Huey and Walmsley?"

"I remember." When Huey was governor or when O. K. Allen was governor, I forget which and it was the same anyway, Huey had sent the National Guard into New Orleans. Walmsley was mayor, and he had set up barricades. There had been fighting.

Her eyes came back full on me. "How would you like to take the Guard in and clear things up?"

"Sure. Sure. Just give me enough authority."

"You'll get the authority."

Steve Jackson

Ada's ultimatum to the dissidents in New Orleans made an eight-column black line in the papers one morning. She gave the old dock and levee board members fifteen days to get out of their offices, and turn them over to the new people (the election by districts for the new Commission Council was not technically involved, but if she and the Old Regulars got the boards, there was no doubt about the election).

If the offices were not turned over in that time, she said, she would send troops in.

I laid down the paper.

So she had finally done it. She had crossed Sylvestre, she had refused to wait for the grinding of the law, she had defied the world. Things were going to happen fast now.

Robert Yancey

Three days after Ada gave me the go-ahead, I brought her the papers. One was an order directing me to proceed. The other was my appointment as commanding officer of the Louisiana National Guard with the rank of major general.

"These'll do it," I said.

Sitting behind her desk, every yellow hair in place, the smooth oval face a piece of white marble, she read the first one and signed it. Then she read the second. Then she looked across the desk to me.

"It needs that," I said. I meant my rank. "We need that to make it work."

She smiled, just a little, with the left corner of her mouth, and said nothing. She knew she would have to sign it, though: she knew it was the only way she could be sure. Still she did not want to.

"You want me to do this little thing for you, don't you?" I said again.

She read it another time, her mouth in the same slight twist, and then she pulled the gold pen very fast from the desk holder and signed it fast, the pen scratching smooth on the white parchment.

"Okay." Her voice was absolutely nothing. "I guess that does it. I guess that makes you it."

I said, "Now you can be sure."

"I can be sure." The way she said it, it could have meant anything.

The minute that pen stopped, I was top man in uniform in Louisiana. I had both the Guard and the state police. I had more medicine than any officer since the Civil War.

Now that she had signed them, she was not thinking about the papers.

"It's firmed up." She pointed at a newspaper on her desk. "They aren't going to get out until somebody makes them."

She felt good about it. She had tasted something big and was licking her chops for something bigger. Now she was standing at the edge of the desk, moving back and forth in short steps. She felt so good she couldn't stand still.

I dropped into a chair. "I guess somebody'll just have to make them."

She looked at me, fast, and one side of her mouth twisted up in a smile, but she said nothing.

The door opened without a knock, my face and hers swung toward it, and Sylvestre Marin, who was supposed to be in Boston Hospital, walked through the doorframe and into the room.

A brown linen suit hung on him loose, he had lost maybe thirty pounds since the attack. His face was thinner, whiter, and had new grooves; his black eyes stood out bigger in it, so the face looked suspended from the eyes.

"Good morning," he said.

Ada was not stopped for more than a second. When she moved, she made it good. "Sylvestre!" She threw a big, white smile, like she had never been so glad to see anybody. She grabbed his shoulders for a second and hugged him lightly. He did not move. She stepped back. "What on earth! It's so good to see you! What a surprise!"

"I'm sure of it." His face dipped, mocking her.

"But what are you doing out of the hospital? Should you be up yet?"

He looked down at her for a second, his smile twisting under his black eyes. Finally he said, "It would seem so." He stopped and looked at me now, his eyes all blackness, and then back to her. "You've been busy, haven't you? Writing bills. Delivering ultimatums. Launching invasions." His short laugh sounded like a hard dry cough. "They have papers in Boston too, you know. Serviced by the Associated Press." He walked over to the desk, saw the order directing me to proceed, and picked it up. He read it, tore it in two, and dropped it in the wastebasket.

"Things have changed since you've been gone." Ada was cool and distant now, but not yet fighting him. "I really think that's necessary now."

"She's right," I said. When he first came in, I felt like a kid caught smoking in the basement. Now I was getting mad. "They've gotten out of hand. They need the old medicine."

Sylvestre eased himself down in the armchair, and let his cane fall loose between his legs. He grinned up at us with his new-thin mean face.

"That's true," she said. "We need direct action now."

He just looked at her, grinning.

"We'll take them. We'll take New Orleans." Her voice climbed in spite of herself. You could tell how she loved the idea and the words. "We'll take it."

Sylvestre, dead-still in his chair, swung around his death's-head white face with the sockets for eyes. They switched from her to me and back to her.

He whispered: "You won't take anything." And he looked at her with his old killer's smile.

She stared at him hard and watchful, and her voice was flat. "Don't you think this is really our best course? Now?"

"No," he said very precisely. "No. I can still turn your indiscretion and ineptitude to my advantage. What I will do—" He hit the words, hard, his voice for the first time rasping like an old man's. "What I will do, is wait for the state Supreme Court to issue its ruling. When they take it to the U.S. Supreme Court, I will wait for that court to rule. I will observe the amenities, and the court will rule for me."

Ada had turned away from him and I watched her face. It had that deep-concentration look I knew well. It was the look of some-one taking the big decision, deciding now is the time to try it, now is the time to put it all on the big play. Later, it seemed so funny. They, we, were just talking and then the bomb exploded. Well, it had been coming. It had been coming a long time.

Ada turned around to Sylvestre. Her face was white-smooth, with-out a line of expression, and her voice had nothing in it at all, and then she did it.

"We will not wait," she said. "I will brook no defiance of the proper executive power of this state. I mean to send the National Guard, of which I am by law commanding officer, into New Orleans. They will take possession of those facilities and functions that are being illegally held. They will turn them over to the bodies created by the State Legislature to exercise these functions."

And there it was. She had done it. She had broken with him. She had seen the chance to take over the state for herself, decided in seconds, and made her move.

And she could—if I went along. If I took the troops in like she wanted. She had used me before. Now she wanted to use me again. She could use me—for a price. I guess she knew that when she did it. I guess she was willing to buy.

Sylvestre looked at her. His mouth curved almost like he was smiling, only he wasn't. His face showed no surprise, nothing at all.

"Oh," he said, very soft. "Oh, I see." He looked at me. "Colonel, have you any, plans, for this particular issue?"

"I just work here," I said. "I just take orders. When I get them in writing. From the governor of the state."

He looked first at Ada, then at me. Then he started to laugh: a low mean laugh.

"You dare," he said. His eyes snapped, he was not even smiling mean now. "You two scum dare." He stood up, and walked to the window, his cane tip hitting the carpet like slow drops of water on earth. He looked out a minute, then turned around and came back to us. "Ever hear of Blanche Jamison?"

And now he did smile, while my guts dropped a thousand feet.

Ada said, "I can't recall the name."

His face swung from one of us to the other, ranging, smiling like the devil himself. "Ever hear of the murder of Blanche Jamison?"

Ada was ice. "What on earth are you talking about?"

He said very casually, "I'm talking about you two murdering Blanche Jamison."

"You lunatic," said Ada.

"*You* female fool. Didn't you think I knew all about you before I ever took you on? Didn't it occur to you I had provided myself with a few, momentos, of your career a long time ago? Didn't it occur to you that I knew about her visits? That I ran my own check when the skeleton turned up? And then the car?"

He was enjoying himself now, he had slipped from the new nasty viciousness into the old smooth viciousness.

"I had to have these assembled rather quickly, but I think they're adequate." He pulled a big manila envelope, folded for narrowness, out of his coat pocket, opened it, and took papers out. "Exhibit A. A list of certain bank withdrawals by Mrs. Dallas, two years ago. You'll note regular withdrawals of a thousand dollars, in the first ten days of every month, over a six-month period. After which they stop abruptly." He moved to another one. "Exhibit B. A notarized statement from the assistant manager of Mrs. Jamison's motel affirming she made monthly trips to Louisiana during the same period of the same months."

He was having a fine time. He was very happy.

"Fool. Senile old fool," Ada said calmly. "Do you think this confetti amounts to anything?"

"Here." He held out another piece of white paper, eyeing it almost affectionately. "I was saving this for last." He handed it to Ada. She took it, her mouth twisting down, but as she read the curve left her mouth, her eyes opened wider, and her face hardened. She handed it to me without a word, and I started to read.

I read the first sentence, and felt the quick shaking weakness in my legs and a big bulb in my throat.

It said the undersigned had seen me kill Blanche Jamison.

The big package had come. In an awful way, everything was on schedule, everything was right.

I had known it would come some day. I felt I was an ant about to be run over by a steam roller. And I had to fight the feeling that I ought to be run over by the roller, that my being run over was what was meant to be.

But I read on, and my fear changed to fury. This was not right. It was all wrong, this thing by God wasn't meant to be. I wanted to kill whoever had signed the paper. If he had been there that second, I think I would have killed him. Because it was a lie, the paper was a lie.

He said he had seen me strangle Blanche Jamison to death in her automobile parked in a motel garage south of Baton Rouge.

"It's a lie." I was boiling. "It's a lying sonofabitching lie."

"Shut up!" Ada must have been afraid I would say: I didn't strangle her, I knifed her; it wasn't in her car, it was outside; it wasn't in a motel garage, it was in the woods across the river.

I might have.

But she had stopped me.

"I saw that signature." Ada was back again in her low frightening voice.

"Louis Lemore? Yes, I did do him a favor some years ago. I got him out of a murder rap before it, materialized. This developed in him a great fervor for good works. He has done several good works since. For me."

"So he signed this lie," said Ada.

Sylvestre smiled. "What is Truth, said jesting Pilate, and would not stay for an answer. But I am not going to debate with you the nature of Truth. Though I will observe parenthetically that it invariably consists of many lies laid end to end. I will only say that I am satisfied as to the authenticity of this document and I think a jury would be. Particularly since Mr. Lemore found a bracelet marked A.M.D. and a brass uniform button marked State of Louisiana at the scene."

I hadn't been in uniform.

"More lies, I never wear bracelets." Ada did not raise her voice. She was smiling at him like he wasn't getting to her at all. "Do you really think anybody will take an ex-pimp's word over the governor's? And the commandant's?"

"Certainly not. All the governor and the commandant would have to do is take the lie detector test. As your legal adviser, the official legal adviser to the government, I would feel impelled to suggest that step to the press. It would dispel immediately the absurd accusations, wouldn't it? It would wipe out the whole annoying problem, wouldn't it?" He laughed. "The case would crack like an eggshell." His laugh now was so low you could hardly hear it. "Just pass the test."

I had frozen inside. He knew. How he knew I could not guess, but he knew what we had done. Even if he did not know how. He had framed us, the evidence was all lies, but it added up to the truth.

"Nevertheless," he said, "I just can't bring myself to see you burned. They burn you, you know. In the electric chair. And if you burn, you might get hysterical and say things better unsaid." He took two steps toward the open window, then turned back toward us. "So here's what I'm going to do for you. I'm putting up ten thousand dollars in Ada's name in a Mexico City bank. I understand, Colonel, that you have acquired certain funds of your own you can transfer. I will wait one week before I present this evidence. In that time, you can be safe in Mexico or South America. They won't extradite you. You won't,"—he slowed, and said the next word very delicately and precisely—"burn. Now, I think this is more than generous. Don't you?"

Neither of us said anything.

"You see"—he smiled his fine friendly smile—"I never take chances. Only fools take chances, only fools believe in luck. A wise man arranges things. That is why I never make mistakes."

"You pompous ass," said Ada, calmly.

His smile warped. "And who knows? With the colonel as your, ah, associate, you might find in Mexico the renaissance of your original, more appropriate, and perhaps still profitable, career. You—"

But she was on him before the words stopped, her open hand cracked across his face, and they stood looking murder at each other from a foot away. Red marks showed deep in his white cheek. She was straining like a fierce animal held by ropes, and I saw the fingers of one hand curve and stiffen like claws. I stepped in quick and grabbed her by both arms.

"Easy," I said. "Easy." It was like the eye in the tree, that day. I was holding her, I was somebody else watching all three of us. While I held and tried to quiet her, I thought that just a minute before, she had been quieting me. He had called her a murderer and she had laughed in his face. He had called her a whore and she wanted to kill him with her hands.

Now he rubbed his red-blotched cheek and laughed at her. "Of course, you can prove your innocence." The low bad laugh. "With the lie detector test." The laugh got louder. "Take the lie detector test. Break up everything with the lie detector test." His voice was shaking with his laugh now. "All you need is the lie detector test."

"Let's go," said Ada.

In the outer office, we heard him laughing through the closed door.

Outside, the November wind was blowing wet in the gray air for there was no sun. It felt like there should have been falling rain, but there was no rain yet, only the evergreens and the green lawn.

On the way to the car, we passed Huey's statue. "What do we do now?" I asked her.

She did not look at me as she said:

"I'm going to kill him."

Steve Jackson

I was dreaming. I was dreaming of tanks rolling down Third Street to the capitol, then nowhere at all but in white mists. I was lying before them, trying to crawl clear, but I could not move, and then it was not me but someone else lying there and I was trying to pull clear whoever it was and I saw it was Ada. I could not move her, and I looked almost straight up at the tank and saw under the driver's black cap the face of Col. Robert Yancey, and as I looked, it changed to Ada's face. Then I looked back at the face of the body I could not move. And that face was still Ada's.

Then something stabbed through the mists like a dagger, and stabbed again, and I knew that it was the doorbell and I had to wake. I swam up through blackness as though coming to the surface from a deep dive, and then I broke the surface and was awake and stumbling through the room to answer the door.

I pushed the buzzer that released the latch, the downstairs door creaked open, and then a woman's sharp-heeled footsteps started up the stairs. I knew who it would be.

I opened the door, yellow light pouring out and down the dark stairway. I suppose I had been waiting for her to come, these many months.

"Come in, Ada."

Rain glistened on her bright hair, and made streaming lines on her tan trench coat. She closed the door carefully and leaned against it, her arms spread only a little, tan against the dark surface of the wood. "Steve, I'm in trouble." Her voice was very calm. Her calm frightened me more than anything else.

"What is it? Here, take off that coat. Sit down."

I took the coat, spread it over a chair to dry, and poured her a glass of straight whisky.

She turned it up, drank, then held it in one hand as she looked up at me from the chair with a frightening bright smile on her death-calm face. "Yes. I'm in quite bad trouble, I think."

I wondered wildly if she were pregnant, and my glance must have shown it, for she laughed.

"No. Nothing so ingenuous. Something quite serious, my dear."

"Tell me."

"I came here to." She was deathly composed. "All of it. Though I think you have guessed the crucial part."

It was half an hour later when she had finished talking.

"What are you going to do?" I said. "Get out or—" I stopped.

"Or stay and get electrocuted?" She smiled very brightly. "Neither. Not as Sylvestre planned it."

"What then?"

"I am going to kill him." She looked at me again with the bright-death smile, and her words sank like stones in water.

I did not answer. I did not know how to answer. I heard the quick thin ticking of the clock, the loud slow thumping of my heart. I finally said, "And then?"

"Then consequence—will become consequence." Her voice was almost gay.

I struggled for the answer, the right answer, knowing as I sought that I would not find it. "Take him up. Get out. Be smart. Anything else is better."

"No." She was still bright, and deathly. "I don't think anything is. I prefer this." Her smile twisted. "I understand it is a nice comfortable chair."

There was no point talking tonight.

"Look. Stay here. We'll talk tomorrow. It may look different then."

"I should be charmed to stay. But it won't look different. Not slightly."

I gave her pajamas and turned down the other twin for her. I brought sleeping pills and a hot toddy when she was in bed.

She looked at them, smiling faintly.

"All right. Good night, Steve."

I felt myself blushing in the dark. She had thought I would sleep with her. I was not sure I could have, then, if I had wanted to.

She took the pills, and drank the drink, and I sat beside her until she was asleep. Then I tiptoed into the living room and opened the double door to the balcony. I stood inside, looking out, watching the dark spears of rain drop slanting through the dim light of the narrow street, listening to them fall unchanging on the roof above and the asphalt below. The starless black was mottling to deep gray when I went to bed.

I thought I had an answer of a kind.

I awoke the next time into full gray light flooding the windows. I jerked upright, saw the other bed was empty, and got up.

I heard Ada's footsteps in the kitchen, went to them, and saw her in front of the stove, cooking bacon, in a white apron abandoned by my Venezuelan widow. Her face was calmly cheerful and lovely; she was a suburban idyll incarnated.

And this was the governor of Louisiana, who had whored for a

living, who had murdered one blackmailer, and who had now de-
termined to kill another and burn in the chair for it.

"Hello." Her voice was clear and gay.

"Good morning." I did not know how to approach what I had
to tell her. What had been steel logic in the wet cold of dawn
simply could not invade here. But of course it had to.

"You looked so surly sleeping that I didn't have the nerve to
wake you," she smiled. "Here's coffee, and breakfast will be ready
quite soon. Now be a good boy and come kiss me."

I did.

It was the first time I had kissed her in more than six years. Her
hair smelled fresh and sweet, and I knew that for me nothing had
really changed.

She moved back, still smiling, her arms about my neck, her face
very close to mine. "Would you like to take me away for a couple of
days? Or maybe just let me stay here? I think I would rather stay
here."

I kissed her again. "Look. I think I've come up with something."

"Have some coffee first."

She poured and set it before me, and worked her fingers in my
hair as I drank. I set the cup down. The kitchen was bright. Ada
was cheerful. And I was going to bring the other in.

"What you were talking about," I said. "Last night."

"Yes?"

"Are you still hell-set on it?"

"Yes." A little of the hardness had come into her voice under the
other things.

"Don't. Take him up and leave the country. I could meet you in
Mexico City. Neither of us is really old. We still have a lot of time."

She smiled, her eyes clouded faintly, and she shook her head.
"No."

"You won't change your mind?"

"No. I won't. Don't talk about it any more. We've got two days.
Don't waste them worrying."

"All right then," I said. "Listen. I have a plan."

I told it. She could plant two people outside the door before she
shot him. They could swear they heard him trying to attack her
with a weapon. She could say later it was because she had found
out he was grafting and had threatened to expose him. She could
throw furniture and paper around to bolster the story.

With the witnesses, and if nothing went wrong, she could beat it.

"And who will these be?" she asked, the smile now crooked.

"Yancey. And me."

"Oh my God. You. What have I done to you?" Her face contorted, and I was sure she was going to cry, but she came out of it. "No. Not with you in it."

"Hell yes with me in it. He has it coming. He ought to be killed. When somebody comes at you with brass knuckles you have a right to protect yourself."

She closed her eyes tightly. "It's a good plan. A very good one." She stopped and breathed, shakily. "But I have a better."

"What?"

"Nothing you're going to be involved in or know about. When you want a room papered you hire a paperhanger, and when you want weeds trimmed you hire a gardener. I should have no trouble in finding a specialist for this problem. At any rate, I'll handle it by myself."

"You need me."

"You are going to have nothing to do with it. If you try, I'll shoot him in broad daylight in front of twenty witnesses. I mean it. Now shut up about it and stay out of it. Please. Please, Steve."

Through the days in the apartment, she was mine again. And I felt a strange sad contentment. She left at dusk on Sunday.

Robert Yancey

I knocked twice on Ada's door, opened it, and walked in. She was on her feet, waiting for me, and keyed high but under control. It was six o'clock Monday afternoon; everyone else in the building but the janitors had gone.

"What's on?" She had sent for me.

"Him," she said. "He's waiting."

"What's to see him about now?" He had us; I had spent the day getting ready to move, writing and signing bank orders for fund transfers. She hadn't said yet she would come with me, but what else could she do? He had us.

"I wanted to talk to him again."

I looked at her close. "All right then. I don't see it'll do any good though."

We went down the corridor, through his reception room, and into his office. He was sitting at the desk, his head sunk between his shoulders, like an old bulldog. Jesus he looked old.

He gave that file-rasp laugh. "The suppliants arrive. You are suppliants, aren't you? You do have a deal, don't you?"

"Yes," said Ada.

His voice changed. "I've already given you your deal."

"I think you ought to listen."

He laughed, mean. "Go ahead, then. I can do with some amusement." He grinned, his head moving from one of us to the other, God he looked mean. He never looked like what he was before the attack. Now everything was there where you could see it. Looking at him, I wondered for a second if I would ever look like that.

"I am asking you to tear up those lies," Ada said.

He laughed again. "You disappoint me. Is that the best you can do?"

"I ask you again. Please tear those things up. I entreat you. I beg you." But there wasn't any begging in her voice.

"What are you wasting my time for?"

"Because I wanted to give you a chance."

"Give *me* a chance?" His mouth made his new ugly grin, and his thin shoulders moved in a coughing chuckle. "And what chance were you going to give me?"

"The chance to live," said Ada. She was very calm. "Once more. I entreat you."

His face changed, twisting in anger, and he stood up, leaning heavy on the desk. "You stupid bitch. Don't think you can. My chauffeur is down in the lot and he knows where I am and who with. I came prepared for hysteria. It won't do you any good. Don't think it can." He was getting worked up.

"Not that you deserve to live. You are a perverted abomination," Ada said. "You are filth."

He moved toward her, his cane raised, hate pouring from his face. He would never have made that move before. The coronary had changed him.

And then he stopped. He lowered the cane and grinned. "Oh no. No my dear Mrs. Dallas you are not going to induce an attack."

"I have no idea of inducing an attack," Ada said very calmly. "I'm going to kill you."

He started. "You—" He stepped forward, then back and relaxed. "No. You wouldn't dare. I won't excite myself."

"Oh I'm not going to kill you now. And not, personally. I'm even giving you the resignation you want, now. But wherever I am, one day I am going to have you killed and you can't stop me."

"Naaayhh—" His face twisted into ugliness.

"I'll have you followed and followed and if it takes a month or a year or ten years my, employees, will come to the place and the time. And you won't have any idea when or where." She stepped closer to him. "It'll be completely unpredictable. You won't like that, will you, Sylvestre? It'll be something you can't predict or control and all you can do is wait."

He made a sound that could have been a snarl or a cough, and his lips pulled back over his teeth. He looked not only angry but afraid. I had never seen him afraid before. "No you won't, no you won't, I'll use the stuff now. They'll burn you both."

Ada kept on as though she hadn't heard him. "There'll be no way to predict it. You'll know your death is already bought and paid for. But you won't know when, or where. You can't plan. You won't know what to do."

"I'll—you bitch, goddamn you to hell, you bitch . . ."

"You can't do anything," she went on in the same soft voice. "You can't fix it or control it. Do you understand that? You can't do anything about it."

He made a noise like I had never heard a human make and raised his cane again. It was impossible to believe this was Sylvestre. But he was sick, he was very sick, and she had hit him in his sickness.

He swung at her and she stepped back, not seeming to hurry, and the cane whushed through the air and hit the carpet. He stumbled after her.

She said the same soft way, "You can't do anything about it," and he swung again, wildly, and he missed by two feet and as the cane cut the air and fell, he followed it to the floor, face down.

He moved, trying to get up.

Ada stepped almost over him. "It'll be something you can't plan for," she said. "You'll be helpless." He tried to push himself up, rose six inches and dropped again. Now he did not move.

We were standing there, looking down at him, for almost half a minute. Then I knelt and turned him over. His eyes were open and rolled back and I put my ear to his chest to make sure. I stood up. "My God."

She nodded and her eyes closed for a second. I saw her sway on her feet. "You sit down," I said. She let me ease her into a chair.

"A good joke on the old devil," I said, though I did not exactly feel like laughing.

"Yes," she whispered. "Yes. Only fools believe in luck. A wise man arranges things."

I looked at her, I did not know what she was talking about, and then I knew she was mimicking Sylvestre. "Yeah," I said.

"He had it planned so carefully. Everything worked out. Except for the unreliable muscle. What a miserable muscle to upset such excellent plans."

"I'd say you gave that muscle a kind of helping hand." I felt myself shaking, I guess with relief. Nothing and nobody to stop us now.

She did not answer, and suddenly she was crying.

"Yeah," I said. "Only fools believe in luck."

She was crying more loudly.

"I'll call the ambulance," I said.

All we had to worry about now were the other copies of that affidavit. The first thing we did was to go through his desk and his safe in the capitol. Nothing there.

Next was his home office in the parish. I went in next day with a couple of troopers, showed his secretary a forged letter directing us to get the safe combination from her in the event of his unexpected demise, and to take certain things out. The secretary was not even suspicious, for that was just what he might have done. She gave us the combo, I opened the safe, and sure enough, in one neat folder marked B.J. were six copies of that phony statement. I took them, thanked the secretary kindly, and went home and burned them.

Next day I called in Louis Lemore.

"Sit down," I said. "Have a cigarette. Hope you had an easy drive from New Orleans."

"Thanks." He had a smooth dark face with brown eyes that would not stay still in it.

"Well." It was good to be sure, to have all the cards. "Sylvestre's dead."

"Yeah." The eyes bounced from me to one wall to the other and back to me.

"I found a little folder in his desk with some information. However, I don't consider it absolutely necessary to keep the file active." I let that sink in. "I thought you might be interested to hear it." I meant the file on his murder, and I looked at him to see if he understood, and he understood, all right.

The brown eyes stopped in the middle of a bounce, right on me. "I might."

"I have it right here." I pulled it out. "As I say, I see no reason to keep the file active. Unless of course you have some documents that might force a reopening. Like, say, affidavits."

I looked at him hard and he looked back and there was no doubt we understood each other.

"No, sir. I've got no affidavits. I'm not planning to get no affidavits."

"Good. Then I'll just deactivate this and take it home so nobody can open the case again. By mistake."

He understood that, too.

That night I told Ada.

"All clear, baby. That other case is closed. Nobody but you and me, on top of the world and running it forever. Now we'll take New Orleans."

"Forever is a long time," she said.

Tommy Dallas

Earl and I drove all night from Florida for Sylvestre's funeral. I had to go. I guess I couldn't believe it was true until I saw him in the coffin.

I saw him. It was true.

I looked down at the hard face, that didn't look no different from the way it ever had except it was maybe thinner and eyelids like thin paper were closed down over his eyes. In the years I had been with him I had never seen him with his eyes closed before. "Only a fool believes in luck," he had said. And he had tried to kill me, and there he was, and here I was, and what did he have to say about luck now?

It was as good a day as any to be buried.

The sky was gray, and a cold wind came blowing across the tombstones. The gravediggers bent and swung their shovels. I watched the brown dirt pile and spread over the silver-trimmed casket, and I tried to be sorry for Sylvestre because he was dead and a long time ago he had been nice to me. But the only thing I could think was: *You sonofabitch, you tried to do this to me, and here you are and here I am.*

That was no way to think about a dead man, and I tried hard to do better, and I finally got to where I wasn't thinking about Sylvestre at all, only about how cold and damp it was, and how good a straight shot would go, and I sure as hell would go for one the minute this was over.

Something yellow flashed, and I started, and then I knew it was just a flash bulb. I wasn't used to them any more. Somebody was shooting Ada and me together. They hadn't had the chance for that shot in a hell of a long time.

I felt her hand on my arm, for the next picture of course, and I looked at her sideways; at her face, all smooth and white and unpainted under a black half-veil. She looked serious but not sad, I thought; I wondered how she would look if she knew what I had and how I was going to use it.

The yellow flash popped again. "You can move it now," I whispered. "Picture's over."

She did not move her hand, though, and her face did not show that she heard.

I had a sudden crazy thought. "Did you take care of him too?"

Her face still did not change except for her lips coming together a little tighter.

Then I couldn't resist it. "I went to Mobile last week. Stayed at the Paradiso Motel. Very interesting place."

Her face did show something. Not much, but it was there. I had seen it. Let her sweat now, let her sweat good.

Finally the funeral was over, and I was in my Cad where Earl was waiting. I was sure as hell not leaving with her. Let her explain it.

"Stop at that bar," I told Earl, and he did.

It had a sign outside that said: GASTON'S. Inside, the air was heavy with cigar smoke, the lights shone on the bar, and the

whisky was warm going down. Against the back wall was a blackboard with horse-race entries and in front of it sat shirt-sleeved
men playing poker and dominoes. One bunch started laughing, and
the noise filled the whole warm room.

Sylvestre was out there in the ground, dead, and I was in here,
alive.

"Another," I said to the bartender.

Robert Yancey

Two days after Sylvestre's funeral, I
rode down the Air-line Highway in the back seat of a command
car with two stars on my collar and a division of troops behind me.
The whole division of course did not have wheels, but there were
a hell of a lot of wheels, and they were all mine. A dozen light
tanks, and twelve tank destroyers, and more weapons carriers,
jeeps, and trucks than you could count. And all mine.

Christ, if I could have gone into Remagen that way. But we were
only going to New Orleans, and the only lines to attack were flimsy
half-assed barricades, and the only opposing force was some New
Orleans cops.

Of course they would not resist when they saw us. When they
saw us rolling down the street, light tanks, td's, trucks, and troops,
they would back down in a hell of a hurry. Nobody but goddamn
fools would try to stand up to a semimechanized division with
billies and pistols.

I had carried the big redhead, Paxton, along as a special orderly,
not because he was bright but because he said what I wanted to
hear when I wanted to hear it.

"A great day, huh, Colonel?" he said now. "Excuse *me*. I mean
General."

"Think nothing of it." I laughed a little.

"By God, this is the way it ought to be, huh, Col-*General*. You
and a whole damn army behind you."

I laughed.

"Yessir, the day will come when you'll have more than one division back there. General. It'll sure come and when it does why by
God I sure want to be there with you."

"You know, Paxton, you just may be."

"Hot damn," he said. "Hot damn."

I laughed. The command car rolled ahead, not so fast that the rest couldn't keep up. We passed through the outskirts and then the highway became Tulane Avenue, and crossed the big bridge over the dry bed of the old navigation canal. After that Broad Street and then Canal. The main line.

It was then that we rolled up to the line of little wooden carpenters' horses and the blue policemen standing in front.

"Stop here," I told the driver, and I felt the command car ease to a stop, and heard all the vehicles groan to a stop, down the road for miles back. And only a little thin line of New Orleans cops in front.

I started to get out and Paxton touched my arm.

"Hadn't you better stay in the car, sir?"

"Boy, I'm no headquarters general." I got out, and walked by myself up to the captain of police at the barricade.

"You know why we're here," I said.

"I got my own orders, General."

I took the paper out of my inside blouse pocket. "Here is a writ from the Supreme Court of Louisiana. It requires that you turn over without resistance all offices, equipment, and records of the Board of Port Commissioners and the New Orleans Levee Board, members of which have been duly appointed by law by the Governor of Louisiana."

"We got our orders."

"This writ further authorizes the State of Louisiana to take any measures necessary to enforce this writ. Any measures."

"Like I said, General. We got our own orders."

"Look, man. Do you see that stuff back there? Do you want it to turn loose on you?"

His face said he did not want it to turn loose a damn bit. But he said in a very thin and dry voice, "Orders."

"I'll tell you. I don't want any bloodshed. I'll give you thirty minutes to change your mind. Then we're coming through."

I turned sharp and walked back. I felt great with the two stars. Being a general does something for you. It means you've made the real breakthrough, you're one of the ones that run things. Great was the only word.

I climbed back in the command car. "Pull into the shade," I said. "We'll wait thirty minutes. Now bring up the light tanks."

It was hot as hell even in the shade. I felt the sweat soaking my armpits and streaking my face, but I wouldn't take off the blouse. You got to keep a thing like this strictly regulation.

"They ain't really going to try to shoot it out, are they, General?" Paxton said.

Sixteen minutes of the thirty had gone.

"Nah," I said. "Nobody could be that dumb."

But they stood up there and gave no signs of moving.

Then the tanks came up, six of them; grinding, coughing, stopping, the turrets not closed, heads of the drivers showing above the turrets like heads of the tanks themselves, their bulb-headed thin-shafted ninety millimeters pointing out and up at a forty-five-degree angle.

I looked at them, looked at my watch, and waited some more. When twenty-five of the thirty minutes were gone, I got out again and walked over to the captain at the barricades. He was sweating through his blue shirt in big dark patches, his fleshy red face was streaked with sweat, and he was not anxious to start anything at all.

"How about it, Captain?" I said.

His voice missed, and then croaked. "Orders. I got orders."

"Okay." I shrugged my shoulders. "Have it your way."

I went back, not to the command car but to the lead tank, climbed up and got in beside the tank captain.

"You ready?" I said.

"All ready, General."

I made the rev-up sign with my right arm, and heard the grinding motor noise behind me start, pick up, and swell until it was a cement mixer in my ear. I looked at my watch: time now, but I would give them two more minutes. I held up two fingers and waved them at the police captain. He wiped his face with a big white handkerchief. The policemen stood in a straight line before the barricades. I watched the second hand of the watch sweeping the last circle.

Then I said to the tank driver, "Let's go. Dead slow." We did not close the hatch. I waved the ones behind forward with my arm, and we rolled toward the barricade.

"Don't stop and don't speed up," I said. "If they get in your way just keep going."

The orders were already out not to fire unless fired upon. I halfway hoped we would be fired upon.

Past the bulb nose of the long gun I saw the straight line of blue cops, and above and past them the long bridge against the deep hot sky. The cops did not have their guns out. I did not think they would pull them. I heard the tank treads grinding over the concrete. The blue figures did not move. We were thirty feet away.

"Don't slow and don't turn," I yelled in the driver's ear.

The treads kept grinding, the blue shapes came taller and taller, and then the line had shattered and they were walking out of the way, fast, very fast, but not running, as though it was part of a plan, and I guess it was. Then there was nothing in front but the dark stick figure lines of the little carpenters' horses.

I did not even feel them as we hit, thought I heard the wood crunch under the treads. Nobody and nothing could stop us, now.

We rolled along Tulane, dead-slow, the treads grinding the asphalt like a meat chopper. People crowded both sides of the street as far up ahead as you could see, their faces close together in rows like bullets on a cartridge belt. I looked ahead and could see the crowd all together; then I looked straight to the sides and each face was different, each face was somebody. I remembered how it had been when I fought the light-heavyweight for school: the crowd nothing but a big blackness out there, then in a clinch you would look over his shoulder and see faces like they were a foot away, every line, every expression, you could almost hear them thinking, you could hear noise and see their lips yell *Kill him Yancey kill him!* It was that way now when I looked straight to the side. I saw the faces so clear that for a second I felt I was out there with them, watching myself go down the street in a light tank, maybe even thinking, *Look at that bastard, look at him.*

Then at one corner, up ahead maybe two blocks, a figure fragmented off from the crowd, waved both arms, and I thought what the hell. Then I saw it was Ada. I gave the halt signal, and the whole column, the whole division behind me eased and stopped for Ada. She walked to the tank, not hurrying, still moving fast, her white skirt swirling with her steps, and looked up at me looking down over the side of the tank. She was smiling like she had never felt so good.

"Is everything all right?" she said.

"Sure," I said. "Why wouldn't it be?"

She nodded, she was very very satisfied. "Okay," she said. "Get on with it." Still smiling, she stepped back from the tank and walked back to where she had been.

I knew why she had done it. She had wanted to show all New Orleans that the tanks and men were hers, that she had sent them, and she could command them. She wanted to show that it was really her taking the town. And I guess she did, all right. Only they didn't know what I knew. I knew she was as much mine as I was hers.

I started the tank, and knew the division was starting behind me. It was a great feeling.

Steve Jackson

New Orleans crumpled like those little sticks of wood that the eminent Colonel, excuse me, the eminent Major General Robert Yancey ran down in his tank. It was all Ada's. Shared of course by the Old Regulars. But when Ada's division took the streets that day to enforce Ada's laws, no one had any doubt about whom the city, or anything else, belonged to.

I remembered her face as she had watched the tanks crawl down Canal. In her private interior vision, she was clearly up there in the front tank, even if, actually, she had had to settle for a good clear view of her own triumphal procession. The Romans had always had a slave in the chariot to whisper, "Remember, you are only a man." She suffered no such annoying strictures.

She has done it all, I thought. She has completed the thing she started back before she even knew what it was. What was there left for her now?

The first thing was another party, in the Orleans Club. And I went, in tails I had not worn since her debacle in the same place, years before.

She received, quite deliberately, without escort. That last time, she had been the first lady, the wife of a governor who was a hill-billy singer and a parish sheriff before he was a governor. This time, she was herself the anointed governor of Louisiana, whose tanks had just taken the city of New Orleans.

Greeting the guests as they entered was a battery of six males of various official positions, all in white tie except Maj. Gen. Robert Yancey, who was in military full dress with his two shining stars. But Ada awaited the guests alone and apart, like royalty.

Almost all of them came, all who had to live in the city and seek their livelihoods and pleasures in it. There were of course exceptions. Mrs. Henri de la Peyre Navarre did not appear; she had no interest in revenue or fear of reprisal, and she considered herself the only royalty of consequence. But the half-dozen families who supported her, because she was a de la Peyre and Navarre, did come, and others came, and they all made obeisances of a sort—reluctant, stiff, painful as self-flagellation. I recognized from her other party the Webster Reillys, the Benjamin Lewins, Mrs. Dorothea Grant, the William di Frassos, and many others. Not present but well remembered were Dr. Smith, Blair DeNegre, Colonel Bartlett, and Von Paulus.

Also not present were certain other guests from that occasion: for example, Charles Cegiano, Arnie Morris, Charles Lemond, and Louis Lemore.

Ada received them coldly, with a regal inclination of her head, without a word, without a smile.

She did speak to me. "So good of you to come, Steve." She smiled warmly, I moved on, and as at the touch of a switch, her face froze again into imperial ice.

The band played, the punch receded in the great crystal bowls, the party ran its straight decorous decreed chilling course, and was liquidated precisely on schedule.

I was taking my leave of the hostess when she said, "Steve. Come to supper. I want to talk to you."

"Is that an order?"

She smiled, almost apologetically. "Will you please?"

She had the same St. Charles Avenue castle as that agonizing time before. I am sure she had chosen it deliberately. But—she said, as her butler wheeled in white turkey, pink and golden ham, and bucketed champagne—she had only taken it for thirty days.

"No extended whirl this time?" I said.

She smiled with a kind of grim limited satisfaction. "No. Not this time. This time I simply wanted to prove a point."

"And I guess you did that."

"I guess I did," she said, still smiling, and sank back into the red cushioning of a chair that looked not unlike a throne. "I guess I did at that."

"So you won't be staying long then."

"I won't be staying at all. But I could. This time I could. Let me show you." She stood and walked across the room, still in the formidable blue gown—for she had not slipped into something more comfortable, she clearly considered this one quite comfortable enough. She stopped at a white-veneered Louis Quatorze desk, extracted a handful of white envelopes from the drawer, came back and handed them to me. "Look."

I shuffled through them. They were all invitations to parties, the very best parties, given by the very best people.

It was odd, and funny, and pathetic, that the governor of a state should feel that a victory was crowned by a handful of engraved invitations. I suppose it could happen only in New Orleans.

She smiled, wearily, triumphantly, and in a kind of amusement. "Quite flattering, isn't it? Or do you suppose they just might remember Dr. Sterling Smith and DeNegre and Colonel Bartlett? To say nothing of the tanks on Canal Street?"

I shrugged. She had answered herself. And I felt what I had not felt for her since I could remember: pity. She was this instant the spurned Irish Channel waif. She had bludgeoned her way into the recognition she had longed for, and she knew as she received it that it was dead and nothing. For a moment, I wanted to comfort her. But I looked at the carved statuary of her face and the awesome lines of her gown and I knew I could not. How do you comfort an empress?

"No," she said. "I won't go, not to any of them. But they *had* to invite me, they damned well did. I *made* them. Yes, by God, I made them." And now it was triumph alone that shone coldly in her face.

Then she smiled, quite differently, and said, "Let's have some champagne." I poured, and she put her hand on mine as I passed her glass. But that was all.

She returned to Baton Rouge and the capitol the next day in the gubernatorial limousine of mortuarial black behind six siren-shrilling motorcycle policemen. After her departure, I had a feeling of loss, like that I had known the day she left me alone in the hotel room on the island. Something had gone. I felt it begin to go that minute I saw her tanks turn into Canal Street. It was not so much that she had changed as that she had succeeded, completely. Total success sets its winner apart like nothing else.

I wondered if this were the point, the point at which the downturn of power becomes visible, a point that is always reached. This much I had learned from a study on which I had embarked as Ada rose: the study of the trajectories in history of the Men on Horseback. Ada of course was no man (not by a damned sight) and that Cadillac was not a horse even if it had 380 of them under the hood. But except for her biological concavities and convexities, she met the specifications. And while all of them, from Horemheb through Napoleon to Huey, were opportunists and were driven by self, were concerned finally only with self, they worked out larger ends unwittingly. It seemed that the achievement of power depended on how useful they were to the Forces, which did not give a damn about one man or a thousand except as this man or these thousand men were useful to them.

Then, after they had used the Man on Horseback as their spearpoint, the Forces finally left him to himself, and the down curve of the trajectory began.

What was this point? Had she come to it?

Tommy Dallas

I read about her taking New Orleans with tanks in the paper that hit the beach house mailbox at two in the afternoon. The first thing I thought was: Why? Why did she do it? She didn't have to, she had everything already, with a little waiting.

Then I thought, maybe I had missed the perfect chance to use what I had and what I knew. Maybe I hadn't. I didn't really have enough proof yet. But mostly, I wanted to be able to follow through personally. And that would take time.

Then I looked out at the water and thought by God today I start.

I walked down the beach, into the water, and started to swim.
The swells came at me, and I ducked into them just right and took them and kept going. I went out maybe three hundred yards, turned around, swimming slow for the beach, waiting for the first one, and then I saw it coming. I swam fast, and was going fast when it hit, and kept stroking like hell, and felt myself flying on top of it. Then it was gone, and I was swimming alone. I had done it, I had timed myself into it. I waited for the next, and I rode that one, and the one after that, and the first thing you know I had ridden them home, all the way to the beach. I staggered out of the water, my knees buckling just a little, walked a few feet, and lay face up in the sand while the old sun poured it in.

Next night, I decided to try something else. I left Earl and drove to Mobile, almost a couple hundred miles. I put in a call to the same place for the same redhead.

When I left at noon, she said, "You can come back any time you want, Daddy. Just any time."

After two years I was well.

For a long time there I had thought of nothing but getting even with Ada and Sylvestre. I had thought of nothing else. Now, Sylvestre was out of it, Ada remained. It was still the biggest thing in the world but it wasn't the only thing. It was mixed up with a hell of a lot else.

It was getting dark when I got back to Florida. Earl was in the living room. When I walked in, I said:

"Pack our things, boy. We going back to town."

"Back to where, Governor?"

"Back to *town,* I said. To New Orleans."

I wrapped that picture, still on the scrapbook page, put it in a manila folder, and put the folder on the bottom of my bag.

I patted it. It was my ticket, my return ticket.

Robert Yancey

I was bored as hell. And then, when it looked like the situation was absolutely under control, things started to pop up. It was like a blanket stretched over bedsprings, smooth all over, and then over in the far corner a spring goes *poinggg* and pops up and makes a point under the blanket. Then you lift the blanket and push the spring in place and cover it again, and then another spring goes *poinggg,* and you fix that. Then one pops up in the middle of the blanket and another somewhere else and another and another, and you start hitting them with a hammer. And I was the boy that had to hit them.

I told myself that I did not like it, hitting at people one at a time who could not do anything but take it. But I was lying. I did like it. I liked getting in the cars at night and streaking on the white asphalt through the black night over the state to wherever we were going, and I liked whatever it was we were going to do, and I liked coming back feeling I had done something. I liked being in motion, and having an objective, and taking it. I had faced a long time ago that between doing nothing and doing something bad, I would always do the something.

The first time we worked on a man personally, instead of just breaking up his property that was technically illegal, was over in Lafayette parish. The man started making speeches against Ada, and against the administration, and particularly against me. He called me a fascist thug. He owned a hardware store and his name was Etrangere. He had no interests involved, I wondered why he did it, but he did and he didn't stop. One night, without mentioning it to Ada, I took Paxton and a couple of other boys I could trust over in plain clothes.

I watched from the car while they gave it to him:

A little black-headed jerk in a white nightshirt, the white nightshirt all you could see in the dark under the pine trees that made dark long triangles against the stars. The white shape twisting and dancing and reeling in the black. Under open hands that went: *Pow. Pow. Pow.* Each one apart. Each one separate. He did not scream. I heard the *pow pow pow,* and I heard him grunt and gasp, but he did not scream. I was uneasy when he did not. It is more natural to scream. It is healthier.

On the ride back, I felt strange, and surprised, and I guess shocked is the only word, at myself. I had liked watching him get it. I could not remember having liked anything like that before. I had liked a fight, and I had liked winning, but not this. I guess when a man gets started, he can turn into a real bastard. But probably it had been there before. Now that I was committed to operating this way, it just came out. And I was going to operate, I was going to run the state, and nobody was going to stop me. Ada or anybody else.

All the papers in the state were full of the mysterious beating. Everybody blamed me. This made me sore as hell. How did they know? What if it was true, they didn't know.

Ada was furious. She had told me not to do anything about Etrangere, just to ride with it.

"Goddamn you," she said. "What good do you think this does? You'll lose us the people instead of winning them. Let them talk. Let them talk all they want. The worst thing you can do is shut them up with brass knucks."

"You didn't mind those brass knucks rolling down Canal Street, baby."

"Don't call me baby." Her voice was not loud, but it chilled me. Even with me knowing she could do nothing, it chilled me.

But I knew where I stood. So did she.

"I can fire you," she said. "I can fire you and stop this and you won't open your mouth. It's your neck, too."

"Nobody ever said I'd tell about that. There's other things to tell, though." She knew what I meant: about her high-class whoring.

"You." Her face said: *I hate you.*

She hurt my feelings. I said, "I don't like to say things like that. You always crowd me into them. I'm a good guy if you just give me a chance."

She laughed out loud.

"I am. You talk about firing me and expect me just to take it. You shouldn't talk like that to me. We've been through a lot together. We ought to be friends, all the time."

"I recall your friendly actions."

She wouldn't let me forget *that.* When I had made her beg. It seemed so long ago.

Anyway she couldn't stop me. Nobody could stop me. I could do anything I wanted. But I could afford to be generous.

"Okay," I said. "I'll go easy."

But as soon as I let up on the pressure, we started getting backsliders. I had to get back into action. I picked a couple of big spots over by the Texas line, that hadn't contributed the first time I asked. And I took them. I mean I took them good. I wanted to make an example, and I did. We broke up everything but the walls and even arrested some of the customers.

"That ought to do it, General," Paxton said from beside me on the front seat, while we whipped along the white concrete all fringed by dark shapes of the country under the November moon.

"Yeah," I said. "Yeah. I guess it will."

After that, there wasn't much trouble. Only a few holdouts and I would take care of them soon enough.

And I was getting rich. All at once. I had never expected to, and to tell the truth I had never worried too much about it. I was more interested in a lot of things than money. I made them pay because now I could and it gave me a reason to move if they didn't pay. But I hadn't really cared about the dough. What I wanted was action.

When I finally started collecting though I found out I liked having money. It was nice to have, it was power. Then I wanted more. I wanted lots more. I wanted all I could get.

Steve Jackson

As the administration hit harder and harder over the state, to clear up the pockets of resistance, I saw less and less of her. Part of this came from my disapproval of Yancey's activities, for which she was, after all, responsible. Part of it came, I thought, from feelings of guilt or embarrassment she was surely entertaining. At least I hoped she was.

That sudden weekend before Sylvestre's death was sliding further and further away, its residue of warmth growing cooler and cooler. I had not seen her for several weeks, when somebody worked over an old Cajun tavern-keeper in Calcasieu parish, for—it seemed clear —having missed too many payments. To Gen. Robert Yancey? Or to Ada? The question had a certain significance, for me.

After that, I went through back newspapers and clipped every story suggesting either police oppression or "unidentified assailants" violence. They made a considerable package.

All of the incidents had taken place since the tanks took New Orleans. That seemed, then, to have been the point of her complete commitment to violence, which was another way of saying her complete commitment to Yancey.

I still could not believe she had ordered the beatings herself. And yet there they were.

I pasted the clips on sheets of white paper, very neatly, wrote on a cover sheet: "—Thought these might interest you—," signed it, marked it "Personal," and sent it to Gov. Ada Dallas, the Capitol, Baton Rouge, Louisiana.

I did not hear from her immediately. I told myself I did not expect to. Still I was not surprised, in fact I felt an odd and unanticipated sense of completion, when I answered the telephone in my apartment early Saturday afternoon, and heard the voice that was like none other in the world say, "Hello, Steve?"

I agreed to meet her at the Chalmette Duelling Oaks, in an hour.

In Saturday afternoon traffic it took more time than I'd figured. She was already parked, her rented anonymous Pontiac standing solitary before the thick black-trunked trees.

She greeted me with a casual ambiguous hello, and we walked silently between the great twisted oaks, their heavy green foliage a canopy over soft green turf.

"Is this all right?" she asked.

"Fine. I don't have any pistols though."

She smiled with the perfunctoriness that my remark deserved.

I wondered why she had chosen to meet me in New Orleans. I could have gone (and would have gone) into her office in the capitol at high noon, and nobody would have cared if they had noticed. I suppose it was more personal out of the capitol and out of the mansion. Well. What the hell.

She wanted to make an explanation and rid herself of the flyspeck of a burden I had imposed. If I did not accept the explanation, I was a damned fool and the hell with me. If I did, she was justified. Either way she had wiped off the flyspeck.

I sat on the grass against the trunk of one of the oaks, its bark rough and hard and bracing against my spine. She took off her coat, spread it, tweed down, on the ground, and sat gracefully.

"I got your letter," she said. "With enclosures."

"Yes."

I looked at her face, a white sharp cameo with her hair hidden.

She was not looking at me but at something a great distance away.

Still looking at whatever it was, she said, "It's not me. It is not me."

I did not answer.

She spoke again. "Steve, I'm not. I am not having Yancey do these things."

I watched autos pass out on the road, some slowing for a view of the oaks. It was odd nobody was wandering around today.

"Do you believe me?"

"He's your appointee," I said. "Isn't he?"

"Yes. Yes, he is."

"Then how can you avoid responsibility for him?"

"It isn't that simple. I can't fire him."

I heard the cars hum soothingly on the road. The leaves overhead rustled in low whispers, and I heard a jay calling *kauw-kauw-kauw*. For some reason, she shivered.

"Are you cold?" I said. "Take my coat."

"No. It's all right."

I put it over her shoulders, anyway.

"The—" and I stopped. I did not want to say it. I had tried to forget that I knew. But it lay there, cold and dark in the shadows under the oaks.

"You know why I can't stop him. I wish I could, I've tried. But I can't."

"He's ruining you," I said.

"I know. He's like a leopard, he's gone crazy with the blood taste."

"Get rid of him. Before he destroys you."

"Any suggestions?" She smiled crookedly. "Shall I shoot him? Or poison him? Or just hex him?" Her face and voice changed. "Steve, what can I do?"

"Why ask me?"

I saw her smile crooked in the shadow. "Because you're my conscience. Don't you know that?"

"Not by a damned sight." I felt my cheeks burning.

"Anyway I'm asking. What can I do?"

I took a long breath, and considered. "It seems to me there are various possibilities. One, you could fire him. Only you can't. Two, you could resign as governor and the next governor could fire him

and maybe put him in jail. Three, you can go along the way you
are and discourage him as much as you can. Will that do any good?"

"No."

"So you can quit or you can go along. Which?"

She did not answer.

"Which?" I prodded. "Will you quit?"

"No," she said.

I said nothing.

"If I stepped down now, I'd be torn to pieces. You know that.
Once you close your hand on it, you can't let go."

I still did not answer.

"I won't lie to you. Even if I could"—and she faced me directly
—"I wouldn't."

"Then do something, Ada. Soon."

There was no point in saying what we both knew: that the mes-
sianic image of herself had been undergoing a transformation since
the tanks rolled down Canal Street, and that Yancey's activities
were accelerating the process.

But she might beat it yet. She had beaten doom before. I hoped
she would, again.

Robert Yancey

When she called me in, after she got
back from New Orleans, she had that look that said: *I don't care
what you're getting at night, you do what I tell you in the daytime.*

But we both knew she couldn't tell me anything.

I dropped into the big chair and put one leg over its arm.

"Hi," I said.

She pretended to be busy writing something, then she looked up
at me all at once, hard.

"You're ruining us," she said. She got up and walked around the
desk to look down at me. "You're ruining us and I'm not having
any more."

I moved my leg from the arm, easy, and stood up, easy.

"Ruining hell." And I reached in my pocket and pulled out something. "Here."

And I handed her my surprise, or my surprises, for there were four of them.

She took them, all suspicion, opened and ran through them. I watched her eyes go narrow, then wide, then narrow again.

They were bank books, from banks in Texas, Mississippi, Arkansas, under four different women's names: Stella Houston, Eve O'Grady, Eva Dart, and Mary Malone. They had deposit entries coming to $220,000.

"Your half," I said.

Her arm holding the books dropped by her side, and she looked out the window.

I followed her over and looked out myself. It was almost five o'clock, and people were streaming out of the building towards their cars, some in the lane out front and some in the back lot. In the green out there was old Huey, looking like he owned it all. And he had, once. Maybe she was thinking the same thing: that she owned it all. But she only owned part of it. The other part was mine, and it was going to be the biggest part.

"If you want me to give it back—"

She didn't say anything.

"Or if you *really* want me to cut it out—"

She still did not say anything.

"That's three months' work. In two years, you'd have an awful big campaign fund."

Her head swung toward me, and her eyes saw me clearly.

"Yes." Her voice was very precise and deliberate. "It would make a hell of a campaign fund."

"Do you want me to stop, now?"

"No," she said, still clear and careful. "I don't want you to stop collecting. But no more rough stuff. Do you understand me?"

"I got you, hon."

Things finally were going so smooth that I couldn't help wishing for the good old days. Now everything was too wrapped up. All I had to do now was to pick up the money and say, "Thank you."

No more streaking down the old slab in the moonlight, no more good old ax-weight on the arms up high, no more sweet sting on the palms and the bastard reeling when you hit. That was all over and done with.

Now there was:

"Have a cigar, General? A drink, General?"

The brief case full of the old green laid careless across the desk, both of us pretending to pay no attention to it until I picked it up, never counting it inside. I never had to. I knew it would be right. They knew better than to have it less than right.

Sometimes the desk was smooth mahogany under glass, sometimes chipped and scarred oak, sometimes just a wooden rickety-legged table. And the walls behind it might be dark rich panels, or fancy wallpaper, or peeling plaster, or even boards. And the face across it might be smooth and well fleshed and over a hand-painted tie, or it might be wrinkled and hard over a dirty open-throated shirt. We were impartial. We let everybody contribute.

There were no beefs. There was no trouble.

"How's everything, General?"

"Is everything all right, General?"

"You're looking fine, General."

"How is the Governor, General?"

"Give the Governor my best, General."

Or if they thought they were Inside:

"How is Ada? Tell Ada we sure want her to come see us, sometime, real soon."

And that was the way it was. Smooth. Under control. Easy.

And I felt restless and mean, like occupation troops. It was too wrapped up. The state was wrapped up; Ada in the only way I could have her was wrapped up. Now I was just a coupon collector. I had no need to move, no chance to move. I tried to make like piling up the money was a substitute, that getting rich was action. But it wasn't. I could feel the juice inside turning sour, building pressure, dribbling off in those picayune meannesses, again. And I could feel it after me again.

Some days I would not think about it at all. Then it would hit like a projectile *whuh-whuh-whuh*-ing in to the dirt at your feet and bursting in orange and black and wind. All of it: the big dark limb, the jays *caw-caw*-ing in the shadowed woods, the look on her face turning, and the grinding shock of the knife driving. The pile under the coat under the tree, and Ada and me on the ground. Like it had happened the second before. It was real, the only real there was.

It never got dim or blurred at the edges. Once a thing has happened, it doesn't seem to matter whether it was twenty years or twenty minutes ago. Once a thing is dropped into that satchel, it is there. You can't get rid of it. And you can pull twenty years or twenty minutes ago out of the satchel, one as easy as the other.

One night, hearing the rise and fall of her breath beside me, seeing her body white in the dark, I asked Ada:

"Do you ever think about it?"

She knew what I meant, and she said, "No."

I did not say anything else, and a minute later she said, "Why should I? It's forgotten. She deserved it. And nobody cares about her. Nobody will ever make trouble. It's forgotten."

"I wish to hell I could forget it."

"Then just forget it. She finished herself. It wasn't you, or me. It was her. Remember that. It was her. She did it to herself. She and nobody else."

I knew Ada was right. But I had swung the knife. And I could not take my hand out of the satchel, I could not let go that knife I had dropped in it. And I held it not by the handle but by the blade.

Steve Jackson

That day under the oaks was the last real conversation Ada and I had for months. The state was full of harmony. Except for the New Orleans newspapers, there was practically no more vocal opposition to her administration. Everything became very decorous; the shakedowns all wore three-button suits. Or more precisely, well-pressed uniforms.

I did not believe Ada was trying to restrain Yancey's collections. Either she had given up, or lied to me in the first place, or had changed her mind and was now sharing the proceeds. I did not think she had lied—but maybe I was naïve. I admitted, now, I was sometimes capable of enormous naïveté.

But whether she suffered, or accepted, or encouraged, Yancey's activities, they presented to her enemies an opportunity.

One morning when I came into my office, I found a note on my desk: "J.S. wants to see you, 10 o'clock."

As a gesture of independence, I did not enter the green-carpeted antechamber until two minutes after the hour. The peccary-faced secretary of J.S., who was the Boss, looked at me with disapproval, and said, "They're waiting for you," the *you* an epithet, and I went into the sacristy.

J.S. sat massive, jowling, eyes horn-rimmed, behind the long fortification of his desk. Flanking him sat a small gray-haired man with undistinguished and pleasant features, who was the publisher of one of Louisiana's largest newspapers.

"Sit down," J.S. said, not cordially, for I had not been Punctual. "Mr. Spencer, Steve Jackson." It was not an introduction but a presentation.

"How do you do," I said stiffly.

"How do you do?" He was much more courteous than I. "I watch your show regularly, Steve, and may I say, I'm a great admirer." He had a genuine Southern voice, an increasing rarity in New Orleans. He stood to shake hands, and I felt embarrassed at my curtness.

J.S. got the signals. He said, much more pleasantly, "Steve, we've got a problem and we need your help."

"Anything I can do." I hit "can" hard.

He did not answer for a moment but stared intently at the desk, eyebrows pulling down and mouth pursing. Mr. Spencer sat half smiling, decorous, patient.

J.S. said, "Uh, Steve, the state administration has been, been extending itself rather far, much too far lately, and I thought, that is we thought, we thought the time has perhaps come for some, perhaps sweeping, disclosures."

"Yes?" I saw it coming.

"Well, Steve, you've got the biggest Trendex of any of our news shows, and you're still the best reporter in town for my money, so it just looks like you're the boy for the job, Steve."

"What do you want me to do?" I was giving him no help at all.

Mr. Spencer came in with his soft pleasant almost diffident voice. "Steve, we thought that if my paper were to run a series of articles exposing this wave of shakedowns at the same time that you might do some telecasts hitting the same thing, why we just might beat this reelection. We've got more than two years, and if we hit hard we just might do it. My staff could do the basic research and legal checking, though I know you'd want to get in the final licks your-self."

"You're the boy," J.S. said again, more authoritatively.

So, I had been told to go after Ada, with the object her destruc-tion. I wanted to laugh, or cry, at the wild absurdity of it. I had been willing, or thought I had been willing, to kill for her, and not so long ago. Now they wanted me to help destroy her. How funny it would be if they knew, I thought. There was no struggle and no victory. The idea was simply and totally inconceivable.

I said, "No."

J.S. looked at me menacingly; through the distortion of the thick lenses, his eyes looked like brown targets with black bulls'-eyes. "How's that now?" His voice was dangerously soft.

I felt a snap of anger, not unmixed with vanity. Once I had to take that. Now I did not. Now I was Steve Jackson, TV's Crusading Reporter, hot-shot, boy oracle. I had no illusions about my merits. Hot-shots are made, not born. But once they are made, they exist in their own right, and must be reckoned with.

"I said: no."

Through the thick glass the black targets glittered.

"Now see here." The voice strove for absolute authority, but missed it. "You want to keep that show, you cooperate. A dozen guys on this staff would jump at the chance to take your spot, and they wouldn't be hard to get along with."

"Get along with them then. I can walk across the street any time and I'm about ready to think the time is now."

His face went red. He knew it was so, and I could see the struggle: he wanted to fire me thunderously, and he did not want to lose a money-making show.

"Just a minute, Joe." Spencer said it in the gentle voice, and yet I could see J.S. brought up on the leash. Suddenly I realized that Spencer must own the station, too. Why hadn't I guessed? "No one should be asked to act against his own conscience." The word lay there in all its archaic embarrassment. But then I saw he was not embarrassed, and had used it naturally. He said to me with the same easy courtesy. "Steve. Why don't you want to help us on this?"

"That's a fair question," I said. "I was once engaged to Ada Dallas. Is that a fair answer?"

The thoughtful lined pleasant face nodded. "Yes. I'd say it was."

It needed only one more swing to drive the nail to the hub, and I knew intuitively what it was. I said: "I am not going to attack her now. No gentleman could." And I knew that had done it.

"You're right," said the soft voice, and the gray head swung toward J.S. "Let's just get somebody else."

And everybody in the room knew that was an order.

I felt obliged to let Ada know (I told myself) and give her another reason for checking Yancey if she could. She was making a speech in New Orleans that week. We met afterward, in the Court of Two Sisters. From the iron grillwork, the afternoon sun threw black bars across our white table, and across the table, Ada's white face trained toward me, one side blanketed and the other striped by shadow.

"I haven't seen you in a while," she said.

"No."

"I take it you don't approve of me just now."

"I don't approve or disapprove things. I try to figure them out." I stopped. "Now I am trying to figure out whether you were lying to me about Yancey or whether you changed your mind."

"I wasn't lying."

"So you changed your mind."

She didn't answer, which was an answer. After a moment, she said, "It's mostly people in, questionable, activities, you know."

"Uh-huh."

She looked at me squarely. "I need money, Steve."

"What for?"

"You know what for. To go on."

"This need is most gratifying to your enemies."

"What can they do?"

"Don't underestimate them. They're getting something ready."

"Again?"

"They've got nothing to lose. They can go on forever. They just extended me an invitation to participate, in fact."

"Which you turned down."

"Yep."

"Did they threaten you?"

"Only somewhat."

"Old Steve."

I felt uncomfortable, and shaggy, as though someone had just patted my head.

"Be careful," I said.

She smiled, and did pat my hand.

When she left, smiling warmly, I had altered nothing.

Tommy Dallas

I stayed in New Orleans at the St. Charles a while, then I rented a house back in St. Peter's. I hired a private detective agency to dig up some stuff on Ada to go with the picture. I had to be careful, because I did not want them to know what I knew; they might sell it to somebody else. All they knew was I wanted to check on her early life. They came up with some dirt on her family, and her working in a bar once, and that she'd made a lot of weekend trips to Mobile when she was at Newcomb. It wouldn't amount to nothing in court, but with the picture, it was good enough for me. All of this took time, but I had plenty of that.

That picture was still my ticket. I would pull it out every once in a while and look at it. With it I could go all the way; with it I was a real powerhouse. I was going back in politics, and at the right time that picture was going to make me governor again. It would be tit for tat. I would be doing to her what she had done to me. I kept telling myself that.

But this time everything I did, except for that, was going to be on my own. I didn't mean without help, nobody can do it without no help at all. I just wasn't going to be no piece of wood jerked on a string, not ever again.

The sheriff's election in St. Peter's parish was coming up just about the right time, two years before the next governor's election. That was step number one. The first time, Sylvestre had just pushed me in. If I could make it on my own, it would prove something.

Just to be polite, I went to the courthouse and told the boys Sylvestre left behind that I was going to run. They didn't like it; they had other plans.

"Geez, Tommy, it's late, boy. You shouldn't ought to do it this late. If you would of just come to see us sooner. But now we got

Jean in there and we already committed to him. Why don't you just forget about it? This ain't big enough for you any more anyway, you a big man, you been governor."

"Well, gentlemen, I sure value your opinion. I surely do," I said. "However, my mind is made up. I'd certainly value your support, but if you can't see your way clear there will be no hard feelings." They looked very surprised. This was not old Tommy, their faces said.

"Boy you got a lot to lose here, you lose this little piddling parish election and you dead in this state."

I knew that. I had thought a hell of a lot about that. I said, "Thank you for your advice. I certainly appreciate your advice but my mind is made up."

I announced my candidacy, and the New Orleans newspapers made a lot of the Dallas versus Dallas thing, since Sylvestre's old organization was now part of Ada's state organization. This made official what was by this time pretty well known anyway, that Ada and I were separated. Neither of us had made any kind of move for divorce, but they all knew we couldn't since so many voters were Catholic.

The papers made a lot of my fighting the crowd that put me in politics in the first place, but they didn't support me. They treated the election like a sideshow. And all the time I kept thinking I was a fool to try it. I couldn't really win anything, and I could lose the world. But I had to do it. This was more than an election. It was what I had to do to make it stick: being born again in the bomb exploding and the car turnwheeling and me swimming fast on the big waves.

It was tough, all right, but not impossible. The organization wasn't what it was when Sylvestre owned it, and I took some friends out of it and into my new organization. I was able to get enough of my men at the precincts to help count the votes, and I was sure of almost a fair shake anyway. Then I blitzed the parish with the Tommy Dallas Four, just like old times.

It was going to be close, real close. But I figured it up before the election and it looked like I would lose by just about five thousand votes.

Then, something happened. A little grocer named Personne shot himself and his whole family—after he had taken an awful kicking around from someone. Yancey probably. I called it for what it was, as good as murder, and I was just as interested in laying it on the line as I was in winning the election. That shouldn't happen. Not ever. I promised it never would if I went in.

And after that I won the election I thought I had lost. I was sheriff of St. Peter's parish.

It may not have been the governor's spot but it was mine. I belonged to myself. And people who had always thought I was a fool before, now looked at me somehow different.

Steve Jackson

Great doors on tiny hinges swing, and history hangs on horseshoe nails. The history of Ada Dallas, which encompassed not only the history of a state but also the personal history of many people including myself, hung on a horseshoe nail named George Personne.

George Personne was a grocer in St. Peter's parish. He first exposed himself outside the armoring darkness of absolute obscurity when he refused to perform certain campaign chores and to contribute a very token sum to the election fund of the organization's candidate for sheriff. (This was, of course, the organization Sylvestre Marin left behind, and which Tommy Dallas, of all people, was bucking.)

Had George Personne done either, or both, of these things quietly, nothing at all would have happened. He was too small to waste time and effort on. Unfortunately—for him—he was quite vocal in his declarations of independence, and was reminded, gently enough, that the Bank of St. Peter's held paper on his store.

He then made his next mistake. At least, it turned out, for him, to be a quite serious mistake, though in terms of ultimate consequence it may not have been a mistake at all but something else. Which, however, he did not get a chance to comprehend.

This mistake was to go to the newspapers.

The paper he went to in New Orleans was traditionally at war with the St. Peter's organization. And it made much of George Personne. For three days, with pictures, black ink, and interviews, it made much of George Personne who became (for those three days)

St. George battling the dragon. Then his news value was naturally exhausted, and the paper of course could not continue running stories about him when he was last week's news. And so there were no more pictures, black ink, and interviews.

It took him a while to learn that he had been dropped. He kept coming around to the newspaper office. At first the rewrite men listened to him carefully, made notes, and later filed them. Then they listened, did not make notes, and dismissed him quickly. Finally he was turned aside, politely but positively, at the reception desk.

Then he was alone with the parish organization, which of course was also a tentacle of Ada's organization. And now that he had chosen to make a symbol of himself, the organization had no choice in the matter.

The bank called up the note on his grocery and foreclosed. He was unable to get public or private employment, and his family was unable to get public or private relief.

Even then (I learned later), the organization was not vindictive. All he had to do was shout *mea culpa,* blame the lying newspapers for his defection, and he would have been restored to grace and handed a larger and sweeter harp than before.

Or, of course, he could always get out of the state.

He took neither alternative.

What he did take was the gun he kept under the counter, an unimpressive little Hi-Standard .22 target pistol, go home, and, in order, shoot his four-year-old daughter, his seven-year-old son, his wife, and himself.

He was news again. The papers hit every note on the scale: the big line on page one, pictures of the family group In Happier Times, a picture of the gun, and an artist's conception of Tragedy on Fercante Road. The paper which had been his sponsor (those three days) ran a stirring page-one editorial, blaming Ada and the St. Peter's organization and demanding justice.

Of course, I did my show on it, underplaying as much as I could. What a fool he had been, I thought. What a fool not to have taken any one of the other solutions.

But perhaps his cornered little brain had been unable to find them. Or perhaps from some irreducible core of stubbornness or resolution, or simple numbness, he had rejected them. Perhaps he wanted to protest, perhaps he wanted to protest so badly he took the only way he could figure.

He had been a damned fool.

The next morning I made an appointment to see J.S. I had changed my mind. I would participate in the campaign to unseat the state administration. Only I had to tell her myself, first.

Robert Yancey

"What a sucker," I said. "What a god-damn fool. From start to finish."

"He wasn't the only one," Ada said.

It was the day after the little jerk in St. Peter's shot himself and everybody in sight.

"Those characters down there," she said. "If they'd let him alone he would have amounted to nothing. Absolutely nothing. Now—"

"They couldn't have known he was going to knock himself off."

"Why not? It should have occurred to them. I even sent them word to lay off. The day before the poor idiot did it. I suppose I should have sent it sooner." She was walking back and forth, her eyes turned toward the floor. "They should have thought of it. Once a thing starts, you never know where it stops. It goes on and on like circles in water when you throw a rock."

"It wasn't anybody's doing but his own," I said, "and it'll blow over soon enough. They can't blame us."

"But they are, by God." She now moved very quickly toward the wall, and whirled. Her eyebrows pulled together, and her eyes stared gray and hard at the wall two feet away. "They are blaming nobody else."

"Forget it, hon. What can they do?"

She didn't answer, but kept looking at the place on the wall. I stepped over, slipped my arms around her, and started to turn her towards me. But she went stiff, and pulled away.

Now she wasn't thinking about us at all.

"That poor little man," she said. "That poor little fool."

Steve Jackson

I called Ada, made an appointment quite formally, and went to see her in the governor's office in the capitol.

Inside, with the door closed, she said. "It's four o'clock. Why don't we go get a drink?"

"I'd rather not," I said.

"Well." She smiled, a little, but her voice was anxious. "I take it it's serious."

"Serious to me."

And I told her.

I finished, and the office was silent. She turned toward the window and looked out, at the low rooftops under the high clear sky.

"Steve." She did not turn or look at me. "Would you believe that I had nothing to do with this? Would you believe that I sent word to give him a break the day before it happened?"

"Yes," I said. "Yes, I would."

Then she did look at me, and her face was grateful. "Thank you. It's true."

I swallowed. "I know it."

"Why do you want to go against me then?" Her eyes glistened as the light hit them.

All I could say was, "I'm not going against you, personally."

"Against me publicly then." She smiled tiredly. "My administration then. Is that right?"

"Yes."

She shook her head in the same half-weary half-sad manner, and I felt somehow compelled to go on, to justify myself.

I said: "The consequences of your actions have completely run away from the actions themselves. I know you didn't mean to have people knock off their wives and kids and themselves, and you didn't mean to turn a uniformed maniac loose and you didn't mean for one hell of a lot of things to happen. But they have happened and they will happen."

She smiled and I realized quite suddenly that she was almost middle-aged. "Steve. Do you think it would change if I was gone?

Do you really think everything would be like it says in the political science textbooks?"

"No. But Gen. Robert Yancey wouldn't be running loose. If you could control all the things that have come together to make you, it would be different. But it's gone beyond you. You put the wheels in motion, and now you can't stop them. The only way to stop them is to break up the engine."

She smiled again. "To break up Ada Dallas, do you mean?"

"I've tried to explain it. Not you yourself. But you as the core of this—."

"You can break me up any time you want. You could send me to the chair by opening your mouth. But you won't."

I said nothing.

"You could ruin me forever just by opening your mouth on something else. But you won't do that, either. You will just break your neck trying to keep me from getting reelected by digging up fly-specks and yet you would burn, yourself, before you would use what could destroy me in a second. Steve, Steve, there is no one like you." She shook her head, smiling, and now she was crying quite openly as she smiled. "No one." She grabbed my arm so tight I felt each finger in my flesh, and she almost kissed me but she did not. "Go on. Get on with it." She laughed, still crying.

I turned blindly and started for the door.

"Steve."

I turned again at the door. Under the incandescent light the tear paths looked strange and shiny on her cheeks.

"You may be right," she whispered.

She was holding the desk chair tight with one hand, and I could see her skin whiten over her knuckles.

"But you know I can't let go."

"Good-by," I said.

She blew a kiss, and I closed her door, softly behind me.

The fat face under the horn-rimmed glasses tried not to look too pleased as I told him.

"I'm glad you've seen it our way, Steve," he said expansively, the spectacles glinting light as they trained toward the desk top, the thick lips pursing in satisfied gravity. "You can do a lot of good, boy, a lot of good."

"I haven't exactly seen it your way," I said. "But you may be right."

He puzzled the deliberate ambiguity for a second, then brightened. "Sure. Absolutely."

I left him.

So I still had not come to the end of learning, though I had thought I had, many times. Accepting your ration of pain, day into year, was not enough. Under the mounting load of it, you were faced, occasionally, with the opportunity to act. And an even more painful recognition: that the opportunity to act meant the obligation to act.

I was without illusion as to the motives of the station and most of its stockholders. They were against Ada because she was taking dough from their pockets and spreading it around elsewhere. If she had been on their side, anything she did would be all right with them. With most of them. There were, of course, exceptions. Like the anachronistic archaic Mr. Spencer, and a few other holdovers from the Tradition.

That was bull. There was no Tradition. Not really. Spencer simply happened to be an ethical man. Within a very narrow framework. But this was something. When I was young, I had privately reproached everyone for the space they fell short of perfection. Now I found myself congratulating them for whatever fraction of an inch they climbed from absolute zero.

In what was coming, I had already made my own rules, which were quite precisely what Ada had foretold they would be, that afternoon in her office. I would do or say nothing against her personally. But I would hit the public Ada and the malfeasances of her administration. And I would hit that sonofabitch Yancey. I would get him good.

I started to work.

Tommy Dallas

The day after I went into office as sheriff of St. Peter's, I sent for Lattimer, the district attorney. He sent word back that he would be able to work me into his schedule at three o'clock that afternoon, maybe, if I was in his office.

I got him on the telephone.

"Mr. District Attorney," I said, very pleasant. "I was wondering if the Raymond oil strip means anything to you."

"I don't know what you're talking about," he said, very tough.

"Well now. Does Maria Sanchez mean anything? Or maybe Ace Wilkins or Ricco Medina?"

I didn't hear a word in the receiver.

"Any of them ring a bell?" I said, very cheerful and friendly.

He still didn't say anything.

"Maybe you better drop by here right away," I said.

And this time he said in a low hating voice, "All right."

He and Judge Revere had cut themselves into about three-quarters-of-a-million apiece by forming a corporation and buying the Raymond oil strip, which was soaked with oil and belonged to the parish. Maria Sanchez was a widow whose land he had taken away with some fake tax claims, and he had bought it for himself before it was advertised. Ace Wilkins was a strong-arm guy he had used on some rough deals; Ace had broken with him over money and was ready to spill his guts. Ricco Medina was the number-one gangster in Louisiana, and I had sworn statements plus photographs of Lattimer going into his house, not once but twice.

That detective agency had been busy all right since I got back to Louisiana. It had cost me most of the dough I had piled up when I was with Sylvestre. It was kind of funny, and at the same time it seemed the perfect way to spend it. Of course I had picked up the leads on these three when I was with Sylvestre. A man would have to be a lot dumber than they thought I was even, not to have. I just had the agency nail it down.

Lattimer came to the office all right. When he left half an hour later, I had a copy of his resignation. The next day, I did the same with Judge Revere.

A special election for both the empty jobs came up right away. As the chairman of the Democratic Executive Committee, which the sheriff always is in that parish, I was able to kick out all the crooked precinct officers, and get honest people in to count the votes. Two good men were elected, I was surprised by how much. Maybe people had been more tired of being pushed around than they knew themselves.

Then I let out of jail a couple of people who had been framed for

political reasons by Lattimer, I gave Mrs. Sanchez what dope I had
on the land steal so she could sue, and I kicked Sylvestre's men,
who had become Lattimer's men, out of every appointive job they
had. Some of them were still left on the elected boards, but we
could handle them. The whole parish machinery was overhauled,
and the long hold the old crowd had had was broken in just a few
weeks.

What kept on surprising me was how many good people came out
once they had a chance, once somebody had kicked the door down.

I was surprised too by the way the New Orleans papers gave me
a real good press. "A long-needed return to decent government," one
of them said, and another, "Sheriff Dallas is turning out to be quite
a different problem for the political gangs than was Governor
Dallas."

Maybe Sylvestre was wrong about the papers, too, I thought.

One day, I was in New Orleans to talk to the Young Men's Business Club, and coming out of the revolving door of the Baronne
Street entrance of the Roosevelt, I bumped into Ada.

"Well." She smiled in an odd way. "How's the Singing Sheriff?
Excuse me. I mean the Fearless Sheriff."

"I'm fine, Governor. Just fine. How 'bout you?"

She knew how I meant it, and she said, a little different, "Oh, I'm
fine, too."

She looked older: two lines starting between her nose and mouth,
a second chin just beginning to show. Yet, hating her, knowing she
had helped try to kill me, knowing I was going to put her out of
business with what I had, I could not help remembering she was the
best in the hay there ever had been.

I was sore at myself, that I could think that, after everything
that had happened. And because of this, I said, "Been to Mobile
lately?"

"No," she said very calmly. "Not lately."

"Haven't visited the old Paradiso Motel?"

"Not in a while," she said in the same way.

"I was over there, you know." I was trying to make her show
something.

"You mentioned that."

"I picked up a very interesting picture over there."

"Did you?" She was not rising to it the way I wanted.

"Ah-hah. Pretty girl, black hair, named Mary."

She just looked at me, and I was madder and madder because I couldn't scare her. I said, "I don't suppose I ought to of said that. I suppose now I can just sit back and wait for another wreck."

"I don't think you need worry about that," she said. "Who do you think kept, certain people, from moving in when you were tearing things apart down in St. Peter's?" She stopped a second, and I looked away from her.

"Good-by, Tommy," she said. "Good luck."

Watching her walk away, I felt confused for the first time since I got back to Louisiana.

FOUR

Steve Jackson

I started to work, feeling miserable, perpetually insisting to myself that the Governor of Louisiana was someone quite different from Ada. This was the old bit that an officeholder's public and private personalities were different. I was concerned only with the public personality. So I kept reminding myself.

The first place I moved to against the public personality was on an oil lease thing, about which I had certain information. The Pelican Development Company, incorporated quite recently in Delaware, had been low bidder for oil rights on a lot of state tracts. Between the Monday and Friday shows, I flew up to Wilmington, checked the papers of incorporation, and found the stockholders were three members of the state mineral board who were Ada's appointees, an R. T. Young, and a Mrs. Stella Houston. I smiled just a little at that last one.

Back in Louisiana, I checked some more records and found that the Pelican Development Company had sold its lease rights on the tracts to several major companies, for more than four times what it had paid the state. Pelican had also retained an override of one-sixteenth; a royalty on all future production.

I photostated everything and put it on the air. Making no charges, of course, but simply describing in basic English what had happened.

But no one in the administration would comment. Mr. Spencer's paper filed charges of malfeasance in office against the three mineral board commissioners, but I was sure Ada would get those quashed. (And in time she did.) "R. T. Young" and "Stella Houston" were, I proved, aliases. I didn't prove whose.

An effective exposé, but not effective enough. Next I looked for vote fraud. Nowhere on that one. They had been too sophisticated to vote any dead or nonexistent bodies; they had only, where necessary, counted votes their own way. I couldn't find anybody who had been inside, and was now sore, to talk.

Then I started on vice in the parishes.

I had material, and material, and material. I took movies of the exteriors of gambling joints and whorehouses (which I referred to as "disreputable establishments"). I wrote personal participation scripts on the gambling even if I couldn't on the other, and we aroused plenty of indignant priests and ministers to demand reform.

The target for this of course was Yancey, but he said smoothly enough to the press, "I will not interfere with local enforcement unless requested by local authorities."

I was not hurting him enough. The people of Louisiana had grown so accustomed to this view that most of them considered it a normal and not improper procedure.

Then I got a gimmick. I had a local trio record a verse of "Waltzing Matilda," the Australian song that was popular in World War II. I left the part about the "Jolly Swagman," then rewrote the punch lines:

"... and he sang as he tucked those greenbacks in his tuckerbag,
Won't you come waltzing, Matilda, with me."

I would close every show with a "Special for the Jolly Swagman": some item on gambling or vice in the state. Then I'd hold up a prop brief case while the recording played in the background. I avoided libel by not using Yancey's name, but it was clearly understood what and who I meant. That brief case of his was as well known as Huey's little black books had been a quarter-century or so before.

And this worked, because it made him ridiculous. My grapevine told me that it was getting to him, that he was burning.

I was glad. I enjoyed hitting General Yancey any way I could.

But I knew it was not enough. And I knew nothing I could do would be enough. Except the one thing I could not do.

Robert Yancey

Jackson had the knife in me now, twisting, and I couldn't do anything, anything at all. That was what hurt. Not to be able to fight. Just to be a target. In the war I always thought I would not mind dying if I could be moving and fighting. But to be tied up and a target was hell. Maybe that is what hell is, when you can't act.

"That sonofabitch," I told Ada. "I'm tired of it. I'm tired of being made to look like a fool. 'The Jolly Swagman.' I see them hiding grins when I go around, it's lousy for discipline. I even had to get me a box for the cash after he started that tuckerbag crap. I can't use the brief case any more. 'Jolly Swagman!'" I mimicked him. "That twerp."

She laughed hard and loud.

"Goddamn it," I said. "Whose side are you on, anyway?"

"Come off it. He can't hurt you. Remember. Sticks and stones."

"Sticks and stones my ass. He *is* hurting."

"Just tough it out. He's not exactly passing me by either, you know."

"The hell he isn't. He goes the long way round every time he comes near you. I'm his target. And you don't want me even to scare him."

She smiled as though she was proud of something. "You can't scare him."

"I can put the fear of God in him. You want to bet?"

"No. Because you aren't going to be fool enough to try it. If you touched him the whole state would know about it the next day. Then we would be on a spot."

"I'm not so sure. Never underestimate the power of—" My fist hit my hand with a loud smack.

"You *are* a goddamn fool. And now you listen to me. You leave him alone. Absolutely alone. You hear?"

"Okay, hon," I said. "Okay. Sure I'll leave him alone."

And I would, I thought. But I wouldn't guarantee what somebody else might do.

I called Ricco Medina and explained. "Somebody quiet and reliable."

"I got you," he said.

Steve Jackson

I had just turned off Royal, onto my street, a narrow corridor between the low dark buildings. The street dead-ended one block away, lighted only by the open yellow windows of street apartments; I saw the two street lamps were out. Before I could turn, I did not hear but felt them, one on each side. Then I did hear a hoarse voice: "Somebody said to tell you something. Somebody said to tell you you talk too much." Then red exploded and I was drowned by darkness.

When I awoke, I was in a hospital room. Pain beat dull and steady behind my right ear, my face burned in patches, and my body ached indiscriminately. I lay a moment, pinpointing sensations, and remembering. I decided they had done a thorough job.

A nurse materialized in white by the bed, asked how I felt, and said reporters wanted to see me when I felt like it. I told her I felt like it now. She checked with the doctor, let them in and I gave them the story.

Then I went back to sleep. When I came out of it, she brought the big one o'clock edition of the afternoon paper.

The line said in big black ink: TV CRUSADER BRUTALLY BEATEN.

The type said:

"TV Newscaster Steve Jackson—who has been campaigning against violence in politics—was himself the target of it last night."

This would fit right in with the idea I had almost had, back there a few days.

Then I slipped away, and when I returned, my room was in darkness, only the white of the sheet showing in the black. Below on the boulevard, I heard the soft hum of traffic, soft because there was not much between midnight and dawn. Through the window, in the black sky, I could see the white points of stars light-years away, the way they had been before I was hurt, before I was born. No, they only looked the same. They changed every day, every hour, every second, and the changes were precisely recorded in tables. You could navigate by the stars, if you knew how and had the tables.

For no reason, I remembered that poor Tommy Dallas had been in a hospital, and that Ada had probably sent him there, too. Though of course she had not sent me here directly. Not she herself. Probably Yancey had. Maybe she had known nothing of it. But Yancey was part of her. So it was her, after all.

But I was part of her, too.

I watched the sky fade slow to gray, so slow that I felt I was riding a record turned to one-tenth speed. I felt I could speed the record or stop it, I could ride the record anywhere I wanted to go, I could turn it forward or backward.

But I did not speed it or slow it. I let it run at its own speed, and the sky was pale and the stars were gone when I slid into sleep.

It was early afternoon two days later, and I lay in sun-yellowed emptiness, as the nurse came into the door and said, "A Mrs. Cisneros to see you."

"All right," I said, and felt my heart jump like a hunter at brook's edge.

The white-capped nurseface withdrew, and through the narrow space or doorway came on high sharp heels a woman in black knit gown, with low black hair framing dark glasses, who was, of course, Ada Dallas.

She closed the door, and stood quite still, both hands behind her on the doorknob, looking down at me. I could not tell what the eyes showed behind the dark glasses.

"Hello, Steve," she whispered.

"Hello."

She still did not move. She stood frozen as though she could never move.

"Do I have to tell you?" She still whispered, and I could see the blue vein working in the white throat.

"No. You don't have to tell me."

"I'll kill him. I'll—"

"No you won't."

"I'll fix him."

"You won't do that, either," I said from the pillows. "You won't kill him and you can't stop him and next time it's somebody else."

"There won't be any next time." Her face was like chalk under the long black wig.

"You know there will."

"If anybody touches you again I swear I'll shoot them myself."

"Who the hell am I? The thing is it can happen to anybody."

I heard the weary exhalation of her breath, and saw the deep surge and retreat of her black-sheathed bosom. "Nothing is very different here from the way it is everywhere. There are people who run things and there are the others. Except—"

"Except for Yancey, the tanks, and the little grocer?"

"Stop accusing me, Steve. It's the same everywhere. Only the degree is different."

"The degree is everything."

"I'll do better, now. I'll—"

"You can't," I said, brutally.

She did not answer. The deep quivering draw of her breath filled the room.

"I can try," she said. "But I didn't come to fight you. I came to see how—to help if I could."

She came to the bed, sat, and took off the glasses. She laid her hand upon my forehead, and it was cool and soft. I closed my eyes, and drifted deep into the warmth of her presence, the scent of her perfume and the caress of her touch.

We stayed like that, not talking, for a while.

When I came back to work the next week, the station got a permit for and talked me into wearing a gun. I certainly did not plan to use it, but it was good theater. After I started to wear it, the rating jumped way up.

But that first time I felt very awkward indeed, and I could not forget that heavy awkward drag at my hip until I was near the end of the script, and saying:

"The fact that one television reporter is beaten by thugs is not important. What is important is that anyone can be beaten for attacking the administration's conduct of affairs.

"Right now we are on the verge of total dictatorship in this state. We are much closer to it than Germany was in early 1933. Elections are bought and delivered, voters are intimidated, favored groups are swollen with profits. A movement that started as a supposed crusade has become a cynical and corrupt force of selfishness."

After the show, I was going through the night wire copy and I saw it:

Mobile (AP)—A skeleton found here about a year ago has been tentatively identified as the remains of Blanche Jamison, local vice figure.

I read it again, and an idea came. I thought that, finally, I had the way to set her free from Yancey. If she still wanted to be free of him, and I was not sure she wanted to, any more. But it was worth a try.

Though it was not important enough, or interesting enough to Louisiana, for the 10 P.M. newscast, I used it. I read it looking significantly into the camera, and hoped Gen. R. Yancey was watching.

Robert Yancey

She walked into my office, not fast like a cyclone, but slow like a tidal wave. She closed the door, very softly, and looked down at me sitting behind the desk.

Her voice was very soft. "If you do that again, if you touch him ever again, I'll kill you."

"Why, hon." I laid my pencil down. "You don't think—"

"I don't think anything. If he is touched, ever again, you will be killed."

I was hot with anger. "That bastard is killing us and you act like you're in love with him."

Her eyes were very steady on me. "Yes," she said. "And you damn well remember what I tell you."

Then she was gone and I was looking at a closed door.

If she thought I was going to sit still while he clobbered me every week, she better think again.

Then one day it came. The next package. I felt like I had been waiting for it for years. I forgot how many, it seemed forever. I had been waiting so long I never really expected it to come. Waiting was life, waiting was forever. Still I knew it would come, someday.

And now it had.

And I felt—I did not know how I felt. Maybe a little like I did that morning the war was over, when we were under shellfire and waiting to attack. Then the fire stopped, the war was over, and we would never make the attack. All at the same time, I felt that I had been saved and that the world had come to an end. Nothing was as real after the fire stopped as it had been before.

But this was not the same. Something had ended, all right. But the war was not ended, nor the waiting. Nothing had changed except another package had come in. Now I would wait for the next.

What came was a story in the Mobile paper three paragraphs long, which said:

> A skeleton found in a creek near here a year ago was tentatively identified by police today.
>
> They believe the remains are those of Blanche Jamison, 51, notorious call-house madam who was thought to have shifted operations to California.
>
> Officers said she probably met her death in a gang killing. Investigations will continue.

No, nothing had ended.

I was afraid, a little. But more than that, I had the feeling that another cog on a big wheel had slipped into place. And I was satisfied. And that did make me afraid.

But I had the two words to hang onto:

Gang killing. Gang killing. Gang killing.

That was it, that was what would save us.

How could they hook a gang killing in Mobile to the governor of Louisiana? And the commandant of police?

But I knew I would still call at the window for packages. I knew I could never stop. Until...but I didn't want any until. I didn't want to think any until.

Tommy Dallas

After Jackson got beat up, I decided this was the time to use it, instead of waiting for the next election. She was a target now. With what Jackson had on her, and what I had, even her tame Legislature would impeach her.

The thing to do was give it to him, right now.

I thought that now the time had come, I would feel great, I'd be evening up with her for everything.

Only I didn't feel great at all.

I felt sick. I remembered her face and her voice: "I don't think you need to worry about that. Who do you think kept, certain people, from moving in—"

Don't fall for any con of hers. You know what to do, now go ahead and do it.

I made an appointment with Jackson for the end of the week.

Steve Jackson

The morning after my newscast on Blanche Jamison, I drove to Baton Rouge. I wanted to see Yancey and before that I wanted to see Ada. If Yancey did not capitulate immediately, and I did not think he would, I wanted her to know she was in no danger, that the bluff was a bluff. I hoped she would know that anyway. But still the continuing threat might throw a shadow of worry upon her, she thinking not that I would deliberately betray her but that I might overextend in going after Yancey, with the same result. So I went to explain to her, my technical adversary, exactly what I was about—so she would not be worried. And I knew when I did that she might tell Yancey and ruin the whole move.

Ada's little secretary (chosen, doubtless, for her nonspectacularness) gave me a notably malevolent stare when I entered the outer office, and bristled as she finally, on instructions from the office intercom, admitted me.

But Ada was as always. It was I who was strained. And I felt, by God, I felt guilty, as though I were wronging her, and she was forgiving me.

I told her what I had come to tell her.

"I didn't want you to worry," I said.

She smiled. "Did you think I would?"

"You might have." I stopped a moment. "I'd appreciate it if—" I trailed off.

"I won't tell him," she said.

Then I went to the next floor, and Yancey's office. I got in to see him without difficulty.

He had seen the newscast then, he was worried, he wanted to find out what I knew. Or so I thought as I went through his door.

He was sitting behind the desk, pretending to be writing, his face turned down, his dark blond hair smoothly combed and parted. "Just a moment," he said tonelessly. Then very quickly he looked up, and I heard his laugh cut the room like jagged metal.

"Got it lashed down for a good fast draw, boy?" His mouth twisted, and his face showed pleasure at the gun. I saw with surprise that his face had aged; tension lines had distorted the old deceptive smoothness.

"Fast enough." I felt myself coloring, but tried to carry it off.

"What's on your mind?" His smile was gone, and his hard face stared at me unrelieved.

"Did you see my show last night?"

"Maybe I did. Maybe not. Why?"

He was watching me like a pursued animal, at once afraid and deadly.

"You heard that item about Blanche Jamison?"

I had to congratulate him, if silently; he never showed it touched him. "I can't remember that. I was concentrating too hard on that, you know, satchel thing."

"I mentioned that a skeleton found in Mobile was identified as the remains of a Mobile call-house madam named Blanche Jamison."

He shrugged. Oh, he was good. He did not protest too much.

"Never heard of her. Now get down to it. What do you want up here?"

"I got a deal."

"I thought you were the boy that didn't like deals."

"I like this one."

"It must be pretty hot then." He smiled, but thinly. "What is it?" The jagged metal ripped space again.

I said, "I want you to resign."

He started laughing.

"Because if you resign I won't do a show about the murder of Blanche Jamison."

He stopped laughing.

"And if I do the show, this is what I'm going to say."

I told it to him like Ada had told it to me.

He laughed again, thinly. "You just do that. You just do that and we'll just put you under Angola. You do that and you'll be out of the way for a real long time. Go on and do it."

"I mean to. And don't worry about Angola, or any other pen, because I've got what it takes to make it stick."

The laugh faded. "You think anybody would listen five seconds to crap like that?"

"I've got what I need to make them listen."

"What?" It escaped him like a pistol misfire.

"Wait and see. Unless you want to deal."

"You are crazy as hell. Go on and try it and I'll send you a Christmas box at Angola. Every year for the next twenty."

"Okay." I walked to the door. "Okay. Just keep watching my show."

I left his office, walked down the broad white steps, through the green gardens, past Huey's cast-bronze godhood, to the car. In it, I looked through the windshield almost straight up at the white tower, and it seemed to blot out half the blue sky. Then I backed out, turned, and started for New Orleans.

I had nothing at all but Ada's story. I would never use a word of it.

I hoped the bluff would work.

Robert Yancey

Through the window, I watched him walk down the white sidewalks in the green lawn. He looked so thin and harmless. Then I left my office, went down the stairs, and into Ada's trying not to hurry.

Inside, I closed the door hard, and stood in front of it a second with my hand on the knob. I did not know whether I was breathing hard from the fast walk or something else.

"I told you," I said. "Baby did I ever tell you. Now he wants us to get out or burn and he's got what it needs. You told him, goddamn it you told him!"

She looked at me across the desk, her face frozen, as though she didn't care about what I said, as though I was just a small nuisance she would like to flick away with her finger.

"Would you please get hold of yourself," she said. "Of course I didn't tell him. Stop acting like a fool and stop taking me for one and tell me what this is all about. Did he say he was going to use that?"

"Yes, he told me he was going to use that. And he's got it, I mean he has got it all, and *I* didn't tell him."

"I told you neither did I." It was her coldness that got me so. "He knew what she was, he knew her in Mobile. He probably saw her in the capitol one day and somehow he must have figured why. Maybe she told him. He read about the identification and the rest he's guessing. He's got nothing." She stopped again. "I don't think he'll do anything with it at all." She did not say that convincingly.

"You don't think. That's just great. You don't think he'll do it."

"No, I don't."

"You're crazy. Do you know that? You're jelly inside for a guy that'll ruin you and maybe burn you."

Her face did not change as she kept looking at me.

I said, "Well, you think I'm going to sit back and let him burn me, you think again. I'm going to have that boy taken care of but good."

That was the first thing that really hit her. She jumped up and came around the desk and now her face was on fire.

"Oh, that would do it, that would just do it, that would just fix it good!" Her voice was that violent whisper, zinging bullets the way it had in the corridor, that time. "You pull another stupid trick like that beating and we'd really be done for." She stopped, I heard her breath, loud almost as her voice, rise and fall twice. "Now you listen. You just sit back and wait it out and take the chance. Or get out." Her voice changed and lost all of its edge. "Maybe, probably, he won't use it."

"You know it's your chance, too."

"Do you hear me crying?" She was calm again.

I saw now she would not see sense. The thing to do was to pretend to go along. But if I gave in too quick, she would know. "What makes you so sure? Has he told you anything?"

"Yes, he has." Her voice rose again. "He has told me that he thinks I ought to resign. What the hell did you think he'd told me?"

"Maybe more than he told me."

"You fool."

"Okay," I said. "Okay. I just hope to God you know what you're doing." I saw in her face that I had made it stick. She believed me. Now I had to set it up.

Tommy Dallas

I didn't feel good about what I'd decided, to let Jackson have the picture and the information.

As long as I had it, I could do anything I wanted with it. Once I gave it to Jackson, it would be gone. My choices would be all gone. And I wasn't enjoying it the way I expected. This was different than I thought it would be.

I wondered if maybe he knew about her and Mobile already. He had been sweet on her, before. Even now, he wasn't touching her personally, only what she did as governor.

Probably he wouldn't use it if I gave it to him. That must be why I was uneasy about giving it to him. Of course. I didn't believe he would use it.

I would keep it a while longer. I called Jackson up and broke the appointment. Now I had all the possibilities to choose from again. I had a world full of possibilities. Until I picked one.

Steve Jackson

The first threat had not worked. I had to force the bluff right up to the edge. I began a very careful build-up. I started closing every show with "Watch this program November 18, from the steps of the state capitol."

I got Spencer to run a page one story:

TV NEWSCASTER PROMISES

BIG NOVEMBER EXPOSE

And the station bought ads:

"Hear Steve Jackson at the state capitol on November 18—for the biggest shock ever!"

This was repeated, with variations, for more than two weeks. Then I called Yancey and said:

"You've got two weeks."

He said: "You must think you'll like Angola."

Of course I had a story of sorts to slip in the slot if the bluff did not work. It was not a bad story: a young racketeer who had been frozen out of the slots in a southeastern Louisiana parish, had been willing to charge Yancey with collusion. He had even been willing to do it in an affidavit. So I had a parachute. Though of course it would be somewhat less than the Armageddon I was promising.

Robert Yancey

I went to see Ricco Medina.

"It's hot, General," he said. "I think it's maybe a little too hot. I think maybe I would forget about it."

"I don't want to forget about it."

He knew what I could do to him. He shrugged. "Okay, I'll see what we can do."

I was not a killer. I did not want to kill anybody. I did not even want to kill this sonofabitch who was trying to burn me. The fact was I was not killing him. He was killing himself. There was nothing else to do.

Six days later, I called Medina, telephone booth to telephone booth at a time we had arranged.

"No dice," he said. "We tried plenty. We couldn't set it up for a hit. He's got a police guard. No way we can set it up before the eighteenth."

He was probably leveling. I said, "Okay. Forget it then."

I was disappointed, and yet a little relieved. He had to be killed, yet I did not want another one, and I could not help being relieved it hadn't happened. But he had to go. Now I would have to do it myself, I thought, and then the relief was all gone. I did not want to do it. I was not a killer. I was a good guy if they only gave me a chance.

But I had to. And now I had to all by myself.

I started to think about it. I thought about it a couple of days, and I could only come up with one answer.

It had to be right on the capitol steps right before he started the show. I would have to do it, and I would have to make it absolutely foolproof. It would be a planning and logistics problem. The biggest I ever had.

Steve Jackson

The broadcast was only three days away, and I thought now that it would not work. Maybe Ada had told him that I really was not going to use it, maybe that was why he was toughing it out. It was not really intelligent for me to have told her. But I would do exactly the same thing if I had a second chance, or a third, or a tenth. Whatever, the only thing to do was play the hand out. I had the studio technicians make preparations for taking the equipment up to Baton Rouge.

Robert Yancey

A couple of days before he was supposed to explode us, Ada came into my office.

"I've got an idea that you've got an idea," she said. "Don't try it."

"I don't know what you're talking about," I said. "Hon."

"Then I beg your pardon. And don't try it. Hon."

Five minutes after she had gone, I went through another dry run. This was the fourth day I had done it. I would do it twice a day for the next two days. The second night was the eighteenth, the night. Then everything had to be perfect.

This time, I did it all in six minutes.

Tommy Dallas

I knew the time had come to do whatever I was going to do with what I had. To stop thinking about the hundred different things I *could* do and go ahead and do one.

I went through the possibilities. Finally I thought I had the way and the man, and they both were nasty. His name was Howard Masters, and he was a well-known sonofabitch.

He had been kicked off a good paper more than ten years before, and since then he had made a living by doing dirty propaganda work for people too clean to do it themselves. Like for example, spreading around and working into print a story that the Governor of Louisiana had been a whore. He called himself a "public relations" man, even if the real public relations people wouldn't have nothing to do with him. But he made out.

At exactly three o'clock, he came into my office. Oh he looked like something: nice white hair, gold-rimmed glasses, sharp dark-blue suit. Dignified. But his face. It was frozen like a dead man's. His trade was in that face.

Maybe what I thought of him showed because he didn't try to shake hands. He didn't try to shake hands. He dipped his head. "How are you, Governor?"

"Sheriff," I said. "Just sheriff. Sit down."

He sat, hitched up his pants just a little, so neat, and crossed his legs.

"Well, Sheriff, I understood from our telephone conversation I, might be of some service, to you." He talked slow, careful, and polite. Unless you knew, you'd never guess what he was. Not unless you took a good look at his face.

"I think maybe so," I said. "I have some information I want to get around, I need somebody, reliable, to handle it."

"Well." The polite careful voice. "I'm considered quite, reliable, I think." He smiled just a little.

"I know." The way I said it, in spite of myself, might have insulted some people. It never touched him.

"Now what is the nature of this information, Mr. Dallas?"

"I got it right here."

I opened the drawer and looked down at Ada with the black hair and the face in heat and the typed sheets clipped to her. I put my hand into the drawer. I did not feel good a damn bit. In my mind I saw me taking it out, handing it to Masters, his hand closing on it, his back going blue and neat out the door, and with him the thing that would ruin Ada forever.

I pretended for a second not to find it. I was not sure why. Just hand it over, I thought, and you'll have what you want. You'll be all even. You'll be right in there with the smart ones—with Sylvestre and her and Yancey, and Masters—welcome to the lodge. You'll be right in there.

I made my fingers close on it, then they opened, and I brought the hand out empty. I pretended to look through the other drawers. I saw Masters watching with that tiny smile.

"I can't find it," I said. "I guess I left it in the safe at home."

"Oh?"

"I'll call you if I find it."

"I see." I looked at him; he did see. He stood up. "Well, Governor, excuse me, Sheriff, if you find it, you know where to find me."

And the neat blue back went out the door just the way I had seen it in my mind, only he wasn't carrying the bomb and Ada was still in one piece.

The door closed, I did pick up the picture, and I stood up and went to the john at the back of my office.

I ripped the picture in half, then in quarters, then in little bits. I dropped them in the water and watched them sink slow. Then I flushed it, watched the black pieces swirling around, and then going down, while the pipes sucked and gurgled.

No lodge membership for you, I thought, you dumb bastard. But I felt very relieved, like I had been pardoned from a jail sentence for life.

Steve Jackson

We drove up the Air-line in the late blue-and-yellow afternoon and started to set up for the show. Nobody tried to stop us. This time, Yancey was either smart or well advised; stopping us would just have made the story bigger.

I helped the technicians lug the heavy stuff from the truck to the steps. I had nothing else to do. I watched the sun ease down toward trees and housetops like a big red ball lowered slowly on a string. The capitol lawns rolled immaculate green out of the smeared red fire. I could look straight up to the almost-white tower spearing high and sharp and alone in the dying red-streaked blue. Turning, I saw the sidewalks ran like white gauze through the green gardens and around Huey's statue.

Huey stared at these and at the western skyfire in deistic immobility. And as the fire went out and the sky inked from blue to gray to violet, the light that never went off coned downward and yellow at his consecrated unseeing features.

In the dropping dark I watched them work with cameras and lights and wires. I felt I had nothing to do with it, with any of it. I was totally apart and out of it. Yet all of it was for me. The cameras and lights would soon train on me, I was the reason for every action. It occurred to me that a man about to be hanged might have the same feeling of apartness and unreality, as he watched them hammer nails in the scaffold. But I had nothing to fear, for I was not to be hanged. I was pretending to be the hangman. Perhaps both principals had sensations in common. Though not of course the final sensation.

I looked at the sky and now saw faint stars. It was getting toward time.

I was very glad when one of the technicians called, "Hey, Steve, commere and let us set up on you."

Robert Yancey

From my window I watched them all. He moved slow and tall and thin, doing nothing, on the steps he looked frail, almost helpless. It was a good chance then. But my alibis hadn't come.

I watched his back, full towards me, and marked the spot, right between the shoulders, that would be mine. He stood absolutely still for a minute, the back offered like a target, and in that minute I felt closer to him than I had felt towards anybody. Like the woman, only closer, even. He was more than my friend, he was my brother, he was me. Then he moved, the target broke up, and he was just the guy who would burn me if he could.

Steve Jackson

The camera lights suddenly triggered my vision into one yellow explosion. I shut my eyes tight, it passed, almost, and when I opened them I was looking at the white steps going down.

"That's good," the director said. "Stand there when we start."

"How much longer?" I asked.

He looked at his watch. "Half an hour."

I thought of opening the bronze double doors and walking to the telephone booths at the back of the high-domed lobby, to call Yancey one last time. I put my hand to the handle of one door, but they were locked together. I stared for an instant at the panel filigrees on the bronze, showing dark in the edge of light, then I gave it up. I thought of trying the basement entrance by the press-room, but there wasn't time for that. I moved back into the indistinctly bordered circle of light.

Robert Yancey

The door opened and my two troopers walked in: Paxton and Beausang.

"What kept you?" I said.

"General, sir, you said seven-thirty, sir. Only seven twenty-one now."

"Okay, okay, I beg your pardon. Now let's get the hell to work."

I put them on some reports, calling figures to each other, verifying the entries, and so on. I picked those two because they would be completely dependable as witnesses. They were absolutely loyal, I had made sure of that by some very recent promotions and the promise of some more.

I had not told them what I was going to do. I would not have to. They would know what they were supposed to do and say. They would do it and say it, and it would never be mentioned between us.

What they would say was: that I, Gen. Robert Yancey, had been with them in my office at the time Steve Jackson was shot to death.

What they would do was to forget a short trip I made to the latrine. That was all.

I had planned it as carefully as I knew how, which was plenty carefully. I had rehearsed it fifteen times by count in the last week.

I would excuse myself for the latrine, the men's room. On the way out, I would pick up a brief case right at the door of the office. The brief case would have inside an army carbine, broken down into stock and barrel. In the men's room on the next floor, I had hung a civilian overcoat and hat, with gloves in the pocket. I would go into that room in uniform and come out in the coat and hat. Then, I would go to the automatic elevator and take it to floor six. On that floor, I would go to a maintenance supply room; I had a key that fitted them all. This room had a screenless window that looked down to the entrance steps, where the telecast would be. I had picked this because it had a good angle, it was as high up as I could go and fire with accuracy, and because it was outside the area being cleaned by the janitorial crew. I had a copy of their schedule for security reasons, and I checked them three nights to see if they followed it, and they did. They would be on floor nineteen and up at that time on that day. Everything was checked out.

Once in that room, I would take the parts of the carbine, reassemble them (you can put the barrel to the stock in nothing flat), check the sight, and put on the silencer. Then I would go to the window, rest the barrel on the window sill, sight very carefully, almost straight down, to the head of Steve Jackson, pull the trigger once, sight and pull it again for insurance, and it would be done.

I would then break the gun in two pieces, which I could do in four seconds, hide the pieces under the locker by moving out one of the supports, move the support back, walk to the elevator, and take the elevator down to floor three. I would leave the coat in the men's room, walk the last flight, come back to the office, and we would be working when they came in.

I had done it once in six minutes and never more than eight. I had done the second phase of it—after the trigger was pulled—in three.

It was almost safe. The gun was an army gun I had taken from a dead man: ballistics couldn't get me. I had gloves. The alibis were sound. The only element of risk was when I would walk from the elevator to the men's room. If anybody recognized me in that coat and hat it would be definitely suspicious. I could cut this down dropping the coat and hat in the brief case and carrying them from the elevator to the men's room and then to the office that way. There was still a risk, but it was minimal. It was a risk I had to take; it was the best calculated risk in the situation.

I went over it the thousandth time:

Office to men's room. Men's room to elevator. Elevator to six. On six to the maintenance room. In maintenance room, the firing. Maintenance room to elevator. In elevator take off coat and hat and put in brief case. Back to third-floor men's room. Down one flight to office. Which my witnesses would say I never left.

It would work. It would have to work.

Steve Jackson

I looked at my watch: ten minutes. I felt disappointed and slack. I suppose I had been hoping until the end that Yancey would scare. But no Yancey. No deal. I moved around in the dark behind the spots, feeling quite alone.

Robert Yancey

Ten of. Not yet. Make it eight of. Two more minutes. Remember it's just a tactical problem. Think of nothing else. One minute more. Just a problem. Follow the timetable. Thirty seconds. Ten. Five. Four. Three. Two. One. Okay.

I stood up. Paxton and Beausang were working industriously across the aisle, their heads bowed and bare. "Got to hit the latrine," I said. "Back right away."

"Yes, sir, General."

Outside in the corridor one light was burning, at the far end. I walked away from it, watching my shadow go longer and longer on the floor between the narrowing marble walls, and then I turned into the men's room.

They were the first things I saw when I pushed through the second, inner door: a brown tweed topcoat and a brown porkpie hat, hanging on the same hook in the row of hooks on the wall. I snatched them, put on a pair of gloves I had in the pocket, and listened. Nothing. Nobody.

So I moved outside and walked fast, not on tiptoe but muting my steps, to the elevator. I got in the elevator and pushed the little black button marked 6.

The elevator hummed, the numbers flashed red as we passed the floors: 3.

4.

I was on schedule. It was half done.

Half done and nothing wrong.

Nothing would go wrong. If I just didn't miss. Miss, with a telescopic sight? I could hit a tennis ball at that distance with that sight.

4.

5.

If the janitors just weren't around. If. If. If.

Red 6.

The humming stopped.

I was there.

This was not real. The floor was not real, the elevator was not real. The elevator door slid back to open automatically and I stepped out. I wedged the elevator door open with a newspaper from the pocket of the brown tweed coat so it could not start if someone else pushed a button. It is not me, I thought, it is somebody else. It is somebody else and I am looking at it from someplace else.

But it was me, all right. It was me and I looked back while the square of light that was the open elevator narrowed to a rectangle, and then a strip, and then a line of light. I turned my back to it and went down the hall.

The elevator would just stay there, nobody could bring it down.

For a second I saw only pure black, everywhere. Then I felt for the wall and eased along it, the marble cold through my gloves.

My eyes adapted, and I could see shades of darkness and down the corridor a patch of dark blue sky dusted yellow with stars. Then I could see doors in the wall, and brass knobs pale on the doors. I went straight for that patch of sky, because the room, my room, was next to it.

I had rehearsed it.

I knew just what to do.

The door was locked.

I hadn't counted on that, but I was ready for it, I had a master key that fitted every lock in the building.

I slid the key in the lock, heard the cold sound of metal on metal, and turned the cold knob.

The door opened. I was inside. I closed it.

I turned the pencil beam from my fountain-pen flashlight on the brief case. I took out the parts of the carbine, and slid the barrel into the receiver. The catch caught with a smooth dull definite click, and my belly jumped. Then I loaded and was ready.

I picked it up, running my hands lightly over the metal of the barrel, the wood of the stock, and I checked the rounds again. I eased to the window, slid the barrel over the window sill, and knocked off the safety.

I looked down the barrel to the light circle six stories below. He was there, tall and thin, the graying head easy to see through the sight. But he was between two other men, one making motions with his hands, the other wearing a cap and his hands in his pockets. They would have to get out of there in a minute. Then—

Jackson had been standing with his back to me and his face towards the cameras. Now he turned, facing the capitol, and he looked up, straight up, like he was looking at me.

And at once he was part of me again. I was him. I was me, I was the eye watching us both.

The watch said two of.

This is the second time, I thought. It is supposed to get easier. Is it easier? I don't know. I don't know how I feel. This is not real. This is not me. I am not afraid, I am not anything, because this is not really me. I am watching this on a 24-inch screen. I am watching a man in a porkpie hat in the kneeling firing position, holding to his shoulder a gun resting on the window sill.

Then I brought the intersection of the cross hairs to his head and it was real, all right. It was real, I was real, he was real. I was going to kill him. Not sometime, not next week, but now.

The pale green hands on the dark dial showed one minute. In the light circle below, the bareheaded man dropped his hands, the man in the cap took his from his pockets. Jackson said something, they laughed, and then they walked out of it. And now he was alone.

I moved the cross hairs dead-slow, up and down, right and left, until they met where the hair touched his neck.

Steve Jackson

It was time. I tried to look past the lights into the gathering faces beyond them, looking for one face, the face. But I could see only the Cyclops eyes of the spots.

"You all set, Steve?" said the director. He had enjoyed setting it up; he liked a tactical problem.

"Not very," I said, and he laughed.

Then he and the light man moved out of the yellow circle, behind the mounted cameras, and we were ready to start.

Robert Yancey

I held the crossing of the hairs on the back of his head, and I slid my finger off the guard and onto the trigger.

A key turned in the door lock.

I could not move.

The knob turned, I moved fast and low for the dark corner, somebody was in the room, I smelled perfume, and I knew.

"Save the trouble," said Ada. "I know you're there."

My heart began to beat again. "Sure I'm here," I whispered. "Be quiet."

"You had to try it, didn't you?" Her voice was a half whisper, but it was not that rifling bullet-whinging half-whisper of her anger, that I knew well. It was calm and flat and almost dead.

"Did you think I was really going to let him burn me?"

"You aren't going to touch him." Her voice held the same resolute flatness. She moved towards me a couple of steps, her head back, and the moonlight fell on her face. And then her face, and her walk, and her voice fell into a pattern that I knew, and I felt a quick coldness.

She had come prepared. Once you have seen them come like that, you will always know them. I had seen soldiers like that, before they left on special volunteer missions, where their chances of a round trip were just above zero. Maybe it is the way a good man goes to the firing squad.

I stalled. "How did you find me?"

"Did you think you fooled me? I've had you followed for weeks. Tonight I followed you myself." The voice had the same unchanging quietness.

"All right, you're smart; if you're so smart, why are you fighting me? It's both of us together. I'm going to save us."

I moved a step toward the window.

She moved with me. "You are not going to use that gun."

"I'm not going to any chair."

"You are not going to harm him." She went on in that same rock-like, dead-like absolute calm. "And you don't need to go to the chair. You've still got time to go down and tell him you're resigning."

"Me quit to that bastard?" I laughed and heard the brittle thinness of it in the dark. "Will you resign?"

"Yes. I'll resign. If you will I will." She did not even hesitate or stumble over it; she must have thought hard about it. Did she mean it?

I looked at her face in the moonlight. "You mean you'd quit, for him? Leave everything? I don't believe it."

"Not just for him."

"What for then?"

"For me."

I heard her quiet breath after she said it, and I moved again towards the window, and she moved with me again. "You're crazy," I said. "I don't know what's happened to you but you haven't got it any more. You're out of your mind."

"I don't think so." She was halfway between me and the window now, almost but not quite blocking me.

"Well, I'm not quitting and I'm not letting anybody talk that can send me to the chair. Now get out of here and let me do my job."

"You aren't doing anything." The almost expressionless mind-made-up voice.

"He's about to start. Get out of my way."

"No."

And then in the moonlight now bright on her face and body, I saw her right hand bring up her pistol. I could see it clear and glint-ing; it was one of the little .22s that can go in a woman's purse. Much later, remembering everything, remembering how angry I was with her interfering, how bad I wanted her out of the way so I could get him, I remembered I felt a quick shot of pity for her, and I thought, what guts. That little purse gun, that she had got some-where and couldn't possibly use good, and with that she went up against a trained man with a carbine.

"Give it here," she said.

I said, "I guess I got no choice."

I lowered the gun, turned it around like I was going to give it to her stock first, and stretching it out I suddenly whipped it hard up against her hand and heard her low cry of pain and the little gun hit the wall and then clattered on the floor.

She stepped back holding her hand, and I ran two steps to the window, and saw him there in the light by himself, ready to start or maybe already started.

I raised the gun. Then her body, which was not small, came into me, I felt a sharp tearing on each cheek as her nails raked, and I staggered off balance.

"You are not going to do it." In spite of what I had just done to her, her voice showed no pain and no anger, just absolute determina-tion that I was not going to do it.

Now I knew what I had to do. I got my feet under me, came towards her, and hit her chin with the open heel of my left hand. I tried to gauge it, not to hit her too hard because you can kill a woman with a punch, but just hard enough to take her out, and she hit the floor with a jar.

Then I stepped to the window, crouched and braced the muzzle on the sill, brought it towards him down there in the light, and I heard her get off the floor; then, thinking *it wasn't hard enough, hurry,* I brought the hairs on, and heard her coming, and she fell on the gun, twisting it away, and the silencer went pop as her jerk pulled the trigger against my finger.

In the same motion, for there was no stop, everything happened together and was part of everything else, she fell back with the force of the bullet in her and toppled like she had been pushed over the low window sill.

For one-millionth of a second, time stopped. And framed in the window were the back of her legs, white flesh and silk in the dark, and her feet angling up towards the sky.

She had done it on purpose, I thought in the part of a second it took the white shape to pinwheel through the black towards the steps below. The only thing she could do to stop me, and she had done it, and she had known what she had done.

She did not cry out. She must have been dead with the bullet.

I could not move as she pinwheeled down.

Then she hit.

Then I ran.

Steve Jackson

I had read the first few sentences from the prompter and was looking away from the tower when I heard it. Perhaps thirty feet away, perhaps fifty. A heavy thud, indescribable, and I thought as I turned that somebody had tried to get me.

Then I saw the white bundle already flooding red, and I knew at once though I rejected the knowledge. Then it came back and I could not reject it, but ran to confirm by the golden hair that it was Ada.

I was kneeling beside her when they came.

Robert Yancey

The elevator had not moved, it dropped to my floor without a stop, no one saw me as I moved from it to the men's room. I hung the coat and hat on the peg, washed my hands carefully, and saw in the mirror that my face had bloody streaks. Four on one cheek, three on the other.

I washed it, I tried to wash them away, but they wouldn't wash, they showed ugly, red, and sharper than ever.

What to do?

If I ran, they had me.

If they saw the streaks, and checked the skin and flesh under her nails, they had me.

All I could do was stay. Stay and hope they did not think to check.

But I would have to go out there, I would have to, what the hell was I going to do, they had me.

I walked back to my office, turning my head so they would not see as I came in. I had some iodine in the drawer, and I put it on the streaks, hoping to hide them, but I could not. They still showed.

I sat behind the desk, my head down.

Couldn't go out, couldn't stay, what to do, what the hell to do.

Sit and hope and wait.

Paxton saw the streaks and ran over to my desk, bellowing, my God, how he bellowed, did the sonofabitch have to bellow, he bellowed, "What happened, General?"

"Nothing," I said. "I fell down and hit the radiator."

And I might have made it, I had anyway a long chance of making it, if a couple of seconds later that bastard Jackson had not come running into the office without knocking, he should have knocked, I could have hid, he busted in without knocking and looked me full in the face before I could hide.

His eyes opened wide when they saw me, and I knew that it was over.

Steve Jackson

So that was what I had to remember. Steering carefully along the dark unwinding ribbon, rolling on and on under the low gray sky shrouding the low green country, I remembered it all. I had to remember.

By a special polling of the Legislature, dispensation had been accorded for burial in the hallowed ground of the capitol itself. The spot, indeed, was only a few feet away from the bronze god Huey. On the white steps were preachers in black and pallbearers in black, but above the rain-brightened green turf swarmed the glaring motley of mourners indifferent to or beyond ritual.

The grave had been dug, a neat oblong emptiness, bottomed by dark earth, in the green brightness. Two gravediggers, trying to look decorous, stood beside the mounds of earth. Next day, the grave would be returfed, the inscribed white stone would be fitted, and after that tourists would glance at it as they wandered into the tower and say, "Ada Dallas. She was the woman. *You* know." They might look again, or they might not, as they departed, on their way to New Orleans for the Mardi gras or the Sugar Bowl or the Spring Fiesta, which was what they came for.

There were many preachers, one for every faith, there was a choir to sing, there were we who were pallbearers, to carry her where she was going. We stood together, and in the cluster my eyes found the face of Tommy Dallas. It looked older, and less soft, and as though a film, or a blur, had been wiped off. He nodded at me, and his lips said, soundlessly, "Hello, Steve."

The choir sang, the ministers spoke, and I did not hear a word of song or sermon except as a flowing tone of sadness. I looked at the casket, plated in silver and closed. I would have liked to see her, one last time, but the coffin was closed of necessity.

I made myself listen to the preacher who was talking, I could not figure his denomination, and I heard:

"Her noble and selfless devotion to the people of Louisiana..."

This was not so.

"... gave not only her strength but her life in the performance of civic duty..."

Nor was this.

"... a very great woman..."

But this was. In her own very special way that was quite different from what the preacher meant.

I was no longer listening to the dirge words on these steps, but I was tumbling in the long chute that was time, and I hit the landing I wanted to hit. Which was that day, the day the sea came in first blue and then dark and the wind blew wet and the rain started to drive.

I want to make the world know I'm alive. I want to make it say, 'Yes, you're alive, nothing I can do has ever made you not be alive. Whatever I have done to you, you have done something to me.'

And I thought: you did that.

I want to make it acknowledge that I lived, that I made my mark on it, and that nobody can erase it, ever. I want to make it impossible for the world ever to fail to acknowledge that I lived.

It never can, I told her.

I want to pay back everybody. Everybody who ever hurt me,

who ever threw dirt on me. I want to make them eat the dirt. Every grain of it. And I want them to know who I am and what I can do and I want to step on them like that jellyfish there.

And you damned near did that, too.

What hadn't she done?

Nothing.

And what had she?

Everything—almost.

She had made her deal, she had kept it, and then she had wiped it out with the willed and accepted drop to the steps.

She had made her mark on the universe. Starting with nothing but her self. Her self and her luck had been bound together, and had worked in stroke and counterstroke to rocket her into the stratosphere. Until the end, when she plunged alone to earth. And it was not her luck that deserted her. Nor even her self. She had given herself to save me, very deliberately, in what she knew would be her final act.

And that was her mistake. Or her mistake was in loving me. Or not even that. Her mistake finally was in being human, in having within her a cell of humanness that she could never quite destroy. This was what had doomed her. And—if you were religious or maybe if you were just ethical—it was what had redeemed her.

She had been finally doomed and finally saved by the simple insuperable unanswerable fact of being human.

And she had served a purpose. For greatness, even amoral greatness, has a purpose. And I believe that she was herself great, and not only the agent for the Forces. I have to believe in her greatness as I believe in her corruption and her final humanity. Even if it was the greatness of vitality. But greatness can abide only for a time, and in the end it is ordinariness that you must make do with.

She had won her world at an awful price, and she had thrown it away. Perhaps somewhere in the process she had found her reality.

Then I came out of it, and was back on the steps watching the earth fall from the gravediggers' shovels, and the service was over.

The crowd stood idly under the gray sky on the green lawns, passive, paralyzed. Then they dribbled away, slowly, and then they moved away very fast.

I waited for a time, watching the dark shower fall as the shovels turned, and then a hand touched my arm.

It was Tommy Dallas.

"Steve," he said.

He had called me that before. I was surprised, for in spite of what we had shared, he had scarcely known me.

"Yes?"

"You got a minute?" he said. "I want to talk to you about something."

"Not now," I said.

He looked at me closely. I noticed again the new sharpness in his face.

"Okay," he said. "There's plenty of time."

I wondered if there was, for anything. The future becomes the past while you grab at the running water that is the present.

But I said: "That's right. Plenty of time."

And he moved away, perhaps considerately. I wondered what he had felt for her, if he still felt anything. It was hard to tell; the thing has many shapes.

The dirt was still falling from the rhythmic blades: dust, particles, lumps—seconds, hours, years.

I turned my back and walked down the steps.

Tommy Dallas

I was sorry about Ada. I really was. I didn't blame her for the car thing any more. Maybe she really didn't do it, or anyway didn't mean it to work out like it did. It didn't matter. It was the best thing that ever happened to me, the way it turned out.

It had set me free. And when she died I got something of the same feeling. I was sorry, but I felt, too, that another string, a thin little string that I didn't even know was there, had been cut, and I was set free all over again. Only I had lost something too, some piece of myself. Why this was I could not explain. I only knew it was so.

I was sorry, but not really sad. Now that I did not hate Ada any more, I could look at her life and see she had already done what she wanted with it. Not everything, nobody does everything, but she done what counted.

I do not mean she wanted to die. Nobody ever wants to die. But they got to, and if they have done most of what they want to before they do, they amount to something. They count. Ada counted.

And I was going to count. I had made up my mind. What I wanted was to be governor, not just to be elected governor but to *be* governor. There were a couple of years till election, and I'd started running. Setting up the lines, getting things organized, the way Sylvestre had so long ago. And I kept campaigning with the boys, singing the songs, playing the gittar. If it had worked for Sylvestre, it would work for me. It was maybe silly, but it was honest, nobody got hurt. So if it would help me get there, there was nothing the matter with it.

I did not want to be governor just to be governor. When I had been governor before, I was nothing, just like the first time I was sheriff, and I wanted to go back and do it all over again, only on my own. And not as the husband of the late Ada Dallas, though our separation took care of that anyway.

I had proved something when I got elected sheriff and kind of straightened out the parish. Now I wanted to prove something bigger.

Robert Yancey

The parish jail has no real Death Row. I was just in a cell two cells apart from the room where they rigged the chair. (They do not keep the chair in the jail. The state has one chair and sends it around.) But they call the last two or three Death Row, depending on how many are occupied. Now Death Row was the last two cells. I was in one, and in the other, the very last one, was George Johnson, who had killed a cop. And I, of course, had killed a governor. So we were both pretty special.

It had been almost a year since Ada went out the window. The best lawyers that money could buy had been able to get me just that much. No more. There was never a chance of getting more. Not from the second Steve Jackson saw the bleeding iodine-smeared streaks on my face. He made them arrest me ("Just overnight, General. Tomorrow you can institute a false-arrest suit against him"). But tomorrow was when they took flesh from under Ada's

nails, and when the lab said it was mine. With that, and the bleeding
scratches, nobody could expect Paxton and Beausang to stick. Yes,
they said, I had stepped out to the john just for a few minutes. No,
I had not been clawed before. As I say, nobody could blame them
because now it was their necks, too.

Even if it was circumstantial, all of it together was too much.
My lawyers did not even put me on the stand, and they were right,
and of course I would not take the lie detector test.

So I never had a chance. The only hope was that since it was all
circumstantial, I might get guilty without the death penalty. But I
didn't even get that. The jury came back in one hour and twenty-
one minutes, and I was guilty all the way, and the judge sentenced
me, "... until you are dead."

And I felt the punch, I think in my heart I had always known I
would be hit with it that way, and my knees jellied, but I stood up
all right and did not collapse.

I suppose I had been heading towards it all my life.

But it was not right. Because I had not killed Ada. She had killed
herself. If I had been sentenced for killing the old woman, it would
have been somehow *right*. The last package would have come. The
one I had ordered and been waiting for. But the way it was, it was
not right. I had not meant to kill Ada.

I had been in this cell, in Death Row, three months already. I
had had two stays of execution.

"This one is the last one," said the lawyer, the senior partner, the
bald-headed one. "We've done all we can do. I can't offer you any
hope for another."

"Well. You did a good job as it is." And I wrote him a check, a
big one.

"Keep trying though," I said. "There's plenty more where that
came from."

"We'll keep trying. But expect nothing."

And that was a month ago, and I had another month.

My cell had a window facing east. Every morning I woke with
the filtering gray light, and I could see the big black shadow bars
on the concrete floor, a hundred times bigger than the iron ones in
the window. The sky would shade from dark to light, and then I
would stand at the window and watch through the bars the sun

come up over the rooftops: the sky going from gray to pink to orange, then the sun rimming orange over the red roof of a certain house, then inching higher and higher until it was all clear and a solid burning ball. Through the bars, too, I could see the capitol, tall and white and ripping sharp into the pink sky. But it wasn't to blame for everything that had happened. What was?

Also through the window you could smell the freshness of dew and the water the truck sprinkled on the asphalt streets, and from the jail kitchen the scent of coffee boiling and bacon frying.

It was a good world. I knew it now. I guess I had not really know it before. I guess you have to lose before you know what you have lost. It was a good world, and I hated to leave it.

It was even a pretty good jail. As jails go. It was clean, and had no jail-house smell. I had a cot, and a straight chair, and I could sit by the bars separating my cell from the next. I sat there often and had long talks with George Johnson, the cop killer.

And talks, too, with the two guards and the deputy and sometimes the sheriff. Before they had moved me into what they called Death Row, the guards had made fun of me, and had given me the business. "Well, General. What orders today, General? Want us to inspect the chair, General? General, sir, how many volts, General, sir?"

But when they moved me into Death Row, everything changed. The same guards were very quiet and polite, and seemed ashamed of the way they had gone on before. One of them made hot chocolate three times a day, he went into the kitchen and made it himself, because he knew I liked it. He brought it out himself, handed it through the bars, and waited while I drank it. The other would buy a magazine for me every day with his own money. The sheriff and the deputy would come in every so often to see if George Johnson or I wanted anything. They had special meals fixed for us two or three times a week, although this was not according to the books.

Everybody was very nice after I went in Death Row. I guess maybe they felt then that a part of themselves was with me going to it, that they were going to follow one way or another, and before very long, and we were all in it together. That I was dead, and they would have to die.

When I first came in, they had clearly thought that I was a sonofabitch. Now I could tell they did not think so any more.

I did not myself feel like a sonofabitch. Everybody had thought I was, for a long time now. Only I did not feel like it.

This is like the Army. The Army gives you a classification, way up there on the umpteenth floor of the Pentagon, and it ships you around according to the classification, and it doesn't give a damn about whether you like the classification or feel like what the classification says you are. You may hate the classification you get, but up there in that air-conditioned office in the Pentagon, they don't care. They just set the punch setting on the IBM machine for what they want, and the cards whir through the machine, and if your card matches the punch setting and drops out, then you're it.

Even if you do not feel you are really what your card says.

And I guess my card said:

Murderer, Strong-arm Man, General Bastard.

But I did not feel like a murderer, strong-arm man, or bastard. I felt like a good guy. I *was* a good guy. The things that had happened to me had just happened; they were not my fault.

Or were they? Was I really a good guy? Or was I a murderer and slugger all the way down?

I tried to figure it out.

I asked for and got a piece of paper and pencil, and then started to figure it like an Estimate of the Situation, the way they teach you at the War College.

I wanted to go back to the start, but I didn't know where the start was.

Was it when I got so hot for Ada I would do anything to get her?

No. It was before that. I had gotten kicks out of working people over before that, even if I hadn't admitted it. I had been called a sonofabitch a long time before that, and I guess I was.

Was it in the Army when I got command and liked it?

Before that.

I could not figure out where it started. Only that somewhere along the line it had started, and I had gotten pleasure out of inflicting pain.

So I wrote on paper:

Likes to hurt.

And on the other side, I wrote: *Not his fault.*

But I could not be sure that was absolutely accurate, so I put a question mark in parentheses at the side of it.

Next I wrote:

Killed woman.

And I thought about that. That was clear-cut, that was my fault. I hadn't had to kill her. So I wrote on the other side: *His fault.*

And then I thought why I had killed, because I had to have Ada, I had to have her so bad, I would do anything to get her, and I hadn't been able to help that. Then I thought some more, and I put a question mark on the side of that.

Next I wrote:

Beat people up. There didn't seem to be any doubt about that one, so I wrote: *His fault.*

But then I thought that went back to the other thing, that I liked to hurt, which I thought was mostly not my fault, and I had to put a question mark after the last *His fault,* too.

Then I wrote: *Killed Ada.*

It was certainly an accident that I had killed her. But she was killed because I was going to kill Steve Jackson. It had just turned out wrong. So my planning to kill Steve Jackson was my fault. I did not *have* to do it—not unless I wanted to stay alive. But I would not have had to kill him if I had not killed the woman. I would not have had to kill the woman if I had not been hot for Ada. Ada would not have wanted the woman killed if the woman had not been blackmailing her. The woman would not have been blackmailing her if Ada had not hired out as a high-class whore a long time before. And she would not have hired out if she hadn't had to, to have her chance in the world.

It got more and more complicated.

So beside *Killed Ada* I wrote *His fault* with a big question mark. Then I thought some more, and I went back and crossed out the question mark by both of the *Killed* entries.

There was no point in not leveling.

You always have to say yes, you yourself have to say yes, before you kill or before you do anything really bad. And I had said it. I had said *yes.* And I had said it and swung the knife and pulled the trigger.

So I had to take the responsibility for the killings.

And when I took it, when I said, *Yes, it was me, nothing else, nobody else in the end but me,* I felt better.

I felt... relief. I did not have to explain to myself any more, I had done it, it was my responsibility, that was it.

Still there were plenty of other question marks back there in the cause and effect line.

Things were all mixed up, everything was all mixed up. What you did and what was done to you. Your own actions and your luck. The things you could help and the things you could not.

So my heading for the chair was not all my fault.

As long as I did not try to dodge the responsibility for finally saying, *yes,* I could also say the other: It was not all my fault.

It had taken me all my life to figure it out.

There was one thing more to do. I wrote two lines on a sheet of paper: *This is to affirm that I alone am responsible for the death of Blanche*—I stopped, what the hell was her name? Then I remembered—*Jamison.* Then I signed it, *Robert Yancey.*

I folded it, sealed it in an envelope, and wrote on the envelope: *To be opened after the death of Robert Yancey.*

Now the figures were balanced. I felt like an accountant who has the figures absolutely right when the bank examiner comes around. Or maybe like a guy who has gone busted, but has everything on paper for the bankruptcy referee, one hundred per cent accurate. The world focused; it was more real than it had ever been.

The man in the next cell, George Johnson, the cop killer, was everything I used to despise. He had a BCD from the army; he had gotten it for desertion when I was a light colonel commanding an infantry battalion. He had been a hoodlum by profession, and had shot a police officer with two children when they caught him in a supermarket burglary in North Baton Rouge. Once I would have said, "The chair's too easy for a sonofabitch like that. They ought to hang him slow or burn him."

But now I knew there was no difference between him and me. I played gin rummy with him through the bars and I guess I liked him better than I ever liked anybody. He was a good guy, and I could see how luck, bad luck, had pushed him from one thing to another.

But of course he had said *yes* when he pulled the trigger and some other *yeses* up to it and I guess this was why I liked him most of all. Not just because things had been done to him, but because he had done them himself and had to take responsibility for them, which he did.

"I shouldn't of done it," he said, more than once. "I know it now. I don't feel bad about taking the dough, all things considered I don't see how I could do anything but take the dough from one place or another, but I shouldn't of shot him. I didn't have to shoot him. That was my fault. I can't blame nobody but myself for that. I feel really bad about that, I wish I hadn't of done it."

I told him I wished I hadn't killed the old woman even if she was a blackmailer and whore seller.

And after I got the stay, I told him. "Look, George. Let me hire my lawyers for you. They can put it off for a hell of a long time even if they can't beat it. Let me hire them for you."

"I don't think so, Bob. I sure appreciate it, but I don't think so."

He was the first guy who had called me Bob in a long time.

"Come on," I said. "I got plenty dough. Let me retain 'em. They can put it off and off."

"It's been put off, Bob. I'm tired of waiting for it. Now I just want to get it over with."

I did not give it up, I kept trying right up to the end, but he never changed his mind.

And then, almost before he knew it, it was time, and too late to change his mind.

The night before, he asked and got permission to stay in his same cell, next to me, and not be moved to the one just in front of the chair. And all night I sat right next to the bars, so he could talk if he felt like it.

We talked. We talked about everything. We talked about which new car models were best, we talked about the songs back in the thirties, we talked about major league baseball, we talked about everything. Once, in the middle of a sentence, he stopped, and said, "I wish I hadn't done it, Jesus, I wish I hadn't done it"—and then he started talking again about a redheaded girl friend he had had, a long time ago.

Then for a while he did not say anything.

And in the red light from the corridor, I saw his face was buried in the pillow.

"George," I said. "Are you all right?"

He turned his head calmly so his face came out of the pillow. I heard him breathe twice. "I'm all right, Bob."

"That's good."

"Bob." He stopped. "Did you ever—" He sounded embarrassed. Then I heard him laugh in the dim redness. "Well. I guess I'll find out soon enough."

I could tell he did not want to talk any more. The poor bastard. I felt my eyes wet in the dark. I wished I could do something. I wished I could. But I didn't know what. Now was the time nobody can help anybody, the time when you have to do it all by yourself.

He lay there, not talking, the three hours to morning. When the red light went off and the first sun came through the bars, they came to take him away, to that one last room, where he would be shaved and prepared.

I did not get to shake hands.

"Good-by, George," I said. "It won't hurt. You don't feel it, you just float away. Good luck, George."

But he did not hear me. Maybe he was already dead.

They could not get me another stay. I had a month.

The month passed. It passed quick, and it passed slow. Time is a funny thing, and it is funnier in Death Row than anywhere else. It is forever and one second at the same time. And all the time in your life becomes the same. It felt like I had never been anywhere but Death Row, and it also felt like just a minute ago that my old man whipped me with a hickory switch, that I saw the red tracers curving out against the sky at Omaha Beach, that the black dirt from the shellburst spattered my face at Remagen, that I felt the knife go in hard and heard the woman say, "Aaahh," that I took Ada in the woods, that I heard the tank treads on Canal Street, that I saw Ada pinwheeling white through the dark. None of these were either further away or closer than anything else.

It was in Death Row that I sent for Jackson.

He came the next day: the clang of keys in lock, the smooth whir of oiled hinges turning.

He walked in. They were not supposed to let anybody in the D.R. cells. I suppose they figured he was okay.

They closed the door: metal slamming metal. He stood a second in front of it, shadows of bars striping him. He did not know what to say.

"Sit down," I said. There was a chair at the foot of the cot.

He sat and looked at me. He did not look mean or glad to see me where I was.

"You weren't afraid, huh? Back there?"

"No." His eyes were on me, steady and deep, not angry or squinted with the pleasure of winning.

"I wanted to see you," I said.

"Yes."

"I. I had something I wanted to tell you."

"Yes."

His eyes did not move. What was in his voice? Pity?

"I was trying to get you then, that night. She jumped in front. I think she knew what she was doing."

I stopped.

"I thought you would want to know."

"I did know," he said.

I looked away, and then I looked back to his face. It was not pity on it; it was—what was the word?—sympathy? The face said: *it could be me, instead of you.*

Maybe not really.

"One thing," I said. "Were you really going to put it on the air?"

He shook his head. "No. I never had any idea of using it."

"Did you tell Ada you weren't?"

"Yes."

"She never told me. She knew we were safe and she never told me. She let me think. No, she made me think you would."

He did not say anything.

"She even said she would get out if I would. I guess I should have taken her up, huh?" I laughed. Then I said, "It was my fault." I stopped. "Maybe not all of it."

"Not all of it." He knew what I meant. He looked away. "Maybe it could have happened to anybody."

"You know better than that."

He did not answer for a second. Then he said, "No, I don't. I was going to help kill Sylvestre for her."

"But you didn't," I said. "You can't be sure."

"No. I can't be sure."

"And anyway that would have been different."

"Would it?" He looked out the high open window to the sky. "I don't think so."

The guard was at the door. He had already given us extra time. He still did not open it, or say hurry.

"Anyway," I said. "I wanted you to know."

"Thank you." He stood up. "Did you know I tried to get you commuted?"

"No. Why?"

He looked past me, at the wall behind, or something far away.

"Because," he said, and looked away. "Because. I was ready to help kill for her. It was just luck that I didn't. Everybody's the same."

"You know better than that," I said, again. "You have to say yes. You have to be responsible."

He looked back from that distance to me.

"You believe that?" he said.

"I know it."

I heard the key go in the lock, the loud metallic snap of the lock turning. I stood up, so did he, we shook hands.

"Thank you for coming," I said. "Good-by."

He said good-by. In the open door, he turned.

"Maybe you're right," he said. Then he was gone, the door clanged shut, the lock snapped again.

That was the last thing. Now the columns in the ledger were really balanced.

It seemed like five minutes, but I guess it was an hour, two hours, and someone was at the door again. It was the sheriff. He stood at the cell door with two guards, all stiff and their faces solemn and scared. The sheriff slid the key into the lock again, it worked metallically like before, the door swung open. The sheriff looked at me with his sad creased face, and said, "General. It's time."

And I walked between the guards, who could not look at me, for perhaps fifteen feet, to the little cell they called the night-before room. It had four walls, with the back half set off from the front by bars. In the section behind bars was a cot and a toilet. On the other side were two chairs. There was one window on the wall in front of the bars. The sheriff opened the barred door, I went inside, and he closed the door and locked it. Then the guards sat solemnly in the two chairs.

And the last night had started.

I was scared, I was very scared. But I did not feel guilty, not any more.

Maybe this was what I had always wanted and been heading toward, for the whatever-it-was to catch me. Maybe I had wanted to be punished. Or maybe I had wanted to pay for what I had done, everything I had done, which is not the same as being punished. This is saying: Yes, I have bought it, give me the bill, here is the money. I am responsible for everything I have ever done and I admit it. I don't just admit it, I claim it, the good and the bad, and give me the bill now. And this maybe was not too different from the priest saying, "I am heartily sorry for having offended Thee—"

It was time to order my meal. "We'll get you anything you want," one guard said. But all I could think of was steak and french fries and apple pie.

I was very afraid. I could feel the coldness in my belly, and my hands were shaking. I tried to control them but I could not.

"Have a drink," one guard said. He poured it into a paper cup, they were not letting me get my hands on any glass, and passed it through.

It felt like fire going down, and I felt better.

I felt better, too, after eating the steak and potatoes and pie. They had cut the meat for me, and gave me only a wooden fork to eat with, but it was all right. I ate every scrap. I had never been so hungry.

And I had never been so afraid. I was more afraid than I had ever been. But I did not feel like a sonofabitch. I had put the books in order. I felt everything was in order. But I was still afraid, and I hoped I would be able to do all right.

But I did not die. I have heard that you really die the last night, that the thing itself is just a final touch, and it had looked that way with George.

But I did not die.

The guards were very nice. They were there to do anything I wanted to do. If I wanted to be quiet, they would be quiet. If I asked they would play the radio, or read to me, or play cards.

We talked about a lot of things and then we were talking about

But I accepted full responsibility for what I had done. I would keep on choosing and accepting full responsibility for the choice.

And I felt something was completed which had started a long time ago, before Ada, before Nothing, even before I drew the four aces and the shrapnel in one convulsion of sound, wind, and pain.

It seemed the most natural thing in the world, that afternoon, to see Tommy Dallas sitting in a chair across the lobby when I stepped out of the elevator. It was, of course, never extraordinary to find anyone you knew there. Particularly on or after occasions of state, as I guess this had been. And of course the X was working. I believed more than ever now that there was an X, and it worked.

His head swung toward the elevator and his eyes picked me up. He had been waiting for me. I wondered what he wanted. Perhaps to talk, to touch Ada again through the only one left now whose life had also been entwined with hers. We were in a kind of kinship.

We shook hands awkwardly and said hello. Neither of us mentioned Yancey.

"They told me you were up here," he said. "We didn't get together in New Orleans. I thought we might, up here."

"Well," I said. "What's on your mind?"

"Let's have a drink."

We went into the bar, sat at a corner table, and the drinks came. He looked directly at me across the table.

"I'm gonna run again," he said. "For governor."

I was not surprised, but decided I should be. "Well. Good luck."

"I want some help from you."

"From me? You know I can't take sides in a campaign."

"I don't mean the campaign. I mean after."

"You're pretty sure."

He grinned, and colored. "I see what you mean. But it's the truth. I'm going in."

"And what do you want from me?"

"I want you to kind of, advise me, you know."

"Me? I'm not a practical politician. What the hell do you want with me?"

"I know you ain't. That ain't what I want. I want some real high-type advice. You know what I mean?"

"Not worth a damn. What do you mean?"

"I mean I want you to kind of help keep things in line. It takes somebody outside. You know, somebody, somebody, dis-interested."

"You mean rap your boys' fingers when they get naughty?"

"Yeah. That's it, that's just what I mean. Sometimes a guy like you can do a lot more than a guy like me. I'll keep you in touch." He grinned again. "You just be a kind of conscience." He was embarrassed. "I'll appoint you to something. Some board or something."

"Good God," I said. "Me."

I had heard it all. Then I remembered Ada had said something like that before: joking, I thought. "I will be damned." I shook my head, it was too funny. Then I said, "Okay, okay. I can go along with a joke as well as the next guy. I'll make you walk the tightest goddamned rope you ever saw."

"Hell man. Not a rope. I ain't no ropewalker."

"Well, a straight line, then."

He insisted we shake hands. He felt it proved something.

I started back. On the Air-line Highway, the clouds that had been running over intermittently suddenly broke loose and plummeted. Rain fell in hard steady streams that beat on the car and asphalt like fire from a million machine guns. Through the side window I saw water darkly sheeting over the low dark-green swamp, and it poured so heavily on the windshield that the wipers could clear it only for a second. The car rolled through it like a snowplow, under a sky so deeply gray that the world was twilight-dark, though it was only four o'clock.

I smelled the keen fresh rain smell through the crack of the no-draft, and I felt sad, alone, and oddly formal. I came out of the swamp and into the open fields of crops, and the rain eased. When I hit the outskirts of New Orleans, it had stopped. The roadhouse neons cut sharp red-green-white shapes in the black sky, the air was clean and cool and purged, and street lights shone yellow on the wet pavement as I drove deeper into the city.

Two quite different careers of Wirt Williams—in literature and the academic world on one hand and in political journalism on the other—fused uniquely in the writing of his third novel, *Ada Dallas*.

One of Louisiana's top political reporters in the late 1940s, he left newspaper work for fiction writing and college teaching. Presently he is associate professor of English at Los Angeles State College, and past director and resident writer of the college's Pacific Coast Writers' Conference.

Born in Mississippi in 1921, he studied writing with Robert Penn Warren and Cleanth Brooks in 1940–1941 at Louisiana State University. After taking an M.A. at nineteen, he served as assistant news editor and news editor of the Shreveport *Times;* he returned to the *Times* after four war years in the Navy as a political writer. For that paper and later for the New Orleans *Item,* he covered state politics and two sessions of the Louisiana legislature. His "exposés" of inefficiency and corruption in public affairs for the *Item* effected some reforms, and one—an investigation of the state's mental hospital—won him a nomination for the Pulitzer Prize in local reporting and the Heywood Broun Award. He served for three months as city editor of the *Item,* and resigned shortly after to rewrite his first novel.

He entered the famous Writers Workshop at the University of Iowa, and took a Ph.D. in English from that University in 1953.

During his navy career, he was gunnery officer on the U.S.S. *Decatur,* last of the old four-stack destroyers, and captain of a Landing Ship Medium. He returned briefly to the amateur boxing ring in 1947, and was runner-up for the Southern Golden Gloves Heavyweight championship.

His first novel, *The Enemy* (1951), was nominated for the Pulitzer Prize in fiction. It was praised as "a first-rate novel of the way it really was" by Ernest Hemingway, in one of the three or four jacket quotations given by Mr. Hemingway in publishing history. W. Y. Tindall called it "by far the best of all the war books," and Allen Tate described it as "a work of great talent." His second novel, *Love in a Windy Space,* was enthusiastically reviewed in 1957.

Mr. Williams lives in Southern California with his wife, the former Ann Meredith, and their thirteen-year-old daughter, Meredith.